MEGAN'S PROMISE

NEVA COYLE

THOMAS NELSON PUBLISHERS
Nashville • Atlanta • London • Vancouver

Also by Neva Coyle

Fiction

Cari's Secret, 1994

Jen's Pride and Joy, 1995

Nonfiction

The All-New Free To Be Thin

The All-New Free To Be Thin Lifestyle Plan

Learning to Know God

Making Sense of Pain and Struggle

Meeting the Challenges of Change

A New Heart . . . A New Start

Published in Nashville, Tennessee, by Jan Dennis Books, an imprint of Thomas Nelson, Inc., Publishers, and distributed in Canada by Word Communications, Ltd., Richmond, British Columbia.

Scripture quotations are from the KING JAMES VERSION of the Bible.

Library of Congress Cataloging-in-Publication Data

Coyle, Neva, 1943–
Megan's promise : a novel / Neva Coyle.
p. cm.
"A Jan Dennis Book."
ISBN 0-7852-8029-4
I. Title.
PS3553.O957M44 1995
813'.54—dc20

95-19137
CIP

Printed in the United States of America
1 2 3 4 5 6 — 00 99 98 97 96 95

About the Author

Neva Coyle is a full-time freelance writer who is very active in the ministry of her local church. She is happily married and the mother of three grown children. She was born in Redlands, California, the setting for much of *Megan's Promise.* She is also the coauthor of the best-selling book, *Free To Be Thin. Megan's Promise* is the third book in a series of Christian romance novels. The previous books are *Cari's Secret* and *Jen's Pride and Joy.*

CHAPTER ONE

Ignoring the icy blast of Chicago's Christmas season, Megan La Bianca fingered the black velvet and royal blue taffeta swatches between her fingers. She struggled to calm the flutter of excitement tightening her stomach. Carefully she tucked the small fabric squares inside the large white envelope she carried in her purse. On second thought, she pulled the envelope from her bag and removed the airplane ticket she had placed there weeks before.

"Chicago to Ontario, California," she whispered into the quiet apartment. She checked the flight time and once again calculated how much time she'd need to get to the airport, allowing for traffic and possibly weather. She stared at the red inked carbon copies of her ticket and settled on the couch to dream about California, summer weather in winter, and Jen and Dan's wedding.

Without warning, doubt clouded her mind and wrinkled her forehead in a frown. *Rusty,* she sighed, *how will I explain Rusty to Jen?*

Rusty had changed so much in the past few months. Once she hoped—even felt that she and Rusty were falling in love. The changes in him had interrupted that. His sudden popularity since helping solve the Halloran's Department Store security problems had led him into several other high profile cases and his ego was clearly out of control. Megan was happy to hear she would be taking a different flight than Rusty. The few extra days with Jen for a dress fitting and other last minute wedding details would be precious time with her friend, and she wanted to avoid a conflict with Rusty before the wedding. She was determined not to let her problems ruin the special days before Jen's wedding.

Megan stood and walked silently to the frost-covered window of the small apartment she once shared with Jennifer Whipple. Peggy was a good roommate, but a deep and lasting friendship like the one she shared with Jen was rare. Not too many people understood that kind of friendship. Her mother didn't, that was for sure.

"Mama," Megan said painfully turning away from the window to stand in the center of the tiny living room. She turned the ticket over in her hand. Her mother didn't understand why she had to go out to California. Didn't Jen have other friends that could "stand up for her"? Rosa La Bianca missed the entire point. Megan wasn't just going to be a part of a ritual, but a celebration. Jen and Dan Miller were a special couple. Dear friends that meant almost more to Megan than her own family.

"Better not let Mama hear you say that," she warned herself. "*Mama,*" she sighed deeply. "I'll have to face her soon enough, no sense worrying about her now." Tomorrow would be difficult; tonight she decided to let the excitement build.

Megan returned the ticket to its treasured envelope, once again touched the soft swatches, and then tucked them both securely in her purse. Walking to the bedroom, once more she went over her list of things to take to California. She'd be staying three months to help Dan and Jen in their new furniture showroom while Jen settled her home and adjusted to being not only Dan's wife, but also a mother to Dan's only child, Joy. Megan was delighted with the invitation—Rosa was furious.

"Who knows what she'll try to pull to get me to stay home this time," Megan mused sadly. "She's done it before, she'll do it again."

"Mama, don't." Megan turned away from her mother's gaze. "We've been over this a million times."

"But, Megan—" Rosa La Bianca tried to press the issue.

"Don't, Mama. Don't spoil my last few moments at home."

"You're going then?"

"Yes, Mama, I'm going." Megan tried to stand from where

she was seated on the edge of her mother's bed. Rosa reached out and took both of Megan's hands in her own, pulling her back. Megan closed her eyes against the disappointment she felt toward her mother.

"You can't even look at me?" Rosa whined.

"Of course I can." Megan opened her eyes and looked into her mother's face. Rosa's dark eyes were set deeply within her pale face. She even *looked* sick this time.

"You know, I probably won't be here when you return," Rosa said flatly.

"Don't, Mama." Megan wouldn't be manipulated into changing her plans. Not this time.

"I mean it. Every day I get worse. Ask Sophia."

"Let's ask the doctor." Megan quickly stood and shook off Rosa's grasp.

She walked toward the door leading from Rosa's bedroom to the hall. She glanced around the room. When her father was alive, Megan had loved this room. But in the ten years since his death, Rosa kept it dark and wouldn't hear of repainting or papering it. Rosa kept a small night-light in the shape of the Virgin Mary on the mahogany dresser. The dark brown carpet hadn't been cleaned in years, and the matching drapes were always drawn. Megan could hardly remember the pattern of the tan wallpaper, and in this dim light she couldn't see it anymore. Only a small lamp burned on the nightstand beside the four-poster bed where Rosa lay. "Where d'you think you're going?" Rosa propped herself up on one elbow.

"I'm calling Dr. Fitzpatrik." Megan stopped at the doorway and flipped the light switch. The ceiling fixture didn't respond. "Why don't you put in new lightbulbs, Mama?"

"You can't call him now."

"Why not?"

"It's Christmas Eve, that's why. He doesn't want to be bothered today."

Megan checked her watch. "It's only one-thirty."

"It's Christmas Eve."

"Mama, if you're sick, we need to call the doctor."

"*If?* If I'm sick?" Rosa fell back against the stack of pillows propped up against the wall behind the bed.

"Mama, stop it." Megan sighed and returned to straighten the covers on Rosa's bed.

"What's the use?" Rosa moaned sinking deeper into her pillows.

"Mama . . ."

"I mean it. I know what the doctor will say. I'm not running a fever, I can't quite put my finger on where the pain is. I don't have a headache, and I'm not dizzy at the moment. He doesn't have a conscience, I tell ya, he'll just take my money and give me another prescription for Miltown. I'm not paying that quack doctor good money for him to tell me it's my nerves. Tranquilizers don't help a broken heart." Rosa took a sideways glance at her daughter to see if Megan would react.

Megan took a deep breath and turned back toward the bed.

"I don't like your hair that way," Rosa said.

Megan immediately put her hand up and ran it down the smooth style—longer on the sides as they curved along her jawline and shorter in the back, shaped close to her long slender neck. "It's the latest thing."

"It looks like something from the twenties."

"It's easy to take care of."

"Well that's something, anyway." Rosa turned away from Megan and pulled her knees toward her chest. She was so thin and small. Megan noticed she was no bigger than a child when she curled up like that.

"Mama, you need to get out. Come on, Sophia and Ben want you to come over and be with them and the kids tonight."

"You going?"

"No, Mama. I'm going tomorrow. I have to finish packing tonight."

"You can't even spend your last Christmas at home with your family."

"It's not my last Christmas at home, Mama."

"Maybe not yours, but . . ."

"Stop it, Mama."

"I mean it, Megan. I may not see another Christmas."

"Then why don't you get up and get yourself dressed? Have a very Merry Christmas if it's to be your last."

"Don't get fresh—it's your mother you're talking to."

"Mama, you still have time to get ready. Go to early mass and then to Sophia's. Benjie will take you."

"I won't have that young upstart priest, Father O'Brien, makin' his remarks about not seeing me except at Christmas and Easter. I'm not much for religion these days, you know since . . . Go on. Do what you have to do. Leave me, if that's your choice."

"Don't do this, Mama."

"Do what? Is it my fault I'm sick to death because of you?"

"I'll be back in March. Think you can live until Easter?"

"Megan Marie, don't you use that tone with me."

"Mama . . . I love you."

"Funny way you have to show it."

Megan took a deep sigh and decided it was useless to try to make her mother feel better. Whenever Rosa couldn't get her way with intimidation, she tried guilt. Predicting her death was the one weapon she saved for rare occasions. Megan remembered her using it only twice before: once when Megan refused to accompany her to visit her father's grave on one of her mother's weekly visits and again when Sophia had some prewedding doubts about marrying Benjamin.

"Go, don't make it any worse by dragging it out. You couldn't make it better now by staying. Not when I know you are dying to go and be rid of me." Rosa curled up tighter and refused to look at her middle daughter. Megan had no intention of giving in to her, but she had hoped for a pleasant Christmas with her family before leaving. "You better tend to your all-important packing."

"Mama, this isn't fair."

"Fair? Let me tell you what's not fair . . ." Rosa turned with a start and sat upright, pointing her finger in Megan's face.

"Now who's using a tone?" Megan jumped to her feet and turned squarely to face her mother.

"I'll ignore that smart-aleck remark, Megan." Rosa threw back her covers and stood. "Look, all I want is a simple and quiet life. Is that too much to ask? Why should I have to worry about a daughter halfway across the country living with God knows what kind of people, meeting who knows what kind of . . . well, men?" Rosa fairly spit out the last word.

"Mama, I've told you. There's nothing to worry about."

"And what do you know, Miss Know-It-All?"

"I'm going to a wedding, Mama, not off to war!"

Rosa slapped Megan across the face. "Don't even say such a thing!" Rosa screamed.

Megan stepped back, stunned. She lifted her hand to soothe the sting left on her cheek by Rosa's hand. Tears sprang to her eyes.

"You cannot stop me from going, Mama. Can't you see that?"

"Then why'd you come here at all?"

"I wanted to spend a few minutes with you, that's all. Just you and me, all by ourselves. I wanted to say good-bye and give you a Christmas present." Megan reached for a small box, brightly wrapped for Christmas. She had chosen a lovely pair of gold earrings for her mother. It took six substantial payments out of Meg's weekly earnings to buy them, but she wanted her mother to have nice things.

"A present is a hollow thing, Megan," Rosa said holding up her hand against the sacrificial gift of her daughter. "What good's a gift if the giver's heart is somewhere else?"

"I have to go." Megan checked her watch again. "It's almost two." She walked slowly toward the door, carefully setting the small package on the dresser.

Passing the open closet door, she caught a glimpse of her father's clothes, which had hung there for the ten years since his death. Her eyes lingered a moment on his hats neatly lining the upper shelf and dropped to wander over his shoes perfectly arranged in pairs, each pair exactly an inch apart. She glanced around the room. With her eyes finally accustomed to the dimly lit room, she noticed again the sad contrast.

Rosa La Bianca kept her late husband's clothes neatly

arranged as if he would be coming back at any moment while her own were strewn carelessly about the room. Joseph La Bianca's clothes hung carefully covered in the clear plastic coverings in which they came home from the cleaners immediately following his death, but Rosa's housedresses lay in a pathetic pile in the corner on the floor. Joseph's robe hung neatly in the closet on a crochet covered hanger while Rosa's robe slumped carelessly from a bed poster. Several pairs of Rosa's shoes were strewn under and around the bed. Her slippers were the only things left neatly waiting beside her bed. The dresser scarf needed washing, and stacked newspapers gathered dust near the door.

"What are you waiting for?" Rosa followed Megan toward the door, grabbing her robe and stepping into her slippers on the way.

"Mama, I . . ." Megan turned slowly toward her diminutive mother. "Please, Mama, all I want is . . ."

"Don't ask me for anything. I ask you only one thing."

Megan closed her eyes. She had heard this spiel hundreds of times, and she braced herself for her mother's well rehearsed plea.

"All *I* want is for you to get a nice husband and settle down. This whole house will be yours someday. You need a husband. What's so wrong with a mother wanting a life for her daughter?"

I don't want this old house. Megan knew she couldn't say the words out loud, but she didn't want this dark, lonely building filled with anger, sadness, and guilt.

"Sophia's got her own house now," Rosa continued, "and, Angelina . . . well, she's too young to know what she wants. I can't even think of Angelina until you're settled. But you—you're old enough to get a good husband and start raising babies. I already had two when I was your age. A life, Megan, a husband—that's all I want for you. Is that too much for a mother to want? I promised your father I would see to it that you find a good husband. I promised him you'd marry Vinny—"

"Mama . . ." Megan protested hopelessly. Rosa had chosen Benjamin for Sophia, and she had chosen Vinny for Megan.

Maybe Benjamin was okay for Sophia, but Vinny? "I have to go, Mama."

"I promised him, Megan."

"I'll see you in March."

"It was the very last thing I said to him."

"I'll be late for my appointment at work."

"If I died today and met your father in heaven, what would I tell him, Megan? He had such hopes for you."

"Bye, Mama."

Megan stepped into the hallway and closed her mother's door behind her. She heard her mother sobbing on the other side.

Megan hated the dark hallway. The entire house had been neglected after her father died, but the upstairs hallway seemed worse than the rest. The wooden floor needed refinishing, and the floral floor runner needed to be replaced. Dust and dankness reeked from the walls covered with wallpaper now cracked and peeling. The mirror at the end of the hall was covered with a hazy film that would not wash off. The only light came from a single twenty-five watt bulb dangling from a grotesque brown cord at the top of the stairs. Rosa took the light covering down to wash it and had never replaced it.

Descending the stairway, Megan found Maria waiting at the landing. "You're breaking her heart, Megan," her aunt said.

"Don't start, Auntie." Megan held up her hand defensively.

"She's my only sister, the only family I have left. I can't stand seeing her so unhappy."

Brushing by her aunt, Megan quickened her step, and Maria followed only a step behind her. "Why can't you just give her what would make her the happiest woman on earth? Is that too much for a daughter to do for her mother?"

Megan reached for the doorknob and felt the cold metal against her palm. The sudden chill of the Chicago winter reminded her that her coat was tossed across the foot of Rosa's bed. "Auntie, go up to her, will you? See if you can calm her down."

"You break her heart and you want me to fix it?"

"Auntie, don't you do this to me too." Maria's face softened. Maria adored her namesake even if she did insist on using the American version of her name. "I left my coat up there," Megan continued. "Will you toss it down?"

"Go back, Megan, go back and get it yourself and make it right with your mother," Maria said.

"I'm going to call a cab, and while I'm waiting you can get my coat, okay?" Megan pleaded. "If you don't, I'll go without it."

"Then it'll be all my fault if you catch your death, I suppose?"

Megan remained silent but raised her eyebrows and looked down her nose at her short, plump aunt. *I can play this game too,* Megan thought.

"Well, then, go call your cab." Maria motioned toward the other end of the house. "Vinny's in the kitchen. He's been waiting to say good-bye to you. Be nice to him, Megan. You might not have feelings for him, but he's crazy about you."

Maria turned and headed slowly up the stairs while Megan started toward the kitchen to use the phone—and to face Vinny.

"Hi, Vinny. I didn't know you were here."

"I wanted to say good-bye, and of course, Merry Christmas, to you, Megan."

"That's nice of you. Merry Christmas to you too."

Megan reached for the phone and dialed the number. After ordering the cab, she turned to face Vinny, who had crept up silently behind her. Spinning her around, he shoved her against the wall, pinning her arms to her sides. Before she could protest, he crushed his mouth on her lips. She sank toward the floor, trying to slip from between his arms. Realizing she would not escape if he pinned her to the floor she suddenly stood up, hitting Vinny's nose with her head. With a yell, he reeled backward, grabbed a towel, and stuck it to his face.

"Vinny! I'm sorry." Megan covered her mouth with her hand. She could barely stifle the laughter rising in her throat.

"I only wanted a Christmas kiss!" Vinny wailed.

"You didn't have to attack me like that!"

"How else?"

"Vinny, don't you start too."

"Would it be so bad, Meggie, you and me?"

"What?" Megan couldn't believe what she was hearing.

"Why do you treat me like I'm dirt?"

"Dirt? Vinny, I have never treated you like dirt. You and I are as close as cousins! Maybe even brother and sister. We've known each other all our lives. I've never treated you like anything but—well, family."

"Dirt." Vinny wiped his nose on the towel. "It feels like dirt."

Megan moved closer to inspect his nose. "You're all right. It's not even bleeding."

"I've loved you since the seventh grade, Meggie. All through high school, even."

"I love you too, Vinny, but we're like family—not sweethearts."

Vinny reached for her again. "Is there a difference?"

The stairs creaked under Maria's feet. Megan stepped bravely toward Vinny. "You're one of my best friends. Don't spoil it." She tried to kiss him on the cheek but he turned and tried to find her lips again. Megan jerked away.

"You're a tease, Megan Marie. One of these days you'll get what's coming to you. Someday you'll meet your own tease." Vinny turned toward the back door leading out to the alley way. "And then you'll know how it feels."

"Vinny, don't leave this way. Our fathers were best friends, after all. We're like family."

"I don't want to be just friends, and I thought someday we wouldn't just be *like* family, we'd be . . ." Vinny dropped the last part of his comment as the cab driver honked the horn.

"I have to go." Megan pushed open the swinging door into the dining room where Maria waited with her coat spread open over the metal hot water register. She slipped her arms into the warm coat and bent to kiss her aunt while buttoning it. She heard the back door slam behind Vinny.

"Bye, Auntie," Megan said in a low tone.

"You're a real heartbreaker, Megan. First your mother,

now Vinny. I'm shocked. I didn't know you were such a selfish person."

Megan shoved her hands into her pockets and pulled out her gloves. Hearing the cab's insistent horn, she grabbed her purse off the chair near the front door and pushed her way out the door, across the frozen front porch, and into the snapping cold December afternoon. She was already late for her appointment with Mr. Paulson. Climbing into the cab, she took one last look back toward her two-story childhood home and watched it fade into its place among the other houses lining the street.

CHAPTER TWO

Once again Megan checked her watch. Oh, well, she didn't look forward to this next encounter anymore than she had looked forward to seeing her mother.

Taking a deep breath, she checked her mirror. "Vinny!" she whispered under her breath as she rubbed her smeared lipstick. At the amused look of the cabby watching her in the rearview mirror, she wrapped her arms tightly around her slender middle and fought back tears.

By the time she reached Halloran's, she had regained some of her composure. As she stepped out of the cab, she helped herself to a deep breath of the cold winter air. She paid no attention to the last-minute Christmas shoppers rushing about or the incessant ringing of the Salvation Army volunteer's bell as she crossed the street to Halloran's main entrance. She didn't pause to take in the splendor of the blue and green decorations lavishly adorning the store where she had spent the best part of the last two years.

"Merry Christmas, Meg!" called a friendly clerk from behind the jewelry counter. Meg had worked there for over a year before being transferred to the security office. "Hey, I love your hair!"

Megan waved and smiled to the sales girl, then stepped on the escalator toward the second-floor offices.

Peggy caught sight of Megan's approach and paused to wait for her on the second floor. "Hi, Megan! Merry Christmas."

"Hi, Peg. And Merry Christmas to you too."

"You headed for Playful Paulson's Playpen?" Peggy teased.

"Don't laugh, Peg. You'll be summoned there sooner or later."

"Not me. He goes for the skinny, young ones."

"That's not funny."

"He's been—well, how shall I put this? Let's say he's feeling a lot of 'Christmas cheer' if you know what I mean."

Megan stopped. "You mean he's been drinking?"

"Not has been, *is*!" Peg pulled Megan out of the main aisle and into the children's department. "I hear he has a bottle. A regular party has been going on in there for most of the day. One guest at a time, of course, if you know what I mean."

"Oh brother!" Megan slumped back, resting slightly on a sale table full of children's pajamas. "Can't he just mail me my paycheck?"

"He could, but he won't. He wants to wrestle you for it." Peggy smiled. "Want me to go with you?"

"He'll just make you go back to the floor." Megan took off her gloves and stuffed them back into her pockets. She squared her shoulders and lifted her chin. "Might as well get this over with. See you back at the apartment?"

"Right after we close." Peggy walked with Megan toward the door leading to Mark Paulson's office. "Oh yes, I forgot," Peg said. "His secretary has the day off. You're on your own in there, Meg. Keep your dukes up."

"Great," Megan mumbled. She shoved open the glass door to the secretary's office. Pausing, she took a deep breath, let it out slowly, and headed toward "Playful Paulson's Playpen."

"Megan, my dear. Come in, come in. I've been watching the clock until you came. You naughty girl, you're late." Mark Paulson's voice was tinged with false cheer and his speech was slightly slurred. "I thought you might have forgotten. I have your check waiting for you right here." He waved an envelope toward Megan, then put it deliberately down on his desk. "But first, it's Christmas! A time for friends to be together and share a little toast. Let me get you a glass of champagne."

Oh, brother, Megan thought, *first Vinny, now this.*

"No thanks, Mr. Paulson, I don't drink."

"Surely, a glass of champagne. That's not what you call *drinking* for heaven's sake. That's celebration!"

He handed Megan a clear plastic cup half filled with the

light amber liquid. Megan noticed the little bubbles float to the top as she quietly set the cup on the table near the brown leather sofa. Dan Miller would be appalled if he could see this. She wanted to say so, but decided against it.

"No, thank you, Mr. Paulson. I just came to get my check and to turn in my keys." Megan fumbled in her purse to get the key ring. She had neglected to separate the store keys from her own the night before and regretted the oversight now. She began to take the store keys off the ring and bent back a fingernail in the process.

"Ouch!" she said as she stuck her finger in her mouth involuntarily.

"Here," Paulson said, seizing the opportunity to move closer to her. "Let me help you." He reached for the key ring while he ran his other hand across her shoulder and around her neck taking hold of her coat collar and tugging it backward. "Let me take your coat, dear."

Meg tried to step away, but he caught her arm. "Don't be like that, Megan. Try to be a little more friendly. After all, I have your keys. You won't get in your apartment without them, now will you?" He shook them teasingly.

She spun around to face him. "Let me have my keys, Mr. Paulson."

"Let's see you smile then, shall we?" Mark Paulson stepped toward her, closing the distance between them.

"Mr. Paulson, I came here for my check and to turn in my keys. I'd like to do that if you don't mind."

"Speaking of your check . . ." Paulson stepped back and turned toward his desk, where he had placed the envelope with Megan's name on it. Dropping her keys on top of the envelope, he smiled sickly at her. "I thought you might be able to use a little, shall we say, 'Christmas bonus'?" He tapped the envelope with his index finger.

"Oh?" Megan's suspicions now rose to meet her already high level of contempt for this new manager of Halloran's. Halloran's was always generous with their employees at Christmas time—that is until Dan Miller decided to sell the store and left for California.

"Couldn't you use some extra cash, Megan?"

"Depends." Megan was getting tired of the game he was attempting to force her to play.

"On what?" Mark Paulson moved to once more stand in front of her. He reached for the top button of her coat and she pushed his hand away.

"On how much I have to pay for it." Megan's anger was getting harder to control.

"Oh, you don't have to pay for it, Megan. But you could show a little appreciation." Paulson's glassy eyes raked over Megan's mouth and dropped to her throat. He grabbed her by the arms and pulled her toward him. "You could begin by at least being friendly. You know—take off your coat and stay a little while. Not long—I have another appointment in fifteen minutes. I find you very attractive, Megan." He lowered his face toward hers.

"Fifteen minutes?" Megan tilted her face toward him and smiled. Leaning into him, she felt him relax and sensed his lack of balance. Placing both hands flat on his chest she whispered, "Do you now?" As he tried to circle her waist with his hands, she shoved him backwards as hard as she could. "Forget it!" Megan lunged toward the desk and grabbed her keys and the envelope.

"You little—!" Paulson regained his balance and grabbed for her as she tried to dart past him. But he caught her arm and spun her around to face him again. She shoved the keys in her pocket but dropped the envelope on the floor. She knew instinctively she should not bend to pick it up. Slowly, without taking his eyes from hers, Paulson retreived the envelope. "You're not a cooperative young woman, Megan!"

"And you, Paulson, are not a very nice man." Both Megan and Paulson turned toward the masculine voice coming from the direction of the doorway. Without taking his eyes from Paulson's, Stephen Bennett noticed him slip something into his pocket. He continued without even looking in Megan's direction, "Get out of here. I have some business with Mr. Paulson."

"But—my . . ." Meg started hesitantly toward the door.

"Get out of here. I'm about to lose my temper, and it won't be a pretty sight."

Megan's heart pounded in her throat. She needed that money. She came here to get it, and she wasn't about to leave without it.

"I came to—"

Stephen spun around to face her. "I said get out!" The veins on his neck stood out, and she could see his temper in the redness creeping up his neck. His blue eyes snapped with anger. "Do it," he whispered hoarsely. "Now!" he barked. Megan started. She backed toward the door, dropped one of her gloves, and stepped on it as she left Paulson's office.

Shaken, she paused and glanced over her shoulder as the door to the inner office closed firmly. She heard Paulson say, "Bennett, you're early!"

The young man's reply was angry. "No, Paulson, I'd say I was just in time!"

She couldn't bear to stay and listen to what was being said; for once her insatiable curiosity didn't pull her back. She left the office and quickly crossed the sales floor to the back stairway. When she reached the main floor, she slipped through the side exit and hailed a cab. The cold winter air slapped her face as hard as she had wanted to slap Paulson's. Her anger burned almost as brightly as her embarrassment. Fishing deep in her pockets, she let out a moan as she discovered one of her leather gloves missing.

Oh well, she comforted herself, *day after tomorrow I'll be in sunny California.* She could easily do without her gloves then. But doing without the money—that wouldn't be as easy.

Megan had barely finished her packing and stacked the suitcases by the door when Peggy Smith barged in overloaded with packages. Frances, Peg's roommate-to-be while Meg was away, followed with as many packages of her own.

"It's starting to snow out there," Frances said. "Perfect for Christmas Eve!"

Peggy grabbed Meg's arms. "You should have seen the look on old Paulson's face when that guy got through with him. He was all red faced and quite humble when I went in."

"How do you know what happened?" Meg asked.

"We saw you escaping and decided to see what was going

on. That's when we thought of going in as a secretary's stand-in."

"You went in?"

"I did," Peg laughed. "After all, Mr. Bennett had a business appointment and Mr. Paulson's secretary was off, so I thought I'd better see if they needed coffee or anything."

"Right." Frances picked up the story. "Mr. Paulson needed coffee to help sober him up, and Mr. Bennett looked like he needed a drink to calm him down!" The two collapsed in gales of laughter.

"And?" Meg asked.

"And Mr. Paulson was getting his just desserts."

"Mr. Bennett was telling him off, in no uncertain terms, if you know what I mean," Peggy added.

"Telling him off?" Meg didn't understand.

"Exactly!" Peggy said, her voiced tinged with excitement. "He told him exactly what he thought of people in a position of authority and responsibility who—let me see if I can remember his exact words . . ."

"*Abuse*," prompted Frances.

"Yeah, *abuse* that authority and responsibility. Who misuse their power for their own ends and don't give a blankety blank for who they hurt."

"No kidding?" Meg slumped back on the couch.

"No kidding!" The two friends said at once.

"You should have been there, Meg," Frances said. "Peggy literally stood at the door, listening to every word. She barely got out of the way in time when Mr. Bennett left."

"With his papers unsigned, yet." Peggy added.

"What papers?"

"Yeah, something to do with the sale of Halloran's," Frances said. "We're not sure exactly. But it was certainly a big deal to Mr. Paulson. He tried to apologize—"

"A dozen times or more," Peg interrupted her friend.

"Poor Paulson!" Frances continued. "I can't help but feel a little sorry for him. One minute he's feeling no pain at all, and the next . . ."

"*All* he's feeling is pain." Peg finished the sentence. "No kidding." Megan grew thoughtful.

Mr. Paulson's comeuppance provided quite a bit of levity among the friends as they wrapped the presents for Fran's and Peggy's families.

"You all finished with your wrapping?" Peggy asked Megan.

"Yeah, I finished a couple of days ago. I didn't dare leave it to the last minute with all I have to do to get ready. My brother-in-law stopped by last night and picked all the gifts up for me so I wouldn't have to lug them with me tomorrow."

"What are you doing tonight, Meg?" Peggy and Frances were headed out for family gatherings and didn't want to leave her home alone.

"I usually spend Christmas Eve with my mother. She ordinarily cooks a traditional Italian dinner. But this year she canceled out on us."

"Oh, she all right?" Frances asked.

"She's pouting about me going to Jen's wedding."

"I see."

"No, you couldn't possibly. Nobody can grandstand like my mother."

"Playing it to the hilt is she?" asked Peggy.

"That's an understatement. She claims it will kill her."

"Oh, my goodness." Frances stared at Megan with wide eyes. "What will you do?"

"Catch the eight-fifty-five flight to Ontario, California, that's what I'm going to do. That is, after I spend Christmas afternoon at my sister's."

"Want to come with me and endure my family tonight, Meg?" Peggy was more than happy to have Meg's company, and her family always welcomed anyone into their circle.

"No, thanks anyway. I'm bushed. I've had quite a day." She let her mind wander back over the argument with her mother and then began to giggle over the scene in the kitchen with Vinny.

"What's so funny?"

"Nothing. It's just been a terrible day, that's all."

"You can laugh about it?" Frances said as she began tearing extra wrapping paper into little pieces.

"What else can I do?"

"Celebrate, I guess," Frances said and threw the paper scraps at Meg. The three girls impulsively began to throw wads of wrapping paper, tissue paper, and anything else they could find. They stuck bows in each other's hair, and before they were through the apartment looked as it if had been vandalized.

After Frances and Peggy left, Meg settled down on the couch in front of the TV to catch the end of *Miracle on 34th Street* before she cleaned up the mess.

A knock on her door sent her running, assuming one of her gift-laden friends had forgotten something. She threw open the door.

"Now what?" she virtually yelled.

"Hello again." Stephen Bennett smiled slightly and leaned against the door frame.

Meg's mouth opened in shock.

"I'm Stephen Bennett. I'm from Jeff Bennett's office. I'm here in Chicago to represent Dan Miller."

"You're who? What?" Meg frowned, then relaxed. "Wait a minute. You're Cari Bennett's brother-in-law? You work with Jeff, right?"

"Right. I came to get some urgent papers signed, and well, as you know, my meeting with Mr. Paulson didn't go exactly as planned."

Meg noticed Stephen's fleeting grin.

"I don't suppose this is yours?" He dangled a brown leather glove in front of Megan.

"Oh yes, thank you, it is. I thought I had lost it."

"You dropped it on your way out of Paulson's office."

"I didn't notice."

"I didn't think so."

An awkward silence fell between them. "I don't suppose you'd like to . . ." Meg stopped, suddenly remembering the wrapping paper disaster left in the room behind her.

"I suppose you think I'd like to keep standing out here in the hallway."

"Oh, no. It's just that—"

"Thank you. I accept your invitation." Stephen swept past Meg into the small living room. Normally quite reserved and even what some would consider a bit too proper, he was surprised at even being here, and now he was inviting himself into her apartment.

Meg's face reddened as he glanced around the room and let out a low whistle. "What happened to this place?"

"We had a paper fight," Meg admitted quietly.

"We?"

"My roommates and me, I mean I—I mean, well, my roommates and myself. We had a little wrapping paper left over, and we . . ."

"You found something else to do with it?"

"Well, yeah, kind of." Megan was not exactly uncomfortable or embarrassed. She couldn't put her finger on what she was feeling. She knew she liked it, that was enough.

Stephen unbuttoned his coat. "May I?" He gestured with his lapels.

"Of course, I'm sorry. I'm surprised . . . well, you know, to see you again."

"If I remember right, you were surprised to see me the first time."

"Oh boy, was I. But relieved, I can tell you that much for sure. How can I ever thank you?" Meg regretted the words immediately.

"No need for that." Stephen cleared wadded paper from the couch. "Where should I put this?"

"Here, let me take that."

"I'd better hold on to it until you get a paper bag or something. It could spring loose at any moment." He laughed, and Meg liked the sound.

Meg retrieved a few brown grocery bags from the kitchen, and Stephen helped her pick up the paper mess. When they finished, he said, "I guess I'd better be going. You probably have plans, Christmas Eve and all."

"No," Meg said quickly, too quickly perhaps. "I mean I did have plans, but they fell through."

"Oh?"

"Yeah, I'm just planning to sit here and have a quiet evening. My friends will be back later tonight, but for now, I'm not doing anything at all."

"Would you like to go out somewhere?" Stephen asked. "Maybe we could get a bite to eat or something."

"I don't know if anything is open. I never go out on Christmas Eve. I'm usually at my mother's, with family—you know."

But Stephen didn't know. He was usually looking for a diner or hanging out in a bar, though he didn't drink, just to avoid being alone.

"Something's bound to be open. You know, a diner or an all-night coffee shop?" he asked.

"Sure. It's worth a try. I'll get my coat." Meg reached for her coat and wrapped a scarf around her head. She quickly pulled on her snow boots, and on the way out the door she said, "Thanks for this," as she waved her glove toward Stephen.

"You're very welcome, I'm sure." And while he meant every word, he didn't feel so sure.

"Hey look, it's still snowing." Meg stared up at the dizzying flurry of snowflakes. Stephen noticed how they clung to her dark bangs and her woolen scarf.

"I never thought I'd see a white Christmas." Stephen had never expected to spend Christmas Eve in Chicago, let alone to walk in the snow on Christmas Eve with such a delightful young woman.

Over coffee Stephen brought Meg up-to-date on Jen's wedding plans and filled her in on as much as he knew about Dan Miller's new furniture showroom. "He's a smart businessman. That I can say for sure."

"He's good to work for, too." Meg sipped her coffee.

"Not like Paw-some Paulson, eh?"

Meg laughed, and Stephen knew then that his decision to wait until Thursday before flying back to California was the right one.

"Thank you," Meg said, suddenly serious.

"For what?" Stephen asked.

"For coming into the office just when you did." Meg frowned slightly, and Stephen decided that she looked beautiful even then.

"Just luck, I guess."

"Whatever. I can't say what would have happened to me if you hadn't mysteriously appeared."

"To you?" Stephen feigned surprise. "It was Paulson I was concerned about. Another few minutes and no telling what condition I might have found him in. I imagine you can come out fighting and clawing if you're backed into a tight enough corner."

"Yeah? Well then, let Mr. Paulson thank you."

"I don't think that's what he wants to say to me right now." Leaning over the table Stephen motioned Meg to come closer. "I think I spoiled his Christmas," he whispered.

"You did?" Meg whispered back.

"I think I did." Stephen leaned back, and the expression on his face told Megan he wasn't the slightest bit sorry about it.

"How'd you do that?"

"I took the papers out of my briefcase, and instead of getting his signature on them, I told him I'd have to discuss the situation I had witnessed with Mr. Miller before the deal would be closed."

"How'd he take that?"

"Like a baby whose hands have been soundly slapped."

"You mean—"

"I mean he stuck out his lower lip, and I think I saw it even tremble a little."

"No," Megan said. "I can't hardly believe it."

"So what do you think of that?"

"I think you deserve a medal, Mr. Bennett—a medal of honor!"

"No applause, please." Stephen bowed in mock humility.

"Then let me bake you some Christmas cookies!"

"What, at this time of night?"

"It's only eight-thirty. And it's Christmas Eve. We could begin a tradition."

"A tradition." Stephen liked the idea. "Okay, let's get with it then." He knew he'd need to find a room before too long. He'd call Dan from Meg's apartment, then he'd call around for a hotel.

"Hey, this is serious snow, isn't it?" Stephen asked as they left the nearly deserted diner.

"Snow is never serious to us, Mr. Bennett. Maybe to a suntanned Californian . . ." Meg dodged Stephen's snowball and quickly stooped to make one of her own. But before she could throw it Stephen slipped and landed in the snow.

Meg laughed and extended a hand to help him up. "No thanks, lady, I don't trust you."

"Then you're on your own, mister." She hurried away, glad for her boots, for which Stephen's leather penny loafers were no match. She ran to the corner and flung her arms around a lamppost. She looked back and laughed at Stephen slipping and sliding his way toward her.

Back in the apartment, Stephen took off his shoes and rubbed his toes. "I think I'm not properly dressed for winter." Meg agreed and went to find a warm blanket for his freezing feet. Coming back into the room, she discovered him talking to Dan Miller on the phone. Stephen handed the phone to Meg as soon as he finished reporting to Dan Meg's trouble with Paulson.

"Jen?" Meg's eyes filled with tears at the sound of the voice of her friend so far away. "Is it really you?"

"It's really me, Meg. I can't wait for you to get here. Sarah Jenkins is insisting you stay in her guest room when you come, and you're going to love it there. Cari's baby is a darling. And Joy is so happy; she's the delight of everyone, especially my dad." Jen's voice trailed off slightly. "Meg?"

"I hear you, Jen."

"I can't believe you ran into Stephen. He was only supposed to be there a few hours and then catch a late flight home."

"Well, I guess he changed his mind." Meg looked across the room to Stephen, who had his feet wrapped in the afghan and was contentedly watching her as she talked. She could feel the blush beginning to creep up her neck and was hoping it wouldn't show.

"How's your mother?" Jen asked.

"She's angry, as usual. She . . . well, we'll talk about it later, when we're together. Can you believe it, Jen? I'll be there in less than two days!"

"Dan wants to talk to you, don't hang up. I'll see you soon. Take care, and Merry Christmas, Megan!"

"Merry Christmas to you too, Jennifer." Meg paused and glanced back at Stephen while she waited for Dan Miller's voice to come across the wire.

"Yes, I think so. I have my ticket, I packed my clothes, but I am probably bringing too much. I don't know what I'll need. Is it really like summer there?"

Stephen smiled and decided he might like to show Megan some of the California sights, especially the coastline he loved so dearly.

"I don't know. That would be wonderful. Okay, yeah. Here, I'll let you talk to him yourself." Meg held out the phone to Stephen. "Dan wants to ask you about your travel plans now that you've missed your plane."

Stephen looked at Megan the entire time he spoke with Dan. "That's exactly what I thought I'd do. By the looks of it, she'll need a U-haul just to get to the airport anyway. She can use all the help she can get—or let's say, I'll give her all the help she needs." At that Meg couldn't keep from blushing and was grateful for the excuse to go into the kitchen and roll out the cookie dough.

Stephen finished his conversation with Dan and came into the kitchen. He turned a chair around and straddled it, settling down to watch Megan make cookies.

"You think making Christmas cookies is a spectator sport, mister?" Meg teased.

"Isn't it?"

"Not on your life." She took a clean apron out of the drawer and handed it to him. He took the apron with one hand and caught her hand with the other. She didn't resist. He noticed how her long her lashes were as she dropped her eyes for a moment.

"Megan," he began.

"Yes," she responded.

"If you tell one soul about this—one single, solitary person—I promise, I will . . ."

"Promise what, Mr. Bennett?"

"I'll make your entire life one long miserable experience."

"Think you'll know me that long?"

"It may be a long shot, but there might be a chance of that." Megan caught the smile in his eyes.

"Sounds more like a threat than a promise to me." Meg laughed, pulling her hand away.

"Take it any way you want."

"I'll give it some thought," Meg said confidently, but her hand shook as she handed Stephen a cookie cutter. His grin broke into a wide smile.

"I hope you do that, Miss . . . Miss Megan." Totally fascinated by her, Stephen realized he hadn't even remembered to ask her how to pronounce her last name.

Stephen and Meg started baking, discussing each cookie's design, deciding just how much colored sugar to apply as if each one were a masterpiece. Hours later, Meg caught an unconscious glimpse of the clock above the refrigerator, then took a sudden second look when she realized what time it was.

"My goodness," Stephen said, following her eyes to the clock. "Time really does fly when you're having fun."

"Frances and Peggy are really late. They both thought they'd be in by midnight at the latest. It's after two. I wonder what's keeping them."

Stephen glanced out the window just as the phone rang.

"What?" Meg's voice sounded an alarm inside Stephen.

"What's wrong?" he asked coming around to stand beside her.

"It's Peggy. She and Frances are stuck at her parent's house. It's snowing so hard no one can get out."

"Who're you talking to?" Peggy asked.

"Oh—well," Meg said into the phone. Peggy and Frances didn't know about her unexpected guest. Stephen watched with amusement, knowing Meg's roommate was asking about him and wondering how she would try to explain who he was and why he was here. "You don't want to know. You'll never guess, so don't even try. No, don't worry. No, I'll be all right. Yes, I can handle it. Merry Christmas to you too." Meg carefully placed the receiver back in its cradle.

"Well?" Stephen smiled.

"You think this is funny, don't you?"

"I haven't had this much fun on Christmas Eve in my entire life." He wasn't stretching the truth at all.

"Oh, really?" Meg heard alarms going off in every section of her brain, but her heart was overjoyed with the fun of it all.

"Excuse me, I think my last batch of cookies is ready," Stephen said as he casually went back into the kitchen. "Don't want them to burn."

Meg reached for the television knob. "I think we'd better catch up on the news." Switching the dial, all she could find were test patterns and empty channels hissing at her from a snowy blank screen. "Maybe the radio."

Rotating the radio dial, Megan quickly passed over Christmas music thinking it beautiful but not too informative. Stephen busied himself with colored grains of sugar and loved seeing her so suddenly uncomfortable.

"And now for an update on the weather." Meg's fingers held the dial steady as if she might lose the signal at the slightest motion. "Chicago is enchantingly covered with a white blanket of snow this Christmas Eve—or more accurately this Christmas morning. The twenty-two inches that have fallen in the last few hours have brought the entire city to a standstill. All is calm, and all is bright in the windy city tonight. I hope you're planning to be up all night, I know I will . . ." The announcer paused a moment. "Won't you join me?"

"Megan, I should call for a hotel. Is there one nearby? I'm sure I can't get a cab—the snow—the hour." Stephen could barely suppress his smile as he tried to appear serious.

"You're having the time of your life, aren't you, Mr. Bennett?" Megan hoped he would not force her to admit she was having the most enjoyable Christmas she could remember—at least in the ten years since her father died.

"Well, I'm not used to plopping myself on some strange

woman's doorstep and staying the night. I mean, how would it look to the neighbors?"

"Keep it up, mister, and you'll find yourself walking out into the snow."

"I mean, a girl's reputation could be ruined . . . her good name smudged, her honor tarnished." Stephen laughed and ducked as she sent a pot holder sailing past his head.

"Listen, I'll make you a deal," Meg said.

"A deal?" Stephen inquired. "What kind of a deal?"

"You don't tell anyone we stayed alone all night at my apartment, and I'll keep my mouth shut about the apron."

"I don't know about that. I'll have to give this some serious thought."

"Fine, you do that." Megan stomped out of the room and returned with a blanket and a pillow. "Here," she said, thrusting them toward Stephen, "I think we'd better get some sleep. Who knows, we may be here a while."

Stephen lay on the couch long after the sounds of Megan moving around in the next room had stopped. This was some Christmas. *Who knows, we may be here a while,* he remembered Megan saying. *Not an entirely unpleasant thought,* Stephen decided. *No, not unpleasant at all.* Pulling the blanket closer to his face, he detected a hint of Megan's perfume on the blanket. *In fact,* he said to himself, *this is great.*

CHAPTER THREE

Megan stretched lazily. The smell of coffee drifted to her room, and she suddenly remembered Stephen sleeping in the living room. She bolted from her bed and grabbed Peggy's robe. Heading into the kitchen, she ran into Stephen coming out with a cup of coffee in his hand.

"Good morning," he said cheerfully.

"Morning." Megan squinted at the clock. "What time is it?"

"Ten-thirty." Stephen sipped at the steaming coffee.

"You're kidding."

"We were up kind of late. I guess we both needed sleep."

"When did you get up?" she asked.

"Oh, an hour or so ago."

"I'm sorry, do you want to . . . well, the bathroom's through the bedroom."

"I know."

"You do?"

"I've already had a shower." Stephen watched her blush and found it amusing. "Does that embarrass you?"

"Well, I was . . . I mean, I was sleeping."

"I know."

Megan squirmed.

"You came in my room?"

"Not exactly." Stephen took another sip from his cup.

"What does that mean?"

"I went *through* your room. You're a very sound sleeper." He loved teasing her.

"I can't believe it." Megan started back toward the bedroom.

"What did you want me to do, Megan?" She stopped but didn't turn around. She wasn't about to let him see how unnerved she was. "The snow is about ten feet deep by now." He laughed as she stomped into the bedroom and shut the door soundly.

"Oh, no!" she moaned out loud. "What am I going to do with him all day today?" she asked the bedroom wall. It was a fair question, and a difficult one as well. Her family would want to know where this mysterious young man came from and where he was staying while he was in Chicago, and she was sure all the La Bianca eyebrows would hit the ceiling if they discovered Stephen planned to accompany her all the way to California. *Mother would have a heart attack for real!* Meg thought.

"Megan?" Stephen knocked softly on her door.

"What?"

"Breakfast is almost ready." She knew he was smiling just by the tone of his voice. "How do you like your eggs?"

Stephen presented her with a breakfast of scrambled eggs, blueberry muffins baked from a mix he had found in the cupboard, and a small dish of fruit cocktail. He poured her a cup of coffee and as he sat down Megan glared at him.

"You lied to me," she accused.

"I did not."

"Last night when we were making cookies, you pretended you had never been in a kitchen before. I can see this morning that wasn't quite the right . . ." Megan let her voice drop.

"That's not the same as a lie."

"It is."

"Is not." As a matter of fact, Stephen knew his way around the kitchen quite well. After all, had he not developed such skills he would never have had breakfast, nor many suppers for that matter.

"How do you define a lie, then?" Megan asked between mouthfuls.

"You didn't ask—you assumed." Stephen buttered another muffin, and before he popped half of it in his mouth, he said, "Don't ever assume, that's a mistake."

"I'll try to remember that little piece of advice," Megan said.

"See to it that you do."

The snow had stopped sometime around five-thirty. Snow removal crews were out, and all but emergency vehicles were kept off the streets. If all went well and if the clouds kept from dumping any more snow on the city, the main streets and highways would be open by tomorrow morning. The airport would be open by noon that same day, and by the time holiday travelers could get there, planes would be landing and departing on schedule.

"So, then," Dan Miller said when Stephen called him Christmas morning, "if you can get to the airport, you can get home."

"That's about the size of it, Dan." Stephen smiled at Meg. "We're ready, and once we're at the airport we're halfway there."

Dan had connections in Chicago, and with just a few phone calls he had arranged for a friend in a four-wheel-drive vehicle to come the next morning to take Stephen and Meg to the airport.

Stephen settled in front of the TV while Meg phoned her family.

"You can get to the airport, but you can't get across town." Rosa's accusing tone came across the phone with as much impact on Megan as if she were standing in the room.

"Mama, I told you, nothing is running today at all. I can't take a cab, and Benjie would get a ticket if he tried to come and get me." *Does she have to be so unreasonable?*

"I don't guess I'll be going either then," Rosa whined.

"Mama, don't be silly—Sophie's house is just a step or two away. Go, be with the kids. It's Christmas."

"I'll see how I feel a little later. And you? A fine Christmas for you there all alone."

"I'm not alone." Megan regretted the words immediately.

"Oh?"

"No, a friend is here with me." Megan interpreted her mother's silence as a command to continue the explanation. She groped for the right words. "A friend I met at work. A friend of Jen and Dan's. We're traveling together to the wedding tomorrow." Megan shot a darting look toward Stephen. She knew he was enjoying her evasive explanation, but he never took his eyes from the TV set.

"I'd better go now, Mama. I want to call Sophie and wish her a Merry Christmas. Tell Angelina for me, okay?"

After Megan finished calling Sophie, she walked into the kitchen. Stephen stayed in the living room, engrossed in a football game. Meg didn't know how to interpret Sophia's reaction to the news she wasn't going to be with them this year. *What was it I heard in her tone? Envy? Impossible.* Sophia carried most of the responsibility for the family holiday gatherings on her shoulders. Mama helped, of course, making menu and gift suggestions—if you could call them suggestions. She even helped wash the dishes when she felt up to it. Maybe it *was* envy Meg heard in Sophie's voice. Perhaps Sophie would like to be snowbound and away from the family on Christmas—just once.

"Something wrong?" Stephen's voice startled her from the kitchen doorway.

"No, not really. It's just that I've always been with my family on Christmas. It's different, that's all."

"Homesick?" Stephen didn't know what it was like to have a family to miss. What he missed was having a family at all—that is, before he and Jeff had grown closer.

"No, that's for sure." How could Megan explain to Stephen how she felt when she was not completely sure. "It's just that I'm outside looking in this year. Usually, I'm inside, wishing to get out."

"You were talking to your mother?" Stephen reached for the coffee pot and wrinkled his nose at the empty sloshing sound.

"Yes. She's not very happy with me." Meg took the pot from Stephen and rinsed it out, measuring absentmindedly as she put fresh coffee into the pot. Putting it back together, she set it on the burner.

"That's an interesting way to make coffee," Stephen observed.

"It is?"

"Yeah, I usually put water in it."

Without comment Megan yanked the pot off the stove, took the insides out, filled the pot with water, and placed it back on the burner.

Stephen watched her expressionless face. "Wish you could meet my family," she said offhandedly.

"I'm not much for families." Stephen turned and returned to his place in front of the TV.

Megan followed, stopping in the doorway. "I'm sorry."

"For what?"

"Assuming you'd like to meet my family. I do that too much, I know."

"It's not your family, Meg, it's families in general. Hey, you better get back in here, your team is losing."

"My team? How do you know which one is my team?"

"Because I'm a Viking's fan, that's why." Stephen made the announcement matter-of-factly.

"I'll choose my own team, thank you," she said quietly. She turned and went back in the kitchen. Stephen looked to the doorway, which a moment ago was filled with her presence, and he suddenly felt sorry—but for what? He didn't have a clue.

"Want to go for a walk?" Stephen wasn't used to staying indoors for hours on end.

"Your shoes dry?" Megan asked.

"I'm sure they are. I parked them under that contraption over night." Stephen pointed to the hot water heating system's register standing in the far corner.

"You're on." Meg reached for her coat and slipped into her boots so naturally that Stephen marvelled at how something that would be such a bother to him came so easily for her. "Let's go see if that diner is still open. I'd like a piece of pie."

"What? With no dinner first?"

"With my mother not watching over me, I'd like to eat dessert first."

The cold air blasted the young couple as they walked toward the diner. A few stragglers wandered the streets, but the diner was locked up tight when they arrived.

"Let's go back, Megan." Stephen was shivering. "I'm freezing."

"Sissy!" Megan knew how to get Stephen warm. He needed to move faster. She took off running toward her apartment.

"Oh no you don't." Stephen grabbed her by the collar. He tried to stop and hold Megan back too, but she kept moving and Stephen slid behind her on the sidewalk. "You've got traction on those army boots of yours," he yelled just before they fell together in a snowbank. Megan rolled over and lay in the snow laughing as Stephen scrambled to his feet and furiously brushed the snow off his pants. He hadn't planned on being in Chicago overnight, and he wasn't about to be wrapped in a blanket while his pants dried by the heater.

Back at the apartment, Megan rummaged through the refrigerator and found enough bologna for two sandwiches. Hot chocolate completed the simple meal. Later she popped popcorn, and the smell filled the entire apartment. Stephen challenged her to a game of Scrabble, and afterward she accused him of being a good speller but a bad sport.

Meg tried to call her mother again, but Aunt Maria said Rosa was in bed with a headache.

At eight-thirty they watched a special Christmas program on TV, and by ten Stephen was dozing on the couch while Megan sat in a bean bag chair she had dragged into the middle of the living room floor. She watched Stephen's eyes close and listened to his breathing deepen into a long, even rhythm. Quietly she got up from her place on the floor and turned off the TV. Reaching over Stephen, she clicked off the lamp on the table next to the couch.

"Where are you going?" Stephen asked sleepily.

"I thought I'd head for bed."

"Can we sit here a while?"

Meg straightened up and stretched to relieve the tension in her back from sitting on the floor so long. "I guess so," she said quietly.

Frances and Peggy had decorated a miniature tree earlier in the week, and the few little lights intertwined in its branches twinkled from its perch in the window. "It's nice here, Megan. I hate for it to end," Stephen's voice was barely above a husky whisper.

"Not your usual kind of Christmas, I bet," Megan said softly.

"Nor yours."

"It's been fun, Stephen. It really has."

Stephen took her hand and pulled her gently to sit beside him. She didn't resist when he encircled her in his arms and held her while they watched the little blinking tree lights in silence.

Megan moved to a more comfortable position, and Stephen nuzzled his face in her dark hair. Megan moved a little away from him and turned to look directly into his blue eyes. Stephen reached up and traced her jawline with his finger and slid his hand behind her head, letting her thick dark hair find its way through his fingers.

"Stephen," she asked quietly, "would you like to kiss me?"

"I most certainly would," he whispered and pulled her toward him.

"Merry Christmas!" Peggy burst in the front door of the apartment with Frances immediately behind.

Megan jumped to her feet just as Peggy switched on the light. Peggy looked from Megan to Stephen, and her mouth dropped open as her eyes grew wide.

"Oh my goodness!" Peggy dropped her bags and packages in a heap on the floor.

"Megan . . ." Frances was backing toward the door. "I'm so sorry. We didn't know. We thought you were here all alone." Frances continued her rapid-fire explanation as she took off her coat and then reached for Peggy's abandoned boxes and bags. "We should have called."

Stephen sat motionless on the couch, covering his mouth with the back of his hand. Megan could see his shoulders shaking slightly; he was about to erupt in laughter. She put her own hand to her mouth to try to stop the giggle swelling up in her throat. Peggy stood as if frozen to the spot, staring openly at Stephen.

"Hello," Stephen stood and said calmly, controlling himself. "I'm Stephen Bennett, from Jeff Bennett's office. I'm here representing Mr. Dan Miller in the final stage of the sale of Halloran's."

"Oh my goodness," Peggy whispered. Nodding her head, she said, "I know who you are."

"Yes, I saw you at the store, didn't I?"

"Stephen, meet my roommate Peggy and her new roommate Frances." Megan managed to make the introduction formally and without laughing.

"But what I don't know is," Peggy said ignoring his question and Meg's introduction, "what are you doing here?"

"I'm snowbound," Stephen said simply.

"Oh, I see." Peggy turned and stomped into the bedroom. The three others remained motionless until they heard the bathroom door slam and Peggy's loud moan before they released the laughter they each had been suppressing. In a few moments Peggy returned sheepishly.

"I'm so embarrassed. I mean I had no idea you two knew each other." Stephen relaxed back onto the couch without a word, waiting to see how Megan would explain his presence. Peggy looked from one to the other as she waited for one of them to say something.

"How'd you get home?" Megan's voice almost squeaked with the question.

Stephen shot Megan a surprised look. *Great move,* he thought, *change the subject.*

"My uncle Morgan is a cab driver. He took it as a personal challenge to get us back tonight," Frances said over her shoulder as she headed for the kitchen to put away the Christmas goodies her aunt sent home with them. "Hey, you guys, had any Christmas food?"

Peggy followed her into the kitchen, "This coffee fresh?"

Megan glanced after her two dear friends, but she turned back to meet Stephen's gaze when she felt him touch her hand. "You owe me a kiss, Miss Megan," he whispered. "One of these days, I'll collect it too." He smiled down at Megan, then walked into the kitchen.

"What'd you bring?" he said as he poked around in the bags.

"Hey, I want to tell you how much we admire what you did

to old Paulson yesterday." Peggy smiled at Stephen as she poured the last bit of coffee into a cup.

Was that only yesterday? To Megan it felt like last week or maybe even last year. Listening to the excited chatter coming from her kitchen, she felt like she had had the most wonderful Christmas of her entire life. She had not opened even one package or witnessed a single family squabble. She did not even have to help her mother to bed with a sick headache. *Could it be you can really have a Christmas without such traditions?* Meg wondered.

Stephen glanced back into the living room where Megan still stood and caught the smile she gave him. Then he returned the gift—with a smile of his own.

CHAPTER FOUR

"Hello, Auntie?" Megan shifted her purse and coat, which were slung across her arm, and stuck her finger in her ear to shut out the sounds of the bustling Chicago O'Hare airport. "It's me, Megan. I want to talk to Mama."

Megan twisted awkwardly, trying to push her body even further inside the phone booth. "I said I want to talk to Mama." She paused. "Please, Auntie, I'm at the airport. My plane is taking off in a few minutes, and I wanted to talk to her before I leave."

"What did you say? She—I—yes, I know how she feels about this trip, Auntie. She's overreacting. No, Auntie, I won't. She won't talk to me then?" Megan's eyes blurred with unshed tears. She didn't know if she was more hurt or angry. "I have to go. I'll write. Yes, yes, of course I will. Okay, bye."

Megan hung up the phone, picked up her cosmetic case, and walked slowly toward the gate. She looked in every direction, but there was no sign of Stephen. She was not exactly sure what she was supposed to do. This wasn't exactly what she had planned or expected.

She glanced at her watch and checked it against the big clock hanging from the ceiling. Only ten minutes left before departure time. Most of the other passengers had boarded already. She didn't dare delay much longer. *Where could he be?*

Megan stepped closer to the attendant checking tickets at the jetway entrance.

"You coming with us, miss?" the attendant smiled at Megan.

"I'm supposed to," Megan said. "But someone else is supposed to be here too. I can't imagine where he is."

"You need to board, miss."

Megan took a deep breath and handed the young uniformed woman her ticket. "Two-A, first class section, second seat on your right, next to the window."

"Thanks." Megan took one last look around the gate area, hoping to see Stephen. She should have objected more strongly to meeting at the airport instead of going with him this morning.

Dan Miller had called early this morning and talked first briefly to Megan then to Stephen. Another detail had come up at the last minute, Dan explained, something Stephen could easily take care of if they took a later flight. Dan arranged for someone to come and take Megan to the airport later in the morning, and Stephen managed to get a cab downtown. Meg and Stephen planned to meet at the gate in plenty of time to board together.

"If I'm not there," Stephen had said at the last minute, "go on without me. I'll catch the very next flight. I think there's one every hour or so. Don't worry. If I don't see you on that plane, I'll see you in sunny California."

Megan now wished she had insisted on going with Stephen to see Mr. Paulson. At least she could have demanded her paycheck. Paulson wouldn't have dared refuse—not in front of Stephen. She hesitated before actually stepping in the plane, but another friendly flight attendant hurried her along.

She settled herself as best she could, wishing Stephen were here to lift her coat and cosmetic case into the overhead storage compartment. Helpful attendants took her extra baggage and instructed her to buckle her seat belt. She heard the whir of the jet engines come to life, and she put her hand across her stomach as the aircraft began to vibrate with power. An attendant responded to the captain's order to prepare the door for departure, and Meg closed her eyes with the disappointment of knowing Stephen wasn't going to make the flight.

"Oops!" the flight attendant suddenly stepped to one side to make room. "You almost didn't—"

"I had plenty of time!" Megan heard his voice before she

saw him poke his head around the corner. He saw her immediately. His hair was wind-blown, and his face, flushed from running through the airport, broke into a full smile.

"This seat taken, lady?" Stephen said with mock formality.

"Please take your seat, sir," the flight attendant said firmly.

"Stephen, I thought you weren't going to make it." Megan didn't know what excited her more, the sudden jerk of the airplane as it backed away from the terminal or Stephen's last-minute arrival.

"I wouldn't have missed it for the world." Stephen smoothed his hair back into place with one hand and reached into his pocket to find his comb with the other. Catching his breath, he leaned his head back on the seat. "Whew!"

"That was a close one," the flight attendant said as she came back up the aisle. "I thought your little lady here was going on her honeymoon all alone."

"Oh, it's not—"

"Not on your life, ma'am!" Stephen grabbed Megan and pulled her close. "I'd never let that happen."

"Stephen!" Megan pulled away from him. "Stop it! You're embarrassing me." She glanced toward the flight attendant and opened her mouth to correct her misinterpretation.

"Ssh!" Stephen warned. "You want her to think we're off on a trip to California together—and not married? The shame of it all."

Megan blushed and turned away just as the aircraft began to lumber its way down the runway. She felt slightly dizzy as the ground outside the small window dropped out from under the plane and the force of the takeoff pushed her deeper into the soft leather seat.

She jumped and grabbed Stephen's arm at the large thump she heard and felt beneath her feet. "Take it easy, Megan, that's just the landing gear."

"The what?"

"The wheels. They have just folded up inside the bottom of the plane."

"Oh, that's all." Megan let go of Stephen's arm and started to relax.

"Let's just hope . . ." he said as he reached into the forward pocket for a magazine. Out of the corner of his eye he saw Megan's head spin around to face him.

"Hope what?"

"Well," Stephen teased, "let's just hope they can get them down again. You know, when we get to California."

"Oh, stop it!" Megan poked him soundly with her elbow and turned once again to the fascinating sights outside her window.

Stephen noticed how her thick, dark hair swung forward when she lowered her head, the way it followed her fine jawline and swept in a gentle curve around her cheek. She could turn her head quickly and her gorgeous, shining hair would gracefully follow the movement then perfectly frame her delicate face again almost immediately. He watched as she lifted her slender hand and unconsciously tucked her hair behind her small, perfect ear. Only then did Stephen see the simple gold hoop that pierced her tiny earlobe.

"Oh look!" Megan turned to get Stephen to look at the mounds of billowing blinding white just now visible as the aircraft climbed through the cloud cover. "The sun is shining!" Megan clasped her hands excitedly under her chin. Before Stephen could look into her deep brown eyes, she had turned quickly back to the window. Stephen leaned forward just in time for her hair to brush his face.

Megan didn't appear to notice how close Stephen was to her; but the close observer could see the quickening of her pulse at the base of her throat.

The late afternoon sun was beginning to set, and its bright rays cast a magical mixture of pinks and purples through the clouds spread before Megan like gigantic mounds of cotton candy. Heading west and south meant the sunset would be a prolonged and spectacular experience for Megan.

"Stephen?" Megan asked without turning from the window.

"Hmm?" He had reclined his seat to rest and try to digest the events of the day.

"Do you believe in God?"

"May I get you a cocktail, miss?" The flight attendant

leaned in front of Stephen and put down the tray from the seat back in front of her.

"We'll have ginger ale." Stephen ordered for both of them.

"Two ginger ales." The stewardess handed Megan a clear plastic cup filled with the chilled beige liquid.

"It's like a party," Megan said happily. "I think you should make a toast." She held her glass up and waited.

"To Christmas traditions." Stephen raised his cup and touched hers lightly with his own. "May we get rid of the old ones and make lots more new ones."

Megan smiled and sipped her soft drink, then fell silent. "Do you?"

"Do I what?"

"Believe in God?"

"I didn't used to."

"But you do now?" Megan searched his face and waited for his answer.

"I do," he said simply.

"Why?" Megan stirred the ice around in her cup with her finger.

"Because I've seen Him."

"You've what?"

"I've seen Him." Stephen's answer was simple and direct.

"Where?"

"In my brother, Jeff. In his wife, Caroline, too. In Sarah Jenkins and her husband, James. In Grandma Nelson—that's Cari's grandmother."

"And in Jesus too?" Megan didn't look up at Stephen.

"In Jesus, most of all." Stephen didn't ever talk about the changes he had experienced or the past he more than willingly left behind when he invited Christ into his life. It was a very private thing. Jeff had understood his need, called it sin, and told him Christ died to take it away and give him a life of worth and purpose. The elder brother had led the younger to Christ within the first few weeks of their reunion.

"I do too," Meg said softly. "I found out about Him, well, as a child, I guess. But I didn't understand anything about Him until I met Jen. She was so different, so truthful and—I don't know—alive." Meg handed her empty glass to the attendant; Stephen kept his and asked for a refill.

"Jen explained to me that it wasn't enough to know *about* Christ, but that I needed to *know* Him personally. I'd never heard that you could do that before." Megan grew pensive. "I've really missed her. We used to have such wonderful talks."

"I hardly know her at all. I've been working on this deal with Dan, though. I like him, and so does Jeff."

Megan dropped her voice even lower and looked around to see if anyone could overhear what she was about to ask Stephen next. "Do you . . . I mean have you ever . . . you know, prayed and had God . . . well . . ."

"Answer my prayer? Sure. I met you didn't I?"

"No . . . I don't mean . . ."

"Well, what do you mean?" Stephen drained his cup.

"You won't think I'm crazy?"

"I already think you're partly crazy."

"I'm serious."

"Sorry." Stephen straightened up in his seat and reached down to pull up his socks.

"Promise you won't think I'm crazy."

"I promise."

"I think that when you pray, you know, you talk to God. Right?"

"Right."

"Well, early this morning, before anyone got up, I went in to take a shower. I had something really important to speak to God about."

"Oh?" Stephen lifted one eyebrow as he glanced at Megan's intense expression.

"Something only He and I know about—it's private."

"So you're not going to tell me," Stephen guessed.

"That's not the point. I was praying, telling God all about this little—well, not so little really. I really dumped it all on Him. My anger, frustration, fear—everything and then . . ." Megan glanced around again, just to make sure no one else could hear. "I think God spoke to me."

"Really?" Stephen knew she was serious and tried not to discourage her by smiling.

"Really. You think I'm crazy don't you?"

"I didn't say that."

"I'm not kidding. It wasn't an out loud kind of voice. It was more like an inside connection of some kind." Megan laid her hand on her chest. "I had peace."

"And?"

"And I knew I wasn't supposed to worry about it—you know, what I had told God about—anymore. I know He's going to take care of it for me."

"I bet I can guess what it was."

"What *what* was?"

"What you prayed about."

"I don't want to talk about it. It's really something I have to—"

Stephen reached in his jacket pocket and produced a simple window envelope addressed to Megan. He laid it in her lap.

"My paycheck!" Megan couldn't believe her eyes. "How'd you get this . . . when?"

Stephen had also been awake in the early morning hours. In the silence he mentally turned over the details of the scene with Meg in Paulson's office. Something bothered him, and he couldn't put his finger on it. He remembered Jeff saying that he not only shared the details of his business decisions and problems with the Lord but that he waited for God's answer too. Stephen simply had breathed a quick prayer for God to show him what it was all about. Then he knew, he had to see Paulson once again. Dan's phone call gave him a reason to go back and face the unpleasant man again, and Stephen took the opportunity to ask Paulson what he had stuffed in his pocket when Meg took her keys and left.

"He was all apologetic about it of course. Says I totally misunderstood what was happening between the two of you when I came in."

Stephen went on to explain that he had insisted he would give the envelope to Megan and that Paulson had been more than enthusiastic about the idea.

Megan clutched the check as a child would a favorite teddy

bear. Her eyes closed and Stephen saw a tear fall down her cheek. "I really need this. Thank you," she said.

"Don't thank me," Stephen said quietly. "Thank Him."

"I just did." Megan's smile made Stephen's heart beat a little faster.

"Think I could collect on what you owe me, Miss Megan?"

"Not here!" Megan whispered insistently.

"Why not?" Stephen leaned toward her. "We're honeymooning, remember?"

"I don't think so!" she exclaimed. "I've only known you two days."

"Two and a half," he corrected. "But it seems like forever."

"That doesn't count," Megan said.

"It does for me." Stephen took her hand and touched her fingertips to his lips. "It does for me."

CHAPTER FIVE

Meg stretched, barely on the edge of sleep. She snuggled her face deeper into her pillow, trying to shut out the morning light. Slowly she opened her eyes, then quickly shut them again. For a moment she lay disoriented, not sure where she was.

The smell of coffee and Jen's ready laugh from the other room brought her fully awake. *Jen!* she remembered, *I'm in California for her wedding!*

Meg straightened the covers on her bed but made no move toward getting up. Instead she lay on her back, staring up at the delicate pattern on the off-white lace canopy above. "My mother's living room curtains," Sarah Jenkins had explained the night before. "I hope I haven't overdone it, but since Jeff and Cari were married, well, James thought I ought to redo Jeff's room—any way I wanted." Meg recalled the adoring way James had looked at his wife of over forty years. "I have been saving this lace ever since my mother went to be with the Lord. I wanted to do something special with it."

It's very special, Meg thought. The windows were draped with side panels of the matching lace and window cornices were covered with the same honey-colored satin quilting as the bedspread.

The head and footboards were made from rock maple and the highboy chest and dresser were a perfect match. A thick honey-colored fluffy oval rug waited for Meg's bare feet and the deep forest green wall-to-wall carpet provided a rich base for the room's feminine decor. Meg couldn't even remember turning out the hobnail glass bedside lamp before she went to sleep.

"Hey!" Meg jumped at the sound of Jen's voice as she came in the bedroom door. "We have a busy day ahead of us. Get your lazy bones outta that bed!"

Jen looked as good this morning as she had last night when she and Dan picked up Meg and Stephen at the airport. All tan and rested, Meg had observed before she noticed the large sparkling diamond on Jen's left hand. Dan and Stephen put the two young women in the back seat of Dan's large luxury car. "If we don't put them together, we'll have to listen to their gossip all the way home," Dan had laughed. Dan plied Stephen with questions about his observations of the business at Halloran's while Jen chattered to Meg, filling her in on wedding plans and details still to be attended to.

Meg's mind returned to the present. She heard Jen say, "You have a fitting today with the seamstress. Cari's dress is already done. It's so beautiful, Meg, just wait until you see it." Jen constantly carried a notebook full of swatches, business cards, and to-do lists. She climbed on the bed next to Meg, and together they examined Jen's choices of colors and discussed the flowers. "Since it's a New Year's Eve wedding," Jen said, "I thought it might be nice to keep it really simple—but, you know, elegant." Meg noticed how Jen beamed with excitement. "At first, I wanted to have the whole wedding party in black and white—you know, sort of like a complete tuxedo effect. Dan doesn't care. He just wants to get married! My mother, on the other hand . . . Meg, you listening?"

"Of course I am. It's just all so overwhelming, that's all. All these plans and stepping into the middle of it—it's like opening your door and getting sucked into a tornado!"

"I'm sorry, Meg. I would let you have the entire morning to yourself if I could. But Sylvia, that's the lady who's making the dresses, needs to see you today. Just in case she has to make alterations on your dress."

"It's okay—really!" Meg tried to assure Jen. "It's just that, well, you know, Stephen and I were cooped up in my apartment for two days, and with no parties or family dinners or anything—well . . ."

"You'll make up for it this week, that's for sure!" Jen stood and pulled Megan toward the bathroom door. "Get yourself beautiful, and see if you can do it in twenty minutes!" She pushed Megan toward the sink and turned to go. "Dan and

Stephen are going to meet us for lunch. Rusty arrives tonight, and from then on, it's no rest for any of us."

"Rusty?" Meg could barely conceal her dread of seeing him.

"Yes. You didn't forget? He's standing up for Dan. It's Cari and Jeff, you and Rusty. That's the whole wedding party." Jen looked at Meg. "I thought you knew. Is there a problem?"

Meg shook her head. "No, of course not. It's just that I haven't seen Rusty in a while." Megan turned toward the bathroom, choosing her words and tone carefully. "I'd better get myself ready. Let's not keep the lady waiting; I don't want a nervous seamstress poking pins in me!"

Shutting the bathroom door quietly behind her, Meg leaned back on it and closed her eyes. *Rusty!* The memory of their evening time together still haunted her.

"You don't know what you want, Megan." Meg could still hear his gruff whisper as he pulled her tightly to him. "I know you even better than you know yourself. Can't you trust me enough to know what you want and need?" Meg shuddered.

"Can't you tell how I feel about you?" he had asked. She felt again the pressure of Rusty's lips on hers as he kissed her that night—so long ago, a world away.

"Do you love me, Rusty?" Megan longed to hear the words.

"Let me say it this way," Rusty said as he kissed her again.

"No." Megan wasn't to be put off so easily. "No, I want to hear you say it."

"I'm not so good at words," Rusty said. "A demonstration is much more effective, don't you agree?"

Megan pulled away from his embrace. She wanted a man to love her enough to tell her so. She wanted to be held in his arms and she wanted his kisses, of course, but she also wanted more—much more. Rusty didn't quite see it that way.

"Women!" He was clearly angry with her. "I can't figure you at all, Meg." He grabbed her arm and pulled her toward him; Meg remembered the force he had used and how it frightened her. "We've been seeing each other for almost a year," Rusty said. "Doesn't that prove something to you?"

"Yes, it does." Megan still couldn't believe she had the strength to say it so calmly. "It proves," she recalled the words exactly, "that I've been dating a man for almost a year who can say everything except that he loves me." She rubbed her arm now in memory of how tightly Rusty had held it as she pulled away from him that night. "I will not marry a man who cannot say it, Rusty. I guess you haven't heard me before. Please, hear me now." Megan felt now just as she did that night. "I will not live my life with a man who has to find ways to prove it with presents, or who has to buy a new house to speak for him."

"Megan," Rusty had interrupted her, "I told you—you never have to worry, I will never cheat on you. I'll be good to you and can give you a nice house—a new one, out in the suburbs. I probably won't ever be rich like Dan and Jen, but I make a decent living. I'm a generous man, I won't hold back anything. I'll let you have as many babies as you want. I *promise* I will—"

"No, Rusty, I don't want the promise of a new house or guaranteed access to a bank account. I don't want a husband who will 'give me babies.' I want a husband who will say he loves me and can promise to keep on loving me. It's plain and clear—it's so simple. I don't want things, I don't want to have his babies. I want to have his heart."

"But it's all the same, honey. Don't you see that?" Rusty tried a softer tone, but Megan had stood her ground then, and she would stand it again if necessary.

"Not to me it isn't." Megan took a step away from Rusty, turned, then handed him his coat. "It's not the same to me."

"Megan?" Jen's gentle knock on the door interrupted Meg's memory. She quickly wiped the tears from her cheeks and stepped toward the sink to splash her face with cold water. "Meg, you all right?"

Jen pushed the door open slowly. "Megan, everything okay?"

Meg tried her best to suppress the sobs she felt welling up within her chest. She turned slowly and looked into the trusting, pure face of her dearest friend. "Megan, what's wrong?" Jen pulled Meg into her arms. "What's wrong?"

Meg felt all the resistance pass from her body when Jen embraced her. Sobs broke from her throat and ripped at her ribs.

"There, there." Jen soothed Meg's dark hair with loving strokes. "Let's go sit down and you tell me what's bothering you."

Jen led her gently to the side of the lovely lace canopy bed. The two friends sat together for a long moment while Meg tried to compose herself. She reached for a tissue from the bedside table and blew her nose, then wiped her eyes with the back of her hand. Megan took a deep breath and then looked at Jen's face.

"Jen, I have so much to tell you!" she cried. "I can't even decide where to begin." She certainly wasn't going to tell her about Rusty. Nothing would spoil this week for Jen and Dan, as far as Meg was concerned. She would manage the awkwardness of being with Rusty somehow.

"What's hurting you so deeply?" Jen's tone reflected her concern.

"It's just that—I didn't get to spend Christmas with my family." Meg knew she was dangerously close to telling a lie. "The snowstorm . . . and, well, it's my mother. She's not happy with my being here. I told you that from the beginning." She turned and looked into Jen's eyes trying to reassure her. "I'm not a bit sorry that I've come. But, well, to put it mildly, she hasn't made it easy. She says this decision has made her so unhappy that it's made her sick." Meg wound the tissue into a tight wad. "But then, you know Rosa—it's her usual tactic. She gets sick and Auntie Maria jumps at her beck and call. Sophie and Benjie cater to her every whim, or at least Sophie does, and Benjie just lets it happen. They can't see that she uses them all. Well, this time I stood up to her. It wasn't easy. Auntie wasn't any help either." Meg's eyes filled with tears again. "Mama wouldn't even talk to me when I called her from the airport before I left." Meg took a deep breath and rolled her shoulders back as if shaking off Rosa's last effort to control her.

"I don't care, it's so good to be here, Jen." Meg smiled at her friend. "I've been so anxious, waiting and all. I guess I can't believe this is finally happening—that I'm really here, with you!" The two girls stood and hugged tightly once more.

"Well, you're here, and it's for real!" Jen didn't want to hurry or pressure her friend any more than absolutely necessary. "Listen, do you want me to call Dan and cancel lunch? We could spend it together, just you and me."

"No!" Megan knew it would be her last chance to be alone with Stephen—well, almost alone—before Rusty got here. She needed to be with him; she felt somehow he would give her strength, and she wanted to tell him about Rusty. She was afraid to hope that it would even matter to him. Turning, she grabbed a hairbrush out of her purse, which lay on the chair by the bathroom door. "Ten minutes! I can do this in ten minutes! Go ahead, time me!"

Jen watched her friend disappear into the bathroom. While Meg washed her face, Jen spread up the covers on the bed and swung Meg's suitcase onto the little upholstered bench at the foot of the bed. "I'll help you unpack, okay?"

"Thanks, Jen. I was too tired last night," Meg said through a mouthful of toothpaste. "I hope I brought the right stuff."

"This is California, sweetie," Jen laughed. "Nothing is right, nothing is wrong. Nothing's in, nothing's out."

"What should I wear?" Meg asked.

Jen picked a pair of corduroy slacks and a matching V-neck pullover sweater. "Got something to go with this tan outfit?" she called to Meg.

"It's beige, Jen, not tan." Meg's mood was lifting.

"I see. Well then, what goes with beige? Got a pin or something?" Jen laughed.

"The navy print scarf and—no, the red one, in there." Meg pointed to the top section of her suitcase as she slipped into her clothes. Then she dug in the corner of the case and produced a new pair of red slip-ons and a matching clutch. With the scarf loosely tied around her neck, she applied red lipstick, puckered at her reflection in the mirror, and spun around for Jen's inspection.

"Perfect. You'll look great for exactly thirty minutes—then you have to undress again for Sylvia." Jen laughed as she pushed her friend out the door. "I still say it's tan."

Across town Dan glanced at his watch. Jeff and Stephen looked up from the papers spread on the conference table between them. Jeff winked in Stephen's direction. "We'll never get through this if you can't concentrate," he told Dan.

"They'll be at the seamstress's shop right about now." Dan smiled at the two men who were poring over the paperwork involved with Dan's sale of Halloran's.

"And you'll be at the cleaner's if we don't finish this before noon," Stephen laughed.

"Noon?" Jeff asked.

"We're meeting the girls for lunch," Dan answered. "Say, why don't you call Cari and join us? Jen is anxious for Cari and Meg to meet. It would be perfect."

Jeff caught the slight frown as it crossed Stephen's forehead. "No, I don't think so. The baby fussed all night. We'll all be at Sarah's tonight for dinner. Anyway, a restaurant isn't the best place for a crying baby."

Jeff watched Stephen's face relax. "Besides, it's the last time you'll get to be with Jen before the crowd gets here. People are coming from all over, right? Let's see, when are your folks due in?"

"Tomorrow morning sometime. They called early this morning from St. George, Utah. They'll be in Las Vegas tonight and drive on in from there."

"Driving?" Jeff asked.

"Yeah, they want to do the Rose Parade thing and all. It's the first real vacation they've had in years. The farm kept them pretty tied down. Now that they've retired, they want to slow down a bit and do some traveling."

"And Rusty?" Jeff watched Stephen out of the corner of his eye and saw that the name meant nothing to him.

"Tonight." Dan began pacing. "He's renting a car at the airport and driving over. I expect he'll call around six or so for directions."

"He has Sarah's number?"

"Yeah. He wants to see Meg as soon as possible."

"Oh?" Jeff asked, keeping an eye on his younger brother's face.

"Yeah. You know they've been going out quite a while, almost a year now."

Stephen froze, but only Jeff noticed.

"Serious?"

"I don't know. That Rusty's not one to be tied down, if you ask me," Dan said. "But you never can tell, Meg's a mighty pretty girl. If anyone can rope in ol' Russ, it's her."

Returning to their work, Jeff thought Stephen's shoulders drooped a little, as if he were suddenly tired—or maybe disappointed. Jeff didn't know which, but he'd find out soon enough. He and his younger brother may not have been raised together, but since Stephen moved to Redlands last year, they had grown close. Stephen's uncanny business sense and Jeff's law practice led them to discover that they even worked well together. Stephen had proved a valuable negotiator for several of Jeff's clients, and Jeff called on him often when he needed an objective third party for mediation or negotiation and even an occasional investigation. Jeff also knew Stephen trusted him enough to refer to his business clients who had legal problems. Hopefully, Stephen trusted Jeff enough to share his thoughts about Megan La Bianca.

Jeff had been the one to suggest that Dan send Stephen to Chicago to see what he could observe at the store before the January first deadline for the sale. Dan had a growing sense that something wasn't quite right in the whole deal. With his wedding only a few days away, it was impossible for Dan to leave, so Stephen went to have a look around, to keep his eyes and ears open.

Paulson's intoxicated advances toward Megan hadn't made a favorable impression on Stephen, nor in fact, with the investment group buying Halloran's. The problem was serious enough to justify a ninety-day extension on the deal. His buyers were unhappy to hear about Paulson's misbehavior, and they assured Dan they would replace him as soon as possible. "Hey, it's lunchtime," Dan observed. "I'm starved!"

"For the sight of one Jennifer Whipple, I assume," Jeff said teasingly. "How about you?" Jeff addressed the question toward his brother.

"I have found it's best never to assume." Stephen's voice was flat and matter-of-fact, belying the hint of anger in his eyes. Jeff wanted to ask him about it, but Dan's eagerness to meet Jen and Megan meant that particular conversation would have to wait until later.

CHAPTER SIX

"Oh, Jen." Meg was still in awe over her friend's unconventional choice of bridesmaid's dresses. "I can't believe how beautiful it is. Who would have ever thought to have dark colors at a wedding!"

"Not dark," Jen teased, "*deep.*" The two friends were still laughing when the two men entered the restaurant and found their way to the table.

"Good afternoon, ladies." Dan greeted them both politely then bent to kiss Jen on the top of the head. "How'd the fitting go?"

"Dan, you should see her—she looks beautiful in the color." Jen turned toward her friend, "Cari's hair is not as dark as yours, and her eyes are blue, but she loves the color, and it looks good on her too."

"Hi." Stephen looked directly at Meg.

"Hi."

Meg felt her cheeks warm involuntarily.

"Sleep well, Meg?" Dan asked.

"Oh, yes."

"I had to get her up this morning." Jen scooted closer to Dan. "I guess everyone is not quite as excited about the wedding as I am." She wrinkled her nose in Dan's direction.

"I am," he said, smiling down at his fiancée.

"Listen, you two," Stephen said, "we've got a whole lunch ahead of us. Try not to spoil our appetites, okay?"

All through lunch, during the happy chatter over lists of things still to be done today, Meg caught Stephen staring at her then looking away quickly if she glanced in his direction. He seemed quiet and distant, even a little angry. Dan excused himself, needing to get back to the house he purchased a few months ago to make sure everything was ready for his family's arrival. Jen decided to walk him to the car and to call the caterer to make sure she was on time for their appointment at two-thirty. "I have a few more errands to run, so if she's going to be late, I'll change my plans. I don't need to be waiting for anyone today."

Meg watched them disappear through the restaurant and let her eyes drop to her half-empty plate.

"You didn't eat very much." Stephen moved to the opposite side of the table to face Meg, sat back, and put his arm on the back of the booth.

"I'm not that hungry." Megan found the courage to look into his eyes for a moment then turned her gaze away. *Why does he unnerve me so much?*

Stephen picked up a spoon and examined it carefully as he asked, "Who's Rusty?"

Megan reached for the glass of ice water waiting beside her plate. Her mouth suddenly dry, she sipped it slowly and carefully placed the glass in exactly the same place it came from. "He's standing up for Dan. Dan knew him in Chicago."

"I see." Stephen carefully arranged the unused silverware in order in front of him. The silence hung heavy between them.

"And . . ." Megan paused. She didn't know how or what to tell Stephen about Rusty.

"And?"

"Hey, Megan." Jennifer hurried across the room toward the table. "Just as I thought, the caterer is running about twenty to thirty minutes behind schedule. I have just enough time to go by Serr's and pick up my cake knife and guest book. They came in yesterday." Jen checked her list as she talked. Stephen just kept looking at Meg, wanting an answer to his question.

Megan looked at him and shrugged, glancing in Jen's direction. *What can I say?* She wanted to tell him, *He's a guy I thought I might be interested in. But he's just like all the other guys I've known up until now—and not at all like you.* But this was neither the time nor the place. Jen was busy with her list, and Meg was here for Jen.

"If we leave right now, I'll just make it." Jen checked her watch. "Let's get on with our mission!" Her eyes twinkled with the excitement of all the details yet to complete before the wedding.

Meg scooted toward the edge of the booth she had shared with Stephen all during lunch. She looked over at him, silently pleading with him for understanding. "I have to go," Meg said quietly.

"I know." Stephen looked toward the doorway where Jen had paused, glancing over her shoulder toward them.

"See you tonight?" Jen called back.

"No, I don't think so."

"Why not?" Meg asked.

"I don't have the habit of invading another man's territory, Megan. I don't think it's right."

"Megan, we have to go." Jen hadn't heard what Stephen said. "Meg?"

"Coming." Megan walked slowly toward the door, wishing she knew what to say to Stephen. But the situation was impossible. Any further conversation would have to wait.

Meg turned back toward the table. "See you later?" Her question was more than a question; Stephen read the invitation in her eyes.

"You might." Stephen hesitated, then smiled. "Of course, I'll have to meet Rusty sometime. Tonight is as good a time as any I guess. I'll see you at Sarah's, not for dinner, though—later."

Meg's whole body relaxed. Stephen would come to the Jenkins' and somehow Rusty would get the message that her life was about to go on without him. Maybe even begin, really begin for the first time.

At five minutes past six, Rusty called and spoke to Dan. They chatted like two friends looking forward to seeing each other. After their brief conversation and Dan giving him explicit directions from the Ontario Airport to Redlands, Rusty asked to speak to Megan.

"She's not here at the moment," Dan said. "She and Cari are out strolling Cari's baby." Dan checked his watch, "Yeah, about forty-five minutes, depending on traffic. You'll still have a bit of rush hour congestion yet, but it should be thinning some by the time you hit the freeway." Jen smiled at Dan from the kitchen doorway. "Go ahead, check into your hotel . . . Yeah, take the Tennessee Street exit, turn left. It's right there on the left."

He hung up the phone and headed toward Jennifer to steal a kiss before the rest of the family started crowding the dining room. About ten minutes later, Meg and Cari returned from their stroll, and before long the commotion of friends and family happily together occupied Meg's attention, and she pushed thoughts of anything else from her mind.

Laughter and good-natured teasing filled the conversation around the table. Jen had known that Cari and Megan would become friends and was delighted to see that it was happening almost instantly.

James called for quiet while he said the blessing.

"Our wonderful Father," he began. Megan had never heard anyone address God so freely before. "We are so very grateful for the food You've placed before us. But even more so, we're grateful for those who have gathered here to share it with us. Thank You for Dan and Jen and the miracle of Your love that brought them together. Thank You for Jeff, Cari, and our little baby, Grace." Meg felt her throat tighten and her eyes fill with tears. "Bless the newest of our family of friends, Megan, Lord. Let her feel Your love and warmth of our welcome while she's with us." Megan was shocked, and she closed her eyes tighter to keep the tears back. "And for dear Sarah, who has so lovingly prepared this meal and who daily graces our lives with special touches of love, we praise You. Thank You too, our God, for Your Precious Son Jesus, and the new life He has given to us all, for it is in His Name we pray. Amen."

Sarah leaned over and patted James's hand. Jeff looked at his "chosen" parents, and Megan sensed the love he felt for them both. Jen leaned closer to Meg and whispered, "They raised Jeff. Aren't they wonderful?"

Wonderful wasn't the word for it, but Megan couldn't think of one better. She watched, amazed, when the baby fussed and Jeff restrained Cari from getting up. "I'll take care of her, you eat." But Sarah wouldn't hear of it. She insisted that both Cari and Jeff eat while she tended to her granddaughter.

At home, they wouldn't believe this, Megan told herself, *not even if they saw it.* She thought about the difference between this family gathering and the typical Thanksgiving dinner at Sophia's house.

"Can't you keep that brat quiet?" Benjie would yell at Sophie, who was already trying to balance two-year-old Tad on her lap. Then when she decided to take the restless baby away from the table, he'd snap, "Can't you even sit at the table with me on a holiday?"

"Hey, get me another beer, will ya?" he'd command later from his recliner as he watched a football game. Sophie would wipe her hands and walk the entire length of the kitchen, dining room, and living room with his beer. "This isn't very cold," he'd sometimes say, "see if there's another one in the back of the fridge." Never taking his eyes off the TV, he didn't even notice when she was tired. Even when she was pregnant, he expected her to wait on him like that.

"Megan?"

"I'm sorry, what?" Meg hadn't heard Jeff's last comments.

"Rusty called from the airport. He'll be here around eight."

"Oh," Meg said simply, then noticing Jen's confused expression she quickly added, "His plane got in on time then?"

"A little early, I'd guess." Jeff turned to Sarah and James. "Rusty worked for Dan for a while." He didn't try to explain anything further. "He's also a friend of Meg's."

Meg was grateful that he dropped it at that.

She turned her attention to Cari and changed the subject. The two of them began to share experiences and tell stories about Jen, blaming her for every mishap they had ever encountered together. But the look on Jen's face indicated that Meg couldn't put her off indefinitely. She would demand further explanation. Meg hoped she would be able to avoid it altogether, but she knew her persistent friend.

"Rusty!" Meg froze when she heard Dan's excited greeting from the front porch, where the men had gone to relax while the women discussed the wedding. "Come in, come say hi to Jen and, of course, to Meg."

Rusty's long legs carried him across the large room in a few easy strides. "Hi, Jen," he said, waving to her without taking his eyes of Meg.

"Hi yourself," Jen laughed.

"How's my girl?" he said to Megan. Not waiting for an answer he pulled her from her chair, lifted her in a tight embrace, and swung her around.

"Rusty, put me down." Megan tried to wiggle from his arms.

"Miss me?" he asked.

"Rusty, put me down."

"Excuse me, folks, I need a moment with my girl," Rusty said as he carried her across the front room, out the front door, and onto the porch. Setting her down, he caught her off guard, and instead of letting her go he tightened his hold on her, lowered his face toward hers, and covered her lips with his kiss.

"Stop it," Meg whispered loudly, "you're embarrassing me."

"Sure I am." Rusty laughed, and Meg escaped his grasp just as she heard a voice behind them.

"Good evening," he said, extending his right hand toward Rusty, "I'm Stephen Bennett, a friend of the family. And you are?"

Rusty stepped closer to Stephen and stretched himself as tall as possible, though he didn't quite come to Stephen's height. "I'm—"

Dan appeared just then and stepped between the men to make proper introductions. Megan took the opportunity to escape back into the house. She ran straight to her room, with Jen and Cari close behind.

"Who in the world is that?" Cari asked.

"That is Rusty—Mr. Egomaniac." Meg's eyes snapped with anger.

"He's a friend of Dan's," Jen offered. "I guess we don't know him as well as . . . or at least, I don't."

"This is going to be quite a wedding, if you ask me." Cari's eyes were full of teasing. "You and Dan will have to spend all your time trying to keep your groomsman and one of the ushers away from each other and away from your bridesmaid, all at the same time!"

"Oh my goodness, Jen." Meg's voice was tinged with the tears that filled her eyes. "I'm so sorry. What'll we do now?"

"We'll let Dan deal with them, that's what. Jeff will help him. How exciting, Meg. Two suitors!" Jen laughed at her friend.

"It's not funny, Jennifer. It's not at all funny."

"You're right, it's not funny—it's hilarious!" Jen and Cari began to laugh so hard that Meg found it impossible not to join them.

"I hope we're still laughing when this is over," Meg said.

Cari sobered, "So do I."

Only Jen still smiled. "It doesn't matter to me. I'm going on my honeymoon," she said with a put-on air, and with exaggerated grace she swept from the room.

"Great, she'll be no help at all!"

"And I'm the mother of a small child," Cari said. "I mustn't get myself into dangerous situations." Cari patted Meg's head, then on her way out the door she said, "You're on your own in this one." Meg heard her giggle slightly as she closed the door behind her.

Throwing herself over the bed, Megan smashed her fist into the satin pillow perched prettily on the bed, wishing it were Rusty's face.

CHAPTER SEVEN

On Saturday Meg, Jen, and Cari spent their time with more last-minute wedding details, shopping, and acting like three teenagers. Meg felt right at home with Cari. While Jen and Dan were away on their honeymoon, she hoped to find an opportunity to take Cari into her confidence about the situation with Rusty; she even thought she might share with Cari the problems she was having with her mother. In the meantime, she enjoyed an exhausting day with an old friend and a new one. By Saturday night, Megan was glad to be in her room before nine-thirty.

"Meg, it's Rusty, dear." Sarah's voice called from the hall. "He's on the phone."

Meg opened the door to her room and stared down the hall. Sarah approached the hallway, "It's Rusty, Megan. He's on the—" Sarah caught the distressed expression on the young woman's face.

"Why Megan, you don't have to speak to him if you don't want too. I'll just make your apologies." She turned back toward the phone.

"No, Sarah, it's all right." This was not Sarah's problem, Meg thought, it was hers. "I'll talk to him."

"Hi." Rusty's voice was softer and more gentle than what was natural for him.

"Hello, Russ."

"I'm sorry about last night. I was just so excited to see you."

"You could have seen me in Chicago. It's been over two months, Rusty—you embarrassed me."

"You're too sensitive, Meg. Women love to be swept off their feet."

"And you know what women love, don't you, Rusty?"

"I've been *told* that women . . . well, never mind. I didn't call you to argue. I'm going to Disneyland tomorrow and want you to come with me. Can I pick you up at eight-thirty?"

"Sorry, no."

"No?" Rusty's voice was back to the strong tone that Megan was all too familiar with.

"No. I have other plans." Megan had looked forward to being with this unique group of people who felt more like a family than friends. They were planning to attend church together, then having a potluck dinner at Cari's grandmother's house afterward.

"Like what?"

"Church, then I'm invited out for dinner." Megan didn't want to give him too much information. She didn't want him barging in on their dinner without an invitation or wrangling one out of Dan or Jeff just to be with her.

"Oh, that. Yeah, I was invited too. But I'm not one for big family gatherings, and I can go to church in Chicago. I can't see Disneyland in Chicago, though. Neither can you. Come on, what d'you say?"

"I already said it. No."

"You'd love Disneyland!" Rusty was insistent.

"I don't want to go." Meg shot an angry glance to the ceiling, unaware that Sarah was listening from the kitchen. "Listen to me, Rusty. I have other plans. What's so hard to understand?"

"Well, let's do something on Monday, then. If I'm going to see Mickey Mouse tomorrow alone, the least you could do is go to the mountains with me on Monday."

"Monday is the day before the wedding, Rusty. I'm not going anywhere with anyone. I came here to be with Jen and Dan. Didn't you?"

"Come on, Meg, they're so in love they don't even know anyone else is around. If we show up for the rehearsal, that's all they care about."

"Rusty, you have a few things to learn about friendship, you have even more things to learn about women—me specifically!" Megan could barely contain her anger. "And you have a really good time at Disneyland. Do me a favor, will you? Look up Goofy while you're there—you and he will get along just fine!" Megan hung up the phone emphatically, turned, and stomped back to her room. She wrapped her arms tightly around her stomach and sat down in the chair. Instinctively, she pulled her knees up and hugged them to her chest.

"Meg?" Sarah spoke softly from beyond the bedroom door.

"Yes," Meg replied without lifting her face.

"May I come in, dear?" But Sarah hadn't waited for an answer. She was already inside and moved across the room to kneel beside her troubled young guest. "Megan, what's wrong, honey? Can you tell me?"

Meg lifted her eyes to Sarah's face and her emotions gave way to the tender comfort she saw there. Sarah held out her arms to Megan, and Meg slowly let herself be wrapped in the woman's embrace. Safely within Sarah's arms, Meg released more of the sobs that had been inside her for weeks.

Sarah knew Meg needed to take her time and to tell only what she felt safe in sharing. "I'm so sorry you're hurting, Megan." Sarah said softly. "Is there anything I can do? I'm a very good listener—and I keep my mouth shut. What you share with me won't go any farther, unless *you* want it to."

Megan didn't know where to begin. Her whole life was in such confusion. With Sarah's patient urging, she let it all tumble out. There was Rusty, obviously, but also Vinny, Sophie and Benjie, and of course, her mother.

"I don't know, Sarah," Megan said at last, "can you make any sense out of this?"

"It's not for me to make sense out of, Megan. You're the one who has to find the answers." Sarah's kind voice softened her next comment: "It's you, Megan, who has the answers right there—" Sarah pointed toward Meg's chest—"in your heart."

"But my heart feels so empty, Sarah. Like there's nothing there at all."

"Then maybe that's the real problem—that your heart feels empty. What do you think it would take to fill that emptiness?" Sarah straightened and rubbed her back. "It's been a long day. Why don't you try to get some sleep. You can think about what I just said." Sarah paused, looking at her young friend. "Or pray about it."

Megan slid between the cool sheets, and Sarah tucked her in as she had many others who were either in trouble or just needing the comfort of a friend's warm hospitality. Meg couldn't ever remember being tucked in—not since her grandmother came to visit right after her father's death. The young teenager and the elderly woman had shared their tragic loss together.

"That's what my Grandma Meggie said the night . . ."

"Your grandmother's name is Meggie?" Sarah smiled. "I wondered where you got the name."

"It's English. My father's mother was English. My father named me after her. My mother wasn't happy about that at all." Megan laughed. "She thinks we should all have Italian names. She'd like nothing better than to have me change it. It's probably the only time Daddy stood up to my mother and got away with it."

"You're half English then?"

"Oh, no. My grandfather was Italian—full blooded. Daddy was half English."

"Caused quite a stir in both families back then, I guess," Sarah said.

"I think so. My mother had very little to do with my father's side of the family. She let me visit every once in a while, but it wasn't because she wanted to. I know that for sure."

Sarah didn't push Megan for any further explanation. She could see that the young woman's conflicts went deeper than Sarah could possibly know. No wonder Meg felt such emptiness. With a history of family conflict, Sarah could only imagine the stress Megan had been exposed to. She needed nurturing, something Meg had never had—and something Sarah was very good at. These three months would be wonderful for both of them, Sarah decided.

"Good night, Megan. Tomorrow you'll have a wonderful day. We'll see to that." Sarah leaned over and kissed Megan lightly on the forehead, then turned out the light as she left the room.

"Now, a story is told . . ." The young preacher began his message but Megan wasn't listening. She was still caught up in the wonder of the music that she had heard just moments before. Two young women had come from the audience to stand behind the simple pulpit and sing a duet so lovely that Megan had trouble keeping the tears from her eyes. Suddenly she was caught off guard with the laughter she heard ripple through the small congregation at the pastor's story. She looked around in disbelief. People laughing in church? How odd, how wonderful! These people loved their religion.

Meg knew Jen's faith was not fake, but she thought that kind of faith was possible only because Jennifer was such a special person. It was not hard to imagine that God had singled her out to have a special relationship with Him. But everyone in this room seemed to have that kind of relationship with God.

Looking to one side of the church, she caught Stephen looking at her. He smiled; she smiled in return, then turned her attention to the minister's message.

Afterward, she was anxious to speak with Sarah again. Could it be that she had heard right? Could you begin again? Was this what accepting Christ was really all about—a way to have a new life, a new birth? Not to just know about Christ, or even accept Him as Savior like Jen had led her to do. But to really *know* Him?

"Megan, aren't you hungry?" Jen asked at Sunday dinner.

Stephen looked at Megan's face and then at her nearly untouched dinner on her plate. He had noticed the way she had followed every conversation, had laughed at every funny joke and moaned at every bad one. It had not been that long ago that he felt much the same way that she did now. She had no way of knowing how much Stephen understood her.

"Everything ready for the wedding, Jennifer?" Virginia Rhoades asked from her place at the head of the table.

"Almost, Grandma Ginny," Jen said. Megan was grateful Jen's attention was turned away from her. "All I have to do now is make sure the groom gets there on time."

"Don't worry, Jen," James said, passing the salad to Jeff, "that's Jeff's job, right, son?"

"Might need some help, though," Jeff laughed. "I'm afraid he's been making plans to skip town."

"Not on your life," Dan said, beaming at the group that also included his parents, his sister and her family, as well as Dan's six-year-old daughter, Joy. "Wild horses couldn't keep us from marrying Jen, right, Joy?"

Joy clung to Jen's arm, and Meg remembered the career plans Jen had when they first met three years ago—plans that didn't include being a mother. Yet here she was—marrying Dan and getting a daughter too.

"God knows more what we want than we do," Jen had said when Megan asked about her marriage plans. "I couldn't be happier that He changed my plans and blessed me with Dan and Joy."

Sounds like Rusty, Meg thought. *He says he knows more what I want than I do . . .* Her thoughts were interrupted by a sudden squeal from baby Grace, much to the delight of everyone at the table.

"She's certainly got her own opinions," James said. "Just like her mother." He winked at Cari, and she stuck her chin out in mock insult.

"It's good for a girl to know her mind, Papa James," Cari replied, "and she can't start too soon, if you ask me."

"What'd I tell you?" James laughed.

Once again, the banter and the happy sounds around the table enchanted Meg. It was so easy to relax when every dish brought to share was appreciated and enjoyed instead of criticized, as so often happened when her family was together.

"I can always count on you to make my favorite," Jeff smiled at Sarah.

"What do you mean yours?" came the comment from the other end of the table.

"It's her specialty," James said proudly patting his wife's hand. "That and her chili—no one makes chili like my Sarah."

"What do you think of all this?" Jen whispered.

"It's really something," Megan said simply. "It's really different." Looking across the table, Meg caught Stephen's smile. He knew what she meant—he had spoken exactly the same words to his brother almost a year ago.

CHAPTER EIGHT

On Monday evening, the wedding rehearsal was as confused and fun-filled as it should have been, or so Sarah Jenkins said. Jen's parents were tentative, even reserved, and her father beamed with pride. Meg pushed away tears as she thought of her own father.

As children, Megan and her older sister Sophia would sneak up into the attic and drag out the old clothes and gowns from a former generation. The sisters often entered the make-believe world of romance and weddings, never once dreaming that their own father wouldn't attend their special days. No one could have guessed that he wouldn't be alive to give away any of his three daughters. How suddenly the accident happened, how quickly he died, and how drastically their lives all changed that day. The pain lingered a long time for Megan Marie La Bianca. Sharing this day with Jen, seeing her on the arm of her father, brought it painfully to the surface. She fought desperately to hide her tears.

"Do you silly women always have to cry at weddings?" Rusty teased as they walked down the center aisle as instructed by the pastor's wife. Meg pulled her arm from its proper place in his and punched him on the shoulder. "Hey! She hit me!" Rusty complained loudly. "Jen, make your bridesmaid here behave herself, will ya?"

"Listen, you two," Dan intervened, "we'll have to separate you at dinner if you don't straighten up."

"Fine with me," Megan said.

"What?" Rusty feigned shock. "You can't mean that, Megan, my love."

"Oh, but I do." Megan shot a pleading glance at Jen.

"She's just worked up that we're not getting married this

time around." Rusty stepped beside her and threw his arm casually around her shoulders. "Listen, Meg, you got a new spiffy dress, we're just a few hours from Vegas—what say we skip the reception tomorrow and get ourselves hitched?" Meg shook off his arm and stepped away from him. Rusty looked around, enjoying being the center of attention. "She loves me, can't you tell?"

"I can't." Stephen spoke up from the far corner of the small church.

"What's that?" Rusty couldn't tell exactly who made the comment, but he thought it was Stephen.

"Hey, it's getting late!" Jeff stepped forward. "The dinner reservations are for nine. It's almost eight-fifteen. If there's anything else you want to go through before tomorrow night, you better speak up—or, as the minister will say again later, forever hold your peace." Jen walked quickly to Meg's side and Cari stepped to the other.

"I think it'll go just fine," the minister's wife said. "Most weddings do." Her voice held a false sense of cheer. "Now, Jen, bring your bridesmaids and come along with me. I'll show you where you'll be getting dressed." She took Megan by the arm and gently led her out with Jen and Cari following obediently.

"You got a problem there, pal?" Rusty followed Stephen down the church steps toward the curb.

"Me?" Stephen turned to face Rusty head on. "No sir. I'm not the one with the problem."

"What do you mean by that crack?"

Dan came alongside Rusty and put his hand on his shoulder. "Take it easy, Russ, okay?"

"Let him explain that wisecrack first."

"I said, I'm not the one with the problem. What's so hard to understand about that?"

"Come on, Steve." Jeff touched his brother's arm. "Back off, okay?"

Stephen saw the unspoken warning in his brother's eyes. "Sure," he said flatly, "sure." Then seeing the concern on Dan's face, Stephen extended his hand toward Rusty. "Sorry, Russ, I guess I spoke out of turn."

Rusty stood motionless for a moment. "Listen, Bennett, Meg and I have been a regular thing for a long time. You've done more than speak out of turn. Stay away from her."

Stephen stuck his hand in his pocket. "When I hear that from her, I will."

"Listen, you!" Rusty lunged toward Stephen, and Dan quickly stepped between the two men.

"Knock it off, Russ!" Dan warned.

"Then you just keep him away from Megan, Miller. I'm warning you. You keep him away from my girl."

"Wait a minute." Dan felt the anger creep up his neck and begin to burn around his ears. "I don't remember hearing Meg say she was 'your girl.' I don't see a ring on her finger, Russ."

"You know I plan to marry Meg. I've planned to marry her from the beginning."

"Does Meg know that?"

"That's between Meg and me." Russ shrugged away from Dan's reach. "It's a long story."

"I see. And if an engagement is in the near future, why was Megan so willing to come to Redlands for three months?"

"Stay out of our business, Dan," Rusty warned.

"But you just asked me to keep Steve away from her." Dan leaned casually against his car parked at the curb. "That doesn't sound like staying out of your business to me."

"He better stay away from my girl, Miller." Rusty approached Dan, stopping just inches from him. "Or I'll hold you personally responsible."

"You warning me again, Russ?" Dan didn't change his relaxed position against the car.

"Take it any way you want." Rusty's dark eyes snapped with anger.

"I'm not going to take it at all." Dan crossed his arms across his chest. "No sir, I don't think I like the way you have shoved your weight around since you came here, Russ. Don't like it a bit. In fact, I think it would be best if you didn't come to dinner with us. You need time to calm down, to cool your temper a bit before the wedding. I don't want anything to spoil tomorrow for Jen." Dan stood away from the car and turned to squarely face Rusty. "Or for Meg, either," he continued. "Your bullheaded approach may work in Chicago, but it won't work here. Now, I'm warning you. Get rid of the attitude, Russ. Or—"

"Or what, Dan?" Rusty asked belligerently.

"Or drop your tux by my house on your way to the airport."

Rusty stared at the faces of the men surrounding them on the sidewalk. "I thought you were my friend," he said huskily.

"Yeah, that's what I thought too," Dan answered.

"When's the next plane out?"

"Midnight," Jeff said coming to stand beside Dan. "You still have time to catch it if you hurry."

Rusty spun to face Dan's car, raised his fist, and brought it down with such force that he left a dent in the roof. Then with a piercing look at Dan, he walked toward his rented convertible. The men watched in silence as he shoved the car into gear and squealed the tires as he peeled away from the curb.

"Guess you're short a groomsman," Jeff said.

"Oh, maybe one of the ushers wouldn't mind doing double duty." He smiled in Stephen's direction.

"Maybe not," Stephen laughed. "On one condition—just keep the rest of your goons away from my girl."

Dan groaned and covered his ears with his hands. "Don't let me hear anyone say that again—and please, don't let Jen or Megan hear about any of this!"

The small banquet room at the Mission Inn was more beautiful than anything Megan had ever seen before. Not as elegant as her cousin Margarite's sit-down reception at the Chelsea in Gary, Indiana, but the Mission Inn's Spanish decor was certainly more romantic.

"He's not coming," Stephen whispered to Megan.

"What?" Meg whispered back.

"You're watching the door, and it's not going to help. He's not coming."

"What are you talking about?"

"Your Chicago private eye isn't coming," he repeated.

"What?" Megan's loud whisper brought inquisitive glances their way, and Stephen smiled at the curious friends.

"I'll tell you later." Stephen turned his attention toward Jen's father, who had stood to give a speech. "Shh."

With great effort Megan turned her attention to Jen's father.

"My friends," Mr. Whipple began, "I can't tell you how happy Mrs. Whipple and I am, uh, are, that you have come to share in this happy moment as we celebrate our Jen's decision to marry Mr. Dan Miller." Mr. Whipple smiled toward Jen then raised his glass. "We're not drinking people, of course, but I think a toast is in order. I propose a toast to Dan Miller and his excellent choice of Jennifer as his bride. She's beautiful and talented—a bit on the spirited and ambitious side, I must admit—but nonetheless, a cherished daughter. And, since we couldn't do a thing with her, we gladly give her to you. May God have mercy on your soul!"

Megan's eyes opened wide with astonishment and turned expecting to see Jennifer mortified and embarrassed. Instead she found her friend beaming with adoration at her father. Jen's mother covered her mouth with her handkerchief, discreetly trying to smother her laughter.

Megan watched as Mr. Whipple's expression turned serious; she saw a tear fall unashamedly down his cheek. "All kidding aside, Dan, if God blesses you with this precious young woman just half as much as He has blessed me with her lovely mother, He will have outdone Himself for sure."

Megan saw Mrs. Whipple take Jen's hand in her own and raise it to her lips for a gentle lingering, tender moment. She watched Jen reach around her mother's shoulders for a warm embrace then extend her hand over to pinch her father on the leg. Then, the scene blurred through Meg's tears.

"To Jen and Dan. God's richest blessings be yours. And of course, we extend our blessing to Joy. It's not every man who can give his daughter away in marriage and become a grandpa at the same time."

"Here, here!" Jeff's strong voice echoed the sentiment of

the warm relationships between the people gathered to honor Dan and Jen.

Over the edge of her glass, Megan looked at the circle of close friends sitting at the long banquet table. She sat in silence, listening. Stephen saw the tears gathered in her dark eyes and knew why Rusty was so possessive—even if he was out of line. He finally reached for her hand. "Want to see the courtyard?" Without waiting for an answer he scooted his chair back and pulled her to her feet.

As Stephen and Meg went out the side door, Dan put his arm on the back of Jen's chair and leaned toward her. "We may have a slight change in the wedding party. Do you mind?"

"No," she said heaving a long sigh, "I certainly don't." She cast a furtive glance around the room then back into the face of her beloved bridegroom. "Is everything all right?"

"Everything's perfect. Don't you worry about it one little bit, sweetheart. Tomorrow is your day—our day. I'm not going to let anything, or anyone, spoil it for us." Dan bent forward and kissed Jen gently.

"Or for Meg, either?" Jen's face was shadowed with concern for her friend.

"For Meg, either." Dan said. "I promise."

Stephen guided Megan across the expansive lobby and through a set of double French doors. Once they were outside, he took her hand, and they walked slowly toward the middle of the tiled courtyard.

"Look up," Stephen said.

Even though they were surrounded by high walls, Meg could see the stars. She looked at the heavily plastered walls of the four-story hotel and noted the wrought iron grillwork planted with long, trailing ivy below each window.

"Are those window boxes?" she asked.

"I guess so, I don't know." Stephen took the Spanish architecture for granted. "I guess you could call them that."

"What kind of ivy is that?"

"I couldn't tell you. It grows everywhere."

"I noticed. Nothing stays green year round where I live."

Megan couldn't get enough of the beautiful courtyard. "Look at the palm trees growing right through the cement."

"That's not cement, it's Mexican tile," Stephen whispered as he leaned toward her.

"Oh, sorry." Megan smiled at his gentle correction.

"Tell me about Chicago." Stephen said.

"What's to say? It's the Windy City—I suppose you know that."

"I don't mean the city. I want to know about your life—about you."

"There's really not much to tell. I've lived there all my life. In the same house, across the street from the Catholic school where I went from kindergarten all the way to graduation. We saw the same friends, my parents played cribbage every weekend with the same neighbors. I guess if I would use one word to describe my life it would be *routine*. You know, the same week after week, year after year." Megan took her eyes from the charming surroundings and discovered Stephen watching her intently. His close attention caught her off guard, making her slightly self-conscious. "What about you?" she asked.

"Not too much to tell, either. My life was constant as well. Constant change, constant crisis, constantly on the move."

"No kidding? Sounds exciting," Megan said.

"It wasn't, believe me. I could've used some sameness." Stephen became pensive and thoughtful. "I never made many friends—we moved too much and it didn't seem worth the effort. Not when you knew you'd probably be leaving soon."

"Guess that explains why you're so close to your brother."

"That's new. We weren't raised together."

"What?"

"It's a long story. One I'd rather not get into right now. I want to know about you. Tell me about Rusty."

"Rusty." Megan took a long deep breath. "Rusty was the first guy I ever dated outside the neighborhood. My mother almost had a nervous breakdown over him." As briefly as she could, Meg told Stephen about meeting Rusty through Dan and Jen while they all worked to solve the mystery of a rash of thefts at Halloran's. "And it was through Rusty that I met Bobby."

"Bobby?" Stephen felt another pang of jealousy stab his heart.

"Bobby was called in to help on the case. He's more the intellectual type. Or at least he wants everyone to think he is."

"You dated Bobby too?"

"For a while."

"Was it serious?"

"Bobby isn't the serious type."

"What type is he?"

"He wanted all the benefits with none of the bother."

"What does that mean?"

"Bobby, like I said, is the intellectual type. He called marriage 'nothing more than a piece of paper.' He wants to live with someone first. Then when you know you're compatible, maybe marriage. He sees marriage as an institution—an unnecessary institution."

"And Rusty—how does he see marriage?"

"As a trap." Megan turned to face Stephen. "I haven't discussed this with anyone before. I was hoping to talk to Jen about all this. But with the wedding and all, it didn't seem right to bother her with all my problems."

"So you're talking to me," Stephen said matter-of-factly.

"Yeah, I guess I am."

"Isn't that okay?"

"I don't know, is it?"

"I think it is," Stephen smiled down into her warm dark eyes. "Let me see if I have this straight. Rusty, though he pursues you and talks marriage, is really only saying he's willing to let you trap him. Right?"

"I never saw it quite like that before, but I guess you could say that," Megan said, smiling.

"And Bobby—" Stephen looked back at the stars and away from the lovely face that distracted him so much. "Bobby advocates nonbinding trial marriage. A relationship that if it doesn't work out—or proves to be too much work—either party can walk away from—no strings, no complications, no commitment. Correct?"

"That's about it." Megan walked a little distance away, then turned to face Stephen again. "Then there's Vinny."

Stephen's heart jumped. "Vinny?"

"A guy from the neighborhood. I've known Vinny all my life. Our fathers were best friends."

"Oh really?"

"He's my mother's choice."

"Your mother's choice?" Stephen asked incredulously.

"Since we were kids. She always talked like it was meant to be. She still does."

"No kidding?"

"No kidding."

"You mean that still happens?"

"What still happens?"

"Arranged marriages."

"If my mother had her way it would. She picked Benjie for my sister Sophia."

"And is Sophia happy?"

"Happy? I don't think so. I don't think Sophia even knows she could be happy. She loves her kids, waits on Benjie hand and foot, and caters to my mother's every whim. She's too busy to even think about being happy." Megan paused, and Stephen saw the troubling frown crowd her beautiful features. "I don't want that kind of life."

"What *do* you want?"

"Something different. Something more. I want to be happy."

"Would it take so much, Megan? To make you happy, I mean?"

"I don't think so. I feel happy now." Megan raised her eyes to meet Stephen's.

He closed the distance between them and took her hand. "Miss Megan, I think I'd like that kiss you promised me."

"I think I'd like that too," Megan said.

Stephen looked deeply into her eyes and she searched the depth of his gaze. Slowly he lowered his face toward hers.

"There you are!" Jeff's voice seemed to echo throughout

the whole courtyard. He stood in the open doorway to the hotel lobby. "We're getting ready to go. We've all got a big day ahead of us tomorrow, and it's almost midnight."

"Be right there," Stephen called back.

Jeff quietly closed the door and stood just inside to ward off any of the others who might go in search of the couple in the courtyard.

Megan dropped her eyes from Stephen's and pulled away from him.

"Listen, Megan," Stephen said, "you and I both know this *will* happen."

"I'm beginning to wonder if it's supposed to," Megan said. As she turned to walk toward the lobby entrance Stephen caught her by the hand and spun her around to face him. Quickly he encircled her in his arms and without hesitation touched her lips briefly with his.

"It's inevitable," he said softly into her ear. "That's just a preview—the main feature will follow soon—very soon."

"Where's Megan and Stephen?" Jen asked as she tried to push past Jeff.

"They're coming," he said. "There's really no hurry, is there? You think you'll sleep tonight anyway?"

"What's going on?" Jen grinned at Jeff

"None of your business," Jeff answered in mock seriousness. But it didn't matter. Jen knew Megan would tell her sooner or later.

CHAPTER NINE

"It's for you, Jen." Sarah's cheerful voice belied her concern. "It's Sister Walters."

Megan caught Jen's eye as she went to take the call. "It's probably just a last minute detail we forgot to go over. I'll be right back."

Megan glanced toward Cari, who was bouncing Grace on her knee. Cari caught Megan's worried expression.

"Don't worry, Meg, nothing's going to go wrong—not today." Meg was pleased when Sarah invited Jen and Cari along with both of their mothers over for a patio brunch. After Rusty's mysterious no-show at the rehearsal dinner, Meg was uneasy. The six women eating and talking together had calmed her—until the phone rang.

"Well, we have a last minute glitch," Jen said upon her return.

"What's the matter, dear?" Mrs. Whipple said, her coffee cup poised in midair.

"It's Adrienne Mitchell. She's been rushed to the hospital with appendicitis.

"Adrienne Mitchell?" Cari's mother asked.

"The soloist, Eleanor," Sarah said.

"Oh my," Eleanor responded, "that's quite a glitch."

Jen's happy expression had been replaced by a frown. "I guess I can get married without a soloist, but I really wanted my wedding to be perfect."

"And perfect it shall be. I know just the person to replace her." Cari's eyes sparkled with excitement.

"You do?" Jen couldn't believe she could find a substitute on such short notice. "It's only a few hours before the wedding, Cari. How do you expect to pull this off? *You* going to sing?"

"Yeah, right." Cari stood and went around to embrace her friend. "Listen, Jen, I know it sounds far-fetched, but just listen, okay. You remember Sharon?"

"Sharon Mason?" Jen's eyes grew wide with astonishment.

"Yes. She went to high school with Jen." Cari explained to Megan.

"Does she still sing?" Jen asked.

"Like a meadowlark, honey." Jen's mother chimed in with her support for Cari's idea.

"She is coming to the wedding anyway," Cari said.

"Yeah, she's helping with the cake." Jen frowned in disbelief at Cari's idea. "But to *sing*?"

"Honestly, Jen, she has a beautiful voice. She's been singing a lot in church."

"She's quite in demand for funerals," Jen's mother added.

"Oh, great. I don't exactly want a funeral song for my wedding."

"She probably knows a wedding song or two. Why not give her a call?"

Jen shot a helpless look at Megan.

"Don't look at me—I don't even know Sharon Mason. And I certainly don't sing."

"Well, I guess I could . . . I mean, what if she doesn't know the songs I picked?"

"She might know something that would do," Eleanor added.

"Okay, let me see if I am hearing you all correctly. If she can sing, okay, great. And if she doesn't know the songs I want, I just have to be flexible—right?"

"We can always count on you to be practical, Jen," Cari laughed.

"Somehow the romance of my wedding day seems to be hanging in the balance." Jen started toward the house to make her call.

"Don't worry, Jen," Cari called. "The romance doesn't start until *after* the wedding anyway." The women joined in a chorus of laughter.

"Cari!" Jen stopped and spun around to face her friend.

"Look," Cari squealed, "the redhead blushes!"

Just after eight o'clock that evening, Cari and Jen stood as close to the door as they could and cracked it open just enough to hear Sharon Mason's clear, rich voice fill the small chapel.

Sharon's voice lifted the words of "Oh Promise Me" in beautiful melody.

"Listen, Meg." Cari pulled Megan closer, and the three crunched together to listen.

"Jen," Sarah Jenkins said from the other side of the room, "it's time to put that veil on, or you'll be goin' down the aisle without it."

The two bridesmaids checked themselves before the long mirror once more, touching their hair and faces lightly to make invisible corrections.

"Okay," said a breathless Mrs. Walters as she entered the small, crowded room, "the men are just coming in. Oh Jen, Sharon sang beautifully. Now remember, once the men are in, you walk slowly. You remember the pace, don't you?" The minister's wife looked over the rim of her glasses at Meg and Cari. "Now, Meg you go first, and you meet your young man at the altar." Meg felt her stomach tighten. "He'll walk you to your place on the side of the platform and then take his own. When he's there, Cari, dear, you begin your walk down the aisle. Jeff will meet you—"

"I know, Sister Walters. We've met there before."

"Oh, yes, so you have," the minister's wife giggled. "Then, Jen dear, Sharon will sing once more, before the wedding march begins, is that right?"

Jen nodded as Sarah pinned the lovely veil into her thick red tresses.

"Okay, here we go then." Mrs. Walters gently pushed Meg and Cari out the door. "I'll see you right outside this door when you're ready. I think the father of the bride wants to come in now."

Meg paused as Mr. Whipple stopped in the doorway of the nursery-turned-dressing room. The fresh pain of knowing that her father would never come into her dressing room or walk down the aisle at her wedding suddenly overwhelmed her. That coupled with the dread of facing Rusty at the front of the church made Megan's knees buckle. Cari caught her as she stumbled forward.

"Meg? You okay?" Cari whispered.

"I'll be all right—I just need a minute."

"You don't have a minute. You're supposed to be going down the aisle now."

Meg pulled herself to her entire five feet four inches and straightened her shoulders. She lifted her chin in the defiant way she often had as a child when she stood up to her mother.

"Atta girl!" Cari whispered as she gave Megan a gentle shove toward the center aisle.

Megan walked slowly and deliberately kept her gaze on the center candelabra on the platform. She refused to look at Rusty, though she was aware of the tuxedo clad figure awaiting her at the altar.

Only when she felt him gently take her elbow did she dare drop her eyes. "You can relax, Megan," Stephen whispered. Meg stared straight ahead in disbelief as he escorted her to the small piece of masking tape that marked her spot on the carpet. Only when Stephen took the place marked for Rusty on the opposite end of the platform and turned to face her could she let her eyes meet his and her mouth relax into a smile. Even while Jeff and Cari took their places, Meg kept her eyes riveted on Stephen's face. He didn't even try to cover the smug grin he wore.

Sharon sang once more as the wedding party stood. Meg still couldn't take her eyes from Stephen's.

It was Cari who finally touched Meg's arm and nodded in the direction of the center aisle as Jen stood in the back of the church on the arm of her father.

Tears sprang to Megan's eyes—tears of happiness for Jen, of course, but tears of relief for herself as well. She didn't even notice Rusty sitting in the corner near the back of the darkened church. Rusty, however, noticed her. He also noticed the way she stared, smiling, at Stephen. He didn't miss the way Stephen was looking at her either.

Mrs. Whipple, cued by the deep chords of the organ as the wedding march began, stood and turned to get a better look at her daughter. The congregation followed her lead. Rusty didn't stand. Silently, he seethed and slouched deeper into the pew.

Jennifer walked slowly toward the altar of the chapel. Her simple Empire waist taffeta dress rustled with each step. The sparkle in her eyes was evident even beneath the layer of sheer illusion that tumbled forward from the small glistening crown nestled in her red hair. The plain train of her dress filled the aisle behind her and multiple layers of sheer veiling fell gracefully to just below her knees.

Cari had never seen her friend look so beautiful. Meg's heart raced with excitement and love for Jen. Dan stood breathless and in awe of the beauty of his bride. Jeff beamed at Cari, and Stephen couldn't take his eyes off Megan.

Rusty still sat, glaring at the back of the woman who stood in the pew in front of him. Megan had rebuffed him. Stephen Bennett had humiliated him. He intended to have a talk with each of them. After the wedding, of course, but certainly before the evening ended. Privately if possible, but publicly if necessary.

CHAPTER TEN

"You may kiss your bride," the minister said. Rusty squirmed in his seat. "And now, may I present Mr. and Mrs. Dan Miller." The wedding guests broke out in applause, and Rusty slipped unnoticed from his place in the darkened chapel and out the front door.

"I need a drink!" he said as he slid behind the wheel of the convertible.

Just past eleven, after the last picture had been snapped, the last wedding gift opened, and the once beautiful wedding cake lay in heaps of crumbs, Dan Miller stood with Jen, now wearing a striking light green woolen suit, at his side. "Dear friends, my wife and I want to wish you a very happy new year. But now, we want to begin this new year together."

"And alone!" Jeff's deep voice interrupted. The circle of close friends and family laughed together.

"Yes, alone." Dan caught Jen's hand and pulled her toward the side door.

"See you next year, everyone!" he called over his shoulder as he put Jen into the car waiting at the curb.

Most of the wedding guests went back inside, but Megan stood alone on the sidewalk until she could no longer see Dan's car. Slowly, she turned back toward the small church's fellowship hall. Stephen waited for her on the steps. Neither of them realized that Rusty watched from his car.

"Cold?" Stephen asked as she came closer.

"No, not really. I can't believe you can actually stand outside like this on New Year's Eve without a coat." Megan glanced at the bright stars glistening in the dark sky.

"Most of us can't. You're used to much different winter weather than this."

"Yeah, at home this would be spring." Megan involuntarily folded her arms tightly across her middle.

"See? You are cold," Stephen said. Reaching out he put his arm about her shoulders and turned her gently toward the building.

Meg didn't resist his closeness and allowed herself to be escorted back inside with the others.

Sarah Jenkins and Cari had already begun to put the wedding gifts back inside their boxes, making sure each gift was correctly tagged with the sender's name. Jen's mother and Bess Miller sat in a corner chatting warmly. Joy slept soundly in her Grandpa Ben's arms. Jeff was helping Jen's father and James Jenkins fold up chairs to make it easier to walk around in the room. Most of the wedding guests had already left. Only a few decided to wait to ring in the New Year together at midnight.

"Want some more punch?" Stephen asked Megan.

"No, I don't think so. Thanks anyway."

"I'll just help myself to some. Be right back."

"You're pretty used to helping yourself, I'd say." Rusty spoke loudly enough that everyone in the room could hear.

"Rusty!" Megan was surprised. "I thought you—"

"Left," Rusty finished her sentence. "Oh, no. I came to California to attend Dan's wedding. I didn't want to miss it."

Stephen moved protectively nearer to Megan. "Well," he said, "the wedding's over. We're just about to call it a day here."

"Good." Rusty reached for Megan's arm. "Then you won't mind if I take my girl home."

Jeff watched the exchange from across the room. James Jenkins paused with a folded chair still in his hands. Cari quickly crossed the room to stand on the other side of Meg, opposite Stephen.

"Let go of me, Rusty," Megan said, trying to free her arm from his grasp.

"You're coming with me, Megan. We have a few things to talk about."

"We'll talk tomorrow, Russ. Not now."

"I said, let's go," Rusty insisted.

"No." Megan's refusal was clear to everyone but Rusty.

"You don't mean that," Rusty said.

"I think she does," Stephen said calmly.

"You stay out of this." Rusty let go of Meg's arm, tightened his hand into a fist, and thrust it toward Stephen's jaw.

"No!" Megan screamed. Without thinking, she stepped in front of Stephen and into Rusty's oncoming fist.

Megan's head flung backward at the impact. Stephen caught her before she fell, and Jeff and James immediately crossed the room, grabbing Rusty by both arms. Without a word, they walked him to his car.

"Now, young man," James said, "I don't know how you treat women where you come from, but that's not the way we treat them here."

"Listen, you." Rusty turned toward Jeff. "You keep your brother away from Megan. She's my girl, understand? You just keep him away, I'm warning you."

Jeff knew then from the smell of his breath that Rusty had been drinking. "Hey, man, you all right to drive?"

"I've only had a few beers. It takes more than that to get me drunk, believe me." Rusty shook free of their grasp.

"Let's call a cab, Jeff," James said.

"No, way." Rusty swung himself over the door and slid behind the wheel of the convertible. Starting the engine, he rammed the car into gear and roared away from the curb. Almost immediately he slammed on the brakes, screeched to a stop, then shoved the gearshift into reverse. He backed down the middle of the street and stopped alongside the two men.

"I'm telling you, keep him away!" he warned as he once again yanked the gear shift. Flooring the accelerator, Rusty squealed the tires and sped away.

"We should have called a cab," James said.

"Too late for that." Jeff's mouth broke into a mischievous grin. "So, let's call the cops."

"You get the license number?"

"Right here," Jeff tapped his temple.

"Think we should?" James could hardly contain the laughter.

"I think, Brother Jenkins, it is our civic duty." James and Jeff headed into the church and found the phone.

"You okay?" Cari brought Meg another cold compress made of paper towels and ice from the church kitchen.

"I think so." Meg's answer was weak.

Meg could barely hold back her tears. Her eye was swelling, her feet hurt, she was tired, and she was embarrassed. Reaching for the headpiece that matched her dress, she found it drooped to one side. She pulled out the pins holding it on and took off the satin bow and netting that sat so perfectly upon her head just a few hours ago.

"Maybe we ought to get out of here," Stephen said.

"That's a good idea, Stephen. Would you mind taking Megan back to the Jenkins'?" Cari asked.

"I wouldn't mind in the least."

"But don't you need us to help you here?" Meg asked.

"Not at all," Sarah answered from behind them. "Here's a key, Megan. Let yourself in the back door. The light switch is right there on the right." Turning to Stephen, she continued, "You can make some coffee, if you'd like. Don't leave her alone. Lock the door when you go in. And maybe you should stay in the back of the house. We'll be along in an hour or two."

Stephen took the keys dangling from Sarah's hand. "Thanks."

Cari helped Megan gather up her things and walked with her and Stephen to his car. Jeff followed them out and gently took his young wife in his arms as they watched them drive away.

"I hope Rusty doesn't bother her anymore," Cari said softly.

"Oh, he probably won't, not tonight anyway."

"I hope you're right."

"Trust me, I don't think he'll bother anyone tonight."

"What makes you so sure?" Cari turned to face Jeff directly.

"Oh, I don't know. Let's just say there's an extra sharp eye out for drunk drivers tonight." Jeff's broad grin was unmistakable, even in the darkness.

"Especially if they are driving a convertible?" Cari asked.

"You're such a smart woman, Caroline," Jeff said as he pulled her close and kissed her.

Once inside Sarah's warm and friendly kitchen, Stephen made coffee while Megan went to check her eye in the mirror. She took the opportunity to change and when she returned she was wearing deep turquoise slacks and a matching sweater.

Stephen poured two cups of steaming black coffee and began to open cupboard doors looking for the sugar bowl.

"Up there," Megan said pointing to the cupboard above the toaster.

"Are you in love with Rusty?" Stephen asked quietly as he dumped the second spoonful of sugar into his cup.

"Well, that's direct." Megan sipped her black coffee.

"Are you?" Stephen leaned against the kitchen counter, and Meg took a seat facing him on the opposite side of the small kitchen table.

"I'm not sure how I feel about Rusty." Megan stared into her coffee.

"Can you tell me about him?"

"I guess." Meg swirled the dark brown contents of the mug in her hands. "Like I told you before, I met him a while back when Dan was having trouble at the store. He was brought in from the outside, I was on the inside. We worked together."

"I see." Stephen studied Meg's face as she talked. Offhandedly, he observed that her eye, while a bit swollen, might not even show a bruise.

"We dated a while." Megan paused, and Stephen didn't rush her. "I really hoped—well, I thought there might be a future for me with Rusty. He seemed so in charge. So capable."

"So pushy," Stephen said as he took a seat at the table.

"Yeah, he can be that. But then, lots of guys I know back home are pushy. They have to be in control. Benjie is completely in control of Sophia."

"Sophia?"

"My sister. I was supposed to go to her house on Christmas Day, remember?"

"Oh, yeah." Stephen smiled broadly. "I remember."

"Benjie is my brother-in-law."

"Well, if that's what your sister wants, fine. But you?"

"I don't think my sister ever thought about what she wanted. Benjie was from the neighborhood. My mother and his mother are friends. They had Benjie and Sophie married before they were out of grade school."

"I still can't get over those arranged marriages—they really do still happen?"

"Not arranged, exactly. More like encouraged—*strongly* encouraged, if you know what I mean."

"No, I'm afraid I don't."

"My mother has a way of getting what she wants. She uses every weapon she can think of."

"Weapon?"

"Well, she mostly uses guilt."

"Whose guilt?"

"It works like this; I can still hear her say it. 'I promised your father, Megan. What do you want me to say to him when I see him in heaven? That you wouldn't listen to me? That the one thing that would let him lie peacefully in his grave you could, but wouldn't, give him? Is that what you want me to say to him?'" Megan could imitate her mother's strong Italian accent and animated hand motions perfectly.

"Wow." Stephen sat back in his chair and folded his arms neatly across his chest.

"Yeah, wow." Megan frowned and took a deep breath.

"Why does she say those things to you?"

"Because she wants me to marry Vinny."

"Oh yeah, Vinny. Tell me more about Vinny."

"He's the son of my father's best friend. We were raised on the same block. My mother always was pushing Vinny and me together. From the time we were barely in junior high, she talked about Vinny and me. It got even worse after my dad died."

"And, what does Vinny say about all this?"

"Vinny? How do I explain Vinny?" Megan tenderly touched her sore eye and cheekbone.

"I didn't mean you had to explain Vinny, Meg." Stephen leaned forward to rest his elbows on the table between them. "You don't owe me any explanations at all. Not even about Rusty. I'm just curious that's all."

"About what?" Megan smiled at Stephen.

"About you. More than curious, really. If I were going to be totally honest—"

"And you are, no doubt."

"I am." Stephen smiled and reached across the table toward her. "You'll find that out about me, Megan. I'm totally honest."

Megan looked at his outstretched hand, then looked up into his blue eyes. Without taking her eyes from his, she slipped her hand toward his, and their fingers easily intertwined.

"Are you?" Stephen asked.

"Am I what?"

"Totally honest?"

"Yes," Megan said then discovered a lump had jumped into her throat. "At least I think I am."

"Let's see, shall we?" Stephen once again spread his mouth into a wide smile.

"What do you mean?"

"I think you promised me a kiss once." Stephen turned his head ever so slightly and looked at her gentle mouth curved in the slightest smile.

"I did?"

"You're hedging."

"I am not. I'm trying to remember."

"So you don't remember?"

"I didn't say that."

"Then you do remember?"

"I remember." Megan's voice was barely above a whisper. Stephen reached toward her and touched her chin with his finger.

"Do you intend to make good on that promise?"

Megan dropped her eyes to look at his strong hand securely tangled in hers. She took another breath and closed her eyes.

"Well?"

"I always keep my word, Mr. Bennett."

"I'm glad to hear that." Stephen stood and shoved his chair back. "I intend to hold you to that promise."

Megan watched him stand and fought the urge to meet him halfway. Before she made up her mind, she heard Sarah and James's car come up the drive.

"Guess the folks are home," Stephen said without taking his eyes from hers.

"Guess so," Megan said.

"Guess we'll have to continue this conversation another time, then."

"Guess so," Meg repeated.

Stephen glanced at his watch. "It's after midnight. Happy New Year, Megan."

"Yes, I think you're right," Megan said.

Stephen grinned and winked at her. "I know I'm right," he said. "And I want to make you a promise now—" Stephen didn't finish his sentence but turned to greet Sarah and James as they came in.

"Is there more of that stuff?" James asked pointing to their half-empty cups.

After half an hour with the four of them sitting talking over coffee, Stephen walked toward the back door. "Guess I'll be going." Sarah and James said their good nights and tactfully left the kitchen and headed for the living room.

Stephen crooked his finger at Megan. She walked slowly toward him and put her hand in his. "Walk me to the door?"

"Sure." Megan's heartbeat quickened.

"About that promise—I promise you that I will hold you to your promise." Stephen tugged on her hand and pulled her closer as he slipped his arm around her slender waist. "And," he said emphatically, "I promise you this, I am a very patient man."

Stephen laid his cheek against hers and pulled her into a gentle embrace. He turned slowly and touched with his lips ever so lightly the place where her high cheekbone had collided with Rusty's fist. Sliding one hand around his neck, and the other around his ribs, Megan relaxed against him.

"Happy New Year, Stephen," she whispered into his ear.

"So far, it's the best one ever," he said huskily.

Raising his face and moving a bit away from her, he once again caught her hand in his. With the back of his other hand he stroked her cheek.

"And," he continued, "it's only just begun."

CHAPTER ELEVEN

"What's that all about?" Stephen asked Cari just after Megan bolted through the room.

"It's her mother. She tried to call home, but her mom won't talk to her."

"Still?"

Cari shrugged and shifted the baby from one hip to the other. "I guess they had some sort of falling out."

"I think it's more than that." Stephen looked toward the closed door of Megan's room. "Think you should talk to her?"

"Not until she's ready, Stephen. Until then it wouldn't do any good to try." Cari looked into the pained face of her brother-in-law. "Just give her time."

Stephen shrugged helplessly and turned back toward the dining room.

"Hey you two." Jeff's voice rang strong above throughout the house. "It's time for our annual game of Yahtzee. I feel like this is my year to win."

Cari and Stephen looked at each other and grinned. Jeff had said the same thing last New Year's Day. Within just a few short years they had developed a closeness that some families who have been together for generations never do.

Eleanor reached for the baby, and Cari gladly let her mother take her. James, content after a day of football and Sarah's cooking, read the newspaper from his recliner in the living room. Jeff had taken Grandma Ginny home earlier, and some friends were staying with her so that Eleanor could have some time with the family.

Jen's parents, exhausted from the strain of the wedding, had excused themselves right after dinner, and Dan's parents had driven to Pasadena to view the floats on display following the Rose Parade.

"*If* you win, big brother—" Stephen said.

"It will be because we feel sorry for you and let you win." Cari finished Stephen's sentence.

"Oh, right. Like you did last year, I suppose?" Jeff threw back his head and laughed heartily.

Meg sat up at Sarah's knock on the door. "Meg, dear, may I come in?"

"Sure, Sarah." Meg reached for a tissue and quickly wiped both eyes and blew her nose.

"What's wrong, sweetheart?" Sarah sat beside the young woman and slid a protective arm about Meg's shoulders.

"It's the same old thing," Meg said. "It's my mother. She still won't talk to me."

"What do you mean, still?"

"I called her from the airport in Chicago and my aunt said she didn't want to come to the phone. I had called to see if she was feeling better and to say good-bye before my plane left."

"And she wouldn't talk to you?"

"She didn't want me to come out here. She thinks I'll find a reason to stay and that she'll never see me again."

"Could any of that be true?"

"I only came for Jen's sake. These three months are for her. Oh, I have to admit I was more than willing to do it. Who wouldn't want to come to sunny California in the dead of winter?"

"And your mother?"

"She wants all of us to stay close to home. She's afraid that if something happened to her, or to any of us for that matter, we'd be—you know—apart."

"Is there any danger of that? I mean she isn't sick or anything, is she?"

"Oh Sarah, who knows? She's pulled this so many times before. In high school I wanted to go to cheerleading camp, and she was sure she was having a heart attack. So I didn't go. I wanted to go to a cabin up on the shore with a friend's family, and she came down with a sick headache, so I stayed home. It happens all the time."

"And was she having problems this time?"

"I went to see her the day before Christmas. She was in bed. She said she was sick and I wanted to see for myself, so I took a cab over and sat with her foı a while. I tried to get her to call the doctor, but she wouldn't hear of it. I was planning to be with the whole family on Christmas Day, over at my sister's. But then the storm came, and we didn't get out at all."

"Stephen and you?"

"Not just Stephen and me. The whole city was paralyzed. She didn't understand at all. She was so mad that I didn't come the day before and stay all night at her place. She just doesn't understand. She uses everything she can to keep us tied to her."

"All of you?" Sarah asked.

"At least Sophie and me. She let's Angie, my younger sister, do anything she wants. It's almost as if she doesn't really care what Angie does at all."

"Is that true?"

"No, it really isn't. It's just that Angie fights with her and Mama gives in. Sophia does whatever Mama wants—and I, well, I try to do whatever I can to accommodate her. But sometimes it can't be helped. I didn't plan that storm. But to hear her, you'd think I did."

"Sounds to me like she's afraid she'll lose you, Megan." Sarah gave Meg a quick squeeze. "I think all mothers go through that with their children."

"Why won't she talk to me, Sarah? I'm almost two thousand miles away, and she won't even talk to me on the phone." Megan's eyes filled with tears.

"I don't know, Megan. But fear can do awful things to people, things they sometimes regret later. The main thing is for you to let her be herself—"

"But I feel like she's trying to smother me!"

"I didn't say let her do whatever she wants—don't let her have her way, necessarily. But know that she's like this, and don't expect her to change. Do you have any reason not to believe this won't blow over in a little while?"

"It'll never blow over, Sarah, I can guarantee you that. Every Christmas from now on she'll bring it up again. She'll light a candle—I can almost see her now. She'll light a candle and say how good it is that we're all together again. 'But,' she'll say, 'there was one Christmas when it wasn't so good because we were not all together. You know what Christmas that was?' And before anyone can answer she'll say, 'That was the Christmas Megan chose to break my heart and spend the holiday with a stranger instead of here with her family.'"

"Oh Megan," Sarah laughed gently, "I doubt that she'll do that."

"You don't know her, Sarah. She will, year after year, just like a tradition, she'll bring it up and she'll never let me forget it."

Sarah believed in bringing up children so that they outgrew their parents and could stand on their own two feet. She couldn't possibly understand how a mother could purposely cripple her children and make them afraid to be on their own.

"Listen, Megan. You can't change your mother. But you mustn't stop trying to keep the lines of communication open. Why not drop her a note or a card? I'm sure she'd be thrilled to get something from you." Sarah stood and pulled Megan to her feet and into a warm embrace. "But in the meantime, there's a mean and vicious game of Yahtzee going on out in the dining room. Why not join the others?"

"You think I should? I mean you think it'd be all right if—"

"If you had a good time?" Sarah finished Meg's question. "I think you owe it to yourself. Will it make things right at home for you to come all this way and be miserable?"

"No," Meg said hesitantly.

"Well, then. Go wash your face and run a comb through that beautiful thick hair of yours and get out there. Jeff could use some new competition. He sounded a little too confident, if you ask me."

"Is she coming?" Stephen asked as soon as Sarah was a little distance from Meg's door.

"She'll be here in a minute," Sarah answered. "She's a little homesick, I think. It's the first time she's been so far from home. Just be patient and understanding, okay?"

Stephen was willing to be patient, but he couldn't understand. He didn't know what it was like to be homesick; but he knew all too well what it was like to be sick of home.

CHAPTER TWELVE

Before the end of the next week, Meg had settled into a welcome routine. She found working at Dan and Jen's store quite different from her job at Halloran's. She liked the casual friendly atmosphere and Jen's touches were obvious everywhere, not only in the displays and furniture arrangements but in the decor of the store itself.

Jen had put together furniture displays to show off each item's best features, and spot lighting from the ceiling gave dramatic but warm emphasis on some of the more expensive pieces.

Jen had also created what she called a "boutique" in a back corner of the store, where they sold accessories to complement the lines of furniture they carried. Her taste was impeccable, and the novelty of this addition to the store drew many potential customers.

Meg walked among the furniture groupings and became acquainted with their names, ordering procedures, and available fabrics. Now and then she took an item from the boutique shelves that she thought would accent a certain setting and placed it in the furniture display area.

With nothing much else to do, Meg decided to experiment. Using a little persuasion, she began by setting the dining table in the front store window with Sarah's good china. At the print shop up the street she had a small placard printed: "This table is set with the wedding china of Sarah Jenkins – 1935." Cari thought it was a wonderful display and made Meg promise to display her grandmother's next.

"Look here." Sarah held out the *Redlands Facts* to show Meg one evening when she came home for supper. "My dishes are in the paper."

Meg deposited her purse and sweater on a nearby chair and came to look over Sarah's shoulder as she read aloud:

The wedding china of Sarah Jenkins is featured on display this week at Miller's Home Shoppe and Boutique. Mrs. Jenkins was given most of the china by several members of the Jenkins family when she and her husband, James, married in 1935. In the years following, the Jenkins have added several interesting pieces for special occasions and anniversaries. Mr. Jenkins gave Sarah the sweet little covered jam dish on their first anniversary. The soup tureen and ladle were purchased in honor of their twenty-fifth wedding anniversary. This year the Jenkins will celebrate their thirtieth year of marriage. Congratulations, Mr. and Mrs. Jenkins on your anniversary, and also to Miller's for such a warm and meaningful display.

"What?" Meg said. "How did this happen?"

"The women's page reporter was downtown and saw the card on the table. She called yesterday and asked about the china. And then she asked if I minded if she wrote a feature story on it." Sarah's face was glowing with pride.

"I can't believe it!" Meg said. "You couldn't pay for this kind of advertising. Why didn't you tell me last night?"

"I didn't want to spoil the surprise."

"And all this time I thought I was using your dishes to show off our most expensive dining room ensemble—the dining room furniture was only showing off your dishes!"

"Not only that," Sarah continued, "but a lady from over in East Highlands called and said she had a covered candy dish that matches my pattern. I wasn't able to get it at the time, and they don't make them anymore. She wants me to have it."

"How much does she want for it?"

"She doesn't want anything for it. She said it belongs with the whole set and that it seems out of place with her things. She's kept it packed away for years."

"That's incredible!" Meg's eyes sparkled with excitement, and the idea of displaying Virginia Rhoades's china next made her wonder whether she had stumbled onto a clever feature that Dan could use in his weekly newspaper ads.

"Why don't you send this to your mother," Sarah suggested. "Be sure to tell her it was your idea. It'll make her proud, I'm sure of it."

"I don't think so," Megan said. "You don't know my mother."

"Oh, go on. She might surprise you," Sarah urged. "Mothers love to see things like this. Doesn't she know Jen?"

"Well, yes."

"Then, go ahead. Send it to her." Sarah reached toward the magazine rack beside James's chair. "I just happen to have an extra copy or two."

"Okay, I will. I'll do it right now."

Five days later, Rosa La Bianca took a deep breath and felt it catch somewhere deep within her middle.

"Again," the doctor said.

Once more she took a deep breath, and this time she couldn't suppress the cough that racked through her ribs.

"How long has this been going on?" The doctor didn't look at his patient but at Sophia, who sat nervously in a chair near by.

"Since before Christmas."

"That long? Two, three weeks?"

"Yeah, three." Sophia waited while he turned back to Rosa.

"Why didn't you call me sooner?"

"I didn't want to bother you," Rosa said nobly.

"Since when?"

"It was Christmas Eve, my daughter—not this one, Megan. She wanted me to call, but she was busy. She had to go back to work and—"

"I was home, Mama. You could have called me."

"Yeah, sure. A mother with two young babies and the day before Christmas, no less. Like you're supposed to drop everything and take your mother to the doctor with all you had to do."

"Angie could have—"

"Angie! She's about as useful in a crisis as . . ."

"It wasn't a crisis, Rosa. At least it wasn't then," the doctor said.

"It is now?" Sophia looked frightened.

"I'm not sure. We'll not know for certain until we get a chest X ray. Pneumonia is not something you ignore, Rosa."

"I didn't know it was pneumonia."

"What did you think it was?"

"I thought it was . . ." Rosa glanced across the room at her oldest daughter. "I thought it was my heart."

"I see. And you thought you could handle a heart attack by yourself." The doctor's tone was patronizing.

"Not a heart attack, not really, anyway."

"What then?"

"A broken heart. My daughter Meg, she—"

"Mama," Sophia interrupted, "Meg didn't cause this." Turning to the doctor she explained further. "Meg had the nerve to go against my mother's will."

"Sophia! How dare you speak like that!"

"Calm down, Rosa. You're not the first mother whose daughter had a mind of her own. They do grow up and leave home, you know—don't they, Sophia?" His gaze caught Sophia off guard.

"Well, some do. Others just move down the street."

"See, Rosa, you still have a daughter nearby. Anyone else living in the house with you?"

"My aunt Maria."

"He was talking to me Sophia, I can still answer for myself. Yes, my sister Maria. And of course, Angelina, my baby."

"Angie is not a baby anymore, Mama. She's twenty."

"Good, then you have people around you to help you. You'll be in bed for another few weeks, you'll need good care. Otherwise, I could—"

"No. No hospitals. I'm not dying yet." Rosa's tone was determined.

"I'll prescribe some medicine for you. You take it, you hear me?" Rosa shrugged her shoulders. "I want you to go downstairs now and have that X ray. The nurse will bring you a wheelchair. She'll go with you. I'll have the X ray results by tomorrow, and we'll decide then if we have to change the treatment. In the meantime, bed rest. Lots of liquid, hot soup and so forth. Also, I'll order a room vaporizer sent out. It should be delivered tomorrow. It will help you breathe easier."

Later that afternoon, Sophia got Rosa back upstairs in her bed and calmed Maria down enough to get her busy making soup. She checked the mail and found the letter from Meg. Thinking it would cheer Rosa up, she bounded back up the stairs with it and sat on the bed beside her mother and watched impatiently as her mother's weakened hands struggled to open the envelope.

Sophia waited impatiently as Rosa's eyes scanned the words. Finished with the letter, Rosa laid back even deeper into her pillows.

"Well?" Sophia said.

"Well, yourself. What? You can't read for yourself? Here, see it with your own eyes. She's two thousand miles away and having herself a real fun time while her own mother lays in her bed sick—maybe even dying—of pneumonia."

Sophia paid little attention to Rosa's words as she took in every word Meg had written. Sophia devoured the little newspaper clipping and then returned to read the letter again.

"Lucky Meg, huh, Sophie?" Rosa asked.

"What do you mean, Mama?"

"Living it up out there with the likes of Dan Miller and all that money he got out of old Mrs. O'Halloran. Living like the rich, I'd guess. And you, poor Sophie, stuck here with your old sick Mama."

"I'm not stuck here, Mama. I've got my family, my babies, too. Remember?"

"How could I forget? I'll guess I'll get along until you find time to come by once and a while. Me and Maria. We'll do our best not to be a bother to you."

"You're not a bother, Mama. And besides, there's Angie. She'll pitch in."

"Don't count too much on Angie, Sophia. She's not as good at taking care of things as you are."

"She would be if . . ." Sophia caught herself before she finished the sentence.

"Now, Sophie, she's only going to be young once. Let her

have her fun while she can. You'd think you'd be the first to tell her to have fun while she can. She'll be tied down soon enough—you know that."

"She's twenty, Mama."

"She's a baby. I don't want you bothering her."

"Mama, let me call Meg. She'd want to know that you're so sick."

"I told her at Christmas, and it didn't make any difference then—it won't matter to her now. No. I won't have you calling her. She made her choice and—sad to say—I wasn't it." Rosa looked at the childhood pictures of her three daughters in the frame above the highboy. "It's a shame," she said softly. "It's a crying shame. You give birth—you give life itself to them. You sacrifice to give them the best schools, good clothes, a nice place to live. You make sure they have the best friends and then what happens? They break your heart, that's what. Look at your own babies, Sophie, and know this: someday they'll break your heart."

Rosa's breathing rattled within her chest.

"Lay back now, Mama, and rest. Okay? Auntie Maria's fixing you some supper. I'll be back after the kids are in bed."

"Don't bother to come back tonight. You've got your Benjie to think about. I won't have you neglecting your husband on my account."

"You'd have Megan give up three whole months in California, though, wouldn't you?"

"Pardon me?"

"What would Benjie miss if I came back later? A cold beer, which he could get himself if he'd get up out of the chair for once."

"You heard me, Sophia, I won't have you neglecting my son-in-law on my account. I've had my say. Now go home to your family. I'll take my supper and then I'll go to bed. I don't want you coming back over here tonight."

Later that evening, after Sophie had fed and settled her babies for the night, she served Benjie his dinner in front of the TV as she usually did on wrestling night. Then she bundled herself against the cold night air and prepared to go back and check on Rosa.

"What do you think you're doin'?" Benjie yelled at Sophia as she reached for her coat.

"I'm going back over to check on Mama. I'll only be gone a few minutes. The kids are sleeping."

"Why can't one of your sisters take care of her?"

"You know why."

"That Angie, she's never home. And, Megan—well, who knows when we'll ever see her again?"

"I'll be right back, Benjie. You want something before I go?"

"No, go on. If I want anything, I'll get it myself. Where's the *TV Guide*?"

"It's in the side pocket of your chair. See? Right there."

Sophia let herself out the back door, quickly crossed the alley, and made her way carefully past Frank's house. Vinny was putting his car in the garage and called to her.

"What're you doin' out this late by yourself?"

"Just going to check on Mama."

"How's she doin'?"

"Doc says she has pneumonia."

"No kiddin'?"

"She'll be all right. Just has to take her medicine and stay in bed." Sophia pulled her coat tighter.

Vinny let down the garage door and secured the padlock. "Hey, let me know if you guys need anything, okay?"

"Thanks, Vinny. Say hi to Frank for me."

"Yeah, sure, I'll do that." Vinny started toward his house, then turned back to Sophia. "Hey, Sophie, wait up. I'll walk you on over."

CHAPTER THIRTEEN

"How's she doin'?" Vinny asked as Sophia came back into the kitchen.

"She's worn out from going to the doctor. Auntie Maria's with her now. She'll probably sleep pretty good."

"How bad is she?"

"Who knows? I don't think even the doctor can tell for sure. They took X rays today, so we'll know more when the doctor calls tomorrow."

"You look tired, Sophie." Vinny reached toward Sophie and casually smoothed a lock of her dark hair away from her face.

"I am, Vin, I am really tired."

"Want some coffee?"

"I really should get back. I told Benjie I'd just be a few minutes."

"He's watching wrestling, I bet."

"Yeah, he is. Same time, same station, every week." Sophia's frown deepened. "You know," she said, "on second thought, I think I'd like that coffee."

"Let me get it, you sit." Vinny jumped up and quickly set a steaming cup in front of Sophia.

"Thanks, Vin—you're a real pal."

"Sophie?"

"Yeah?"

"You hear anything from Megan?"

"No. Not much. Mama got a letter today. The first one, I think."

"She hasn't called or anything until today?" Vinny didn't even try to hide his feelings.

"I think she's called. But Mama won't talk to her. Said she didn't have anything new to say."

"What'd she say—in the letter, I mean. She doin' okay?"

"Sounds like she's doing great. She sent Mama a clipping out of the paper about the store where she works. She did a special display and they wrote about it."

"That must have made Rosa proud." Vinny sipped his own coffee.

"No, Vinny, it didn't. It made her mad."

"Mad?" Vinny looked at Sophia. "Or jealous?"

"Who knows?" Sophia shook her head.

"Did you know I saw Meg just before she left? When she came by the day before Christmas."

Sophia watched Vinny's face and tried to guess what he was going to say next.

"I was a real—well, let's just say I wasn't on my best behavior." Vinny swirled the last of his coffee, then drained the cup completely. "I made a complete fool out of myself, Sophie."

Sophia remained silent, waiting.

"I was a total jerk to her. I was drunk."

"You, Vinny? I haven't ever known you to drink."

"Yeah, a real shocker to me too." Vinny's expression clouded with shame. "I'll never do it again, that's for sure."

"What'd Frank say?"

"Dad? Nothing. He just looked at me and shook his head. Later on, when I got sick, he put me to bed. He must have cleaned it all up after I passed out." Vinny settled back in his chair. "The next morning I had quite a headache. When I came downstairs he was in the kitchen. He handed me a cup of coffee and said, 'Sit.'" Vinny's mouth pulled to one side in a hint of a boyish grin.

"After a while, he just said, 'Now, was that worth it?' I said, 'No.' He said, 'There'll be no drunks in this house, understand?'" Vinny put his elbows on the table and leaned forward. "He means it too. Dad never held with any heavy drinking, or women chasing and that stuff."

"He's a good man, Vinny." Sophia loved Frank; he was more like an uncle than a neighbor.

"Yeah, he is."

"Why didn't he ever marry again—you know, after your mom died?"

"He never wanted anyone other than her. He really loved her—still does for that matter."

Sophia stood and reached for her coat. "Is that the way you love Megan?"

"I don't know. I've been thinking about that ever since Christmas. How do you know how you feel about someone you've always thought you'd grow up to marry? I never questioned it. Your mom and my mom were always so sure it was 'meant to be.' Rosa never stops saying so. But Dad always said that when you love a woman like he loved my mother you don't even look at other women."

"You ever look at other girls, Vinny?"

"Yeah, I guess I do."

"And?"

"And I feel guilty about that. Rosa would kill me if she knew."

"She's really good at it isn't she?"

"Good at what?"

"Controlling everyone around her like they were her puppets."

"Not Meg," Vinny said, "and not my dad either."

"Your dad? You think she'd like to control your dad?"

"Marry him is more like it."

"Yeah, I guess you're right about that." Sophia glanced at the clock above the refrigerator. "It's getting late. I better go."

Vinny helped her into her coat and shrugged into his own parka. Outside in the silent, snow-covered backyard, he spoke again. "You going to call Megan?"

"Mama won't let me."

"How can she stop you?"

"I'd never cross her, Vinny. She'd make life even more miserable than it already is." They walked slowly in silence for another minute or two before Vinny spoke again.

"Why don't you write her a letter then?"

"I thought of that. But you know Mama, she'd never forgive me for that either."

"You have Meg's address?"

"It's on the letter that came today."

"Would it be all right if I wrote then?"

Sophia stopped and looked at the young man in the moonlight. "You miss her?"

"Yeah, I really do. But more than that, I need to apologize. I could tell her about your mother. Nothing too drastic, just that she's really sick this time—you know, and what the doctor said."

"I'll get the address for you tomorrow."

"Thanks, Sophie."

"No, Vinny, thank you. I really appreciate your walking me home."

"Hey, Sophie?" Vinny said softly as she walked away toward her own back door.

"Yeah," she answered as she turned around.

"Is your life really that miserable?"

"How would I know?" Sophie said. "I don't have anything to compare it to."

"Yeah, I see what you mean."

"Night, Vinny."

"Take it easy, Sophie."

"A date?" Meg asked with surprise. "A real, genuine date?"

"That's what I said, ma'am," Stephen said.

Meg moved the receiver from one ear to the other, then sat on the small stool that Sarah kept near the phone.

"I guess it'd be okay," Megan teased.

"I just thought that since we've already known each other almost a month—"

"Three weeks," Megan corrected.

"Yes, almost a month. I thought you'd like to see a movie and go out for burgers and sodas afterwards."

"It sounds like fun, Stephen. I'd love it."

"Good. Pick you up in half an hour."

"You mean tonight?"

"You have other plans?"

"No, not really. I just thought I'd . . ." Megan thought of the decorating magazines and manufacturers' catalogs stacked beside her bed. "No, nothing. I'll be ready in thirty minutes."

Megan quickly chose her deep green woolen slacks and a white cable-knit bulky sweater. She slipped her feet into her favorite brown penny loafers and rummaged in her jewelry box for the pin that matched her small gold earrings. As an afterthought, she slipped on a jade colored bangle bracelet.

Stephen arrived just as Megan slipped her toothbrush into the holder. She hastily ran a dark shade of rose-colored lipstick over her lips and pursed them together onto a tissue. Grabbing her hairbrush, she brushed her shiny brown-black hair and tucked one side behind her ear. Before she left the bedroom, she quickly dabbed a drop of her most expensive perfume behind each ear. She gave herself a last-minute examination in the full-length mirror in the hall before she entered the living room. Just as she came in, Stephen and James were discussing the validity of the wrestling matches on TV.

"I think it's all a show," Stephen said. "No one could take that kind of beating and walk away from it if it were real."

"You'd say the same about the Roller Derby then, I bet." James chided.

"Probably," Stephen laughed. He liked James and Sarah. Once he had gotten over his jealousy that Jeff had lived with them while he had been returned to their mother's care—or lack of it—he came to feel more and more like part of their family too.

"Hey, there's our girl," James said approvingly as Megan came closer. "Don't you look pretty tonight!"

Megan warmed under James attention. She could feel a blush beginning at the base of her neck and creeping slowly toward her face.

"I say, Miss Megan, you certainly do look very pretty. James," Stephen said without taking his eyes from Megan, "you sure know how to call 'em."

"I also know how to take care of them, young man. You have this young woman home at a decent hour."

"Yes sir!" Stephen said, giving James a sharp salute.

"Go on, you two," Sarah said coming into the room as she wiped her hands on a tea towel. "Don't you give him any mind. They're both of age, James, and too grown-up to be given any curfew."

But Megan loved the protective tone in James's voice when he spoke to Stephen. "Grown up or not, Megan's under my roof and in my care. See to it that you treat her with respect, Bennett, or you'll answer to me." James shook a rolled up newspaper playfully in Stephen's direction.

"I wouldn't treat her any other way, sir, I assure you." Turning to Megan, Stephen offered his arm. "Shall we go, miss?" Then he lowered his voice into a hoarse whisper, "Before the old coot changes his mind about letting you out at all?"

Megan's eyes danced with delight. Being doted on by two men was a rare luxury. James stood and grabbed for Megan's arm just as Stephen encircled her with his own and walked her quickly out the door. On the porch, Megan stopped suddenly, taking Stephen by surprise. She glanced into Stephen's eyes, then did a quick about-face and raced back inside, flinging herself into James's arms. She lightly touched his cheek with a brief kiss and just as quickly spun around again and rejoined Stephen on the porch.

"Good night," she called happily over her shoulder. "Don't wait up for me."

"You heard me, young lady," James chided as Stephen opened the car door and politely helped her in. "You get yourself in by a decent hour."

Megan threw a kiss toward the couple who so warmly opened both their home and their hearts to her. James circled Sarah's waist with his strong arm, and the two of them stood on the porch and waved Stephen and Megan off on their first official date.

"Do you always cry at movies?" Stephen asked after they had placed their order at the drive-in.

"Not always," Megan said. "Only when the endings are happy."

"Not when they're sad?"

"I never go to movies that have sad endings, so I don't really know."

"Play it safe, do you?"

"I don't go to movies to see sad stories."

"I see." Stephen looked at the clear, smooth color of Megan's exquisite complexion.

"Do you?" Meg asked.

"Do I what?"

"Like movies with sad endings?"

"No, I don't."

"See, you play it safe too."

"Not always."

"What do you mean by that?"

"I'm certainly not playing it safe right now."

"Now?" Megan looked at the few cars parked around them. "This looks like a safe place to me."

"Not this," Stephen said as he glanced around outside the car. "This," he said, gesturing back and forth between them. "This is very risky for me."

"This?" Megan asked, repeating his hand movement. "You don't feel safe with me? What? Do you think you're in danger with me?"

"Oh yes, Megan. Very real and very present danger."

"That'll be four sixty-five," the waitress said, smiling at Stephen as she hooked the small tray onto the car window. Megan waited until she was sure the waitress was beyond hearing before she spoke. "How am I a danger to you?" she demanded.

"Let's just eat our burgers before they get cold, okay. I've said too much as it is." Stephen handed Megan a paper-wrapped hamburger and reached across in front of her to open the glove compartment. Megan caught his hand, forcing him to stop midair, but he didn't look at her.

"We will finish this conversation, Stephen."

"Maybe," he said, looking at her hand on his. "Maybe not."

"We will." Megan withdrew her hand and unwrapped a portion of her hamburger. She nibbled at the warm, soft bun and realized Stephen was watching her. "What are you looking at?"

"Do you mind if I say a blessing before we eat?"

"No." Megan was stunned. "Of course not."

"Dear Lord," Stephen said softly, "we ask Your blessing on this food, and on our evening. We ask You to, well, to bless our relationship as well. Amen."

Megan dropped her eyes and stared at the hamburger in her hands. Stephen unwrapped his hamburger and took a large bite. Swallowing, he noticed Megan wasn't eating. "What's the matter?"

"That was sweet, Stephen," she said. "I never had a date do that before."

"Can I tell you a secret?" Stephen looked around to make sure no one could hear what he was about to tell her.

"Sure."

Stephen leaned toward her and motioned her to come closer. When her face was only inches from his he whispered, "I never did it before, either."

Megan turned her head toward him and flashed a smile wider than any Stephen had ever seen. He took another big bite of his burger, and with his mouth full, he pointed at her hamburger and said, "Eat."

Megan took a bite of her own sandwich and wondered if she'd be able to swallow it. She wasn't sure she could get it past the excitement growing in her chest.

CHAPTER FOURTEEN

Several times during the next few weeks Megan thought she couldn't have been happier. James and Sarah doted on her. Vinny's letter of apology let her relax. Jen and Dan, back from their honeymoon, had all their close friends over for a chili supper—which Sarah insisted on preparing. Joy was attending first grade and happily called Jen her mommy.

Jeff and Cari announced that they were expecting another baby. Stephen called almost every evening and took her out on two more official dates and made it a point to be at her side at every informal gathering.

Megan attended the small church with Sarah and James, loving to be with those who enjoyed the faith that was quickly becoming her own. Sarah and James patiently answered all her questions about God and the miracle of what they called "the new birth" as best they could, and they gently urged her to accept by faith those things which still puzzled her.

Megan couldn't have imagined a life more perfect. Even the news of her mother's pneumonia didn't trouble her once she shared it with Sarah and James, who prayed for Rosa now at every meal they shared together. The six weeks past seemed like always, and the six weeks stretching out in front of her seemed like forever. Only once in a while did she feel a painful reminder of home.

Because of Sarah's gentle encouragement, Megan wrote home every three or four days. Even though there was no response from her family, she kept her letters newsy and upbeat. She hoped they would brighten her mother's mood during her recovery.

One Thursday afternoon she came home from work to find a letter from Sophia waiting on her pillow. Sarah and

James had taken a meal to a family from their church, and Megan was expecting Stephen to pick her up momentarily. She refreshed her makeup, brushed her teeth and hair, and took Sophia's unopened letter into the living room to read it while she waited for Stephen. But before she could open the envelope, Stephen rang the doorbell, and she laid the letter unopened on the lamp table beside James's chair to read later.

Stephen took her to dinner and then to a symphony performance at the University of Redlands. The chamber orchestra's concert was especially beautiful, and the intricate music of the string quintet moved Megan almost to tears.

"Do you always cry at the symphony?" Stephen whispered.

"I don't know, this is my first one," she replied.

"Then so far, you always do." Stephen smiled and tucked her hand in his before he turned his attention back to the performing musicians.

In all the times he and Meg had been together since the wedding, Stephen hadn't made the slightest move toward collecting his promised kiss. Seeing how Megan reacted to Rusty's aggressiveness, he had decided to watch for Megan to make the first move or to give him some sort of signal. He wasn't sure what that signal would be, and he hoped he wouldn't miss it when it came.

As they left the auditorium and walked along the broad, tree-canopied sidewalk toward the car, Megan noticed a slight mist filling the night air. She shivered, and Stephen wrapped his arm around her shoulders, pulling her close.

"You're acting like a Californian, Meg."

"I am?"

"Yes, you're shivering, and it's only in the low fifties."

"I wasn't shivering because I was cold," she said. "I was shivering to get you to come closer to me." Megan snuggled closer to Stephen then poked him playfully in the ribs. She made a quick movement to run away, but Stephen's reflexes were too fast for her to make her getaway and he turned her around to face him. She laughed aloud, tossing her hair back with a quick graceful movement of her head, and collapsed against him.

Stephen quickly encircled her with his arms and then in the soft glow of the street lamp in the mist, Stephen looked into Megan's eyes and slowly lowered his face until his lips found hers.

"Megan," he whispered as he lifted his face barely an inch from hers. She smiled at him, then tucked her forehead into the gentle curve of his neck. She breathed deeply against the softness of his turtleneck sweater as she slipped her arms tightly around his waist.

They had both waited and longed for this moment, and neither wanted it to end too quickly. Only when the mist gave way to gentle drops of rain did Stephen release Meg from his embrace.

"I better take you home."

"I guess so."

"James will have my hide if I bring you home soaking wet."

Megan laughed softly at the thought of having such a protector. "Yeah, he might."

Once inside the warmth of the car, Stephen turned to Megan and could barely see her face in the darkness. "Megan," he said, "I have to go to Sacramento tomorrow."

"You do?" Megan's heart dropped.

"I have to go for a client of Jeff's. He's had some trouble with a licensing and zoning issue, and I need to search some state records."

"How long will that take?" Megan couldn't imagine not having Stephen in Redlands.

"It shouldn't take more than six or eight hours unless I run into a dead end or something." Stephen ran his hand behind Megan's head and cradled her soft, thick hair in his hand. "It won't take one moment more than necessary, I guarantee you that. I will catch a flight home as soon as I can."

Megan settled back against the seat as Stephen started the car engine. She could feel the tears swelling in her eyes and was grateful Stephen could not see her face.

"You're awfully quiet," he said as they rounded the corner by the Jenkins' house.

"I was just trying to think what I'll do to keep busy while you're gone."

"I'm sure Jen will be glad to have you to herself for once."

"Yeah, right. She's so busy fixing up her house and making cookies with Joy, she won't—"

"You're wrong."

"How do you know?" Megan said as Stephen pulled his car to a stop in front of the house.

"She complained loud and clear when she found out I was taking you out tonight. She wanted you to come over."

"She didn't say anything about that to me," Megan said.

"I know." Stephen's mouth widened into a broad smile. "Isn't she wonderful?"

"Yeah," Megan had to agree, "she certainly is."

Stephen quickly walked Megan to the porch, where they were sheltered from the rain.

"You'll miss me then?" Stephen asked.

"I'll try," Megan teased. She stood quietly for a moment, facing him, and unconsciously began to play with a button on his blazer.

Stephen took her hand in one of his, then lifted her chin with his free hand. "Megan," he said softly. "I . . . well . . ." he stammered.

"You don't have to say anything."

"Yes, I do." Stephen pulled her close in a warm hug. "Megan, I really care about you," he whispered.

Stephen released her, stepped back, and walked slowly toward the edge of the porch.

"Stephen?" Megan said softly. Stephen turned and faced her.

"Yes?" he whispered.

"I really care about you too."

"I'm glad," he said.

"Me too," she said quietly.

Stepping inside the door, Megan considerately closed it as quietly as she could. She stepped to the table beside James's chair and reached to turn off the lamp Sarah had left on for her. At the very moment she switched it off, her eyes fell on the envelope she had dropped there earlier.

Switching the lamp on again, she picked up the envelope and then decided to read Sophie's letter in her room.

Outside, Stephen watched the lamp go off, on again, and then off once more. He thought Megan was giving him a signal and responded by doing the same with the lights of his car. But Megan didn't notice; she was heading for her room. *A beautiful evening with Stephen and a letter from my sister,* she thought. *What could be more perfect than this?*

Her eyes wandered over Sophia's handwriting, barely comprehending the words she saw.

> *I'm sorry I haven't written sooner, but you know Mama. She's still in the same mood she was in when you saw her before Christmas. She'll have a complete fit when she finds out I have written you now. But there's something you need to know.*
>
> *I know Vinny wrote to you earlier and told you about the pneumonia. It's been long enough for Mama to be getting better and she isn't. In fact she's worse. It took Frank, believe it or not, to get Mama to go back to the doctor. The doctor assumed that she was getting better since he hadn't heard from us.*
>
> *Well, to get to the point, Mama's problems are worse than we thought at first. I don't know how to break this to you any other way—the doctor says Mama has spots on her lungs that indicate something more serious than pneumonia. He says it might even be cancer.*

Before she realized what she was doing, Meg dropped the letter to the floor, wrapped her arms tightly around her ribs, and cried aloud with sobs that racked her whole body. "No!" she screamed. "No!"

Sarah and James arrived at her bedroom door almost immediately. "Megan, dear," Sarah called as she first knocked, then without invitation opened and entered Megan's room with James following close behind.

"Megan," James said, "what's the matter?"

"It's Mama," Megan sobbed. "It's Mama!" Megan collapsed into Sarah's waiting arms.

James spotted Sophia's letter on the floor and picked it up. Without asking permission, he scanned the words written by Megan's older sister.

"Oh, sweetheart, I'm so sorry." He reached for Megan and

handed the letter to Sarah. "Hush there, baby. They don't know yet for sure. First thing in the morning, we'll call, okay? How's that? It's two hours later there than here. What time does Sophia get up?"

"About six-thirty, I guess," Megan said between deep sobs. "She gets Benjie off to work. He leaves around seven-fifteen," Megan began to quiet down and started wiping her tears.

"Okay then," James said, checking his watch. "That's four-thirty, our time. We'll set our alarm and get up and call."

"We'll know something for sure then, Megan. In the meantime, we'll pray." Sarah pulled Megan to sit beside her on the bed. "In times like this, it's not just all we can do—it's what we must do."

"Oh Sarah, I saw the letter earlier, but Stephen was coming and I didn't want to be late. I thought I'd read it after I got back. I even forgot about it until I saw it there by the lamp. I can't believe I didn't open it right when I got home! Mama's right—I'm not much of a daughter, am I?"

"Now, it doesn't make any sense to blame yourself and feel guilty. Doesn't your sister have the phone number here?"

"Sure she does."

"Then why didn't she call?" Sarah asked Megan the question, but exchanged knowing looks with James.

"I don't know. I guess Mama wouldn't let her."

"Your mama is not well, Megan. How could she stop her?"

"You don't know how it is, Sarah. You wouldn't understand." But even though Megan knew how it was, she didn't really understand it either.

"You know what I think?" James said calmly. "I think that if there had been any more news, bad or otherwise, Sophia would have called. Maybe there just isn't anything more to tell you at this point."

"James is right, dear. Once we call in the morning, we'll have all the information, right up to the minute. Right now, you need to get some sleep. Your sweater's damp. Did you get caught out in the rain?"

"Not really." Megan could barely remember the evening she had just spent with Stephen. Her mind was crowded with the accusations of a well trained guilty conscience.

James stepped out of the room until Megan was settled in bed. Then he came back in at Sarah's invitation, and the two of them knelt beside Megan's bed and lifted their young houseguest and her family in prayer. Afterward, James left the room, and Sarah stayed, stroking Megan's hair until she was sure the young woman was asleep. Finally, she joined James in the living room, where he sat waiting in silence.

Once again as husband and wife, they knelt together in the darkened room as they had so many times before. It wasn't the first time James and Sarah had spent the night in prayer for someone God had placed in their home and under their care.

Four hours later, Sarah gently knocked on the bedroom door. "Megan, it's time to make our call."

Megan opened her eyes in the darkness and decided she must have been dreaming, but then Sarah opened the door and quietly came to stand beside the bed. "It's almost five, nearly seven in Chicago. Are you awake?"

"Give me a minute, I'll be right there." Megan swung her feet onto the floor and raced toward the bathroom. Momentarily she returned, grabbed her robe, and pulled on her slippers as she headed for the dining room.

"Oh Meggie . . ." Sophia's voice cracked when she recognized her sister's voice. "I'm so sorry I had to write you. But I don't know what to do."

"How's Mama?"

"She's not well, Megan. The doctor wants to do a biopsy. He can't be sure what's wrong unless he does that, and Mama won't go to the hospital. She says a hospital is for dying people." Sophie began to cry, and then Meg heard Benjie's strong voice.

"Megan? Hi, this is Ben. Your mama's being a real—well, let's just say she's being her same old difficult self. She's wearing your sister out with worry. She won't cooperate with the doctor. Auntie Maria's a mess, crying all the time."

"And Angie?" Megan asked about her younger sister.

"Who knows? She's been gone a week now, with who knows who? We don't even know where, for sure. She's got herself mixed up with some of those hippies at the university. Hanging out and smoking pot, if you ask me."

Megan took a deep breath and let it out slowly. "Listen, Benjie, can you give me Frank's number?"

"Yeah, sure. It's right here, somewhere."

Megan wrote Frank's number on the pad Sarah held out to her. "I think I'll call Frank and get his opinion on all of this."

"Yeah, that's a good idea. Here's Sophie, she wants to talk again."

Megan listened as her sister took the phone. "Meg?"

"I'm here, Sophie."

"I'm scared, Meggie."

"Me too," Megan said. "Listen, Sophie, I want to call Uncle Frank. You think that's okay?"

"Yeah, of course. I think this is hard on him. You know, going through all this once before."

"You think this'll turn out the same way?" Megan asked.

"Megan, the doctor is pretty sure it's cancer. He's so angry with Mama for not coming in sooner. All those times she ran to the doctor and wasn't—" Megan heard Sophia blow her nose. "And now she really *is* sick and won't go."

"This is all my fault, isn't it Sophia?"

"No, Meggie, it's not. She blames you, but it's not your fault. She's wrong, Megan. She's wrong."

"What does she say about Angie?"

"Nothing. She just shrugs her shoulders and says Angie needs her father."

"I don't get it. Angie can be out doing who knows what and she doesn't—"

"But you—that's another story. You, she didn't even want living downtown with Jennifer. Listen, will you call me later after you talk to Frank?"

"Yes, I guess I could. Or I'll ask Frank to call, okay?"

"I forgot—it's long distance. Costing a fortune, I guess."

"We'll worry about that later. I better go now."

Megan immediately placed her call to Frank. "Uncle Frank? It's me, Megan."

"Hi, Meggie, it's Vinny."

"Oh, Vinny, hi. I was hoping to talk to your dad. Is he there?"

"Hi, baby." Uncle Frank's voice was affectionate and warm. Megan wasted no time in asking what Frank thought about the situation.

"I think," Frank said slowly, "that she's really in trouble this time and is scared out of her wits. It's like as long as she refuses to admit it, she'll not have it or something."

"Do you think I should come home?"

"Only you can decide that, Megan. You know how she is. She's not going to be any better just because you come home. All she's been saving up, she'll dump on you the minute you get here."

"I know."

"Sophie, on the other hand," Frank said, "would be really glad to see you. She's had this all alone, you know."

"You mean because of Angie." It was more a statement than a question.

"Yeah, Angie."

"Does she ever come home?"

"Occasionally, mostly when she runs out of money."

"Money? You mean Mama gives her money even though she—"

"Look, Megan, you know how things are with your mama. It doesn't make any sense to me, but there's nothing I can do. Sophie is afraid to even try. You're—" Frank let his sentence drop without finishing.

"I'm the only one who can handle her," Meg said.

"You'll have to fight her, you know."

"I have to try, though, don't I, Uncle Frank?"

"I would if it were me. Listen, whatever you decide let me know, okay? I'll pick you up at the airport if you need me to. Just call—I'll be home all day."

CHAPTER FIFTEEN

Stephen checked his watch. Five-twenty. He'd have to hurry to catch the six-fifteen flight to Sacramento. Thoughts of Megan and their date the night before filled his mind. Distracted, it took him several minutes to realize that the freeway traffic was slowing almost to a crawl. He reached for the radio dial, then changed his mind. He'd rather think of Megan.

Dan checked the alarm clock on his bedside stand as he reached for the ringing telephone. Five-thirty.

"Who was that?" Jen asked sleepily as he hung up the phone.

"James. Megan's mother is seriously ill. Meg is needed at home."

"Now?"

"As soon as possible. I think there's an early flight to Chicago. We can just make it if we hurry."

"I'll go with you."

"What about Joy?"

"I'll call my mom. She's usually up early."

"Or we could take her to Sarah's."

The Jenkins' house was quietly busy with the bustle of getting Megan's things packed, tempered with the seriousness of the situation awaiting Megan in Chicago.

"I shouldn't have come," Megan said softly.

"Oh Megan." Sarah came immediately to her side. "You couldn't have known this was going to happen. You said yourself it was hard to tell when your mother was sick and when she was just trying to get her own way."

"But I read in the Bible that I am supposed to honor my mother."

"And you do. I've never heard a word of disrespect for her come from you." Sarah took both Megan's hands in her own. "Honoring our parents doesn't necessarily mean we give in to every one of their whims or allow ourselves to be controlled by them. It means we give them the respect they deserve—not based on anything they have or haven't done, but just because they brought us into this world. In a way, honoring them is a way of respecting ourselves."

Sarah slipped her arm around Megan's shoulders. "Now understanding her, being patient with her, and knowing what to do for her—maybe even over her own objections—that's going to be quite a challenge for you." Sarah reached for the small Bible she had given Megan just two weeks before. "Here is another passage you might find helpful. Here, let me underline it for you, so you can easily find it again."

Sarah reached for a red pencil and then thumbed through Megan's Bible. Stopping at First Peter, chapter five, Sarah read aloud. "Here, sweetheart, verses six and seven. 'Humble yourselves therefore under the mighty hand of God, that he may exalt you in due time: Casting all your care upon him; for he careth for you.'"

"What does it mean, Sarah?"

"It means that as long as you present yourself openheartedly, humbly before God, you can give Him all the care you are carrying and let Him do the caring for you. You see, Meg, that leaves you free to handle the necessary responsibilities without the heavy emotional burden that times like this present. It doesn't mean that you don't care about your mama. What it does mean is that you care so much you choose to let God carry the heavy emotional load, leaving you unhindered to carry out the more practical things your mama needs you to do."

"How do I do that?"

"You just simply have a conversation with God, or maybe you could write Him a note or letter listing all the things about your mama and the situation that bothers you. Then why not just tuck it here inside your Bible? When you find yourself overloaded with the care of it all, come back to these verses and remind yourself that you have given those cares to God to take care of."

"Thanks, Sarah. I'll write the list on the plane. It'll give me a chance to think it all through ahead of time."

"Speaking of planes, we'd better get on with it or you'll be waiting for the noon flight instead."

Megan tucked the precious book in her small carry-on case beside her leather gloves. She fingered their softness and remembered Stephen's appearance at her apartment door when he returned the one she had dropped at Halloran's on Christmas Eve. She shut her eyes against the memory and then shoved the last pair of her shoes into the corner of her largest suitcase.

"Are you taking everything?" Jen asked, bursting through the bedroom door.

"Well, I thought I'd—"

"You may get to come back, Megan."

"Oh Jen." Megan's eyes filled with tears. "I don't know what will happen when I get home."

"I guess you're right. It's just that I don't want to think that you won't be coming back. It seems you fit so perfectly here. And what about Stephen?"

Megan threw herself into Jen's outstretched arms. Her sobs came with uncontrollable force.

"I can't even reach Stephen to say good-bye. He left early this morning for Sacramento."

Dan, standing in the doorway, took his cue from the look Jen threw his way. "I'll try to page him at the airport. Maybe I can catch him before he gets on the plane."

Stephen consciously loosened his grip on the steering wheel of his car. There was no use getting impatient now. He'd already be at the gate ready to board if the traffic hadn't slowed to a snail's pace. Only part of the freeway had been cleared of an overturned load of navel oranges, and all four lanes of traffic had been forced to funnel into a single lane for passage. There was no need to hurry now. He decided he'd get to the airport, change his ticket, and call Megan before she left for work. He was almost glad for the delay.

"He doesn't answer the page," Dan said, hanging up the phone. "He is probably already on board. His flight leaves in less than fifteen minutes."

Meg's spirits dropped even lower. She had hoped for at least a brief word with Stephen before she left. Was her mother's illness to be on both ends of her brief but increasingly important relationship with Stephen? All at once she realized: going home to her mother wasn't nearly as painful as the thought of leaving Stephen. *I'll make two lists for God,* she said to herself, *one about my mother, and another about Stephen.*

"It's time to go," Dan said, motioning toward the clock in Sarah's kitchen. Six-forty-five. "It'll take us forty minutes if we have no traffic problems. We have to change your ticket and get you checked in. That'll take another twenty minutes or so."

"We're ready, Dan," Jen said. James carried out the two heaviest of Megan's suitcases, and Sarah followed with her carry-on bag and the plastic garment bag containing the dress she had worn at Jen's wedding. Megan carried her heavy winter coat. She decided not to wear it until she absolutely had to, knowing her trip to California would be officially over once she put it on.

Stephen softly tapped his ticket envelope on the counter. "The next plane for Sacramento leaves at eight forty-five. It'll board around eight twenty or so," the woman behind the counter said. "That gives you time for breakfast—it's only a beverage flight."

"Thanks," Stephen said. Glancing at his watch, he compared it with the airport clock suspended in the center of the room. Both clocks registered seven-twenty. He decided to take the ticket agent's advice and have breakfast before he called Megan. "It's early yet, and she's probably still sleeping. I'll wait until seven-forty-five or so."

"Pardon me?" the man standing next to him said.

"Just talking to myself." Stephen smiled and headed for the newsstand to pick up a morning paper.

"We made pretty good time," Dan said as they approached the ticket agent. "Forty minutes flat, including parking."

"Good thing that mess on the freeway was cleaned up," Jen offered. "Nothing quite like thousands of spilled oranges to tie up traffic."

Megan stood quietly, letting Dan arrange her ticket and Jen do all the talking. "Want a magazine or something to read on the flight?" Jen nodded toward the newsstand.

"No," Megan said, patting her carry-on bag. "I already have something to read."

"Well, we've got a little time to spare. They'll be getting ready to board in about fifteen minutes. Want to get a cup of coffee or go right to the gate?"

"Could we go to the gate?" Megan asked. "I get so nervous, thinking I might be late. I'd feel better at the gate."

Stephen put his newspaper aside, picked up his briefcase, and left the coffee shop looking for a phone. Seven-forty-five. If Megan wasn't awake by now, it was time somebody woke her. He smiled at the thought it might be him.

"Oh, Stephen." Sarah's voice was tinged with sadness. "I'm so sorry you missed her. She had to go home—to Chicago. Her mother is gravely ill and her sisters need her."

"She left?"

"She's at the airport now. Dan and Jen are with her."

"The airport? That's where I am. I missed my flight."

"Well, if you hurry, you could probably find her. Ontario airport isn't that big. What do they have now, four or six gates?"

But Stephen wasn't listening to Sarah any longer. His eyes were already scanning the faces filling the small airport's ticketing area. Hanging up the phone, he quickly went to find the flight to Chicago's information on the boards behind the ticketing counter. The only flight to Chicago that morning was leaving from the west gate area, he discovered. Stephen ran through the crowd, bumping into strangers apologetically and leaving people staring after him.

Jen and Megan hugged tightly. "Please, Megan, call us the minute you get home, okay?"

"I'll see how things are first. I'll have to watch expenses. I just don't know right now." Megan didn't tell Jen and Dan her concerns about her younger sister, Angie. The thought crossed her mind that she'd have to remember to add Angie's name to her list of cares. "Listen, will you please, *please*, tell Stephen that I didn't want to go . . ." Megan's voice trailed off, and her eyes once again filled with tears. "Tell him I wanted to talk to him." She began to cry openly and Jen hugged her friend once again.

Stephen ran toward the gate at the end of the open corridor. Nearly knocking a woman off her feet and scattering the contents of her purse across the cement, he paused and hurriedly tried to help her gather her things. "I'm sorry, ma'am."

"Well, you ought to be," the angry woman shot back. "Try to be a bit more careful will you?"

"Yes, ma'am," he promised and once again raced toward Megan's gate.

"You better go," Dan said. "They're almost finished boarding."

Megan looked around and then up at the warm sunshine that had quickly burned away the morning mist. She felt it warm her face and then she turned once again to Jen.

"I hope I'll get to come back here someday." The two friends stared at each other. "I just wish I could have talked to Stephen," she said as the tears once again coursed down her cheeks. "I don't want to go . . ."

She turned and headed toward the waiting plane. One by one she forced her feet to climb the stairway, and without turning, she stepped through the open door and into the aircraft.

"Wait!" Stephen yelled from behind the chain-link fence that preventing him from taking a shortcut to where Megan had just disappeared from sight. "Wait!"

"You have a ticket, sir?" the gate attendant asked.

"No, I have to see someone."

"Sorry, sir. They're closing the door."

"Can't you do something?" he almost screamed at the young woman.

"I'm sorry, sir. There's nothing—"

"Stephen!" Dan's surprised voice came from behind him. "We thought you were already gone."

"I was in the coffee shop. I could have been with her . . . I didn't know." Stephen's voice shook with the tears that ran down his cheeks. "Why does she have to go?"

Jen stepped in front of Stephen and tried to put an arm around his waist. He stepped away from her, refusing to be comforted. He sobbed silently as he watched the huge aircraft pull away, taking the one woman he could honestly say he ever openly and freely permitted himself to care for. Jen stepped closely behind him and put her hand on his shoulder.

"I don't understand," he said wiping the tears from his face with his hand. "We were together last night. She didn't say anything then. Why didn't she tell me she was leaving this morning?"

"She didn't know," Jen said. "She didn't know until she read her sister's letter and then called home this morning."

"How long's she going to be gone?" Stephen asked. He braced himself for the answer.

"I don't know," Jen said softly.

"She's not coming back, is she?" Stephen's sad tone tore at Jen's heart.

"Oh, I hope she does," Jen said too cheerfully.

"She won't," Stephen said flatly. "I know she won't." He turned and walked quickly away from Jen and Dan.

Tears threatened to spill from Jen's eyes, and Dan gently pulled her within the circle of his arms. She buried her face in his strong shoulder and let herself cry. She felt wonderfully grateful, yet almost guilty, for having him when both Megan and Stephen seemed so alone.

CHAPTER SIXTEEN

Megan refused the coffee offered by the cheerful flight attendant and reached into her carry-on bag and found her Bible. She opened it to the verses Sarah had underlined in red pencil.

Oh God, I don't know where to begin. She found a small notebook in her purse and a pen with *Miller's Home Furnishings* printed in gold on the barrel. She turned the pen over, watching the light play against the gold lettering and the dark navy blue plastic, and let her thoughts drift once again back to Redlands.

In her mind's eye she pictured the large clock in front of Wilson's jewelry store and the sweet contented couple that owned and operated it. She thought of the stately palm trees lining Center and Cajon streets. She remembered the pepper trees growing down the center divider of Brookside Avenue and the Spanish architecture of the post office.

Jen had walked her through the sprawling high school campus and proudly guided her on a tour of the Grace Mullin Fine Arts Building—"Just under construction when I was a senior," Jen had said proudly.

"This is Sylvan Park," Jen had told her on another of their excursions. "It's a little cold now, but in the spring, we'll have a family picnic there. Everyone comes. We've tried to reserve a large section on Easter Sunday ever since Cari's grandmother hasn't been up to her traditional Easter dinner."

Then Megan let her thoughts wander to just last night, when she and Stephen walked through the mist toward his car. She closed her eyes and could once again feel his arms around her and his gentle kiss upon her lips.

Oh, Stephen, what will happen to us now? Megan looked out

the window and over the sun-drenched clouds billowing white and fluffy far below the airplane that carried her farther and farther away from the one person she wanted to be near. She took a deep breath as a single tear found its way down her cheek and fell unnoticed into her lap.

Stephen forced his hands to open the briefcase resting in his lap. He tried to focus on the list of questions that his brother Jeff had briefed him on late yesterday afternoon.

He had rushed Jeff's instructions, wanting to hurry home to get ready for his date with Megan. He knew his evening with her would be important. His attraction to her had been strong from the first moment he saw her in Paulson's office at Halloran's, and he realized during their snowbound holiday that his attraction was deepening into feelings that he had not been willing to permit himself to feel before. Now, Stephen knew that he loved Megan La Bianca, and he was determined to tell her so.

He leaned his head back against the seat and closed his eyes. He remembered her face, totally enraptured with the beautiful music of the concert. He could still feel the warmth of her hand as he tucked it into his own. He recalled wanting to wrap her in his arms and how he hesitated, not wanting to rush her the way Rusty did. He relived the moment she came to him last night in the mist and remembered the wonder of their long-awaited kiss.

It was so easy to tell her that I care for her, he thought. *And she feels the same for me.* Stephen bent his head to look out the window of the plane and across the billowy clouds. The whine of the engines reminded him that his plane was carrying him north and another just like it was carrying Megan east. *Oh, Megan,* he said within himself, *please, don't leave me.*

Megan headed to retrieve her luggage before catching a cab to her mother's. She had decided against calling Frank, wanting to have as much time with her thoughts as possible. She'd have to face the realities awaiting her soon enough. Once she was home, she'd talk to Frank.

Home? Megan asked herself when she saw the familiar streets of the neighborhood where she had grown up. *Is this really my home?* She paid the cab driver and stood facing the front of the house she had grown up in. She felt so alone, standing there with her luggage on the sidewalk beside her. "Oh, God," she whispered, "please tell me I don't have to stay here for the rest of my life. Please, promise me!" But immediately she felt guilty for even having such a wish, let alone saying such a prayer.

Slowly, she began the dreaded walk toward her mother's door.

"Hey lady, need a hand?" Vinny's voice rang across the snow-and-ice-covered yards between their houses. Without waiting for an answer, he quickly crossed the distance between them and grabbed her two suitcases.

"Hi, Vinny," she said simply. "How's it going?"

"Okay, I guess."

"I got your letter."

"Yeah, well . . ."

"I was glad to get it, Vinny."

"Thanks," he said. "You better get in. I know it's thirty degrees out, but you're not wearing your coat."

"Yeah," Megan said, shrugging her shoulders, "I guess you're right."

Once inside, Vinny headed for the kitchen to find Auntie Maria. "She's probably cooking something or other. You know Maria." He glanced up the stairway. "You'll want to be going up to see your mom, I suppose."

Megan took a deep breath. "That's why I'm here." She started toward the stairs and turned back to Vinny. "Would you do me a favor and call Sophia? She didn't know when to expect me."

"Sure," he said and walked toward the kitchen.

Megan paused midway up the stairs, took a deep breath, and let the familiarity of her childhood home fill her lungs. She glanced toward the same dim bulb that hung from the same dark brown covered wire in the same dark hallway above. Then she quickened her steps to face the inevitable. No matter how sick her mother was, Meg knew what was coming and she braced herself. No one else she knew could give a tongue lashing like Rosa. *At least,* Meg thought, *I know what to expect.*

Usually, a task such as this turned Stephen into a man with a mission. He loved finding answers to elusive questions in deeds, old permits, and property easements recorded decades ago. On previous occasions he had been led, almost driven, by insatiable curiosity, each bit of information leading him, teasing him to look further. But today was different. Every move he made was born of forced discipline.

Jeff had used him on several occasions in settling land and property line disputes, estate and inheritance squabbles, as well as easement and mineral rights questions. Some of the cases he had worked on led him to obscure and even trivial historical facts that fascinated him as much as finding patterned scratches and drawings carved into the wall of a cave would fascinate an archaeologist.

But not today. Today he was only interested in getting the answers Jeff needed to service his client's needs. He would only gather the barest and most necessary information, and it would take all the energy he had. Then he would find a hotel. There was no reason to hurry back to Redlands tonight, no reason at all. His reason for wanting to get this job done in a single day had left that very morning for Chicago—and he didn't even get to say good-bye. A not-so-unfamiliar ache lay deep within his chest.

Rosa barely opened her eyes when Megan whispered her name. She thought the sound she heard must have been the irritating swooshing of the humidifier the doctor had ordered to run in her room day and night. Then it came again.

"Mama," Megan whispered. "It's me, Megan."

Megan noticed how deeply Rosa's eyes were set into her drawn face.

"What're you doin' here?" Rosa's voice was hoarse, and the words came between shallow breaths.

"I came to see you."

"Well, you've seen me. Now go back to where you really

want to be." Rosa's dark eyes snapped with anger though her voice was barely above a whisper.

"I want to be here—with you."

"I don't need you here."

"Oh, yes you do!" It was Maria's voice from the doorway behind Megan.

"Hello, Auntie."

"Hello, yourself." Maria's tone was gruff and unfriendly. "Sophia called you?"

"No, she didn't." Megan instinctively protected her sister.

"How'd you know to come then?" Rosa demanded.

"I called her. She didn't want to tell me, Mama. I made her."

"What in the world did you call her for?" Rosa asked.

"Well, I wasn't getting an answer from you, now was I?" Megan chided her mother.

"So you took the time and expense to call your sister, did you?" Maria wasn't about to be left out of the argument.

"What difference does it make? I'm home, now."

"For how long this time?" Rosa pouted.

"Mama, don't start. I'm home. This is my home. Can't you just . . ." Megan decided to drop it. "How are you Auntie?"

"Worn out with worry, how'd you expect me to be? Your mama here all by herself and you off somewhere." Maria began straightening the bed covers on Rosa's bed.

"Stop fussin' over me," Rosa said. "Besides, you know how it hurts me when you jiggle the bed."

"Have you had lunch?" Maria asked Meg.

"No, I was on a breakfast flight. But I'm not hungry. I'll wait until dinnertime." Megan checked her watch. Almost twelve-thirty, California time.

"Better get yourself settled in, then," Maria said. "Take your old room. I'm in the middle bedroom so I can be close by if Rosa needs anything in the night."

Vinny stood in the hallway with Megan's suitcases hanging from his hands. "Where do you want these?"

Megan signaled toward the closed door of the bedroom she had shared with Sophia as a child. Vinny waited until she turned the knob and opened the door.

The mattress on the bed was bare and the blankets and bedspread were folded neatly, wrapped in plastic, and placed at the foot of the bed. The drapes were pulled across the window. Megan drew them back and then lifted the heavy window shade, letting in some of the natural light from outside. Frost had formed in exotic patterns on the outer storm window. Peeking over the frosty display, Megan could see Sophia picking her way carefully up the icy alley toward the house.

Megan stood motionless, almost unaware of Vinny's presence in the room. His voice startled her.

"I'm glad you're back, Meggie," he said. "I missed you."

"Oh, Vinny." Megan felt the tears finally give way and fall uncontrollably down her cheeks. Vinny crossed the room and put his arms around Megan. Instinctively she pulled back.

"It's okay, Megan. I know how it is with us. We're good friends, maybe even best friends. I just can't stand to see you like this. I just want to hold you and make it go away." Megan eyed him suspiciously. "Really, I promise you, if you'll just let me hold you a minute, you'll feel better."

Megan didn't resist Vinny then. She welcomed his familiar arms around her and cried unashamedly into his chest until Sophia opened the door.

"Megan," her older sister said softly. "You made it. You're home."

At once the sisters embraced. A new bond now existed between them. They had gone against their mother's wishes, for her own good. And they needed each other now in a way that they hadn't since their father died a decade ago.

"As you can see," Megan said, waving her hand toward the bed, "I wasn't expected."

"Yeah, I know. Mama ordered Auntie to pack away all your things and put them in the attic. Auntie was more than happy to oblige."

"Those two," Vinny said. "They love to make things just as bad as they can, don't they?"

"Only until something really bad happens. Then they do everything they can to pretend it isn't so."

"Oh well, most of the stuff I want is at my apartment anyway. I'll try to get over there in a day or so." Megan turned to her sister. "How bad is it for Mama?" she asked.

Sophia's eyes brimmed with unshed tears. "It's pretty bad—at least the doctor thinks it might be."

"She won't let him do a biopsy to find out for sure," Megan said to Vinny. "She won't go to the hospital."

"Maybe my dad ought to talk to her," Vinny offered.

"You think he would?" Sophia asked.

"You think it would make any difference?" Megan said.

"It might," Vinny said. "It's worth a try. But I want to warn you, Meggie, he's already mad at you."

"Me? What did I do to him?"

"You didn't call from the airport. He didn't want you to have to take a cab."

Megan didn't have the heart to tell Vinny she had her own reasons for wanting to come home alone. "Oh well," she said, "might as well have him mad at me too."

"If it's any comfort to you, Megan, I'm not mad at you. I'm so glad you're home." Sophia hugged her sister again.

"Me too," Vinny said.

How could Megan ever tell her sister and her childhood friend that this house, this city would never be home to her again. Not after being in Redlands. Not after last night. Not after Stephen.

"Well, one thing is certain." Megan eyed them both. "We've got our work cut out for us with her. We'd better stick together, that's for sure. If she ever finds a way to come between us—we're sunk."

"Here's to the team, then," Vinny said, holding out his arms and pulling the sisters close.

"By the way," Megan said, "where's Angie?"

"Oh, Angie," Sophia said. "I was hoping that subject could be avoided for a little while."

"Okay then, we won't talk about Angie today. But soon, Sophie, I'll have to know what's going on."

CHAPTER SEVENTEEN

Stephen paced his sparsely furnished room. He picked up the phone to call Jeff and then changed his mind. *What does it matter?* he reasoned. *He's busy with Cari and his own life. I have to sort this out for myself.* Grabbing his jacket, he headed out into the night. After all, Sacramento must have something to offer on a Friday night.

He made his way downtown on the bus. Strolling past the tourist traps, he found a quiet seafood restaurant with a lovely city view. He couldn't make up his mind what to order. The waitress suggested the captain's choice, a seafood variety platter; he acquiesced, settled back, and looked out the window while he waited for his food.

A heavily made-up woman sitting at the bar spotted him and watched him for a few minutes. Finally she walked slowly by his table and made her way to the ladies' room. On the way back she stopped beside him.

"You're even better looking than I thought," she said.

"Pardon me?" Stephen was taken completely off guard.

"All alone?"

"Yes."

"Want some company?" she asked.

"No," he said flatly, looking her in the eye.

"You sure?"

"Absolutely." Stephen's disgusted tone underscored the word. "Well, you don't have to get testy, sugar," she said sweetly.

Stephen turned back to his view of the city lights. He watched the reflection in the window as she stood by his table a moment longer, then sauntered away. For a moment he felt smug; then he realized that he enjoyed what he had just done. He actually liked rejecting her. Glancing over his shoulder, he saw her talking to another man at the bar. *She didn't even feel it,* he thought. It was probably better that way, he decided with a shrug. It was certainly better than what he felt. *Oh, Megan. Why does loving someone always have to be so painful?*

Megan warmed the room by turning the faucetlike handle on the hot water register in the corner. She listened to the clunking noises coming from the old, efficient heating system. Eventually she heard the familiar sighing sound of a bit of steam escaping somewhere within the pipes.

She lay down on the bed, and the springs squeaked deep within the old-fashioned mattress. When she felt a mattress button dig into her shoulder through the sheet, she knew she would have to resume her search for more padding the next day.

The street lamp in the alley cast an eerie light in her room. She could have pulled the window shade and the draperies, but she hated the gloom of this house. In the semidarkness, she could see the wallpaper peeling away from the wall near the ceiling. It had been that way since her high school days. Rosa refused to redecorate. "Why should I spend the money on a room that you'll only leave when you graduate?" Megan knew then, as she did now, that Rosa would have given her the money to repaper if she would only have promised to stay. In fact, this little game was Rosa's way to get Megan to make such a promise. Megan really didn't plan to leave then, but she wasn't about to give Rosa anything to hold over her if she should change her mind.

Megan's eyes searched the familiar cracks in the ceiling plaster. They were more severe now than before, and Megan noticed a patch of plaster that would probably fall if she ever slammed the door.

Once or twice during the night Meg roused to hear Maria padding about checking on Rosa or tending to her needs. Lying awake, Meg tried to picture her mother as a young woman—the way she was before Meg's father had died. She dug deep within her memory, but she failed to retrieve any happy image of her mother. All the smiles she could remember were the ones Rosa managed whenever she let someone take her picture or when Frank's family came for dinner or an evening of cribbage. All of Megan's other memories of Rosa revolved around her constant nagging or her perfectionism in keeping her house and her little garden in the backyard.

Megan's years in this house seemed a lifetime ago. It was strange to think that Stephen didn't know anything about this part of her life.

"Stephen," she whispered into her pillow. "Oh, Stephen." Turning onto her side, she curled up and pulled a second pillow into her arms. His face, only last night so close, was now two thousand miles away.

In his hotel room, Stephen lay on top of the covers of the bed. The familiar feeling of being alone threatened to engulf him, and he instinctively knew what he had to do. He had perfected his plan with years of practice. This wasn't the first time someone important had left him on his own without warning. After all, Diedra Bennett Davis Smith Gonzales Powers Bennett had taught him well. Yes, his mother, with her succession of boyfriends and husbands, had taught him how not to care when it hurt too much.

He decided against hurrying back to Redlands. After all, wasn't that part of the strategy against pain? Whenever his mother was gone, he hadn't hurried home. Why should he? He had no idea when—or even if—she'd return. There was no reason to go back to an empty apartment, trailer house, or cheap motel room only to be alone again.

No, he wouldn't go home tomorrow. Instead he would explore Sacramento's old town. He loved history, so he would set out on a quest to learn as much as he could in a single day about California's historical capital city. He had no idea what he would do on Sunday; he didn't want to think that far ahead. He'd take it as it came. Getting back to Redlands on Monday would be soon enough. He could even delay longer if he wanted to, saying he needed to double-check the work he was doing for Jeff.

He wasn't really prepared for staying over. The last time he had a trip unexpectedly delayed was at Christmas. The uninvited memory of Chicago pained him. Suddenly he stood up, quickly undressed, and slipped between the sheets. Grabbing a pillow he held it tight to his face. Involuntarily his pain surfaced and escaped silently into the softness. Then, spent from crying, Stephen rolled over and slept.

Megan slept very little and welcomed the lightness of a new day. She checked her watch. Six-thirty, California time. She grabbed her heavy robe and pulled socks on her feet before putting on her bedroom slippers. She walked as quietly as she could through the dark hallway and down the stairs toward the kitchen. Even in the very early morning she could see the dust and smell the musty odor of the unkept house. One thing she had learned well from her mother was housecleaning. This place needed it. Sophia was too overloaded with her own housekeeping responsibilities to help, and Angie—well, Angie was obviously too busy.

After putting the coffee pot on the stove to perk, Megan stared at the phone. It wasn't too early to call. She knew Jen would be wondering about her and what she found when she got home. Maybe she should call Stephen. Her heart quickened at the thought. She'd call Jen first, then maybe she'd try to call Stephen.

"Megan!" Jen's voice was excited, and Megan thought she also heard a tinge of relief. "We've just been sitting here talking about you."

"Well, I'm here," Megan said.

"And?" Jen's tone indicated the intensity of the question.

"And it's just as bad as we thought. My mother looks terrible and her attitude is worse. She's still angry at me."

"For what?"

"For leaving, I guess. For leaving her sick and even for coming home." Megan sighed and leaned against the doorway leading to the dining room. "Who really knows why she's angry at me. She's always been angry, I think. Not just at me. She just uses me to vent it."

The two friends fell into a momentary silence.

"Have you heard from Stephen?" Megan finally asked.

"I was just trying to think of a way to tell you about him."

Megan's stomach tightened. "What do you mean?"

"He missed his plane. He got held up in traffic when that truckload of oranges spilled on the freeway." Jen paused for a moment. "Megan, he was at the airport the entire time we were." Jen waited for Megan's response.

"But, why . . . I mean, how did we miss him?"

"He was in the coffee shop."

"If we had gone for coffee we would have seen him." Megan closed her eyes against the pain of how close she came to seeing him once more before she left. "You saw him?"

"He called Sarah's to talk to you and found out you were at the airport. He came running to the gate just as you boarded. He was really upset, Megan."

"I wanted to see him," Megan said. "I didn't want to leave." Tears filled Megan's eyes.

"I know that."

"I really miss you. All of you. I *really* miss him."

"We miss you, too."

"Have you heard from him?"

"We haven't. I don't know if Jeff has or not. He was supposed to come home last night, wasn't he?"

"Yeah, we were going to play Monopoly with James and Sarah—but then . . ."

"Well, maybe he called Jeff," Jen said. "I'll call and talk to Cari later. Is it okay if I give him your phone number?"

"Of course. You know, Jen, I haven't ever felt this way about anyone before."

"Not even Rusty?"

"Not even Rusty." Megan glanced toward the stove and saw the dark color of the coffee perking on the burner. She stretched the phone cord as far as she could then reached her free arm to turn the burner off. The blue flame quenched, the coffee perked a few times more, then quietly settled down.

"Have you told him?"

"Well, sort of."

"I see. It's none of my business, I know. But, I just wanted to know how to talk to him when I see him."

"Tell him my feelings haven't changed. I came home because I had to, not because I wanted to."

"I think he knows that already," Jen said.

"Will you make sure he does?"

"Sure."

Jen and Megan ended their conversation just as Sophia came in the back door.

"I just had to come over and make sure you were really here," Sophia said.

"I'm here," Megan responded. "I'm not sure I want to be, but I am."

"I'm sorry, Megan." Sophia began to cry and Megan immediately regretted her remark.

"I'm not sorry I came for your sake, Sophie. But Mama just makes it all so difficult."

"You know what makes it so hard for the rest of us?" the older sister asked. "She only wants you when you're not here. Nothing anyone can do will please her. She always says 'You shouldn't have to do that. Megan should be here to take care of this.' But then when you come, she—"

"She tells me to go away."

"Do you understand her at all?" Sophia wiped her nose on a napkin from the ceramic holder on the counter. "Why does she make out to the rest of us that you're her favorite and then . . ."

"To me she acts like she can't stand me." Megan poured two cups of coffee and sat opposite her sister. "It's like this, as near as I can figure. She wants me to handle things. But the way she goes about it makes me feel so guilty that I do it without her having to ask. Then if I resent it or don't want to do it and say so, then she says, 'Who asked you?'" Megan sipped her coffee. "Do I understand her? No, Sophie, I can't say I do. I understand *what* she does, but I don't understand *why*."

"Maybe we'll never know."

"Maybe. But I'd sure like to, wouldn't you?"

"I guess."

"Now, tell me about the kids, and Benjie. How's it going?"

"Okay, I guess. He's been pretty patient with Mama like this and all. He's even taken an interest in reading to the kids so I can come over here once in a while. You know, to make sure the house is locked up at night and everything." Sophia moved toward the coffee pot for a refill. "Vinny's been great, too."

"Vinny?"

"He watches for me at night so I don't have to walk home alone. Once he even called and offered to make what he calls 'the bedcheck' so I didn't have to go out."

"What'd Mama say about that?"

"You know, her usual. 'Couldn't find even a minute to come over and say good night? Oh well, I know you've got too much to do already. I don't want you neglecting Benjie on my account.'" Megan laughed at Sophie's perfect imitation of Rosa's accusing tone. "She thinks all I have to think about is either Benjie or her. What d'you suppose she'd say if she knew I didn't come because I was too tired and simply didn't want to. I took a long, hot bath and spent some time alone reading a magazine while Benjie put the kids to bed."

"Oh, heaven forbid you should take a minute for yourself." Megan laughed.

"What? You're having a party down here this early in the morning with your sick mama up there needing nourishment? Can't you two think of anyone other than yourselves for once?"

Maria's entrance brought back the real reason Megan had come home so suddenly.

"Want some coffee, Auntie?" Megan said reaching for a cup.

"With my sister up there all alone needing her breakfast?"

"You sit and have your coffee. I'll make her breakfast," Sophia said.

"Don't you have enough to do with your own babies? Let your sister here do it. She's not on vacation anymore. You've done enough already."

"I know," Megan said, "let's do it together. Then Auntie,

you sit here with your coffee. While we're cooking breakfast, you make a shopping list. What do you think we need?"

"Let's not go overboard," Maria said. "We're trying to make every penny stretch. We're not made of money like your fancy California friends are."

"You let me worry about the money, okay?" Megan had saved quite a bit. Living with the Jenkins allowed her to put what she earned working for Dan and Jen away for when she would eventually come home to look for another job. She wasn't sure how long that would take, and she had wanted to be prepared.

"Well, someone has to, that's for sure." Maria's curt declaration caused Megan to try to catch Sophia's eye. Sophia, however, was trying to avoid the subject as long as possible. She certainly didn't want to discuss Angelina in front of Auntie Maria.

After breakfast Sophia announced that she had arranged for a neighbor to watch the kids for most of the day. Benjie had offered to go out and get a pizza for supper in order to free Sophia to help Megan sort out the situation at home. Benjie's mother was available on Sunday to keep the kids and make dinner for the whole family.

"Look at this house, Sophie," Megan said. "It's going to take the both of us to put it right."

"I'll tackle this floor," Maria said.

"Listen, Auntie," Megan tried to be as tactful as possible. "If you'd just tend to Mama, keep her company—you know, make her comfortable—that would really be a big help."

"Sounds like a conspiracy happening here," Vinny said, walking through the back door without knocking. "What can I do?"

"Well," Meg smiled at Sophie, "there is the back walk that needs shoveling."

"It is pretty icy out there," Sophia agreed.

"Great. I offer to help and you send me outside to get me out of the way." Vinny walked to the now empty coffee pot. Shaking it slightly he grinned at the two sisters. "Make you a deal. You make a new pot of coffee, and I'll have the walk done before it's finished perking."

"Deal," Sophia and Megan said in chorus. "I'll do better than that," added Megan. "You finish the back walk before that pot is finished perking and I'll make you some of Mama's cinnamon rolls."

"Ah, a wager?" asked Vinny.

"You on?" Megan asked.

"You bet." Vinny picked up his jacket on the way out, slammed the door as he hurdled the back steps, and jumped the fence between the yards.

"Where's he going?"

"Frank bought a snowblower. Vinny's been using it every now and then to keep the walks dry. You've been suckered, Meggie." Sophia's face lit up with delight.

"And you let it happen."

"Couldn't have stopped it if I'd tried."

"Right! For that, you get the upstairs bathroom," Megan declared, pointing to the floor above. Sophia bent to look beneath the kitchen sink for cleaning supplies, and Megan couldn't resist snapping her in the seat with a tea towel.

"Megan," Sophia screamed as she jumped to stand, "you'll be sorry you did that." Sophia lunged at her sister, who took refuge behind a distraught Auntie Maria.

"Girls!" she scolded. "You behave yourselves. You've got a sick mother upstairs. Now don't upset her with your foolishness."

Megan put both arms around her aunt's neck and began plying her cheeks with kisses. "Oh, don't tell on us, Auntie. Please don't tell."

"Get away from me, girl," Maria said almost laughing. "You're too big for such antics."

"Too big to spank, huh, Auntie?" Megan said refusing to let her aunt escape her tight grasp.

"Let me go, Megan Maria," Maria said emphasizing the Italian version of her namesake's middle name.

"Go on, then. Say it," Megan teased. "Say we're too big to spank."

Sophia watched, admiring Megan's bold treatment of her mother's sister. "Tell us, Auntie," Sophia joined in, "who's the oldest, you or Mama?"

"Get away from me, Megan," Maria scolded. "Let me go and I'll tell you."

"Uh-oh, Meggie, we're about to learn a family secret here." It was more a family joke than a secret.

"If I let go will you tell us?"

"Let me go and see," Maria said.

Megan released her grip. "Now, tell us," Megan feigned a pleading tone, "the family secret. Is Mama older or you?"

"You know, we're both so old, it's hard to tell. I just can't remember," Maria said, backing out of the kitchen door and into the dining room. "And you come one step closer and I'll bean you one," she added, holding up the cane she kept hanging on the doorknob. "Now, I'm goin' on up to your mama. You two behave yourselves down here and get to your chores."

"It really is in bad shape," Sophia said observing the condition of the house. "I've just been so busy with my own little family and so worried about Mama, I guess I just didn't notice."

"It's not your fault, Sophie. After all Angie lives here. Why doesn't she take care of things?" Megan walked to face her sister. "By the way, now that Angelina's name has come up, where the heck is she anyway?"

"Our little sister hasn't been home in over a week. I have no idea where she is or who she's with. But I am sure she'll be back. She always manages to find her way home when she runs out of money."

"Isn't she working?"

"Who knows? She says she's taking classes at the university—Benjie says she's just hanging around down there with the hippies. Her life is her own and her own business. She's made that quite clear to both Benjie and me."

"Well, so it is. But then, she needn't ask Mama for money either. Let her finance her own, as you say, *business*."

"More power to you, Megan. How do you plan to carry this off?"

"I'll get hold of Mama's money somehow myself and put it in my checking account."

"You know Mama doesn't hold with checking accounts."

"Then she still keeps it up there in the box in her closet?"

"And some under the paper lining of her handkerchief drawer."

"Well now, I guess we'll just have to move Mama into another room while we do a thorough cleaning, won't we?"

"Sounds like the place we should start if you ask me," Sophia said.

"Let's clean the back bedroom, change the sheets and put a TV in there for Mama. We'll call it her day room. Then we won't take no for an answer. We'll move her and clean her room. When was the last time her bed was changed?"

"Oh, Megan, I don't even want to think about that."

In a way, Megan and Stephen were more alike than either of them realized. Both managed to put their personal pain on hold while they made a mission out of the mundane. Thoughts of California and the delayed promise it held for Megan would wait until later. First, she had a job to do. A place to put all her energy, both physically and emotionally. A way to forget—for the moment.

CHAPTER EIGHTEEN

By Sunday afternoon, Stephen had to admit that he wasn't as good at pushing his pain away with business or activity as he once was. Megan wasn't as easy to forget as Diedra had been. But then, he had plenty of practice with his mother. Megan was another story.

Catching the five-fifteen plane, Stephen arrived in Ontario, retrieved his car from long-term parking, and was headed for Redlands by six forty-five. He headed straight for Jeff and Cari's, not wanting to face the loneliness of his room just yet.

"Why don't you call her?" Jeff urged after he and Stephen had discussed their business issues.

"I don't know." Stephen sat in the easy chair in the corner of his brother's living room. "I guess I could."

"You *guess*?" Cari said handing him a cup of cocoa.

"It's too painful."

"To call her?" Cari asked.

"Being apart."

"Does she know how you feel about her?" Jeff asked.

"I think so."

"You *think*?"

"You don't understand, Cari," Stephen told his sister-in-law.

"Help me, then, will you?"

"I don't know if I can."

"Maybe I can shed some light here," Jeff said. Reaching for one of Cari's Toll House cookies, Jeff dunked it in his cocoa, then shoved the entire cookie in his mouth.

"I don't want you to let Grace see you do that," Cari

warned. "She's imitating most everything these days," she explained to Stephen.

"My guess," Jeff said, returning his attention to Stephen, "is that it wouldn't have mattered if you had seen Megan before she left or not."

"I'm not sure I know what you mean."

"Just this. You know she had no choice. Had she seen you, she still would have had to go."

"Yeah, I guess you're right about that."

"So the issue is not that she had to go without seeing you first." Jeff paused, watching his brother's reaction. "The real issue is that she went at all."

"But," interrupted Cari, defending Megan's decision, "she had no choice."

"We know that, honey," Jeff said. "Choice or not, she went. Am I right, Stevie?"

Stephen winced both at the accuracy of Jeff's statement and at the use of his childhood nickname. "Probably."

"I don't understand," Cari said.

"Stephen isn't mad at Megan for going," Jeff explained without taking his eyes from his brother's pained expression. "He's angry at the *fact* of her going."

"It seems there's so much of life we can't control," Stephen said quietly. "So much it's best not to even try."

"What do you mean, Stephen?" Cari leaned forward, trying to understand her brother-in-law.

"I'm not sure, Cari." Stephen looked at the two of them. Their obvious love for one another made Stephen's heart ache for Megan's closeness even more. "Maybe it's wrong," he ventured further, "to want Megan to leave her life there and come be a part of my life here."

"Wrong?" Cari asked. "I'd go anywhere in the whole world to be with Jeff."

"Well, maybe not wrong, then. Maybe just impossible."

"People do live apart from their families, Stephen," Cari said.

"You don't have to tell me that, Cari," Stephen said curtly.

"I'm sorry, I didn't mean—"

"He knows you didn't, sweetheart." Jeff shot his brother

a warning look. "He knows you lived apart from your mother for a while. Just like I did and just like he did."

"And it's too painful," Stephen said. "I couldn't ask Megan to go through that kind of pain for me."

"Maybe being separated from her family wouldn't be as painful as being separated from you." Cari almost whispered her comment.

Stephen's head shot up and Jeff thought he saw hope in his brother's eyes for the first time since he appeared at their door an hour ago.

"You think so?"

"I'm not the one to ask."

"Jeff?"

"Don't ask me either. It's Megan you ought to be asking." Jeff drank the last of his cocoa and handed the empty mug to Cari. "The phone's right in there. Why don't you give her a call?"

"I don't have the number," Stephen said helplessly.

"I bet Jen does," Cari offered on her way to the kitchen. "Her number's on the little blackboard out here," she said nodding toward the doorway. "Want me to call and get it?"

Stephen's broad smile gave Cari her answer.

It had been a long day for Megan, and she rubbed her back as she stood in the middle of Rosa's room. Sophia had gone home only a few minutes earlier, and they had made plans to continue their cleaning project first thing in the morning. Sophia's neighbor had insisted she could leave the children as many days next week as necessary, and Benjie offered to bring Chinese take-out food home for supper so the sisters wouldn't have to think of cooking.

"Might as well get it done," Benjie had remarked. "Then our lives can return to normal."

Frank had come over earlier that afternoon and carried Rosa into the back bedroom. Once the girls got her settled and began to clean her room, they realized that it would take more than the afternoon to finish.

"I don't think she'll give you much trouble," Frank had

said earlier. "She's not really up to being moved twice in one day. Besides she's nearer your room back there, Megan."

"There are twin beds in that room, Frank," Maria said. "I'll make up the other one and sleep back there with her."

"Fine by me," Frank said, "but I'm not in charge here." He nodded toward Megan.

"That—" Megan stopped, realizing the full impact of Frank's insinuation. "That would be nice of you, Auntie."

With Maria and Rosa tucked in for the night, Megan surveyed the room. The bed, now stripped, had been vacuumed completely. Frank and Vinny had moved it to the middle of the room, dismantled it and took the mattresses outdoors for a good airing out. They had also carried the stacks of newspapers and magazines out to the garage. Sophia had rubbed the old poster head- and footboards with furniture oil until it shined. Then she started on the nightstands and announced that the highboy would have to wait until tomorrow. After that, Frank and Vinny moved the mattresses back in and reassembled the bed.

Megan had waxed the foot and a half of hard wood flooring surrounding the floral wool carpet and polished the dark stained wood baseboards. She also polished the wood trim, then washed the painted doors with Spic and Span. Once the walls had been dusted and the carpet vacuumed, the room began to look and smell clean; Megan herself felt grimy and dirty.

Megan looked forward to a long soak in the large claw-footed bathtub. While the water ran, she walked back to the bedroom and one by one opened the drawers in the highboy. One drawer stuck slightly as she opened it, and she decided that if they were going to do it right, they might as well take out the contents and rub the drawer runners with soap. She managed to work the drawer loose, and carried it with its contents to the bed. Then she decided to check on her bath water.

Sitting on the side of the tub she ran her hand through the hot water. Satisfied, she turned the squeaking faucets until the water stopped. It was then she heard the phone ring.

Running downstairs, she made her way quickly through the dark, familiar house toward the ringing phone.

"Hello?" All she heard was a dial tone. *Too late,* she said to herself. *No telling how long it was ringing.* Megan switched on the light and opened the refrigerator door to look for a soda when Vinny knocked lightly on the back door.

"I saw your light on," he said as Megan unhooked the door chain.

"I came down to answer the phone."

"Oh," he said.

"I didn't make it."

"Why don't you get one put in upstairs?"

"Never thought of it," Megan said, glancing toward the ceiling. "Mama wouldn't have one up there when we were growing up. She didn't want us making calls she couldn't overhear."

Vinny laughed and found a soda for himself, then joined Megan sitting at the table. "No kidding?"

Megan nodded. "So we just came down here after she was asleep." Megan took a sip of the cold drink. "Sometimes we talked for hours."

"You guys were bad." Vinny laughed at the thought of Meg and her sisters fooling Rosa. "How'd you get down here without her hearing you on the stairs?"

"Only the center squeaks, Vinny. We walked on the edges."

"Who do you suppose it was?" he asked.

"Who what was?"

"On the phone?"

"I have no idea," Megan said. "I can only hope—" She stopped mid-sentence.

"You meet someone in California?"

"No, Vinny. As a matter of fact, I met someone here, just before I left."

"Here?"

"Yeah, but he's from there."

Vinny's forehead wrinkled with unspoken confusion.

"It's hard to explain. He came to Chicago to take care of some business for Mr. Miller—you know, at Halloran's."

"He works for Halloran's?"

"No."

"For Mr. Miller then?"

"Not really. He works with his brother, who is Mr. Miller's lawyer. He came to check out a few things before the sale of Halloran's was final."

"I see."

"He's really nice, Vinny. I think you'd like him."

"You like him?"

"Yes," she said softly, "very much."

"Must have been hard to come home." Vinny's statement was more of a question.

"It was, Vinny. He was away on business." She decided not to go into the whole story. "I didn't get to say good-bye."

"Ouch!" Vinny's face winced with understanding.

"How about you?"

"Me?"

"You got your eye on somebody?"

"Besides you?" he teased.

"Come on, Vinny, be serious."

"I am, Megan." He reached across the table and took her hand before she could move away. "No kidding. Will you just listen to me for a minute?" he asked, sensing her sudden discomfort.

"Vinny, I—"

"Megan, stop it. You always think you know what I'm going to say and you always assume you're not going to like what you hear. Just hear me out this time, will you?"

Megan decided she owed Vinny at least this much. She relaxed and didn't try to pull her hand away again.

"I wrote and told you how ashamed I was of how I acted the day before Christmas. I'm really sorry about that, Megan."

"You don't—"

"You're supposed to listen, remember?" he asked and she nodded. "Well, I got to thinking later—not that day, of course. And come to think of it, not the next day either. I had too big a headache the next day." Vinny laughed and began to play with her fingers.

"I guess it was the next week or so, I began to think about

what you said. I have loved you for so long, I don't remember ever not loving you. But you were right, we've been raised more like cousins."

"Our dads were just like brothers, Vinny."

"But your mother," Vinny said, glancing toward the ceiling, "she was so determined. Did you know she paid for our prom tickets?"

"What?" Megan's voice rang with shock.

"She did. I didn't have a job that year, and my dad always said I had to finance my own dates. She thought we ought to go to the prom together. In fact, she said if I didn't take you, who would? She gave me the money, but she told my dad I worked for it."

"I don't believe this."

"Believe it, Meggie. It gets worse."

"I don't think I want to hear this."

"I think you should. She offered me her ring. You know, the one your dad gave her."

"My grandmother's ring?"

"Yeah, that's the one. She said you loved your grandmother, and that she'd promised your dad the only way you'd get the ring is if I gave it to you as an engagement ring.

"Anyway, I said I couldn't do it that night. She was really pushy. I decided to talk it over with my dad, and he took the ring and said he'd speak to Rosa about it. I never heard either of them mention it again. In fact your mother didn't speak to me for weeks afterward, remember?"

"I thought she was mad because we didn't come home until four A.M."

"Yeah, right," Vinny said.

"You haven't answered my question, Vin. Is there anyone special in your life?"

"Not yet, but I hope there will be someday. It's strange talking to you about this, Meggie."

"It is? Why?"

"Because it's strange for me to even think about anyone else. You don't know the turmoil I was in at Christmas."

"I never saw you drunk before," Megan said.

"I never was before. And I can tell you this, I won't be

again. Not as long as I live at my dad's house anyway. He made that very clear.

"You know, I'm glad that we're still friends. After all these years of being certain I would spend my life with you, right here in this house—It is really strange."

"Boy, how many other people in our neighborhood are doing what they were trained to do rather than what they want to do?"

"One I know of for sure," Vinny said.

"Oh? Who?"

"Sophia," he said, watching for Megan's reaction.

"Yeah, I know." Megan's expression clouded with concern for her sister.

"You think she's happy, Meggie?"

"It's not what I think—"

"I know, it's what she thinks." Vinny shifted uneasily in his chair. "Do you know what she thinks?"

"I never asked her."

"I did."

"You what?" Megan was surprised at Vinny's admission.

"I asked her. She doesn't know."

"She what?"

"She doesn't know if she's happy or not."

"She said that?"

"She said she never thought about it. Doesn't know what to compare her life to. She was always told she would marry Benjie. That was it—it was settled. I don't think it ever occurred to her that she had a choice."

"I can't believe this."

"Believe it, Meggie," Vinny said. "It almost happened to us—well, to me anyway." He fell silent for a moment, then continued. "But you saw things differently, didn't you?"

"I just don't want to be forced into any decision that I can't be sure isn't mine."

"I understand that now," he said.

"Who knows, if Mama hadn't insisted on shoving us together, maybe we would've, you know, gotten together on our own."

"You think so?" Vinny asked.

"I don't know for sure. But I do know this: it would have always been a question whether or not we were together because Mama wanted it or because we wanted it. I want a relationship where *I've* made the strongest commitment—not her."

"Listen, it's late. You going to call it a day pretty soon?"

"I think so, I just wanted to take the dresser drawers out and put them on Mama's bed so Sophia can start on them first thing in the morning."

"Want some help?"

"You're not too tired?"

"Nah, the caffeine in this Coke will keep me up a while anyway. Might as well make myself useful. Have to work tomorrow, so I can't help you then. Let's have a look at what you need done."

On the way upstairs, Vinny made Megan promise she'd look into having a phone extension installed upstairs. "With your Mama so sick and everything." He didn't tell Megan, but his real concern was for the safety of women alone in the house at night.

CHAPTER NINETEEN

"Look at this, Vin," Megan said.

Vinny set the drawer he was carrying on the floor and came to sit beside Megan on her mother's bed. "What do you make of that?"

"It's money," Megan said.

"I know what it is," he said. "Where'd it come from?"

"Stuck to the bottom of the drawer in this envelope."

"How long's it been there?"

"Who knows?" Megan turned the yellowed envelope over for closer inspection. "Looks like it's been there for years."

"How much?"

Megan started counting the hundred dollar bills. "Fifteen, sixteen, seventeen, eighteen, nineteen, twenty."

Vinny released a soft whistle. "Wow, two thousand bucks. I never saw that many hundreds in my whole life. They look brand new." Vinny took one from Megan's hand. "Look, Meg, the date of issue is nineteen fifty-two."

"That was before my dad died."

"Has it been there all this time?" Vinny asked.

"Who knows?" Megan carefully tucked the bills back in their envelope and began to pick up the other drawers. "Look here," she said holding up another small drawer from the top of the chest and displaying another envelope taped securely to the bottom.

"I don't believe it," Vinny said, carefully prying the brittle tape loose.

"You want to count it?"

"You better. I don't think I can be trusted around all this money."

"Oh, Vinny, someone as honest as you?"

"Yeah, but now I've got my eye on a one of those new little Mustangs. Better keep me and that money apart."

Megan laughed. "Let's keep looking. Who knows what we'll find lurking here?"

"The shadow knows," Vinny said eerily.

"She's either not home, or not answering the phone," Stephen told Cari when he hung up the phone.

"I hope that doesn't mean her mother's worse or in the hospital or something," Cari said.

"What did Jen say when you talked to her?" Jeff asked his wife.

"She just said Megan told her the situation was serious. She thought Megan was crying. She said Meg didn't want to be there and it was causing her some feelings of guilt."

"Good grief," Stephen commented, "she'd feel guilty if she didn't go and she feels guilty for going and not wanting to. How do you deal with that?"

"With a close relationship with the Lord," Cari said. "Haven't we all learned that ourselves?"

"Yeah, I guess we have." Stephen walked away from the phone and back into the living room. "I just want to make sure she knows—you know, to make sure she . . ."

"She'll have to discover it for herself," Jeff said. "Just like we all did."

"But you helped me," Cari said.

"And me too," Stephen added.

"Yes. But not really. I just helped you see it for yourself. If you hadn't, no matter what I said or did, it wouldn't have helped. Megan has to come to that place too."

"But who is there to help her the way you helped us?" Stephen asked. "She's all alone since Jen came back here."

"I guess we'll just have to trust God to bring someone to help her," Cari said. "Like Jeff helped me."

"I don't think I can pray that prayer," Stephen said. "I can't even think it—much less pray it."

Cari and Jeff looked at each other knowingly. "You're in love with her, aren't you, Steve?" Jeff said.

"Yeah, I am. And I'm not sure I like it. I mean, when she

was here it was wonderful. I really thought I'd like to tell her . . ."

"That's a big step," Jeff said.

"A big risk, you mean."

"Love isn't a risk," Cari said. "It's an investment."

"Yeah, sure. Like I said—a risk."

"This whole thing brings back memories, doesn't it?" Jeff decided to be direct with his younger brother.

"Yeah, I guess it does."

"How many times did she leave without telling you where she was going or when she'd be back?"

"I lost count," Stephen said.

"Me too." Jeff took his brother's elbow and guided him toward the sofa.

"But you had James and Sarah," Stephen said.

"Yes. And, I'm grateful. But remember, I didn't have them until I was almost twelve. You were just a little tyke."

"I can't even remember you ever living with us."

"And James and Sarah's was the last place I lived, Steve. Not the first."

Cari wondered if she should leave the brothers alone. "Listen, I think I'll check on Grace. If you two don't mind, I'll leave you alone."

"I don't hear anything, honey. I'd like you to stay, if you would." Jeff's expression pleaded with his wife.

"Sure," she said, sitting in the chair nearest the sofa.

"Stephen, I remember one birthday when Diedra came—only one. I sat hour after hour waiting for her each year. She'd promise me she'd come and then she'd never show. One time, when I was about six or so, I cried so hard my foster father spanked me and put me to bed. He told me I was acting like a spoiled brat. I thought maybe I was."

Jeff slipped his arm around his brother's shoulders. Stephen sat motionless. "We've never discussed this before," Jeff continued, "but many times I envied you."

"You envied me?" Stephen didn't even try to hide his surprise.

"You got to stay with her," Jeff said hoarsely. "I was sent away." He wiped the tear from his eye before it could fall down his cheek. Cari felt her throat tighten. "I thought there must be something wrong with me. I thought you were the lucky one."

"Oh, no," Stephen moaned.

"I thought so until long after I moved in with James and Sarah. I can honestly say that they were the only foster parents that really loved me. They invested themselves in me, Stephen. They took a great risk in loving me, because I didn't know how to love back. I didn't know how to trust anyone, I didn't know how to care or to be polite. All I knew was to be so afraid of losing them that I tried not to let them get too close."

Cari shifted in her seat, and Jeff smiled in her direction.

"But they are so wonderful," Stephen said. "So kind and they'd never do anything to hurt you. Anyone could see that."

"Anyone but me," Jeff said. "I was afraid to see it for a long time. But they never gave up on me. They just kept loving me, no matter what. They kept giving, I kept refusing, they kept on giving."

"When did you finally let yourself care about them?"

"When I went away to college." Jeff relaxed against the soft sofa cushions. "Sarah cried for an entire week before I left. I have no idea how long afterwards. I thought I had hurt her in some way. Finally she and James sat me down and told me that she was crying because she didn't want me to go. That they'd both miss me. That's when I realized how much they loved me.

"They begged me to come back and see them whenever I possibly could," Jeff said. His eyes filled with tears. "You know something? I heard them begging me the same way I had begged Diedra. That's when I decided."

"Decided what?" Stephen asked.

"I decided right then and there that I was never going to do to anyone what Diedra had done to me. I realized for the first time in my life—after living with James and Sarah for six years—that Sarah was my mother, that she cared more for me than Diedra ever could. And, I decided something else."

"What?" Stephen looked intently at his older brother.

"I decided that someday I'd love you the same way Sarah and James loved me."

Stephen leaned forward, resting his elbows on his knees. Quiet at first, he covered his face with his hands and wept openly. Jeff moved to kneel in front of his younger brother. He wrapped both arms around him and let him cry out his pain.

Cari sat motionless in the chair opposite the two men. It was all she could do to keep her own tears from turning into audible sobs.

"And now," Jeff said at last, "I want you to be able to love someone the way I love Cari."

"I do too." Stephen said wiping his eyes with his open hands. "I want to love Megan that way, Jeff. I really do."

"Okay, then. Don't blame her for leaving. She didn't want to go—isn't that what she told Jen?" Jeff glanced at his wife. Cari nodded.

"I just don't know how to handle the pain, Jeff," Stephen said. "I don't want to put any pressure on her for going. I just want to hear her say she'll come back."

"I don't think she can say that—not just now."

Stephen's face furrowed with a frown. "Why not?"

"Because her mother's condition is uncertain. She's got responsibilities, Stephen."

"But if she loves me . . ."

"Don't make her choose between her feelings for you and her responsibility for her mother. Does it really have to be either her mother or you?" Jeff again glanced at Cari, who nodded in agreement. "Does your love for her require her to be here right now or never?"

Stephen searched his brother's face, trying to understand. "I guess not," he said. "It's just that she's so far away. Back there in familiar territory with who knows how many guys hanging around."

"Oh, I see." Jeff stood to his feet and pulled Cari up and into his arms. "Tell me, Cari, do you love me?"

"You know I do, silly."

"Then tell this thickheaded brother of mine something, will you?"

"I'll try."

"How many suitors would it take for you to stop loving me?"

"Oh, Jeff. Don't be ridiculous."

"Tell him—and make it quick before I start to worry."

"You know, Stephen, once I met Jeff it wouldn't have mattered how many guys wanted to ask me out. I was doomed."

Jeff gave Cari a warning glare.

"Okay, I was *destined* to be a one-man woman. All kidding aside. When I fell for him, it was all over."

Jeff gave his wife a warm squeeze before releasing her and returning to sit beside his brother.

"You think Megan might feel that way about me?"

"All the signs were there," Cari said. "She looked like she was falling in love to me."

"What about Rusty?" Stephen directed his question to Cari.

"I think Rusty cut himself out of the race for good. She was embarrassed to tears and angry beyond words at his behavior."

"And Vinny?"

"Who's Vinny?" Cari asked. "I didn't hear her say a word about him."

"He's someone she's known most of her life."

"But not someone important enough to mention," Cari said.

"Do you think she would?" Stephen asked.

"If he was important to her? Of course she would." Cari came to sit nearer her brother-in-law. "Listen to me, Stephen. Do you honestly think Megan would have given you the time of day if she was hoping for a lasting relationship with someone else when she got home?"

"I didn't think of that," he said. "She is pretty open, isn't she?"

"Too open for her own good. She couldn't hide a secret if she tried. She's too, well—"

"Transparent. Strong and opinionated—among other things," Stephen said. "I guess that's why I have come to care so much for her. I also think that's why I want to be near her. She thinks she comes across as confident, but anyone can see she's just bluffing. I want to . . ." Stephen's voice faltered.

"Protect her," Jeff finished for him.

"Yeah, but I'm not sure from what. Maybe I'm afraid she'll get herself into trouble someday. You know, say the wrong thing to the wrong person."

"You really love her, don't you?" Cari asked.

"I'm only sorry I didn't tell her so."

"You didn't tell her?"

"I had the chance and I blew it, Cari. I said I 'cared for' her."

"Well," encouraged Cari, "that's a beginning."

"But now she's gone."

"She's not gone, Stephen," Jeff said forcefully. "She's just away."

"Yikes," Cari moaned. "That sounds like a verse from a sympathy card."

"Yeah, I guess it did. But when someone's dead, they're gone. Megan's not dead. She's just not here."

"For the time being," Cari added.

"But for how long?" Stephen asked.

"That is something no one can answer right now. Probably not even Megan," Jeff said.

"You know," Cari said, "there is something quite romantic about a long distance relationship."

"How would you know?" Jeff asked.

"You called me several times from L.A., remember?"

"Yeah, wanting to come home and marry you immediately."

"But wasn't it fun?"

"Only to remember," Jeff said. "I certainly was miserable at the time."

"See?" Cari asked brightly. "There you are."

"You mean this misery is romantic?" Stephen said.

"Exactly." Cari leaned back looking as smug as Jeff had ever seen her.

"You have Megan's number, now use it!" Jeff scolded.

"Maybe you're right."

"It's worth a try, isn't it?" Cari asked.

"I guess," Stephen said.

"She's worth it, isn't she?" Cari asked.

"Yes, I think she is."

"Then, keep on trying until you reach her. Make a date for when you'll call again. Don't let the distance between you keep her from knowing how you feel about her." Cari's eyes danced with delight.

"This could cost a fortune!" Stephen moaned.

"Relax, Stephen," Cari warned. "It's nothing compared to the cost of a wedding. She'll have to pay her fair share, believe me!"

"I'll try tomorrow, it's too late now. It's already past ten here, after midnight in Chicago. She's probably already in bed by now."

"How much is in that one?" Megan asked Vinny.

"Fifty-five hundred," he said.

"That makes—let's see—" Meg read the column of numbers she had written down. "Two thousand, thirty-five hundred, eighteen hundred, seven fifty, nine hundred, twenty-six hundred, and fifty-five hundred." Megan then began adding. "Vinny, there's seventeen thousand and fifty dollars here!"

"Shh." Vinny warned reaching for the light switch. "I hear something."

Megan sat perfectly still and listened while Maria helped Rosa to the bathroom and then back to bed again.

"Meggie," Vinny whispered when they heard the bedroom door down the hallway close tightly, "she can hardly walk."

"It's really bad, Vinny. I'm going to call the doctor tomorrow. I'm afraid of what he'll say."

"You think she'll go to the hospital?"

"Not without making a hysterical scene."

Vinny turned his attention to the money lying in neat piles around Megan on Rosa's bare mattress. "What are you going to do with all this?"

"I don't know, Vinny. It makes me nervous just knowing it's in the house. What do you think I should do?"

"Get it to the bank, that's what," Vinny said.

"I know that, dummy. But what do I do with it right now?"

"Call an armored car," Vinny laughed.

"You're a big help," she said. Megan opened Rosa's closet door and rummaged around for something to put the money in. Finding a shoe box on her father's side of the shelf, Megan stretched but couldn't reach it. Vinny came and easily reached above her head and pulled the box down.

"Yikes, Megan, it's heavy," he said, handing the box to her.

"Look, Vinny," Megan whispered. She stood motionless with the top of the shoe box in one hand and the box resting in the crook of her other arm.

"A gun?" Vinny took the box from Megan and picked up the small pistol carefully. "How long you think she's kept that thing up there?"

"Not her," Megan said. "Daddy."

"But he's been gone for . . ."

"I know, but look at this closet. It's the same as the day he died, except now his clothes are covered in plastic."

"She expecting him to come back or something?"

"Who knows? I don't know why she does anything."

"We'd better tell my dad about all this, Megan."

"Now?"

"Well, not now. It's after midnight. But soon, okay?"

"Right. But what about now?" Megan silently wished they hadn't taken out the drawers in the first place.

"Listen. How about putting it all under the gun, back in the box and keeping it under your bed?"

"I don't think so, Vinny." Megan took a step back. "I don't think I want to sleep with that much money or a gun under my bed."

"You want me to stay here?" Vinny offered.

"Could you?"

"Why not?"

"No reason, I guess." Megan looked uneasy with the idea.

"Look, Megan, you're perfectly safe with me. We're just friends. Or did you forget already?"

"No, of course not. Where will you sleep?"

"I can go downstairs on the sofa. Look, I'll take the money and the gun with me. I'll put them somewhere."

"In the kitchen," Megan decided. "Come on."

Together they crept down the stairs, keeping to the side so they wouldn't squeak. Sneaking through the house, Megan felt like a teenager again. When they reached the kitchen, Megan closed the swinging door to the dining room behind her.

"Up there," she whispered, pointing to a small, high cabinet door.

"Why are you whispering?" Vinny whispered back.

"I don't know," she responded and pointed to the box in Vinny's hands. "I guess I'll stop when the you-know-what is safely stashed away."

Vinny retrieved the stepladder from the pantry closet and climbed up carefully. "What's in here, anyway?" he said as he opened the cupboard.

"I haven't the slightest idea," Megan said.

"Booze."

"What?"

"Booze. Look." Vinny handed Megan a bottle of scotch.

"How old is that?" Megan wondered almost aloud.

"Do you suppose it's been here since—"

"Probably." Megan never knew her mother to use any kind of alcohol except wine for cooking.

"Shall we see what else is up here?" Vinny asked from his perch on top of the ladder.

"No," she whispered loudly. "I've found enough family secrets tonight to keep me for quite a while. Come on down."

Vinny replaced the ladder in the pantry, and Megan sneaked back upstairs for a couple of blankets.

"I'm glad you're going to stay, Vinny," she said when she returned. "When I think of Mama and Auntie Maria here by themselves with all that money, it scares me half to death."

"When are you going to tell her about it?"

"I haven't thought that through just yet. What if she doesn't know anything about it?"

"You think she doesn't?"

"I don't know for sure. Just a hunch. Think I'll feel her out a little first."

"And Sophie?" Vinny asked. "I don't think you should keep this from her, do you?"

"No, probably not. I'm a little nervous about telling anyone just yet. Let me think about this for a while, but I'll tell her soon. I don't want Auntie knowing."

"Or Angie."

"Especially not Angie," Megan said. She turned and creeped back upstairs.

Suddenly tired to the bone, Megan looked forward to bed. Taking off her clothes, she remembered her bath. *Not tonight,* she decided. *I know I'm filthy,* she mused, *but it'll have to wait until morning.*

"I wonder," she whispered into the semidarkness of her room, "if this is what they mean by filthy rich."

CHAPTER TWENTY

Within a few days, Megan was growing increasingly curious about the money. She decided to have a look around in the attic, to go through the things stored there for any clue as to why Joseph would have hidden the money in the first place, and in the second place, why Rosa was obviously unaware of it.

"Have you told Sophie?" Vinny asked one morning over coffee.

"Told me what?" Sophie said reaching for a donut to dunk in hers.

"I haven't told her yet, Vinny," Megan said, casting him a glaring look.

"Don't you think you should?" Vinny asked without returning her gaze.

"Tell me what?" Sophie repeated.

"Look, Sophie." Megan made sure Maria was still upstairs giving Rosa her breakfast. "I have to tell you something, and you have to promise to keep it to yourself."

"Come on, Meggie," Vinny urged, "she has a right to know too."

"Let me do this my way, okay, Vinny?" Megan turned to face her sister directly. "Remember the other day when we were cleaning Mama's room?"

"Of course."

"Well, you were coming back the next day to polish the chest, so I thought I'd take everything out of the drawers ahead of time. You know, to make it easier to get started."

"And I offered to help," Vinny said, feigning pride.

"We all know what a great guy you are, Vinny," Sophie said, laughing.

"Well, Vinny and I started dumping the drawers on the bed, you know, to save a little time. And we saw an envelope taped on the bottom."

"What was it, a letter or something?"

"Or something!" Vinny let out a low whistle.

"Listen, Sophia, you have to promise you won't tell anyone."

"Oh, come on, Meg, who would I tell?"

"I'm not kidding. I'm not going to tell you any more until you promise me you will keep it to yourself, for now anyway."

"Okay, I promise," Sophia said with a grin that spread into her eyes. "Cross my heart."

"It was money, Sophie."

"Money?"

"You heard right," Vinny said. "Money."

"Well, maybe Mama was saving for a new coat or something. Maybe it's her Christmas fund. You know she never did any shopping last year."

"I don't think so," Megan said.

"Why not?"

"Because the bills were all hundreds."

"What?" Sophia's eyes opened wide.

"Hundreds," Megan repeated.

"No kidding?"

"That's not all," Vinny said, nodding for Megan to continue. "We found seven envelopes."

"Seven?" Sophia couldn't believe what she was hearing.

"I counted over seventeen thousand dollars," Megan whispered.

"Where in the world did it come from?" Sophia's head spun with the incredible information.

"I haven't a clue," Megan said.

"Oh, yes you do," Vinny corrected.

Sophia looked from Vinny to Megan, waiting for further explanation.

"What Vinny means is that the tape that held the envelopes on was really old and yellowed. And the envelopes were yellow on one side, but not on the side next to the drawer. And—"

"Here's the best part." Vinny's eyes widened with excitement.

"Go on, Megan," Sophia instructed.

"Well, the bills all feel new. You know no wrinkles or anything."

"So?"

"But . . ." Vinny said.

"But," Megan interrupted, "we looked at the date. All the bills are at least ten years old—some even older."

"Oh, my goodness." Sophia shook her head. Vinny and Megan waited for the same realization to hit Sophia. "Papa."

Megan sat back in her chair and nodded. "I think so. But what I can't figure out is *why*. Or even *when*."

"Where is the money now?" Sophia asked. But before Vinny could stand up, she held up her hand in protest. "No, don't tell me. I don't want to know."

The phone rang and Megan reached for it. She heard Maria speaking Italian to one of her old family friends. She hung up quietly.

"Who was that?"

"One of Auntie's friends."

"How's the phone working out?"

"It's great. They fussed and fussed. Of course, Mama said we shouldn't spend the money, but then . . ." the trio laughed at the thought of an extra two dollars a month for the two additional extensions. "We could pay for the phones for over eight thousand months and never even feel it!"

"Does Uncle Frank know about this?"

"Not yet," Vinny said.

"I didn't want to tell anyone until I told you," Megan said.

"I don't think we should tell Angie, do you?" Sophia asked her sister.

"You know more about that than me." Megan became a bit more serious.

"I don't think you should," Vinny said.

"And I don't want Benjie knowing about this." She looked at the two sitting with her and they nodded their agreement.

"But Uncle Frank?" Megan asked.

"I think he should be told," Sophia said. "He'll know what

to do with it. He might even know where it came from." She looked directly at Megan. "What do you plan to do now?"

"Me?" Megan said arching her eyebrows. "Don't you mean we?"

"No," Sophia said. "I'm staying out of it. If I even got close to that money, Benjie would smell it for sure. You can talk to me about it, but I'm afraid you're on your own." Turning to Vinny she added, "You'll help her, right, Vin?"

"I think it's exciting. Who knows what skeletons we'll drag out of the next closet?"

"Stop it, Vinny," Megan warned.

"Well, what do you plan to do next?"

"I want to have a look around in the attic," Megan said. "I thought I'd try to find the family picture albums. You know, the ones Mama put away after Papa died."

"It's cold up there," Sophia said.

"All you have to do is open the stairway door for a couple of days and let the heat up there," Vinny said.

"Or take up a heater." Megan opened the pantry closet door. "I found this in the basement." She displayed an old electric heater. Vinny examined it closely and said he'd better test it first and perhaps change the worn plug.

"That's all we'd need now, a fire," he said, throwing on his jacket. "I'll be back in a flash."

"You going to tell Uncle Frank?" Sophia and Megan asked almost in unison.

"Me?" Vinny looked at the two sisters. "Yeah, I'll tell him. See you later."

"This is quite a mess, isn't it?" Sophia said.

"Not yet," Megan said. "It may be just that Papa wanted to save money and didn't trust banks."

"Or Mama," Sophia added.

"Makes you wonder, doesn't it?" Megan asked.

"Wonder what?" Maria said entering the room. "Where's Vinny? I thought he was down here with you girls."

"He had to go home. He's repairing a heater," Sophia said.

"Oh? Good for him. He's such a handyman, that boy. You could do worse, Megan."

"He's a friend, Auntie. Nothing more."

"And what's so wrong with that? It's a good marriage that's built on friendship. Marriage lasts longer than romance, you know. Friendship is good."

Megan shot her sister a knowing look. "Look Auntie," Sophia said, "Megan will have to look for work before too long, and we thought it'd be a good time to give the entire house—even the attic and the basement—a good cleaning."

"A spring cleaning in the dead of winter? You girls!"

"An early spring cleaning," Sophia said. "You think that'd be all right with Mama?"

"Ask her yourself. Last I looked, she still had her hearing. I'm just a guest in this house."

"Auntie," Megan scolded. "You've been here longer than either Sophie or me."

"Maybe my welcome's all wore out, then?"

Sophia rose and went to put her arms around her aunt's shoulders. "Maybe you're tired of us, Auntie. Is that it? You've had enough of us?"

"So where would you go?" Megan joined in. "Off to some tropical paradise maybe?"

"You maybe got a secret admirer we don't know about?" Sophia asked.

"Is that it, Auntie? You got yourself a beau?" Megan teased.

"Now listen to the both of you," Maria said, her eyes dancing with merriment. "Going on in such a way." Her Italian accent grew thicker than usual.

"That's it, isn't it?" Megan continued. "You've got yourself a beau and you've been tied down here with the likes of us. Who is he, Auntie? Anyone we know?"

"That's enough out of the two of you," Maria warned sternly, but the sparkle in her eyes belied the pleasure she got from her two nieces teasing her this way. "Now, remember your poor Mama up there. She's not a bit well. We needn't be making fun down here, with her up there so sick."

Megan sobered instantly. "Do you think she's better? Even a little?"

"No, Megan, I don't. I think she's worse if anything." Maria sat heavily on the nearest chair. "We had quite a night of it, Megan. Didn't you hear us?"

The night before Megan had fallen into a deep sleep almost immediately. Long days of cleaning, vacuuming floors and furniture, and polishing woodwork left her exhausted, her muscles aching. "I didn't hear anything, Auntie. I fell asleep before my head ever hit the pillow. I'm sorry. I should leave my door open. Why didn't you call me?"

"You need your sleep. You seem so intent on tackling this old house from top to bottom. I didn't want to disturb you."

"But what about you, Auntie?" Sophia asked. "You insist on taking care of Mama yourself day and night. We need to arrange something so you can get a good night's sleep yourself."

"I'll sleep in there with her tonight," Megan said. "You sleep in your own room."

"It's not necessary," Maria protested.

"Yes, it is," Megan insisted. "I sure don't want you getting down too."

"I could do with a whole night's sleep," Maria said pensively.

"There, then it's settled," announced Sophia.

"But only tonight," Maria said.

"We'll trade off," Megan offered. "That way we'll each get a whole night off, then a whole night on."

"I wish I could help—" Sophia stared to say.

"Never!" Maria was appalled. "Your place is home in bed beside your husband. Your mama would never forgive us if we let you come and Benjie was, well, you know—lonely."

"That's right," Sophia mused. "No matter whatever else is going on in the world, Benjie's needs come first."

"It's a wife's duty, Sophia. Many a sorry and divorced woman forgot that—sometimes just for a moment. And sometimes a moment is all it takes."

Sophia shook her head and headed for the basement. "I think I'll start downstairs. Who knows when anyone's cleaned down there."

"Last fall," Maria said proudly. "I cleaned the basement real good. Put up the clothesline and even cleaned out the old coal bin."

"By yourself?" Megan asked astonished at her aunt's admission.

"And were you here to help me?"

"Auntie—"

"No, you were too busy with that job of yours and of course, your friends."

"Auntie."

"Never mind. It wasn't too bad. Nobody's used that old coal bin for years. Not since the oil burner was put in. It just needed sweeping. Anything stored down there would mold in the summer anyway." Maria turned her attention to Megan. "And you?"

"I thought I'd start in the attic." Megan waited for Maria's response.

"I don't know what's up there. I've never been up there. Thought it wasn't any of my stuff anyway, so why bother?"

"Mama had Megan's stuff moved up there," said Sophia.

"That's right, Frank came and carried up the boxes. Rosa called him. Don't know why she bothered him. Vinny could have done it just as well."

"Or Benjie," offered Sophia.

"Well, your mama doesn't want to bother Benjie unless she absolutely has to."

"Tell me about it," Sophia complained.

"Mind yourself, Sophia," Maria warned.

"I'll be downstairs." Sophia disappeared down the stairs.

"Go check on your mama before you go poking around in the attic. You'll be too dirty before long," Maria said.

Upstairs, Megan tiptoed into the back bedroom where Rosa had decided to stay once she was moved. Megan noticed her eyes were closed and her breath was labored and raspy. She stood for a moment before Rosa spoke.

"You want something, Megan?" Her voice was a coarse whisper.

"No, Mama. I'm just checking on you." Megan tried to sound cheerful and loving.

"For what? I'm still breathing, if that's what you want to know."

"Can I get you anything?" Megan asked.

"Where's Maria?"

"Downstairs."

"You can get Maria."

"Mama, let me. Maria's having a cup of coffee. Can I get something for you?"

"I want my sister's company. Is that too much to ask?"

"She'll be up in a few minutes. Can I open the window shade? It's dark in here."

"Suit yourself."

Megan crossed the room and carefully raised the window shade a few inches. "It's sunny out, Mama."

"Hmph," Rosa grunted.

"It'll be spring soon."

Rosa didn't answer, she simply gave a feeble wave of her hand.

"Sophia and I have decided to give the house 'a good top to bottom,'" Megan said, using her mother's own words for a thorough cleaning. "Do you mind?"

"Of course not," Rosa whispered. "It should have been done a year ago."

"Yeah, well, so we skipped a year. We're doing it now."

"Fine," the woman said flatly.

"Mama?" Megan began tentatively. Rosa barely opened her eyes, but Megan knew she could see her. "Would you mind if I packed Papa's things and put them in the attic?" Megan half expected her mother to raise up on one elbow and order her out of her room. Instead she was shocked at Rosa's response.

"I don't care. Soon you'll be packing mine as well. Might as well get to it."

"Mama—" Megan tried to argue.

"Let me sleep, Megan. You tire me." With that she closed her eyes and turned her head away from her daughter. Instead of leaving, Megan stepped closer and took her mother's hand, noticing how thin and cold it was. Suddenly she bent and pressed her lips against the bony fingers. Rosa opened her eyes for a moment, but she didn't look at Megan. Then she pulled her hand away and stuck it under the covers. "Tell Maria I'm sleeping," she said.

Megan's eyes involuntarily filled with tears, and she quietly left the room.

CHAPTER TWENTY-ONE

"Stephen? Dan Miller here," Dan said into the phone.

"You're up early for a merchant," Stephen teased good-naturedly. Seven A.M. wasn't too early to be up, but it certainly was a little early for phone calls.

"I've had some bad news. The sale of Halloran's isn't going well." Dan shifted the phone from one ear to the other. "In fact, it looks like it isn't going at all."

"What's the deal?" Stephen asked.

"The whole deal's about to fall through, that's what," Dan said.

"I'm sorry, Dan." Stephen said, "But I'm not surprised—not really."

"Yeah, I guess I'm not either."

"What's your plan now?"

"Jen and I've been talking it over, and we've decided that we'd be better off to just close the store once and for all and put the property on the market as real estate."

"That's not a bad idea, Dan. I wondered why you didn't do that in the first place."

"Well, it's a long story. Halloran's belonged to my first wife's family. It really belongs to Joy now. I'm the trustee for the estate. I had to be sure it was in Joy's best interest to do this. But she's so young. I doubt that it would be in her best interest to try to preserve something she might not even want to be a part of when she grows up. Besides, there's really no way to run the business from here. What's more, suburban shopping centers are really making a negative impact on stores like Halloran's."

"It's a trend. Maybe it'll reverse itself."

"And maybe not. Who can predict how it will go?" Dan

paused, then continued. "Anyway, we've made our decision. We were wondering how you felt about going back to Chicago for a few weeks to oversee the closeout?"

Stephen felt his insides tighten. "I'm not sure I'm the right one for that, Dan."

"It's not too difficult. Just be on the premises, make sure we don't lose our shirts in the process. We'll contact some of the stores in the area and try to get rid of the fixtures, the displays, and so forth."

Stephen closed his eyes. He'd be near Megan. He would be able to see her and to find out for sure what was happening between them. He'd had no excuse for taking a trip to Chicago, even though he had considered it. Now Dan Miller was offering him something better than an excuse—a reason.

"Wait a minute, Dan. Why me?" Stephen thought it might just be Jen's plot to encourage his relationship with Megan. "This Jen's idea?"

"No, not really, although she heartily agrees with it. No, it was Jeff's suggestion. He's aware of the situation and the complexities concerning Joy's inheritance. He suggested that we send someone close to us, someone who would be willing to go there to represent not only me, but Joy's interests as well."

"Can I give it some thought?"

"Sure. Twenty-four hours enough?"

"That's not very much time, Dan."

"Forty-eight, then. I can't give you more time than I have. I just got the call yesterday. The investment group has given me only seven days to have someone on-site. Today is day number two. If you say you can't go, I'll have only three days to find someone else."

Stephen knew he would go. But he wanted to talk to Jeff before he gave Dan his answer. He wanted Jeff's opinion firsthand.

"That's a big job for someone who knows nothing about retail to do all alone," Stephen said.

"Oh, you won't be alone," Dan replied. "I'm going along for the first week or so. Jen is going too. She may stay until the very end. Could take more than a month. I'll be back and forth before it's finished, I pretty sure of that. My folks said they'd love to come back out and stay with Joy."

"Bit by the California bug, huh?" Stephen said.

"Just looking for a good excuse to pack the wagons and head west, I'm afraid."

"You know what they say? 'How're you going to keep them down on the farm once they've seen Southern Cal?'"

"That's about right too. I know I'm not sorry I'll never shovel another spoonful of an Iowa snowfall."

"Now you just have to cut through the smog."

"What smog?"

"Spoken like a native."

"Why don't you stop by on the way to the office?" Dan said. "I'll fill you in on the rest of the details."

Stephen wanted to speak with Megan. As much as he wanted to see her, he wasn't about to show up in Chicago unannounced. Stephen Bennett never assumed. He took a deep breath and let it out slowly before dialing the number Jen had given him.

"I'm sorry." It was Maria who answered the phone. "She's not available."

"Can you tell me when she will be available?" Stephen asked.

"No, I can't," Maria said curtly. "She's busy, she's with Vinny."

"I see."

"And who are you, young man?"

"Stephen Bennett."

"I see. Well, Mr. Bennett, I don't know when she'll be available."

"Will you tell her I called?"

"Is there a message, Mr. Bennett?"

"No, not really. Just that I called."

"Who was that?" Rosa asked before a coughing spasm hit her. "Stephen Bennett," Maria said. "Does his name ring a bell with you?"

Rosa shook her head. "I suppose he's someone she knew at work." Rosa's voice was now almost always a whisper.

"I don't think so," Maria said. Coming closer to her sister, she leaned near Rosa's ear. "I think," she whispered, "he might have been calling long distance."

Rosa's deep-set eyes opened wider and she looked directly into Maria's. "Don't tell her," Rosa said.

"But he asked me to tell her he called."

"Did he say leave her a message?"

"No, not really."

"Then forget the phone ever rang," Rosa whispered. "I mean it, Maria." Her voice cracked as she tried to speak aloud, then collapsed into another fit of coughing, throwing Maria into a dither of panic and worry.

"Vinny, look here," Megan said as she rummaged through an old cardboard box. "My Camp Fire girl uniform."

"Get any badges?"

"Only a few. I was not real good at this stuff. I did earn a nature badge for collecting and identifying leaves."

"If I remember right, I should have had that badge."

"Shh. Someone might hear you."

"Your mama, you mean. Didn't you ever tell her I got all those leaves and helped you label them?"

"No, of course not." Megan looked at him tenderly. "You know, Vinny, you really helped me out of a lot of scrapes with Mama."

"Forget it."

"No, I won't. I won't ever forget it. You're a good friend, Vincent."

"Yeah, right."

"No, I mean it." Megan stood and motioned toward the heater. Vinny had repaired the plug and brought up an extension cord to heat the attic so that she could work. "See? Even now you're looking out for me. Thanks."

"Don't mention it," he said, suddenly shy.

"Why Vinny, you're embarrassed!" Megan was delighted.

"I'm not."

"Look at you! You don't even know how to handle a compliment from me."

"Well, Megan, you've been such a brat most of your life. I'm not used to you being nice to me, that's all."

"Has it been that bad?"

"Worse," he said, sticking his lower lip out in a mock pout.

"Oh, Vinny. I'm sorry." Megan came to stand beside him. Without thinking, she impulsively threw her arms around his neck. Vinny wrapped his arms around her waist and closed his eyes, enjoying her nearness.

"Megan, I've wanted to hold you for a long time—a very long time."

"Vinny," she said, trying to back out of his embrace. "Don't."

"Megan, can't I kiss you just this once?"

"It would be like kissing your sister," she reasoned with him.

"How would I know?" he argued. "I don't have a sister."

"Vinny," she pleaded.

"Just once," he begged.

"I don't know . . ." she said. But Vinny's mouth smothered her words.

Maria, curious beyond words, crept silently up the stairway toward the muffled voices until she could just peer over the flooring of the attic. She couldn't hear their conversation clearly, but her eyes widened at what she saw.

Maria could hardly wait to report to Rosa. As silently as she came, the woman backed down the stairway and returned to her sister's bedside.

Without lifting his face from Megan's, Vinny began to laugh. She froze, with his lips still firmly on hers, and stared wide-eyed at him. She was contemplating punching him in the stomach. She managed to pull away from him and back safely out of his reach. Vinny lost his balance and tumbled facedown on the old mattress on the floor.

He began to laugh again, then caught both her hands and pulled her down next to him. "You were wrong, Megan, Vinny teased. "I'm pretty sure that was not like kissing anyone's sister." He grinned mischievously. "But I don't think I know for sure. Shall I try again?"

"You said just one!"

"I lied," he said. Megan thrust a well directed fist into the middle of his diaphragm.

"I'd like to speak with Megan, please." Stephen's voice was polite, but insistent.

Maria recognized Stephen's voice when he called the second time. "Sorry, she's still with Vincent."

"Hang up the phone," Rosa ordered in her barely audible whisper. Raising herself slightly on one elbow she pointed at her sister. "Hang up!"

"Could you please give her a message?" Stephen's question was answered with a rude click of the receiver.

"Why not send her a telegram?" Jen asked when Stephen turned from the phone to face her.

"I can't tell what's going on," Stephen said. "I'm confused. Why won't she take my calls? What's she doing with Vinny?" Stephen glanced at his watch. "It's not even noon there. Doesn't he have a job?"

"Are you sure she knows about your calls?" Dan asked.

Stephen looked into the faces of the friends that had become important to him in such a short time. "No, I'm not."

"Maybe Jen's right. Maybe a telegram would be more—well, maybe it'd work." Dan placed his hand on Stephen's shoulder. "It's worth a try, Steve, isn't it?"

"Why not?" Stephen said. "I'll stop by Western Union on my way to the office." He turned to Jen. "I just don't want to intrude."

"You're not intruding, Stephen. I'm positive of that."

"Maybe I ought to give Megan a call," Jen said to her husband after Stephen left.

"Oh?"

"You know, just to find out if she's avoiding Stephen or not."

"Stay out of it, Jen."

"But she's one of my best friends," Jen said.

"I know that. If you want to call and see how she is, that's one thing. But her relationship with Stephen is her business. If she brings it up, okay."

"And if she doesn't?"

"Then keep out of it."

"But I just want to see them happy," Jen cajoled, "like us."

"You mean you want to see them married."

"Isn't that the same thing?"

"For us, yes. But I'm telling you, Stephen and Meg have to find their own way."

"Okay then. But tonight after dinner I'm going to call her. I've been wondering how she's doing."

"You can tell her about the store, and you can tell her we're making plans to come. But not a word about Stephen unless she asks—agreed?"

"I know you're right. It's just that I want her to be happy."

"And you want her to get together with Stephen, and you want her to move out here close to us. Sweetheart, you're not really as unselfish as you make yourself out to be." Actually, Dan loved Jen and would have pushed Megan to move out to Redlands permanently just to make his wife happy. He had to work hard to be objective when it came to Jen having whatever she wanted.

Megan decided not to stay in the attic with Vinny but to return by herself after lunch. Making an excuse to see how Sophia was doing in the basement, she led Vinny away from the dimly lit attic. Sophia, dirty and needing a break, was happy for any excuse to come up from the dingy basement.

After a quick lunch of sandwiches and some of Aunt Maria's homemade minestrone soup Vinny said he had to get to work. "I work three to eleven. I'll stop by on my way home and see how it's going."

"Not tonight, Vinny," Megan said. "I'm planning to take a long bath and go to bed early."

"I'm off tomorrow. I'll see you then," Vinny said.

"Really, Vinny, you don't have to hang around here all the time. You're not our slave, for goodness' sake."

"I don't feel like a slave, Megan. I want to be here just in case—" he shot a quick glance at Sophia before continuing—"you know, just in case you discover another buried treasure or something."

"Shush, Vinny!" Megan warned. "Auntie might hear you."

Vinny moved toward the back door and put on his coat. "She saw us, you know."

Megan's head shot up. "She what?"

"She saw you?" Sophia asked innocently.

"She did not!" Megan said firmly.

"Oh, yes she did. She came partway up the stairs, and she saw us."

"When?" Megan asked, her heart pounding.

"You know when," he teased. He crossed the room and bent low to Megan's face. "When we were making out."

"Megan!" Sophia nearly choked on a cookie.

"We were not making out!" Megan insisted.

"Ask Auntie Maria," he said in a bragging tone. "Ask her what she saw with her own two eyes." Vinny bent and kissed Megan on the cheek. He caught her hand just as she swung at him, then threw his head back and laughed. Turning to Sophia, he said, "Just ask her."

As soon as he was out the door, Megan jumped to her feet and practically threw her dishes in the sink.

"What's he talking about, Megan?" Sophia's voice was tinged with accusation.

"We were not making out!" Megan insisted. "He kissed me, that's all."

"No kidding?"

"It wasn't my idea, Sophie. Believe me. I have never had romantic feelings for Vinny—not ever."

"Well, that's what you've said all along."

"And it's the truth, I swear!" Megan held up her right hand. "Besides—" she started.

"Besides?" Sophia asked.

"Well, I've met someone."

"And?"

"And nothing. I'm here. He's there. And Mama's up there."

"Oh, Meggie."

"Don't," Megan warned, holding up her hand. "Just don't. I came home. It was the right thing to do. I'm here, and the rest will just have to wait until we know what's happening with Mama."

Sophia reached across the table to touch Megan's arm. "And do we know what's *really* happening with Mama?"

"No, not for certain." Megan looked directly into Sophia's eyes. "But I don't have a good feeling about this, do you?"

Sophia's eyes filled with tears, and she hastily wiped them away on the sleeve of her sweatshirt. "I'm afraid, Megan."

"Me too." The sisters sat quietly for a moment, then Megan returned to the attic, and Sophia went to finish cleaning the basement before it was time for Benjie to come home.

Passing Maria in the front hallway, Megan said, "I'll be in the attic, Auntie."

"Alone?" Maria smiled sweetly toward her niece.

"Yes, Auntie, alone."

CHAPTER TWENTY-TWO

Megan began packing her keepsakes back in their boxes. After looking through a couple of high school yearbooks and reading the inscriptions from all her friends, she realized how much she didn't want to stay in Chicago. More to the point, she knew how desperately she wanted to return to California, how much she wanted to be with Stephen. So much had happened within her heart since Christmas Eve. It had been just two short months, but to Megan it seemed like she'd known him all her life.

Megan thought she heard the doorbell ring, but she dismissed it when no one called up the stairs to her. She spied two boxes in the corner that she recognized, and she began moving other cartons and old trunks to get to them.

Sitting on the floor, she began sorting through the pictures of her parents, her sisters, and even her grandparents. She looked up momentarily when she heard Maria hurry into Rosa's room and shut the door. But before she could think about what that might have meant, she turned all her attention back to the pictures in the box and began to organize them into neat piles.

"What's that?" Rosa whispered to her sister.

"A telegram," Maria repeated.

"Who's it for?"

"Megan," Maria said.

"What's it say?"

"I don't know. I didn't open it—it's addressed to her."

"Well, open it," Rosa insisted.

"I'm not sure we should."

"Open it. It may be bad news." Rosa's breaths came short and somewhat shallow. "We may need to soften it for her.

You know how that is, don't you?" Rosa referred to the only other telegram received by anyone in the family.

"Yes, I do." Maria's eyes glazed over with the memory of the hand-delivered message that her husband had been killed on the beach in Normandy.

"Well, then. Wasn't it best we knew first?"

"I guess it was." But Maria often wished that she had been the one to open the envelope, that she had had some privacy when she heard she had become a widow the day before her twenty-first birthday.

"You know it was best. Now go on," Rosa insisted and sank back into her pillows exhausted. "Open it."

Megan put all but the pictures of her parents back into the box. Then she began arranging the stack into what she believed to be chronological order. She saw Joseph and Rosa with what they referred to as the neighborhood gang—the group that hung around the corner drug store and went to the movies and dances together. She saw her father's young face and the black curly hair that he slicked back as best he could. Even with all his effort, a wavy lock of thick black hair had escaped and fallen across his forehead in every picture.

And there was Frank. Megan knew her father and Frank had always best friends. They grew up together in this same neighborhood. Frank bought his parents' house and moved into it before Vinny was born. Joseph had bought this house, two doors down from Frank and Lois, as soon as it came on the market.

Megan picked up a picture of her parents smiling, close together in a tight huddle with Frank and Vinny's mother. Putting that picture aside, she found others. Rosa had been happy then. You could see it in her face. Joseph, Rosa, Frank, and Lois—the foursome was as close as any family could ever hope to be. Rosa saw to that. No matter what the occasion, she insisted on Frank and Lois being included. Megan ran her finger over the image of her father's face. It was flat and cold.

"Papa," she whispered to the picture, "I wish you could tell me about the money." She clasped the photograph close to her chest. "What in the world am I supposed to do with it?"

Megan suddenly felt the same loneliness she felt in the weeks and months following her father's death. So many unanswered questions. They seemed childish to her now but so important to her then. *Why did you have to die? How did such an accident happen? Why couldn't you have worked in a bank where it was safe? Why did you have to work in the train yard where it was so dangerous?* Now other unanswered questions seemed to haunt her. But how could she find words to ask questions she only felt?

"Oh, Papa. I wish you could talk to me."

"Megan," Frank's voice called from below.

"I'm up here."

"Vinny told me you were rummaging around up there," he called from the stairway. "I'll be up as soon as I look in on your mama."

"She's in the back bedroom, Uncle Frank."

Maria stuffed the telegram back inside its envelope and shoved it between the mattresses under Rosa. Straightening her apron she opened the door wide for Frank to enter.

"Frank," Rosa whispered from her bed. "Frankie."

"How's it going, Rosie?"

"I've been better, I can tell you that."

"Haven't we all?" he responded.

"You come to see Meggie?" she asked.

"And you," he said softly.

Maria excused herself and told Frank she'd be downstairs putting on a fresh pot of coffee. He simply nodded, and she left the room.

"Vinny says she's tearing up the place," Frank said.

"You know Megan. Once she gets started she's impossible to stop. It's just that getting her started is nearly as impossible."

"How come you're still back here?" he asked, looking around the small room that had once belonged to Angie.

"The girls decided to clean my room," she said. "But then, you know that, you helped them."

"I only carried the mattresses out and back in. I know your girls are strong, Rosa, but Vinny and me, we wanted to help them out a little." He smiled at Rosa. "So then, why are you still back in this room?"

"I don't think Megan's done in there yet," Rosa whispered. Frank watched as Rosa coughed deeply. He could see the pain cross her face. He'd seen it before when Lois was dying.

"What's the doctor say?"

"Haven't seen him since Megan's been home."

"You haven't?"

"No. Not since the day Sophie took me. Then Megan came and they all got so busy . . ." Her voice trailed off, and Frank could see that the conversation was wearing her out.

"Rest now, Rosa," he said, smoothing her long hair away from her face. "I'll go check on Meggie up there. Let's see if she's into any mischief," he said as he winked at Rosa. "I'll come back in before I leave."

Upstairs, Megan shoved the small box she was about to open back into the corner when she heard footsteps on the stairway. Frank came up and found Megan sitting among the old pictures. "What've you got here?"

"As you can see," Megan answered, "I am visiting yesteryear."

"Vinny told me, you know, about—"

"Shh!" Megan warned and quickly stood up. "Just a minute." She crept quietly down the stairs and closed the door that led into the hallway.

"Sorry," Frank offered, "I didn't think."

"At least now we'll be able to hear her if she opens the door."

"Now, tell me," Frank purposely kept his voice low.

"Didn't Vinny?"

"Yes, but I want to hear it from you."

Megan repeated almost word for word the story Vinny had told his father earlier. Finally, Megan saw Frank shake his head slowly. "I can't believe it. Well, yes I can. He was so determined that . . ."

Megan waited a moment, then urged, "Go on, Uncle Frank."

"I'm not sure what to say. He was just determined to have his own way eventually, I guess. Your mother knows nothing about this?"

"I don't think so."

"You didn't tell her?"

"No. I thought if she knew she'd say something when we told her we took the dresser apart and soaped the drawer runners. She always was complaining that they were tight." Megan sat cross-legged with her elbows on her knees and rested her face in her hands. "If she had taken out the drawers herself, she would have found the money. And then, I thought if she didn't know, there must be a reason. That's what I'm doing up here. Looking for a reason for all this."

"You thought your mother might fix the dresser herself?"

"Well, she could have."

"But then she would have been independent. You know your mother is determined not to be self-sufficient."

"That's a funny thing to say."

"I mean it, Megan. She is as capable a woman as I have ever known, but she is very determined not to be."

"I don't understand."

"You and me both." Frank began sifting through the pictures laying around Megan. "It's just that she always manages to get people to do things she should be able to do for herself—like soaping the drawer runners. On the other hand, she often tackles things she's incapable of doing and, in a way, forces people to rescue her." Frank picked up one of the pictures and began to laugh. "Your Papa, he was a real clown at times."

"Look how happy you all were." Megan pointed at the smiling faces of the four young people.

"Well, we managed to look it anyway, didn't we?"

Megan's face reflected her confusion.

"Megan, honey, do you think everything you see in a picture is real? That every smile is an honest one?"

"I never thought about it."

"Remember this?" Frank held up a picture of Megan, Vinny, Sophia, and Angie.

"Vinny's eighth birthday."

"How old were you?"

"Six and a half."

"No front teeth," Frank reminded her. "And did you want to smile for this picture?"

"No, I didn't. Mama made us all stand there until I smiled. Then she said we all had to stand there until I gave her a wide smile."

"That's my point." Frank glanced around the room. "Can you tell me that smile is not genuine, just by looking at the picture?"

"What are you saying?" Megan asked, examining a couple of the other snapshots a bit more closely.

"Only this: things were not always what they seemed then, and they certainly were not what they appear to be from these old pictures."

"Was my papa happy?"

"He loved you girls more than anything else in the whole world."

"Did he love Mama?"

"I think so," Frank said.

"But?"

"But I don't know. You'd have to ask him. I can't speak for him anymore now than when he was alive. We never discussed Rosa."

"But I can't ask him now."

"No, honey, you can't. I'm not sure you could even if he were here right now."

"Why not?"

"He was a private man," Frank said. "My best friend—like a brother to me. But we never talked about Rosa."

"Was that his decision, or yours?" Megan asked.

"I think it was mutual."

"He was a nice man, wasn't he?" Megan asked, holding a picture at an angle for better light.

"Yes, Megan, he was. A more loyal man I've never met. Loyal and committed to his family. And, if you never knew it, he was partial to you."

"No." Megan smiled.

"Oh yes. You were his little favorite. Your sisters knew it.

Your mama knew it. Your sisters didn't seem to mind, but it drove your mama crazy."

"But he was so careful to make every thing equal."

"Yeah, and he had good reason for that too." Frank glanced toward the stairway. "He never wanted her to take it out on you."

Megan's eyes opened wide with an instant flash of understanding. "Is that why she is harder on me than Angie or Sophie?"

"Think about it, Meggie." Frank stood and stretched his legs a bit before walking slowly down the stairs. "I'm going to check on your mama again. I'm not too pleased with the way she looks. I'll be back in a minute."

Megan began to search her father's face in the photographs once again. Was his broad smile false? She bent forward and lined the pictures up again all in a row, then separated those of the two couples who had been closer than family.

Frank almost always looked lovingly at Lois, who snuggled close and looked adoringly at him. Joseph always looked into the camera. And Rosa, a smile frozen on her face, was almost always—*looking at Frank!* Megan began frantically pulling out every picture that showed the four of them together. In candid snapshots, Rosa was almost always looking at Frank.

More confused than ever, Megan gathered the scattered pictures quickly and stuffed them back into the box. Without thinking, she pulled out a smaller box she had ignored earlier and put it on her lap. Peeling back tape that had so carefully sealed the contents away from the casual observer, she pulled back the flaps and carefully examined the contents.

Turning a padded, hand-tooled leather book over in her hands, she marvelled at the detail of the drawing on the cover—hearts and doves with ribbons caught in their beaks. She saw her father's initials carved carefully in the lower right-hand corner. She slowly opened the front cover and saw the words written there in her father's scrawl: *To Rosa, my love, my life, From Joey.*

Leafing through the next few pages she found her mother's handwriting. *A diary,* she thought, *my mother's diary!*

"Megan!" Frank's strong voice echoed up the stairway and jerked Megan back to the present. "Megan, get down here!"

Not waiting to return the diary to the box, Megan ran toward the stairway. "What's the matter?"

"How long's she been spitting up blood?"

"I didn't know she was!" Megan's heart pounded with panic.

"Get the doctor on the phone," he ordered. "No, never mind!" Frank walked to the new phone on the table between the twin beds.

"Don't," Rosa tried to protest.

"Operator, this is an emergency," Frank shouted into the phone. "Get me an ambulance."

Frank picked up Rosa from the bed as if she were just a child. Megan grabbed the blanket from the bed and tucked it around her mother as Frank carried her down the hall.

"I'll go with her, you call Vinny at work. Tell him to come home and get you. While you're waiting, you get yourself cleaned up, and you and Sophie meet us there." Megan watched, frozen with fear, as Frank carried Rosa toward the front door.

"Where are you going?" Maria's voice revealed her terror.

"To the hospital," Frank said. Megan could hear the siren wail and then fade as the medical vehicle skidded to a halt in front of the house.

"You hear me, Megan? Now," he shouted as he opened the door, "go call Vinny!" Frank effortlessly carried the blanketed bundle out the door and brushed by the surprised ambulance attendants. Only when he was at the back door of the ambulance did he surrender his burden. Frank glanced back at Megan and yelled again, "Now, Megan!" He stepped inside and took a seat near Rosa.

"I can't understand it," Stephen said to Dan and Jen later that afternoon. "We know the telegram was delivered . . ." He paced back and forth in the Millers' store.

"You're sure," Jen said.

"I checked. Someone signed for it."

"I don't understand it either," Jen said.

"Just because somebody signed for it doesn't mean Megan got it," Dan said.

"Right," Jen tried to reassure Stephen. "Maybe she wasn't home. Maybe she hasn't even seen it yet."

"That's a lot of maybes," Stephen said flatly. "Maybe she doesn't want to hear from me after all."

"Don't be silly," Jen said.

"Silly is one thing I've never been called, Jennifer." Stephen's firm voice was tinged with anger.

"Sorry," Jen said quietly, "I only meant that . . ."

"Listen, Jen is going to call Megan later tonight anyway. She can simply ask her what's going on."

"No." Stephen's tone was emphatic.

"Why not?" Jen asked.

"I can't stop you from calling. Megan's your friend, and you have every right to call her whenever you like. But please, I don't want you discussing me."

Jen rolled her eyes, and Dan recognized the look; her temper was rising.

"Whatever you say," Dan said calmly. Jen shot him a fiery glance. "We respect your right to handle your affairs, your *personal* affairs your own way. Don't we, sweetheart?"

"Jen?" Stephen asked firmly.

"Honey?" Dan said.

"Listen, you two. You are both wrong about this. Megan has a right to know that Stephen has been trying to reach her. I know," she said when Stephen tried to interrupt, "I know, what you're about to say. But you have no reason to believe she has even received any of your messages."

"And I don't have any reason to believe she hasn't, either."

Jen stood with both hands firmly planted on her hips and her chin stuck out stubbornly. "You can believe whatever you choose to believe." Infuriated, Jen turned on her heel to walk away from them. "But I will tell you this: if I do talk to Megan and if she says anything to me about you—anything at all—I'm going to ask her what's going on and why she hasn't returned any of your calls."

"No," Stephen said.

"Oh yes, Mr. Bennett. But don't you think for one minute I'm doing it for you. No sir. I'll ask for my own benefit, and for Megan's. Not because you want to know—because obviously you don't—but because *I* want to know." Jen walked quickly away from the two men.

Stephen tried to reach out and grab her arm, "Jen, wait!"

Dan blocked him from reaching Jen. "Let her go, Stephen. She'll simmer down. She gets a little feisty at times, but she'll think it through before she makes the call. Honestly, she will."

Jen knew Dan would try to talk to her once more before she called Megan's house in Chicago. *Maybe I shouldn't wait until after supper,* she thought. *Maybe I'll go straight home and call right now.*

Walking in the house ten minutes later, Jen went immediately to the phone in her kitchen. Glancing at her watch, she muttered to herself, "After all, it is after supper there." Five forty-five, Chicago time, "Well, an early supper anyway."

CHAPTER TWENTY-THREE

"Oh, Jen," Megan cried when she heard her friend's voice. "I can't believe it's you."

"Megan, what's wrong?"

"It's my mother. Uncle Frank just took her to the hospital in an ambulance."

"When?"

"Just now. I came back in to call Vinny to come and get me. I was just reaching for the phone when you called." Megan loved hearing the soothing voice of her friend and hated to cut the conversation short. "Could I call you later? It really is a bad time to talk right now."

"Of course. Listen, is there anything we can do?"

"No," Megan said, "just knowing you're available if anything should happen . . ."

"I'm always near a phone, Meg. Either here at the house or at the store. Call anytime, promise?"

"Sure."

An hour later when Megan arrived at the hospital, Vinny parked the car while Sophia and Megan asked at the front desk for Rosa's room number.

"Room five twenty-four," an emotionless woman said.

Sophia and Megan waited impatiently for Vinny before pressing the elevator's call button. Wordlessly, the three stepped inside the elevator, and Vinny pressed the button marked for Rosa's floor.

"How is she?" Sophia asked Frank once they reached the hallway outside the room.

"The doctor is with her now. Megan, you called him from the house?"

Megan nodded.

"He came right over. He's furious, I can tell you that."

"Why, Uncle Frank?" Sophia asked.

"Because he wasn't called sooner."

"He doesn't know how—well, how difficult she can be, does he, Dad?" Vinny asked.

"He's finding out," Megan said, nodding toward the frazzled nurse leaving Rosa's room.

"Where's Maria?" Frank asked.

"She's home crying her eyes out. She's sure you've done more harm than good taking her away from home," Megan said.

"Any word from Angie?" Frank asked.

"No," Sophia said. "We haven't heard from her since a couple of days after Christmas."

"What's gotten into that girl anyway?" Frank asked.

"She's gotten mixed up with some pretty interesting people," Vinny said. "But don't be too hard on her, okay? It's just the university atmosphere, that's all."

"That's a polite thing to say," Sophia said. Megan remained silent, keeping an eye on Rosa's door.

"Vinny," Frank said, "you think you could find her?"

"I don't know. I guess I could try."

"Why not start at the university? She's living somewhere around there isn't she?"

"Wait a minute," Sophia said, "I might have an address." Rummaging through her purse, she looked for the slip of paper Angelina had given her.

"Never mind, I think I know where to look. Maybe I'll go home and get Benjie first," Vinny said.

"Good idea, son. It might be better to go together."

The doctor came out of Rosa's room just as Vinny disappeared into the elevator. "Are you all here? Is this the entire family?"

"No, my sister's not here yet," Megan said, "but we don't know when—" Megan said.

"Or *if*," Sophia joined in, "she'll be coming."

"And Auntie Maria is at home. That's Mama's sister."

"You're her children?" The girls nodded. "And you?" he asked nodding toward Frank.

"I've known Rosa almost her whole life."

"I see," the doctor said. "Well, we have a very seriously ill woman in there," he nodded toward the half-closed door of Rosa's room. "As I told the young lady here a few weeks back, some of the spots on her lungs looked very suspicious. I wanted to do a biopsy earlier, but you said you wanted to contact your sister."

"Yes, she's here." Sophia nodded toward Megan.

"I see." The doctor rubbed his forehead and gestured toward the empty chairs at the end of the hallway. "Upon my first examination, sometime back around the holidays, I knew that Rosa had pneumonia. I didn't like some of the shadows showing on the X ray, but the congestion in her lungs then made it too complicated to tell for sure. Once we had the pneumonia under control, we needed to look further. I wanted to hospitalize her then, but she is a pretty determined woman—as you probably know."

The small group nodded in understanding.

"You brought her back in to see me, let's see, ten days ago?"

"About that, I guess," Sophia said.

"I told you then we needed to do a biopsy," the doctor said. "Maybe I didn't make myself clear as to the urgency of the matter."

"Yes, you did. But she wouldn't—"

"Well, that's past. Now we're dealing with what's going on today."

Frank told the doctor of his visit with Rosa and the fact she had been spitting blood. He saw it first on her pillowcase, and then she had a spasm while he was in the room.

"I have examined her. Both her liver and her spleen are enlarged. Her entire abdomen is bloated, and she is complaining of headache and a bit of dizziness." He looked at the small family gathered so attentively. "I'm afraid that any news we get from her tests isn't going to be good. My suspicion is that she started with cancer somewhere else and it is now so widespread we've more than likely already lost what chances we might have had earlier."

Megan and Sophia moved closer together for strength and comfort.

"Where do you think it started?"

"I'm not sure. Breast or uterus, maybe. She refused to come in for regular examinations."

"You mean it didn't start in the lungs?" Frank asked.

"Highly unlikely," the doctor answered.

"Then an operation . . ." Megan said.

"Probably isn't indicated." The doctor nodded toward an approaching nurse. "Excuse me."

Sophia and Megan stared at each other without emotion. Frank pulled them both into his arms, and together the three walked toward a window.

"What are we going to do, Uncle Frank?" Megan whispered.

"Wait, I guess," he said.

"Did you reach Megan?" Dan asked.

"Yes, but she couldn't talk. They had just taken her mother to the hospital." Jen turned and faced her husband. "Megan's voice was filled with fear, Dan. I didn't know what to say to her."

"There's really nothing you can say, honey." Dan opened his arms to his young wife. "I'm sure just hearing your voice was some comfort to her. Did she say how bad her mother's condition is?"

"She doesn't know yet."

"You tell Stephen?"

"Not yet," Jen said. "I really don't know anything more than what I just told you."

"Maybe he'd like to hear it, honey. Why not try to give him a call?"

After speaking briefly with Stephen, Jen turned to Dan. "You were right," she said. "He thinks this may explain why Megan hasn't returned his calls."

"How long would it take you to get ready to go to Chicago?" Dan asked.

"I need a few days, at least." Jen began mentally forming a checklist.

"I have a few things to tend to myself, but I think we should plan to go within a few days. Thursday, if possible."

"That soon?"

"I thought I might have a couple days at Halloran's with the staff around, then spend Sunday there without them." Dan's voice was quiet and thoughtful.

"Will it be hard to go back?"

"Not with you there."

"I'll be ready," she said. "What about Stephen?"

"I'm not sure."

"I hope he goes with us."

"Me too," Dan said. "I really need him. However, he might be distracted being in the same town with Megan."

"You think that would be a problem?"

"It would be for me." Dan smiled at his redheaded bride. "In fact, if you remember right, it was."

Frank insisted that Megan and Sophia go back home, but he was adamant about spending the night at Rosa's bedside. The doctor told them she was resting comfortably, thanks to a generous injection of morphine. "She'll sleep soundly, I assure you." Before he turned to go, he looked at Frank and said, "You know, Mr.—"

"Petrossi, Frank Petrossi," Frank said.

"Mr. Petrossi, these girls may need you more tonight than Rosa does. Really, she's sleeping. We're making her as comfortable as possible. We'll try to relieve some of the pressure in her abdomen, and she'll probably be feeling quite a bit better by morning."

Frank hesitated.

"You all need as much rest as you can get," the doctor continued. "In a week or two, you may have some pretty long nights."

"He's right, Uncle Frank," Megan said. "Why don't we all go home. I'll make us some dinner. Then we'll call it a night."

Finally, Frank gave in. After another brief look at Rosa,

they all met outside her door and agreed that she looked more comfortable than she had in weeks.

Walking out the front door of the hospital, they met Vinny walking toward them with Angie. Benjie followed behind.

"Well, Megan," Angie said haughtily, "I see you've come back for the kill."

"Angelina!" Sophia cried.

"It's true."

Frank took Angelina's arm, pulling her roughly along the sidewalk.

"Ow, Uncle Frankie," Angie whined, "you're hurting me."

"I need to paddle you, right here and now."

"Go right ahead," she said, sticking out her tightly covered bottom.

"Behave yourself," Frank scolded.

"Come on, Uncle Frank." She formed her mouth into a pout. "That wouldn't be much fun, now would it?"

"Get the car," Frank called back to Vinny.

"Are the six of us going to fit?" Benjie asked.

"I think so," Vinny said.

"Listen," Benjie suggested, "you two take her in the car. I'll call a cab for the three of us." Frank eyed him questioningly. "I just thought we should keep her away—you know, from them," Benjie explained, nodding toward Megan and Sophia.

"You're right, Ben. Meet you at the house, then."

"Wow! You mean I get the two of you completely to myself? How lucky can a girl get?" Angie said sarcastically.

Back at the house Sophia and Megan waited with dread for Frank and Vinny to arrive with their youngest sister. "I'll make some coffee," Megan said as she started toward the kitchen just as the phone rang.

"Hello?" Stretching the phone cord as far as she could, she grabbed the coffee pot from its place on the burner.

"Megan?"

Megan could scarcely believe her ears. "Stephen?"

"It's me."

"But why—I mean, you're calling me."

"Is this a bad time?"

"Actually, it really is. My mother's been taken to the hospital."

"I know, Jen told me."

"And my sister, Angie . . ." Megan heard some commotion from the living room. "I think my sister has just arrived."

"I've been missing you, Megan," Stephen said.

"You better get in here," Vinny warned as he poked his head around the door. "She's a real basket case."

"I can't talk now, Stephen. I'll have to call you later." Without waiting for his response, Megan hung up the phone and went to face Angie.

"There she is." Angie's voice was loud and shrill. "The family pet. Come here, Megan darling, let me give you a hug."

"Stay away from me," Megan said sharply.

"Of course, my pet," Angie snapped. "Anything you say. Just like always."

Vinny stepped in front of Megan, facing Angie. "Why Vinny! Meggie's great protector. How touching! How sweet!" Angie pursed her lips. "Isn't that cute?" She turned to face a wide-eyed Sophia. "Just like you and your big teddy bear, Benjie."

Frank stepped forward and pulled her roughly to one side. "Angie, for heaven's sake."

"Hey, Uncle Frank, you're hurting me! You always did prefer Megan over me, didn't you, Vinny? Look at the two of you." She lowered her voice to almost a growl. "The two favorites that two whole families have put their entire hopes in while the rest of us can just go to—"

"Angelina!" Maria's voice came sharp and loud from the corner of the living room.

"Auntie!" Angelina faked an enthusiastic tone.

"What has gotten into you?" Maria said frantically.

"Well, whatever do you mean, Auntie?"

Sophia tried to intervene, and Megan took a protective step toward her aunt as well; then suddenly, everyone was yelling at once.

"Stop it!" Frank shouted. "Stop it all of you!" Every eye in the room looked toward the source of the command. At once, they were quiet. "I mean it," he said more softly.

"Wow," Angelina said admiringly. "Right on, Uncle, right on. You're groovin' now, Frankie. Groovin'!"

"It's okay, Auntie," Sophia said soothingly. "Don't mind her. She's—she's not herself."

"Oh, you're wrong, big sister. I'm more myself than I've ever been."

"With your mama laying down there in the hospital! How dare you talk like this!" Maria cried.

"But Uncle Frank made me come!" Angie whined.

"Well, then you can just go." Maria motioned toward the door. "Go on now, go back to the hole you crawled out of."

"No, wait." Sophia motioned to Megan. "Auntie, we're family, we all need to be together.

"Then Angelina," Maria stood erect stretching to her full four feet eleven inches, "You'll go to your room." The small woman pointed toward the upstairs. "And when you come down, you'll change that attitude of yours, do you understand me?"

"But Auntie," Angelina whined.

"But nothing," Maria interrupted. "We've had a rough time of it here and your sisters have been working hard getting this place back into shape while you've been—who knows where?"

"But . . ."

"Go." Maria pointed to the stairway. "Now!"

Angelina sullenly climbed the stairs stamping her foot on every step as she went.

"She'll calm down in a little while," Frank said, inwardly hoping he was right.

Megan felt the stress of the day hit her all at once. Tired beyond anything she had ever felt before, she sat down at the table in the dining room and rested her head on her arms.

"You need to go to bed, Megan," Sophia said.

"So do you," Benjie said quietly to his wife.

Maria sat on the sofa in a daze. "Come on, Auntie," Megan said finally. "Let's see if we can make it up the stairs, shall we?"

"I'll sleep in my own room tonight," Maria said.

"Good idea." Megan took Maria by the arm and gently helped her up the stairs.

After seeing her aunt to her room, Megan stopped at the back bedroom. From the door she spotted the stains on the bed that had alerted Frank earlier that afternoon.

Walking numbly to the bed, she pulled the sheets off and gathered them in a bundle. She didn't notice the yellow envelope that fell to the floor. Without thinking, she tossed the bundled bed covers back on the mattress, turned and left the room.

As Meg slipped between the sheets of her own bed, Stephen's face flickered momentarily through her mind. "I'm just too tired," she whispered. Almost instantly, she was sleeping while Stephen, almost two thousand miles away, paced the floor of his room, trying to decide what to do.

CHAPTER TWENTY-FOUR

Megan checked the alarm clock beside her bed: three fifteen. She wasn't sure what had awakened her, and she lay listening for a few minutes in the darkness. Then it all came back to her. The grave condition of her mother, her younger sister pouting in her room, Uncle Frank asleep downstairs on the sofa. After a few minutes of tossing and turning, she knew she wouldn't sleep and decided to get up. Slipping on her jeans and a flannel shirt, she quietly crept into the attic and turned on the electric heater. Then she pulled out the boxes of family mementoes and pictures once again.

Opening the box she had abandoned earlier, she carefully retrieved Rosa's diary. Her father had hand tooled it for Rosa, probably as a gift early on in their relationship. Despite the sense that she was invading her mother's privacy, she began to read. She was still reading when Frank found her, nearly an hour and a half later.

"Morning," Frank said softly, startling Megan.

"Uncle Frank," she said quickly, closing the book. She stuffed the diary back into its box.

"What's that you have there?"

"Oh, nothing. Just some old stuff."

"What old stuff?"

"Just some more family junk. You know."

"Megan?"

Pushed as much by her curiosity as by Frank's persistence, she decided to approach him directly. "Uncle Frank, I've been reading my mother's diary."

"Oh yeah?"

"Yeah. I guess my father must have given it to her. Look, it's hand-tooled."

"I remember when he did that," Frank said. "I think that book was his last project." Frank extended his hand, expecting Megan to hand over the book.

"I don't think you should—well, you know, the stuff written here is pretty personal."

"I can imagine," he said without withdrawing his hand.

"You know, she must have written these things when she was pretty young."

"No dates?"

"I didn't notice."

"I bet," Frank said, coming closer. "Let me see it, Megan."

"I'm not sure . . ."

"I am." Frank knelt beside her and gently took the diary out of her hand. He settled down on the floor next to Megan.

She watched him closely as he thumbed through the pages, waiting for his face to register his reactions.

"Well," he said finally, "now you know."

"I'm not sure I do, Uncle Frank."

"I dated your mother for a while, Megan. It was only a short while, and I dated others as well. Back then we called it playing the field. I wasn't ready to settle down. I liked all the girls. Then I met Lois, and I fell in love. Really in love." Frank turned the diary over in his hands and examined the covers, front and back. "Your mother, she wasn't too happy about my romance with Lois. She behaved rather—well, shall we say unladylike?"

"I wouldn't know. I wasn't there."

"Right," Frank smiled at her. "You weren't were you?" He dusted the book with his shirt sleeve. "It was then that she set her cap for Joseph. He was my best friend. He had been around the neighborhood as long as I could remember. We were really like brothers. He had always had a crush on Rosa. As long as I can remember, he liked her."

"But she liked you," Megan said.

"We all thought she had gotten past that," Frank continued. "We were all so close. She made it a point to stay close to Lois. Lois found her a bit overbearing at times, but we all just chalked it up to Rosa being Rosa. We overlooked a lot of things that maybe we shouldn't have. But then, hindsight is always clearer, don't you think?" He paused, then decided to continue.

"Then, when Lois got sick, Rosa saw us through it all. She was at our house more than she was here. Joseph didn't like that very much. She talked about you and Vinny someday marrying, like it was all decided. Your papa and I tried to talk to her about it, but she always said she wasn't forcing it, just that she knew it." Frank found talking to Megan about this easier than he might have imagined. "Then after Lois died, Rosa started writing the letters."

"I know," Megan said.

"You do?"

"She wrote about that near the back, see?"

"She thought we'd be together someday, Megan. I swear, I did nothing to encourage her. It was just that she had this idea so stuck in her mind. Then Joey's accident happened, and she went through all sorts of grief—that is, for everyone to see. But at the same time her letters got more—well, quite personal. As soon as she felt the grieving time was respectably over, she invited me to come calling, you might say."

"And did you?"

"No," Frank said quietly, "I didn't."

"Why not?"

"I didn't feel the same way about your mother. It's not that I don't have some affection for her. After all, we grew up in the same neighborhood. She was my best friend's wife. I couldn't have loved you girls any more if you were my very own." Frank ran his hand through his graying hair. "But I didn't feel that kind of interest in Rosa."

"You never married again, Uncle Frank. Why not?"

"I have never stopped loving Lois. I still miss her every day of my life." Frank wiped an uninvited tear from his eye. "I never met anyone—I never felt like that again."

"Did you give yourself a chance to meet someone new?"

"Probably not. No," Frank said. "In a way, I was as obsessed with Lois as your mother ever was with me. If I couldn't have her, I didn't want anyone."

"So has Mama ever let up?"

"Oh, sure. In the last few years. She never brings it up with me anymore. But somehow I think her hopes for you and Vinny—it's hard to explain."

"Do you think Vinny and I would have been her substitute?"

"That's my guess," Frank said. "I've thought so all along."

"Did Papa know?"

"He was a pretty smart man, Megan. I'm pretty sure he did."

"Did he ever talk about it with you?"

"No. He knew how much I loved Lois. He knew I wasn't interested in your mama."

"Do you know she still has his clothes hanging in his closet downstairs?"

"No kidding?"

"I decided to pack them away. I couldn't stand the thought of her making a shrine to him. It bothers me even more now."

"Need some help?" Frank said. "Can I carry boxes out or anything?"

"Sure." Megan stood and helped Frank to his feet. "I'm glad we have you, Uncle Frank. We love you, you know. I don't know what we would've done without you after Papa died."

"Let's get to those boxes," Frank said, "before we call the hospital."

Megan led the way to Rosa and Joseph's room and opened the door. Frank followed her inside, and Megan opened her father's closet. "No use sending these to Goodwill or anything. They're ten years out of date," Megan said, pointing to the boxes where she had carefully placed her father's clothes.

"More like twenty," Frank corrected. "Your papa didn't care to buy himself new clothes unless Rosa made him."

"I've packed most everything, except I can't reach that little box way up there, back in the corner. I almost didn't see it until I stood on the bed to get the light fixture down when I was cleaning."

Frank turned from closing the lids of the large boxes of clothes, stood on his toes, and stretched his arm back to the corner. Barely able to reach it, he coaxed the small box from its hiding place and put it into Megan's hands.

"Hope it's not another gun," she said, smiling. "I can't stand the thought of that thing even in the house." Megan carefully lifted the lid and found only a small key inside. "Wonder what this is for?"

"I think I know," Frank said. "I almost forgot. Your papa gave me a small metal box before he died and told me that I was to hold it for you girls. He wanted me to give it to you if you ever decided to marry Vinny." Frank winked at Megan, "Have you?"

"Uncle Frank," Megan blushed, "I'm certain I will never marry Vinny."

"Are you positive?"

"Quite."

"You have someone else in mind?"

"Maybe," Megan hedged. "But even if I didn't, I have never wanted to marry Vinny. I'm sorry, Uncle Frank. I just don't love him that way."

"I know exactly how you feel, Meggie."

"Yeah." She smiled at him with new understanding. "I know you do."

"I'll get the box."

"But I thought it was only if I was planning to marry Vinny."

"Well now, since that isn't going to happen, I guess I shouldn't wait any longer." Frank turned to go, then called back over his shoulder, "Be right back."

Megan had finished packing her father's belongings and taping the cartons shut by the time Frank returned. She heard the back door slam upon his return. She thought she overheard voices and then remembered Angie. Making her way to the living room, Vinny stopped her from entering the kitchen.

"Let my dad handle her," he said.

"She's my sister, Vinny." Megan tried to push past him.

"I don't think you should go in there," he said.

"Pretty bad, huh?"

"She's still angry, Meggie."

Frank came hurriedly into the living room and thrust a

small metal box into Megan's hands. "Put this someplace. In the attic, maybe—and do it now!"

Megan could hear the raised voices downstairs and crept closer to the stairway to see if she could tell what they were saying. Maria came out of her room, clutching her robe around her middle. "What's all the ruckus about?"

"It's Angie," Megan said quietly. "Uncle Frank sent me up here. I think he wants to handle her himself. I think we'd best stay out of it. Let Uncle Frank and Vinny handle her today. We've got enough to think about with Mama sick and all."

"Any word this morning?"

Megan directed her aunt toward the back bedroom. "Let's call, shall we?"

Opening the door, Megan gently shoved her Aunt Maria inside the room and shut the door behind them. Maria spotted the yellow envelope lying on the floor and the sheets bundled in the middle of the bed. Her first reaction was to cover the telegram with her foot.

"What's that?" Megan said.

"What's what?"

"What's that you're standing on?" Megan bent over and put one hand on the envelope and the other on Maria's ankle. "Get off the paper, Auntie," Megan said.

Maria stood transfixed while Megan retrieved the envelope. "It's been opened. Who's it to?" she asked. Without waiting, she pulled the slip of paper from inside. She read the brief message, and the full impact of what she had found didn't hit her until she had read it again.

Need to talk to you stop Please call asap stop Stephen stop

Megan lifted her eyes from the paper in her hand to meet Maria's frightened stare. "When did this come?"

"Well now, I can't remember exactly," Maria lied.

"It's got yesterday's date on it."

"Well, maybe so." Maria reached for the paper.

"No, Auntie. Not maybe. You knew about this, didn't you?"

Before Maria could answer, the phone on the nightstand rang. "The phone, Megan. It's probably the hospital."

Megan picked up the receiver. "Hello?"

"Megan La Bianca?" the voice asked.

"Yes."

"This is a nurse at Mercy Hospital. Your mother is asking for you, dear. Can you come?"

"Of course," Megan said. "I'll be there as soon as I can."

"I can tell her you're coming, then?"

"I'm on my way." Megan wanted to storm into her mother's room and demand an explanation.

"Where're you going?" Frank asked Megan as she bounded down the stairs.

"Mama's asking for me," she said.

"I'll drive you," Frank said decisively.

"Thanks."

"I can take her, Dad," Vinny offered.

"I'll do it. I want to see Rosa myself."

"But you didn't have breakfast!" Maria whined.

"Hey, Auntie, you can make me some," Vinny said. Megan shot him a grateful look.

Frank noticed Megan's silence and the paper she held tightly in her hand. He waited for a few minutes and then asked her, "What's the matter, Meggie?"

"I can't believe it, Uncle Frank," she said angrily. "I just can't believe this." Megan's eyes filled with tears, and she didn't try to stop them. Suddenly, anger surged from somewhere deep within, and she let it explode in a tirade of words and sobs. Frank didn't try to stop her outburst; he simply pulled the car to the curb and stopped. Once Megan had released most of her hurt and had run out of words, he reached over and pulled her close. She turned away at first, then relaxed against him. Hiding her face in the softness of his lamb's wool collar, Megan sobbed against his chest.

"Megan, I wish I could tell you that what you are about to experience with your mother will be a pleasant, touching mother-daughter moment. However, I know her too well to hold out such hopes. What I'm afraid of is you—how you will react to her. You've got to get a hold on yourself. It will do no good at all for you to lose control in there, in front of her."

"I know. It's just that I'm so mad!"

"I can tell that, little Meggie," Frank said. "You leave little room for doubt about how you feel right now. But listen. Your mother, for all she's done, is a very sick woman. You and I both know she's probably dying."

Megan took a deep breath broken with a sob. "I know. You're right. I'll be okay. I just need a minute."

"You also need to remember something. She's the one who's sick. And she's being eaten alive not only with cancer, but with anger, unforgiveness, and bitterness. It wouldn't be right somehow if you won the argument but ended up just like her, would it?"

"I'm not like her, Uncle Frank."

"Oh, but Megan, you are. In so many ways, you're just like her."

"No!"

"It's true. But don't you see, honey, many of her qualities can be such positive ones. It's her jealousy and the blind ambition to control everyone's life that has made her this way." Frank held Megan a moment longer. "Listen to your old Uncle Frank, okay?"

"Okay." Megan's voice was soft and almost pitiful.

"You're a spitting image of your mother. Maybe your hair's a little lighter, but nevertheless, you look like her. But you don't have to repeat her mistakes. Look for her good qualities, Megan. Her determination. Her ability to keep her family together. Her strength." Frank looked into the eyes of his favorite of all of Joey's daughters. "Nothing would have pleased me more than if you had ended up with Vinny."

"Not you too!"

"But only if it had happened of its own accord. Who knows, maybe Rosa wants to clear up her account with you, Meggie."

"Are you really that naive, Uncle Frank?"

"You never can tell," he said.

"I have my doubts," Megan said.

Frank wouldn't admit it to Megan, but so did he. But for a moment, when they walked in Rosa's room, he thought they might be pleasantly surprised.

"Meggie," Rosa whispered.

"Mama, I'm here now."

"My precious Meggie," she said.

"Frank brought me," Megan told her. "He's with me."

"Frank?"

"Right here, Rosie."

"I want to talk to my daughter. Would you mind?"

"Megan?" Frank said softly.

"I'll be okay."

"Meggie," Rosa said softly once Frank was gone from the room. "I want to talk to you about your papa."

Megan pulled the chair closer and sat with her face as close to Rosa's as possible.

"He loved you so much, Megan. He said you were just like me." Rosa paused, smiling. "I thought you were just like your grandmother, but he said no, you were just like me." Megan remained silent and waited for her mother to gather a little more strength. "I made him a promise, Megan. I promised your papa something. You were very important to him, you know that, don't you?"

"We all were, Mama."

"Yes, but you more than the others. You were his favorite. That's why I made him the promise."

"What promise was that, Mama?"

"It was very important to him, Megan. That's why I promised him the day he died."

"Mama, don't." Megan knew what was coming.

"Hear me out, Megan, please." Rosa clung to Megan's hand. "We both know I don't have much time left. Have I failed him, Megan? Maybe I have. But you can make that right again. Marry Vinny, Megan. I promised your papa. Vinny will be such a good husband. He's just like his daddy. Frank is such a wonderful man. Look at him, Megan, and you'll see what a good husband Vinny will be."

Megan shut her eyes against the guilt rising within her chest—guilt mixed with anger.

"Mama, don't do this," Megan begged.

"I promised your papa, Meggie."

"Megan?" Frank's voice startled her. "You all right?"

"I'm fine," Megan said. "She wants me to marry Vinny, Uncle Frank. She promised Papa."

"Wait for me outside, Megan." Frank's voice was firm. He turned to Rosa. "It's time to let Meggie have her own life, Rosa."

"They're right for each other, Frank. Like we were when we were their age. She's just like me, you said that yourself, many times. I know Vinny loves her, Frank. You could be blind and still see that." Rosa was momentarily seized by a fit of coughing. Frank paced the room then approached her bed once again.

"I'm begging you, Rosie. Let her go. Let *me* go."

"You're such a good man, Frank. Even now, you can't admit that we were meant for each other. So loyal to your best friend, even after all these years. He's dead and gone now, Frank."

"You're wrong, Rosa."

"He's gone and I will be soon." Rosa's voice dropped to barely above a whisper. "Vinny and Megan, now, they're young. They can have what we were denied. Our love can live through them." Rosa closed her eyes and fell into a deep sleep.

"She needs her rest now." The nurse came to stand beside the bed and check the tubes running into Rosa's transparent arms.

"Yeah, we all do." Frank slowly walked to the door and glanced back at Rosa's thin drawn face against the pillow.

"Uncle Frank?" Megan whispered. "You okay?"

"Oh, Megan," he said softly. "The things we do to our kids!" His voice caught in his throat and a tear escaped down his cheek.

"It's okay, I'm here," she said, wrapping her arm around his waist and walking him toward the elevator.

CHAPTER TWENTY-FIVE

As soon as Megan got home, she climbed the stairs and headed for her room to take a nap.

"How'd it go?" Vinny asked.

"Not too well," Frank said. "You know how Rosa is about you two." Vinny nodded. "Well, she won't let it go. Not even now."

"She's still on my side, then?"

"What are you saying?" Frank turned on his only son.

"Is that such a rotten idea, Dad? That one of the La Bianca girls and I might one day . . ."

"Yes, Vincent, it's a very rotten idea."

"I don't know why you'd say such a thing. Do you know how long I've wanted to marry Megan?"

"I know how long you've been brainwashed to want to marry her, that's what I know."

Maria kept her distance, eavesdropping on father and son from a safe place behind the kitchen door.

"That's a terrible thing to say," Vinny shouted.

"It's the truth!" Frank yelled.

"I could love her, Dad."

"Of course, who wouldn't?" Frank said as loudly as before. "But then"—he dropped his voice—"she doesn't love you—not in that way."

"I need to hear that from her," Vinny said.

"Would you believe it then?" Frank grabbed his son by the elbow and shoved him toward the stairway. "Let's get this settled once and for all." Frank's voice had returned to full volume.

"What's going on in there?" Sophia said as she came in the back door.

"Shh!" Maria warned.

"That's Frank's voice, isn't it?"

"Stay out of it," Maria said.

"No, Auntie, not on your life." Sophia brushed by her aunt and followed Frank and Vinny up the stairs to Megan's room.

"Come on, you guys," Megan protested at their sudden entrance. "I'm beat. Let me go to sleep."

"It's time this was settled, Megan. Past time, in fact."

Vinny shook at his father's rage. He'd never seen him so agitated before.

"Tell him, Megan," Frank ordered.

"Tell him what?" she asked.

"Do you love him?"

"Of course, I love him. We've been friends since we were kids."

"Not like that!" Frank yelled. "Do you love him enough to marry him?"

"Please, Uncle Frank!" Megan begged. "Not you, too."

"Then tell him! For mercy's sake, tell him!" he insisted.

"No!" Megan screamed at Frank. "This is more your fault than mine. You tell him yourself!" Immediately Megan wished she could retract the hateful words. "Uncle Frank! I'm sorry. I'm so sorry," Megan cried and rushed to him. "I didn't mean it. Really, Uncle Frank. Please believe me. I'm so sorry."

Vinny stood in shock, watching the two of them. "Obviously," he said finally, "the two of you know something the rest of us don't. Would you like to let us in on the secret?"

Frank surrounded Megan with his arms, and they both wept. Sophia found a chair in the corner and sat without speaking, waiting. Soon Frank released Megan, and the two of them faced Vinny and Sophia.

"Your mother," Frank said, nodding to Sophia, "has had this ridiculous idea for several years that she and I . . ." He couldn't continue.

"It's just this," Megan said, "Mama was in love with Frank, and he didn't love her back. So she married Papa to make him jealous. Then she started a lifelong campaign to make Vinny and me carry out her dream. She thought that Vinny and I could have the life she was denied because Frank married Lois." Megan crawled into the middle of her bed. "Is that about it, Uncle Frank?"

"I'm afraid so."

Vinny paced, and Megan watched his cheeks pulsate as he clenched and unclenched his teeth. "Let me get this straight. You mean," he said, "that she believes Megan and I can marry and fulfill *her* dreams?"

"Your entire life," Frank said. "She's believed it that long."

"I didn't know you were in love with her," Vinny said to his father.

"I wasn't, Vinny. I never was, that's the whole point."

"I really do love Megan," Vinny said. "For as long as I can remember."

"And," Angie said from the doorway, "isn't that the tragedy of it all?"

"Angie," Megan said.

"Vinny loves Megan, but Megan doesn't love Vinny. And so Vinny won't even look at another girl who might love him."

"Angie!" Vinny said.

"Angelina?" said Megan.

"Uncle Frank, Megan, Vinny, Angie!" Sophia shouted, leaping from her chair. "Stop it! This minute! I said stop it!" Everyone looked at the usually soft-spoken Sophia with surprise. "Listen to us! Have you ever heard anything more ridiculous in your life? We're quite a family, I'd say. Half of us want someone who doesn't want us back and the other half—well, some of us have even married not knowing what we want or whether we're wanted or loved. How long does this insanity have to go on?"

Stephen stepped into the darkness of the early morning. Sleep had eluded him most of the night, and he decided to drive toward the desert, hoping to catch a glimpse of the sunrise. Nothing compared with a sunrise over Palm Springs, and he longed for the quiet inspiration it had provided in the past.

"Megan," he said into the quietness of his car. "Oh, God," he whispered, "what am I supposed to do about her?"

Driving along the highway leading up the gentle sloping mountain toward Yucca Valley, he found a place where he could turn off and see the entire desert floor below. He switched off the engine and listened to the stillness. Rolling down his window, he breathed deeply of the quiet desert air and waited.

Within a quarter hour the sun began to rise over the distant mountains, leaving the desert in total darkness yet shining on the mountain peaks at his back. Stephen got out of the car and looked around at the wonder of the awakening morning.

Majestic, he thought as the golden hues bathed the rocks and hills behind him. *The earth is my footstool.* He recalled the words from the Bible, but couldn't remember where. "I don't know which way to turn, Lord," he prayed into the early morning light. "I can't find my way in this. I don't understand Megan's family, and I don't understand why she hasn't returned my calls. I need Your help here, Lord. I really do."

In silence he watched as the sun made its way into the morning sky. Stephen thought about how in the evening shadows lengthened, but in the morning they grow shorter then finally disappeared altogether. For Stephen, the morning seemed to be a picture of God's dependability. He reached into his car and retrieved his Bible. Thumbing through the pages he came upon a verse he had underlined earlier, intending to ask Jeff about its meaning:

Remember ye not the former things, neither consider the things of old. Behold, I will do a new thing; now it shall spring forth; shall ye not know it? I will even make a way in the wilderness, and rivers in the desert. "Isaiah forty-three, eighteen and nineteen," he said aloud. "A new thing." Stephen read the passage a few more times then stepping back inside his car he leaned his head on the steering wheel. "Oh, God. Please speak to me through Your Word and make it clear. I'm not a man of great spiritual understanding. Make it as simple as possible, please."

Stephen checked his watch. He'd have to be going soon if he were to meet Jen and Dan at the store before it opened. He reached for the ignition, *Not yet,* something seemed to whisper within his heart. He let his hand fall away.

Forget the past, don't dwell on how things used to be. Stephen's mother's face seemed to be etched in his memory. *I want to do something new in you.* Stephen knew that the living Lord he had decided to give his life to a few months ago was speaking to him. *And I want to do something new for you.* Stephen listened quietly. *Even now I am bringing it to pass. Just be patient and let Me work. Obey Me, follow Me through doors of opportunity. Watch and see if I don't do a miracle more wonderful than bringing a river across this desert.*

Follow me. It wasn't a new concept to Stephen. One of the first things he read in the Bible was how Jesus called men to follow Him. Now Stephen sensed God was calling him. For the first time in days, Stephen's face broke into a grin. Joy and excitement seemed to stir, then bubble within him. He started the engine, and before he reached the freeway, he almost had the giggles. Within ten miles of Redlands, he was laughing uproarously. He would go to Chicago with Dan and Jen. Hopefully, he wouldn't laugh all the way—at least not so that anyone would notice.

The small family group looked at Sophia in shock. "She's right," Angie said meekly from the corner. "No wonder we're all miserable."

"What are you talking about?" Vinny asked.

Sophia answered. "Just this: we've been managed and manipulated for so long that to do what *we* want is unthinkable. None of us can make even a simple decision without guilt or, at the very least, doubt." Sophia walked calmly toward Frank. "Am I right, or not?"

"You're so right, honey. So very right." Frank walked around the room and looked at each of the children. "I made the decision to marry Lois. It was what I wanted. And I think Joey wanted to marry Rosa. He loved her more than he loved anything—until you girls came along."

"But what about Mama," Megan said. "Did she ever decide to do what she wanted?"

"Oh yes," Frank said, "Not only to do what she wanted but to get everyone else to do what she wanted as well. It can go too far."

"And it has," Megan said. "Mama has gone way too far.

Vinny, look at me. You're a nice guy. But you're simply not my type. I don't want the same things as you want. I don't even want to live the rest of my life here in this city, much less in this neighborhood."

"But I like living here," he complained.

"Fine," Megan said. "Fine for you. But not for me. Oh, Vinny, don't you see? I'm not really rejecting you. I just want something else. We're great friends, but we simply don't fit together."

"I want to stay here," Angie said quietly. "I like this place."

"I think we have some choices to make, all of us." Megan moved to stand beside Sophia. "I think we should all think about what it is we want and come back together and then—"

"Tell everyone?" Frank asked.

"Right," Megan said. "But more than that. We need to be able to say what we want with no one running our ideas down or trying to make us do what they want."

"Do we know how to do that?" Vinny asked.

"It's time we gave it a try, don't you think so, Uncle Frank?"

"Yeah, I really do." He looked at each of the four grown children in the room. "But it has to be what you *want*—not necessarily what you think is the *right* thing to do."

"I already know what I want," Angie said. The entire group fastened their eyes on her. "No, it's not what you think. When's the meeting? I'll tell you all then."

Once the meeting time was set, Megan ran everyone out of her room. She was tired and needed some sleep. She was almost overcome with weariness. Even her bones ached.

"Megan," Frank whispered when everyone else was heading downstairs.

"What."

"Did you open the box?"

"No, not yet."

"When?"

"Later, Uncle Frank. Please, let me sleep."

"Then you'll be going with us?" Jen asked Stephen, barely able to conceal her delight.

"Yes, I will. But you must remember one thing, Jen."

"What's that?"

"I've been praying about Megan and me." He found it uncomfortable to talk about this with Jen. "I am trusting God for direction. Do you understand what I'm saying?"

"I think so."

"Then you'll understand if I ask you to stay out of it?"

"It's not that easy," Jennifer said.

"Listen to him, Jen," Dan said.

"But, it's—"

"Jennifer, what I hear Steve saying is that he has trusted God with his relationship with Megan. If you interfere, how will he know for sure if it was God's plan or yours?"

"If God brought Megan and me together, do you think He needs your help now?" Stephen asked.

"I know you're both right, it's just that sometimes . . ."

"No, honey." Dan put his arms around his wife. "Not sometimes, not anytime. God may use us, but let's not use Him, okay?"

"Agreed?" Stephen asked.

"Okay, I'll try to stay out of it."

"That's not what I'm asking," Stephen said.

"I'm confused then."

"It's not that I don't want you involved. I just want God in control."

"Boy, that's tough. How will I know the difference?"

"Do you remember how my mom handled the situation between you and me?" Dan asked her.

"She didn't handle the situation," Jen corrected her husband.

"Was she involved?"

"Of course." How could Jen forget the way Bess Miller had influenced not only her, but Joy as well?

"That's how."

"I don't know if I can be that discerning."

"Just give it time and prayer, okay? That's all we're asking." Dan kissed his wife on the cheek and pulled her closer.

"My knees could get pretty sore before this is all over," Jen said, and both men laughed at her pained expression.

CHAPTER TWENTY-SIX

Megan awakened several hours later, and for a moment she didn't know where she was. Once she regained her orientation, she searched for the clock on the stand beside her bed. Six-thirty. Was it morning or night? In the darkness she couldn't tell.

The phone was ringing in the back bedroom, and Megan jumped up to answer it.

"Jen!" she exclaimed at the sound of her friend's cheerful voice.

"Megan, I have some news," Jennifer began. Within a few minutes Jen filled Megan in on the plans for her return to Chicago and the closing of Halloran's.

"It's kind of sad, don't you think?" Megan asked.

"I don't know," Jen said. "Maybe it is. For Dan it will be a relief. This has been hanging over his head for quite a while."

"I was thinking more of the people who still work there."

"There's not too many of the people we knew left," Jen said. "Most have gone off to new jobs. They weren't too happy with the way the new management was running things."

"So when can I expect to see you?"

"That's up to you," Jen said. "We're coming on Thursday, that's tomorrow. Everything is moving so fast. I still have so many things to do this afternoon. We'll be checking into a hotel near the store, and I'll call you from there. If I miss you somehow, you can get me at Halloran's most of the time."

"What about the house?" Megan asked, picturing Dorthea O'Halloran's large suburban estate.

"That was sold about a month ago. I guess Dan will be handling the sale of the furnishings once we get there. The new owners take possession in two weeks. We've really got a lot to do."

"Need some help?" Megan offered.

"We might." Jen wanted desperately to tell her that Stephen was coming along for just that purpose. "But what about your mother?"

"It's not good, Jen. I'm afraid there isn't much hope."

"That bad?"

"Worse," she said. "We're trying our best to get things in order here before . . ." Megan paused.

"It's got to be a tough time."

"It is, but we're pulling together as a family, believe it or not."

"I hate to cut this short," Jen said, "but I need to get busy. I'll call you in a day or two."

Megan hung up, disappointed that she didn't get to ask about Stephen. Then she realized that she'd be seeing Jennifer in a few days; she'd ask then.

"Megan? You awake?" Maria was knocking softly on Megan's bedroom door.

"In here, Auntie," she called from the back bedroom. "I was on the phone."

"Oh, I see," Maria answered stiffly.

"It was my friend, Jennifer."

"Oh, Jennifer. How is she?" Maria's tone softened.

"She's fine. She's coming to Chicago." Megan took a minute to fill her aunt in on the details of Jen's trip.

"It's too bad. Halloran's is kind of a landmark. Everything's changing so fast."

"Well, I just came to tell you that everyone's coming for dinner. Uncle Frank took Angie to the hospital to see your mother. Sophia is with her children and arranging for a baby-sitter so she and Benjie can be here without all the bother of the kids. Although in my day, children were certainly not considered a bother."

"Need some help?"

"I could use some, I guess. I made the sauce already. Frank brought over some sausage, and I've got chicken in the oven now. A salad would be nice, don't you think?"

"Got the bread?"

"Yeah, the bakery truck was by earlier and I bought the old man's Italian bread."

"You've gone the whole way, huh, Auntie?"

"Megan, if it's to be a family dinner—"

"I know," Megan laughed at her aunt. "And nobody makes a better family dinner than you."

Megan was putting the last touches on the salad when Sophia arrived. "Benjie will be over in a little while. He's watching the end of the news."

Within a few minutes Angie and Frank got back from the hospital. Angie's face showed signs of stress, and her eyes were swollen from crying. Frank was quiet and solemn.

"How's it going with Mama?" Sophia asked.

"She looks so pale and thin," Angie said.

"How soon is dinner?" Frank asked.

"Almost ready, soon as Benjie gets here," Megan said.

"Benjie's here," he called from the back door. "How soon do we eat?" Vinny followed him in and threw his jacket across a chair in the kitchen.

The family gathered around the table, and Benjie reached for the basket of bread. "Wait," Frank ordered. "I think we need to say a prayer." It was clearly an uncomfortable moment for the group. "Who wants to say a prayer for your mama?" Frank asked without lifting his head or looking at the little group encircling the table.

"I do," whispered Angie, making the sign of the cross.

"Well, then," Frank said, "dispense with the formalities and get on with it. God isn't going to hold you to proper prayer manners at a time like this."

"We need you to help Mama, God. Amen." Angie said quickly.

"And," Sophia added, "us too. If that's not asking too much."

"And God," Frank said coarsely, "please ease Rosa's suffering. Ease her mind," he added.

"Help us, dear heavenly Father," Megan began, "to know Your love through all this. Help us to love each other more.

Help us to understand You more. And bless our food. Amen."

"Amen," the family chorused.

"That was beautiful, Meggie," Vinny whispered.

"Vinny," Angie said, smiling wide, "would you pass the salad?"

For the first time, Megan purposely watched the way Angie looked at Vinny. She stared openly at Angie as if seeing her for the very first time. *Did anyone else hear what Angie said this morning?* she wondered. Angie caught Megan staring at her and dropped her eyes to her plate. She quickly glanced at Vinny and back at Megan. Megan then saw the blush begin at the base of her sister's neck and slowly creep upward. *How long has Angie felt this way about Vinny?* Floods of memories began to race through Megan's mind.

I wish I was going with Vinny to the prom, ninth-grade Angie had said that night in Megan's room. *I wish Vinny was taking me to the football game,* she had said on another occasion. *I think I love Vinny more than you do.* Time and time again, Angie had hinted to Megan about her feelings for Vinny, but Megan hadn't caught the full meaning. It wasn't the prom or the football game or the pizza parlor that Angie wanted—it was to be with Vinny. Just this afternoon, Angie had said, *I like this place.* But just as on so many other occasions, no one paid any attention to what she was really saying.

Megan stared at Vinny. How could he be so blind? Angie adored him, Megan could clearly see that. And no one knew—until now. Now Megan knew. No wonder Angie had been so angry with her mother so much of the time. It wasn't because Rosa gave Megan more attention. It was because Rosa had insisted that Megan and Vinny were meant for each other.

"Megan," Benjie said between overloaded forkfuls of food, "you're not eating. Your food's getting cold."

Angie and Megan's eyes met, and Megan glanced at Vinny then back to Angie. Angie closed her eyes for a moment and swallowed hard. Opening them, she saw her sister smiling at her. Someone knew how she felt about Vinny. Without a word her secret was being shared. Megan saw a nervous smile tug at the corners of Angie's mouth.

After dinner, the entire group pitched in to clear the table and wash the dishes. Maria was silent, almost sullen.

"You want to go see Rosa?" Frank asked.

"What kind of question is that? She is my sister, Frank. Of course I want to go see her."

Megan and Sophia shooed her out of the kitchen, and Angie asked if she could go along too. Vinny offered to stay and help with the last of the kitchen cleanup. "You go too," Megan ordered. "Let us finish up here. Benjie will help."

Sophia frowned and glanced toward her husband, who sat at the table still picking at the remnants of the salad. "Of course he will," she said sarcastically.

Vinny said he didn't mind staying behind, but Megan insisted. "Hey," Megan whispered to Vinny when Angie went upstairs to find a coat, "look out for her, will you?"

"Sure," Vinny said. "Don't I always?"

"Let me put this another way, Vinny." Megan paced back and forth until she heard Angie coming down the stairs. "Vinny, look *at* her," she whispered, "For once in your life, open your eyes."

Vinny looked confused for a moment, then opened his eyes in surprise. "What?"

"You heard me."

Rosa's condition was deteriorating by the hour. She slept most of the time, and when Frank arrived, the nurse pulled him aside. "She's almost comatose. The doctor wants to talk to the family. Here's a number where he can be reached. He'd like to speak to you as soon as possible."

Frank settled Maria beside Rosa's bed and went to find Vinny and Angie in the waiting area before heading for a phone.

Vinny thought about what Megan had said. *Look at her.* Angie sat across the small room from him and leafed through a magazine. Her long brown-black hair parted in the middle hung straight and thick down her back almost to her waist. Her bangs, cut evenly across her forehead, tapered downward at each side to frame her oval face. Vinny noticed her long lashes as her eyes scanned the magazine in her lap. He studied her long fingers as they gracefully turned the pages.

She cast the magazine aside and folded her slender arms across her middle. She crossed her legs, and Vinny noticed how shapely they were; involuntarily, he wished she wouldn't wear her skirts so short.

Angelina looked around the walls of the waiting area until she found the clock, and with a quick toss of her head, she threw her hair back behind her shoulder. Vinny saw her long graceful neck and the small ear set off perfectly by a large golden hoop.

"You're really beautiful," he whispered.

"What?" Angie turned her face toward him, and he looked into her dark brown eyes. "I'm sorry, did you say something?"

"When did you grow up, Angelina?" he said quietly.

"When nobody was looking," she answered.

Vinny felt his pulse quicken and leaned forward in his seat just as Angie caught sight of Frank walking toward them. She stood, and Vinny watched her every movement as she walked toward Frank.

"I've just spoken to the doctor, Angie." Frank's face didn't hide the fact that he had serious news. "They took some spinal fluid this afternoon. The lab has determined that the cancer is now in the spinal fluid—" He paused and Angie saw the brightness of the tears forming in his eyes.

"That's bad, huh?" Angie said.

"I'm afraid so, honey." Frank opened his arms, and Angie leaned against him for comfort. "I'm afraid it won't be long."

"Should we call the others?"

"Let's think this through for a minute. I don't think we should leave her alone. Somebody needs to be here now."

"I'll stay tonight," Angie said.

"Well, it's going to be a long one." Frank paced and ran his hand through his hair and stuck the other one in his pocket. "What if you stay here with her for now. I'll take Maria home and talk to your sisters." He ran his hand down his cheek and across his chin. "Vinny, you stay with Angie, and

I'll shower and shave and catch a few winks and come back in couple of hours."

"Okay," Angie said.

"I don't like the idea of any of you girls being here alone. Promise me you won't go outside the building by yourself."

"I'll stay right here with her, Dad. I promise."

"You watch her, Vinny."

"I will, Dad." Vinny glanced at the tall beauty at his side and protectively put his arm around her waist. He noticed she didn't resist or move away. "I'll stay right here." Vinny pointed at the floor.

Angie watched Frank disappear into Rosa's room, then she turned to Vinny. She dropped her long lashes, and Vinny noticed her tears. He hesitated for a moment then pulled her into his arms. "It's okay, baby," he said. "It's okay to cry." Then he kissed her lightly on the cheek and ever so slightly tightened his grasp around her.

CHAPTER TWENTY-SEVEN

Once the dishes were done and the kitchen cleaned to meet even Auntie Maria's standards, the sisters wandered upstairs to Megan's room.

Walking over to the dresser, Sophia picked up the small metal box Frank gave Megan earlier. "What's this?" she asked.

"I almost forgot about that," Megan said. "I found some keys in Papa's closet. Uncle Frank said he had the box they fit."

"Why did he have the box?"

"Papa gave it to him a long time ago."

"Well, open it, Meggie. Let's see what's inside," Sophia said, shaking the box. "I hear something in there."

Megan found the key and slipped it inside the small lock. "I feel almost strange about this. Think, Sophie, Papa was the last one to put this key in there. It almost makes you feel closer to him, doesn't it?"

Inside, they found a note in Joseph's handwriting:

To whom it may concern; I have left instructions with my friend Frank that this box is only to be opened in the event of my death, the key hidden in such a place that it would be discovered only then. Inside this box are two more keys. One is to a safety deposit box at City Bank and Trust in my name or my daughter Megan's. Only she can open it, or if she is not yet of age, Frank Petrossi, whom I designate as her representative is authorized to open the box.

The other key opens a small trunk I have put in the attic, behind the sliding panel under the far south eave of the house. The contents of that box I also leave to Megan Marie La Bianca. And I instruct no one, under any circumstance, to open that box until she is of legal age.

The enclosed letter addressed to her is to be given her on her twenty-first birthday, and only if she is yet unmarried.

Signed by my own hand,
Joseph La Bianca
June 20, 1954

"My gosh, Sophie, that was just months before he died." Megan looked at her sister and the two girls held their heads close together to read the note again.

"Open the letter, Megan."

Megan's hands shook as she carefully opened the sealed envelope. On several pieces of paper ripped from a spiral notebook Joseph had written these words:

My dear Megan,

First of all, I want to say happy birthday, for this letter is to be given to you on your twenty-first birthday. So now you have become of legal age.

Since your birth, I have been more than aware that your mother wants to plan your entire life for you, as she does Sophia's and probably even little Angelina's. We have had many arguments about this, and I can't think of any other way to stop her than this.

On several occasions I have been able to save a little money and have put it safely in a safety deposit box at the bank. There may be some envelopes hidden beneath the drawers of the tall chest in my bedroom that I was not able to take to the bank for one reason or another.

"A little money!" Megan exclaimed. She read on.

It is for you because I know your mother will try everything in her power to cut you out of what little family inheritance there is if you don't marry Vincent Petrossi. I don't think you should marry Vinny. Not that he isn't a fine boy and will probably grow up to be a wonderful man. But he is not for you.

Megan, you are not to be strapped down to the same life the rest of us have all enjoyed here for three generations, including yours. You, I can see, are destined for other things. You have never been like your sisters. You are a dreamer and you need room to grow into the woman you were meant to be, different from any of the other women in our family.

I made a promise to God, Megan, the day you were christened. Now, you know I am not a religious man nor a praying one, but I made an exception that day. In my prayer, I promised God that I would see to it that you were not tied down to repeat the same old family traditions or make the same old mistakes. I promised God I would use every means within my power to make sure you could form your own traditions and be given the freedom to make your own mistakes.

Megan could barely make out the words on the page. Her tears gave way to sobs and she handed the paper to Sophia. Sophia read aloud.

You, Megan Marie, are different from any of the rest of us. You are more like my own mother's mother, your great-grandmother Eunice Megan Parker. She was a grand old English woman, with fair skin and light hair. She was strong and elegant. But most of all, she talked like she knew God personally. My own mother, English by blood, loved her mother and was stricken with much sadness at her passing. When you were born, some of the light in her life that had died with her mother was rekindled. It happened the day she looked at your fine fair skin and reddish hair.

"My hair's not reddish," cried Megan.

"In the sunlight it is, sort of," Sophia said.

Let Sophia and Angelina carry on the Italian part of the family heritage if that's their choosing. But you, my Meggie, have more English blood in you than the rest of us put together.

I have told your mother of my wishes concerning you. She, of course, is furious. She has her own reasons for wanting you to have a life with Vinny, and those reasons have nothing to do with you, but with me. I have taken a solemn oath and your mother knows it—a promise, Megan—that you will have the freedom to find your own way, to fulfill your own destiny.

Sadly, your mother has made a solemn promise of her own. She has sworn to see to it that you marry Vinny. If you do marry Vinny, promise me it is because he is your choice, not your mother's.

I fought to give you an English name. Now you must fight to have your own life.

Your loving papa,

Joseph Martin La Bianca

P.S. Vinny would make a better husband for Angelina than for you.

In block letters, Joseph had added the following amendment:

> *With this letter, I declare truce. I will no longer argue with Rosa concerning this.*

"What does it all mean, Meggie?"

Megan got up and fingered the little keys strung on the simple chain made of tiny metal beads.

"It means that the promise Mama has tried to make me keep for her isn't a promise at all. It's nothing more than sworn revenge."

"Why does she want revenge on Papa?"

"Because he isn't Frank, I guess."

"You know," Sophia said, "I remember how angry Mama was over the fact that Papa wasn't full-blooded Italian. I guess she really didn't know that Grandma was English."

"How could she not know? They grew up in the same neighborhood."

"Maybe that's why. Maybe nobody thought to tell her. Growing up so close to something, why would anyone have to tell her?" Sophia fingered the letter tenderly. "But what I can't understand is, why would it matter?"

"Oh, Sophie, I feel so guilty that he left this to me."

"No," Sophia said strongly. "Don't feel guilty, that's the promise you can make to me. No guilt. I've had it up to here with guilt," she said, waving her hand above her head. "He had to do it this way. Mama wouldn't let him do it any other."

"Will you go with me to the bank?"

"I don't know. Why not have Frank take you. You can show me later. But, Megan, I don't think you should tell Angelina just yet."

"Why not?"

"I'm not sure she'd feel the same way I do. I have my own family, Benjie, his parents. She still has nothing except us."

"Will you at least go with me?" Megan asked.

Before Sophia could answer, they heard Frank's voice downstairs. "I'll see to Auntie. You go on up if you want."

"I'll wait."

Downstairs the two sisters saw the strain on Maria's face.

Frank looked at them helplessly. He didn't need to tell them, they knew—their mother's condition was worse. They looked at each other and wordlessly agreed that Auntie's comfort came before anything else at the moment.

At the hospital, Vinny peered at Angelina from Rosa's doorway. She tenderly tucked and smoothed the blankets, and every few minutes she held a wet cloth to Rosa's parched lips. Once in a while, Rosa would open her eyes and see her daughter hovering over her.

"Angelina?" Rosa whispered.

"Yes, Mama. I'm here." Angelina's eyes searched out her mother's.

"Where's your sister? Where's Megan?"

"She's at home, Mama. She'll be here in a little while."

"I want to talk to her. Call her for me will you?"

"I'm here, Mama. Meg will be here in a little while." Angelina's eyes filled with tears. "She'll be here later."

"Angelina, my baby," Rosa uttered, "be a good girl, will you? Get your sister, I want to talk to her." Then Rosa closed her eyes and lapsed back into her more peaceful state.

Vinny watched helplessly as Angelina sat beside the bed and put her face against her mother's hand. "I'm here now, Mama. It's me, Angelina," she said through her sobs.

"How's she doing?" Frank asked Vinny upon his return.

"Still asking for Megan," he said.

"Tomorrow," Frank said. "She can see Megan tomorrow."

"Will she make it that long?"

"I don't think anyone knows for sure. But tomorrow's good enough." Frank patted his son on the shoulder. "Take Angie home now, will you, son?"

Vinny was only too happy to take Angelina by the hand and pull her from her mother's bedside. Outside Rosa's room, Frank stooped to look into Angie's eyes.

"She's pretty out of it, sweetheart. Don't pay too much attention to whatever she said, okay?"

"She wants Megan."

"I know," Frank said.

"She always wants me to get out of the way." Angie started to cry softly.

Frank shook his head. "Listen, honey. I'm going to stay with her tonight. You girls can come back tomorrow. Get a good night's sleep, okay? Vinny," he said turning to his son, "you take her home and stay with the girls. If I have to call, I don't want them coming back here alone."

"Sure," Vinny said. "Come on, Angie—I'll take you home." Gently, he helped Angie into her long woolen coat then moved in front of her to fasten the buttons. Stepping behind her, he reached his hands beneath her long hair and pulled it from inside her collar, letting it fall down her back. Angie stood still and let him reach into her pockets and find her mittens and put them on for her one by one. Only then did he put on his own coat.

Frank watched his son carefully guide Angie toward the elevator. Only after they after they had disappeared and the door slid shut did he turn back to sit with Rosa.

"Oh, Rosa. If you could only see them together," Frank whispered. "You would have a nervous breakdown." He couldn't help but smile at the hollow, wrinkled face of his best friend's widow. "You tried so hard to get it to turn out your own way. Too bad you couldn't have seen what was in front of you all the time."

Inside the car, Angie looked straight ahead and Vinny turned on the motor.

"It'll be warm in just a minute or two. Nothing like a Chevy to warm up fast. It won't take long since it's only been sitting here a few minutes." Vinny glanced at Angelina, and in the dim light he saw tears streaming down her face.

Scooting across the seat, Vinny slid his arms around Angie. He pulled her close, put his face next to hers, and felt the wetness of her tears. He nuzzled her hair with his face and tried to ignore the stirring within his heart.

"Angie," he whispered into her hair. "Angie."

"All she wants is Megan," Angie said softly. "All anyone wants is Megan."

"Shh," Vinny said. "That's not true."

"You should have heard her, Vinny. 'Be a good girl, go get your sister,'" Angie quoted her mother.

Vinny tightened his hold on Angelina and then freed one hand to trace her jawline with his finger. When he touched her chin, he gently tipped her face up and looked into her pain-filled eyes. For a long moment he stared at her and then slowly lowered his face until he touched her lips with his. In no hurry to let Angelina go, he could feel her slowly relax against him.

Finally, Angelina pulled away. "Vinny," she whispered hoarsely, "what are you doing?"

"Exactly what I want to do," he said, smiling.

"My mother's laying in there dying and you're—"

"Kissing you."

"Vinny!"

"Feeling guilty, Angelina?"

"Do you know what she'd say if she knew?"

"Yes."

"She'd kill us."

"I know," he said. He pulled her closer and kissed her again.

CHAPTER TWENTY-EIGHT

After Auntie Maria was settled and the two sisters had seen to it that she drank a cup of warm milk, Sophia said good night and returned home with Megan's promise to call her if she heard anything from the hospital. Vinny and Angie were sitting in the car in the alley when she came out.

"Hi, you two," Sophia said. "You just get home?"

"Well . . ." Vinny hedged.

"How's Mama?" Sophia said. She noticed Angie turn away. "Not good, is it?"

"No, Sophia, it isn't," Vinny said. "She wants to see Megan."

"I bet she does."

Angie spun her face around and faced her sister. "What does that mean?"

"I just meant she's been asking for Megan all along. Nothing new, is it, Angie?"

"No," Angie said. "That's nothing new."

"So what's Megan doing?"

"Right this minute?" Sophia tried to avoid the question. "I can't say that I could tell you that for sure."

"Maybe she's up in the attic again." Angelina's tone was almost a pout.

"Well, she's the one who's taken on the job of going through all the stuff up there. Somebody's got to do it." Sophia smiled at her youngest sister. "As you know, I am the one who cleaned the basement."

"Please, don't remind me!" Angelina wailed.

"You staying here tonight?" Sophia asked Vinny.

"Yeah. Dad told me to stick around in case—well, you know, just in case you guys need me." He noticed Sophia shivering. "You better get on home, we'll watch until you get inside."

"Thanks," she said. "Good night."

"Night," Angie and Vinny said in unison and watched Sophia until she was safely inside her house.

"We better go in," Vinny said.

"Yeah, I guess so."

Megan heard the car doors slam shut and waited on the stairway. She thought they'd come looking for her, but when they didn't, she smiled to herself and went up to her room.

Picking up her alarm clock, she saw it was nearly one-thirty. Eleven-thirty in Redlands. Stephen may be in bed, but she didn't think he'd mind if she called. After all, she had the note that said she should as soon as possible. This was as good a time as any.

"Hello?"

"Hi," Megan said.

"Meg?"

"Hi," she repeated.

"I thought maybe you didn't get my message."

"I almost didn't."

"Oh?"

"It doesn't matter, I have it right here in my hand."

"How are things there?"

"My mother is worse," she said quietly.

"I'm sorry, Megan."

"Yeah, me too."

Silence. Then Stephen spoke. "You hear that Halloran's is closing?"

"Jen called. She told me."

"Did she tell you anything else?"

"Yes, she said they were coming. I'll really be glad to see her. I don't know how much time I'll have, though. I'll probably be spending the better part of my days at the hospital. My mother really needs at least one of us there most all the time."

"Is someone there now?"

"Yeah, my Uncle Frank."

"It's a difficult time for you isn't it?" he asked.

"Yes."

"I wish I could make it better for you."

"You can't."

"I know. I just wish I could."

"It's nice to hear your voice."

"Yours too."

Silence.

"You alone?"

"No, not really. My Aunt's here. And my little sister, Angelina. Vinny's here too. He's downstairs."

"Vinny is there?"

"Yeah, he's staying over. You know, just in case we have to go to the hospital or something."

"I see." Stephen wished Vinny would go home, but he really didn't want Megan to be alone. "I wish I could help."

"I know."

"But I can't."

"No, you can't." *I wish you could come,* Megan wanted to say. *I wish you could be the one downstairs in case I needed to face my mother's death tonight.* "I miss you," she said instead.

"You do?"

"Is that a surprise?"

"I guess not. I miss you too." Stephen wanted to be with her that moment. *I'm coming,* he wanted to say. *I want to be there with you right now.* "I'm sorry I missed you at the airport."

"Me too."

"I tried to get them to let me come on the plane."

"You did?"

"Didn't Jen tell you?"

"I haven't talked to her much."

"Oh."

Silence.

"It's really good to hear your voice," Megan said again.

"Yours too." Stephen sat up in bed and noticed the time on his clock radio. "It's late there. Are you all right?"

"I had a lousy night last night. I slept most of the afternoon. I'm not sleepy."

"Tell me where you are right now."

"I'm upstairs," Megan said. "In the back bedroom. We just got extension phones a few days ago."

"So who is it that usually answers the phone?"

"Probably my aunt. What do you mean, 'usually'?"

"Well, I tried to reach you the other day, I guess you didn't get the message then."

"No, I'm afraid not."

Silence.

"Megan," Stephen said after a few moments, "when this is all over . . ."

"I can't even think that far ahead right now."

"I'm sorry. I didn't mean to—"

"It's okay. It's just that my mother's so sick and everything."

"You're right," Stephen said. *I am not going to pressure you. I am going to let God handle this,* he said under his breath.

"I'd better say good night," Megan said reluctantly.

"Yeah, I guess so."

"So, good night then."

"Good night," Stephen said.

Silence.

"Are you going to hang up?" she asked.

"You first," he said.

"I can't," she said.

"Me either."

"On the count of three?" she proposed.

"No cheating?"

"One, two, three." Megan yanked the phone from her ear. She didn't wait to see if Stephen cheated or not.

Stephen listened after the phone line clicked, then went dead. He cheated.

Megan looked at the phone. She wanted to pick it up and dial Stephen's number again. Seeing her father's letter on the bed, she picked it up and reread it. Fingering the small keys on the tiny chain, she put on her sweater and headed for the attic. She knew the area behind the sliding door well. She and her sisters played there as little children. Funny, she didn't remember seeing any locked trunk.

"You better go on up," Vinny said softly in Angie's ear. "I'm supposed to be here to protect you."

"I feel perfectly safe," Angelina whispered back.

"Well, that shows you how unreliable feelings can be." Vinny gently shoved her toward the stairway. "I'll be right down here if you need anything."

Angelina looked teasingly back over her shoulder.

"Go," he said. "I mean it, go!"

Megan met Angie at the top of the stairs. "Hi," she said.

"Hi." Angelina saw that Megan wasn't dressed for bed even though it was almost two. "Aren't you tired?"

"A little," Megan said. "But I'm not sleepy. I slept almost all day. How's Mama?"

"Asking for you."

"Still?"

"Afraid so," Angie said. "She hardly knew I was there."

"That's not right, Angie. It isn't me she wants. Not really."

"No?"

Megan walked a little distance from her sister and opened the door to the attic stairs. "No, she wants me to promise her something. It isn't really me she wants. It's her own way she wants."

"And you're the only one that can give it to her?"

"Not really, but that's the way she sees it." Megan shook her head. "You going to bed?"

"Yeah. But the way she looked, Meggie, it could be a short night—for all of us."

"Vinny staying over?"

"He's downstairs."

Megan turned and went up the attic stairway. Moving the boxes that covered the special hiding place, she wished she had thought to bring a flashlight. She didn't relish the thought of reaching around in the dark attic.

"Have your lost your mind?" Vinny's voice fairly boomed through the silence, and Megan jumped, almost bumping her head on the small opening.

"Oh, Vinny! You scared me to death!"

"What are you doing?"

"Looking for some box or a small trunk. Maybe a small foot locker."

"Like that?" he said pointing to a small navy blue chest stuck away in a distant corner. "Looks like a skate case."

"I thought it was back in there."

"Why'd you think that?"

"Never mind. Does this key fit the lock?"

"I'll tell you in a minute." Vinny moved a few things out of the way and sat down on a larger trunk. "The lock's all scratched up. It looks like someone tried to get it open with a screwdriver."

"Has it been opened?"

"I don't think so," Vinny said. "The key still works."

"Don't open it!"

"Why not?"

"It's mine, that's why!"

"Don't get so edgy, Megan. I helped you with all that money, didn't I?"

"Shh!" Megan scolded.

"And who's going to hear us?"

"Angie doesn't know about the money yet."

"You going to tell her?"

"Probably. But not just yet."

"Why not?"

"It's family business, Vinny."

"I'm just like a brother, remember?"

"Just hand me the box, okay?" Megan's temper was getting short.

Megan took the box and pushed back the thumb catch. The brass latch sprung open. Her heart began to beat faster, and even Vinny had to admit that the mystery of the box was more exciting than the thriller he had been watching on TV downstairs.

"Well, silly, open it!"

"Don't rush me, Vinny."

"Megan, it's almost three o'clock in the morning. Open it for crying out loud."

Megan laughed. "Hey, remember the last time we tried to sneak around up here late at night?"

"Just open the box before I rip it out of your hands and open it myself."

Megan turned her back on Vinny and slowly lifted the lid. Vinny couldn't see over her shoulder and knew he would bump his head on a rafter if he tried to get past her. Slowly, she turned around, and Vinny could see the sweet yet sorrowful expression on her face.

"What is it?"

"A present. Look Vinny, a present."

"Who's it from?"

"Papa," she said almost in a whisper. "He left it for me." Megan lifted the small tissue-wrapped gift from the case and handed it to Vinny. Underneath were what looked like important legal papers and a bank savings book.

Sensing that Megan needed to be alone, Vinny moved the sliding door back into place. Shoving the boxes back against the wall, he turned to go back downstairs. He was suddenly tired.

"Vinny?"

He stopped at the top of the stairs.

"You know I can't marry you, don't you?"

"Yes."

"I really can't, Vinny."

"I know."

"Do you know why?"

"Do you?"

"My father didn't approve of us, Vin."

"Me, you mean."

"No, Vinny, *us.*" She watched the information sink into Vinny. "He really liked you, did you know that?"

"How do you know?"

"He left me a letter. I just got it today."

"No kidding?"

"He called you a fine boy."

"Really?"

"Yeah, he just didn't think that we—you know, that you and me would make a good—well, couple."

"And what do you think?" Vinny asked.

"I think we make good friends," she said. "But we'd make a lousy couple."

"Then you wouldn't mind if I . . . ?"

"Dated someone else?"

"Yeah."

"Anyone I know?"

"Maybe."

"You don't want to say?"

"You going to show me what's in there?" he said, pointing at the gift in her hands.

"No."

"Then I'm not going to say."

"If I showed you what's in here, would you tell me then?"

"Probably not."

"Good, because I'm not showing you anyway."

"Then what's this conversation about?" Vinny started down the stairs. "I'm going to get some sleep."

As she heard Vinny's steps fade, she shivered. Opening the large trunk Vinny had sat on while he unlocked the small case, she found an Army uniform jacket her father had worn in the war. *The Big One,* he had called World War II. *We'll never have another,* he had promised. *We saw to that.*

Shrugging into the long sleeves, Megan wrapped herself in the rough wool and sat down to go through her treasure, her very special inheritance. It had been here all the time, just waiting for her to be ready to receive it. It didn't matter that it was the middle of the night. She wouldn't rush through the contents now. One by one, she would lift the documents from their places. Little by little, she would discover, even savor, her legacy.

CHAPTER TWENTY-NINE

Megan made herself comfortable and opened the small metal case. She took the little wrapped present out and set the case with the remainder of its contents aside.

Papa, she thought, *a present for my twenty-first birthday.* Although Megan was two years past the age marking her legal adulthood, she reveled in the gift her father had so carefully tucked in the case with all these papers.

Unwrapping the small box, she carefully folded the brittle tissue, treasuring every detail of her father's plan. Before she opened the little black box stamped with gold, she knew she would see a piece of jewelry inside. She was quite unprepared, however, for what lay there awaiting her discovery. Carefully, she lifted the ornate rings from their place. Megan could tell they were quite old, though apparently her father had thoroughly cleaned them before he wrapped them.

Examining them closer, Megan saw engraving inside the band. *EMP, my forever love—JP. Eunice Megan Parker!* Great-grandmother's wedding rings! Megan slipped the diamond and sapphire rings on her finger; they fit her hand perfectly. She held them up toward the single bulb hanging over her head and marvelled at their radiance. Then she turned her attention once again to the little box they were in.

Tugging slightly at what seemed to be a loose corner of the satin lining, she found slipped inside a handwritten note. She didn't recognize the distinctive scrawl. *To my precious Eunice, who has brought to my life and heart the brilliance more than a hundred times as bright as the small stones in this ring. Forever, Joseph.* Carefully replacing the note, she reluctantly took off the rings and returned them to the satin setting. She tucked the treasured box in her pocket and began reading the papers and documents her father had so carefully organized and prepared.

Within an hour, Megan realized she had become the owner of several stocks, some bonds, and a couple of railroad annuities. She had no idea how much these investments were worth now. Her name was listed on all the documents as the beneficiary in the event of Joseph's death.

At the bottom of the case was a business card. *Randolph James Packer, Attorney at Law.* Megan guessed the phone number was probably no longer valid, but was sure Uncle Frank had mentioned the Packer Law Firm at one time or another.

Tired and confused, she leaned back on an old mattress and pulled her father's coat closer around her. Within minutes she was sleeping.

She stayed that way until Frank gently shook her.

"Megan," he said softly. "Meggie, wake up."

"Oh, Uncle Frank, I'm so glad you are here. I have so much to tell you!" She was instantly awake, but before she could open the case, Frank laid his hand on her arm and restrained her.

"Megan," he began, tears coursing down his face. "Meggie, it's your mother."

"Mama?"

"She's gone, Meggie."

"No," Megan cried. "She can't be . . ."

"She's gone, honey. It happened about an hour ago. She was awake and spoke to me one minute. Then she fell asleep . . ." Frank's voice broke. He gathered Megan in his arms and wept with her.

"She said something, just before . . ." Frank reached for his handkerchief, blew his nose, and stuffed it back in his pocket. Megan didn't rush him.

"She said your name. She said, 'Tell Megan, never mind.'"

"Never mind?" Megan's wrinkled her forehead trying to make some meaning out of the words. "Never mind? What did she mean by that?"

"I'm not sure, honey. Maybe after we've all had some rest, we'll be able to figure it all out."

"Mama is gone?" Megan asked.

"Yes, sweetie."

"Do the others know?"

"Vinny does. He let me in. I thought we should all be together when I tell the family. But I wanted—" His voice broke again. "I wanted to tell you myself."

"Uncle Frank?" Megan looked at him through her tears. Her mind whirled with confusion and her heart threatened to burst with pain. She patted the mattress beside her. "Will you just sit with me for a little while?"

Frank slumped beside Meg, feeling much older than his age. He was only fifty-six. He had several good years ahead of him yet. But he had just spent the night looking into Rosa's drawn, aged face. She was two years younger than he and Joey. But then the years hadn't been kind to her. She looked at least ten years older.

As Frank leaned against a large trunk, Megan slid easily inside his outstretched arm and put her head on his strong shoulder.

"What are we going to do now?"

"Well, first we're going to make arrangements to bury your mama. Right next to your papa. After the funeral we're going to come home, have lunch together, and . . ." he paused.

"Then what?" Megan asked.

"Then we're going to go on with our lives," he whispered. He was glad for Megan's nearness. She was as close to a daughter as he would ever have. He had known for some time that she would never marry Vinny. It didn't matter. Somehow, that might even have spoiled it.

"Uncle Frank," it was Megan who broke the silence.

"Hmm?"

"Tell me about my papa."

"Oh, Megan," he said softly. Kissing the top of her head, he took a deep breath. "Your papa was about the best friend anyone could ever have. He was loyal—to a fault really. He was a hard worker and he adored his family."

"Where did he get all that money?"

"Well, now I'm not exactly sure about that money. He was also what I would call a private man. He shared as much of his life with me as he did with anybody—probably more. But he kept much of his personal business to himself."

Frank let his mind drift back over their growing up years. "You know, this neighborhood hasn't changed much since we were kids. I lived where I live now. And your papa's family lived just down the block, across the street. Your grandma—now she could bake the best cookies for miles around. Made all the other mamas jealous, I think. You remember your grandma?"

"Of course. She let me stay overnight sometimes."

"A fine woman, now that I think of it. She was widowed too young and should have married again."

"She wasn't the same after Papa died."

"I know. She died of a broken heart more than the sickness that took her, if you ask me," Frank said.

"How did Papa meet Mama?"

"Don't know for sure. She was around as far back as I can remember. Just one of the neighborhood kids. We all grew up together. Joey had his eye on her from the fifth grade on. Never looked at another girl, as far as I know."

"But Mama?" Megan's tone indicated her question.

"Now, your mama, she was a headstrong girl. Quite the neighborhood leader, you might say. Even though Maria was a year or two older . . ."

"Maria is older?"

"Held back a grade, as I recall. Put her in the same grade as your mama. That's when they stopped saying who was the oldest. Anyway, your mama led the entire neighborhood group of girls around like she was the queen or something." Frank let out a sigh. "Now, your mama, she had her cap set for me. I was so ignorant about girls. I didn't even know. Everyone else did it seems. Then when I went away in the army, I met Lois. We fell in love and I brought her home right after we got married. Your mama, well, she carried on like I had outright jilted her. It was right after that she married Joey. I'll never forget that day. Big church wedding and all. Right after Joey kissed her—you know, in the ceremony—she turned and gave me the dirtiest look I ever saw.

From then on she doted on Joey whenever she thought I was watching."

"Didn't Papa know?"

"He knew. But he never let on."

"Why did she keep insisting I was to marry Vinny?"

"That was something she planned long before the two of you were ever born. She wasn't too particular whether Sophia was a boy or a girl. But when she was carrying you, she swore you were going to be a girl and heaven help anyone who said otherwise."

"And Papa?"

"Well now, Meggie, you have to understand how it is for a man. Even more so for us old-country boys. We have it in our minds we have to sire sons. Or it's a reflection—you know, on—"

"I know."

"When Sophia came, it was okay that she was a girl. Joey worshiped the ground she walked on. Did until the day he died. But when Rosa turned up expecting again so soon, Joey just knew it was a boy. He really wanted you to be a boy."

"He was disappointed."

"Only for a minute. Then he saw that shock of red hair you came with and those big brown eyes, and he fell in love. Harder than he ever fell for Rosa, I think. Of course, Rosa knew from the beginning you would be a daughter and told everyone so. Vinny was already walking by that time. She had taken it upon herself to give birth to a bride for him."

"And, Angelina?"

"That was the hardest. Rosa was just as sure she was a boy as she had ever been that you were going to come out a girl. Joey, by then, didn't care. He loved his girls.

"I don't think your Mama ever loved Angelina like she should have. Maybe if Angie had been a boy . . ." Frank's voice trailed off, and Megan knew he was thinking of something else.

"That wasn't fair to Angie."

"No, it wasn't."

"There's something you're not telling me, isn't there?"

"There are some things best left unsaid, Meggie. She's gone, let it go with her."

"I want to know everything. I'm trying to make sense of all this," Megan said, motioning toward the blue case. "Please, Uncle Frank."

"Well, one day just after Angie was born, I got a message Rosa wanted to see me. I went to the hospital and she was holding the baby, ready to come home and waiting for your papa to come and pick them up." Frank's face clouded with pain. "I remember it as if it were yesterday. I walked into the room, convinced she was going to ask me to be Angelina's godfather. You know, like I am to you and Sophia. I suspected that Lois and I would never have any more children. She was already having trouble that way." Megan studied the strong jawline of this man she loved almost as much as she had loved her father.

"I walked in and Rosa told me to take a good look at her. She was a beautiful baby—still is. 'Another girl, Frank,' she said. 'If I were married to you, I'd have five sons by now.'"

Megan sat up and stared at him. Frank shifted slightly and rubbed his eyes with his hand. "What did you say to her?" Megan asked.

"Nothing. I couldn't believe she'd say such a thing. She wasn't getting what she wanted, and she didn't like it at all. Then she said, 'If we can't have sons together, then we'll have grandsons. I swear to you,' she said, 'Megan and Vinny will marry and give us the sons we couldn't have.'"

"Uncle Frank! What did you do?"

"I turned to go. I wanted to get out of there as fast as I could." Frank's voice broke once more. "But I ran right into Joey." Frank leaned forward, and silent sobs shook his whole body. "He had heard every word."

Megan kept quiet, waiting for Frank to continue. "Your papa never was the same after that. He knew it wasn't my doing. He treated me the same as always. But Rosa? No—it wasn't the same between them after that."

"No wonder," Megan said almost too quietly for anyone to hear.

"It became a sparring match. She was determined that

you'd marry Vinny, and he was just as determined you never would. He really didn't have anything against Vinny. In fact, just as you girls were the daughters I never had, Vinny was the son he never had. It was her—he felt he had to protect you from her."

"Uncle Frank, are you aware of how Angelina feels about Vinny?"

"Yes," he said. "I've known for some time. She always tried to get her mother's attention. When that didn't work she tried to get Vinny's."

"Does he even know she's alive?" Megan asked.

"I think he might be starting to wake up to that fact."

"Is there anything we can do to help it along?"

"Yes, there is, Megan. Leave them alone. Let them find each other. If it's meant to be, it will be their choice—not ours."

Megan settled back against Frank's arm. "So Mama's really gone?"

"Yes."

"Does Auntie know?"

"Not yet."

"How are we going to tell her?"

"As gently as we know how. It breaks my heart," he said with a sigh, "to cause that woman any pain."

CHAPTER THIRTY

"I'm sorry to do this to you, Dan," Jeff said over the phone. "But it can't be helped."

"It's no problem, really it's not. Jen and I will go on ahead, and Stephen can join us as soon as possible." And so it was settled. Dan and Jen headed for Chicago, and Stephen returned to Sacramento to do some final record searching for Jeff's client.

At the airport, Stephen embraced Jen and gave Dan a firm pat on the shoulder as he shook his hand. "I'll get there just as soon as I can. I'll do whatever I have to, talk, beg, even bribe for the records I need. Then if possible, I'll ship the papers home special delivery and catch the next flight to Chicago from Sacramento."

"We know you'll do the best you can, Steve," Dan said. "We'll be glad for your help, but really, until we get there and see what has to be done, we can't even tell you what to do."

"Honey," Jen said, "he's in no hurry to join us." She smiled in Stephen's direction. "He wants to see one of your former employees."

The next few days passed in a blur for Megan and her family. Days were marked no longer in hours but in decisions. The family members slept when they could and stayed together as much as possible. Maria surprised them all.

"Please bring the children," she said. "Death has a way of stripping hope from you, and children have a special way of giving it back."

Sophia and Benjie brought their two children over, and they gravitated toward Maria.

"Did she even cry?" Vinny asked Angelina.

"Yeah, but in a very quiet way. I guess she knew it was coming."

"I don't care. Even when you know it's coming, you can't ever be prepared for it."

"She has her own way of grieving," Sophia said when Megan wondered aloud how Maria was really handling her sister's death.

"It's not what I expected," Megan confided to Frank.

At the wake, the three sisters and their aunt, along with Frank and Vinny, gathered for the usual visitation of friends and distant relatives. People in their neighborhood had lived together for several generations, and it was difficult to tell family from friends.

As the long evening was finally coming to an end, Maria stood by the satin-lined casket, looking down at her sister. Megan noticed the tears silently falling down her aunt's cheeks and came to stand beside her, wrapping her arm around her shoulder.

"You were always a problem for her, Megan." Maria's statement took Megan off-guard. "She had such dreams for you."

"Auntie, I . . ."

"But she was always thinking only of herself, never of you." Maria's voice was getting louder, and from across the room Frank noticed Megan's disturbed countenance. "A great deal of your pain and misery I lay at your own feet, my sister." Maria's sudden outburst of anger was clearly directed at the blank, cold expression frozen on Rosa's thin white face. "You could have been spared so much. You could have had such happiness. If only . . ."

"Maria," Frank said abruptly.

"It's true, Franklin Petrossi, and you know it. Megan was Rosa's hope for grandsons. Just as she knew Megan would be a girl, she knew that her grandsons would come from her."

"And Vinny?" Frank wondered how much Maria knew.

"Of course, Vinny. How else was she to dilute the English blood in the family except through Vinny?" Maria reached into the casket and straightened an imaginary wrinkle in Rosa's dress.

"She already has a grandson, Auntie," Megan tried to distract her from saying more.

"Pooh." Maria spat out the word. "Vinny was like her own son, she said that all along."

"Come on, Maria," Frank said. "It's time to go home. You need some rest."

"And my sister doesn't?" Maria's eyes blazed with grief. "She lies here, but she isn't resting, is she? And who is to blame but herself? No one. No one is to blame. She could have gone to her grave peaceful, but she wouldn't give up on trying to get her own way. She wouldn't settle for anything less than the one thing in life she wanted more than anything else. I tried to tell her . . ."

"Maria, come." Frank gently pulled her away from the casket. "Auntie," Megan's heart throbbed for her aunt.

"Maria. Let's go home." Frank took the small woman by the shoulders and forcibly walked her away from Megan's side. Megan's eyes filled with tears, and Sophia came and stood beside her.

Frank guided her out the door and into the car, where Benjie was awaiting.

"Take her home," Frank ordered. "And stay with her."

Inside the chapel, Sophia placed a hand on her sister's shoulder. "Meggie," she said softly, "it's not your fault. You know that. Whatever Mama said"—Sophia nodded toward her mother's body—"whatever she wanted, it has nothing to do with you. Don't you see that? Please, Meggie."

Megan looked again at her mother and began to weep uncontrollably.

Angelina went to stand beside her two sisters at the casket. Vinny watched silently from a seat halfway back. "She didn't know what she was saying," Angie said softly. "She looked on children as possessions meant to please their parents instead of people. Auntie of all people. She really does see us as something more than an extension of Mama."

"Mama came to my house one day," Sophia said, "to talk to me about my family. It was right after Baby Ben was born." Sophia wiped her eyes with a tissue. "She said she wanted me to understand that Auntie never had any children and that she'd never have any grandchildren of her own. She wanted me to have my babies grow up to think of Auntie more as their grandmother than their aunt."

"Then that's why—" Angie started to say.

"That's why they call her Grandy," Sophia said. "Mama decided. She said she'd have lots of grandchildren before long and that she could spare mine for Auntie."

"Is there anyone's life she wasn't in control of?" Angie asked.

"Yes," Megan said gripping the side of the casket. "Yes, there is. Mine. And yours too, Angelina. And Frank's, and Vinny's."

"It has to stop," Frank said from behind the girls. "It has to stop now. Let her need to control our lives be buried with her. Let's go home. Let's turn all the love and understanding she never gave us toward each other now. Let's try to see each other not through her eyes, but through our own."

A few minutes earlier, Jen Miller slipped in the chapel unnoticed. Finding a seat near the back, she watched while the family comforted each other.

"Jen!" Megan broke from the center of the group and rushed toward her friend. "Jen."

The two friends flung themselves into a tight embrace. "I'm so glad to see you, Megan," Jen said.

"Not as glad as I am to see you." Megan sobbed painfully once again. Finally, she turned to introduce Jennifer to her family.

"We've met before," Sophia said extending her hand.

"We're just on our way home," Frank said. "Won't you join us?"

"Oh, Jen, could you?" Megan begged. "It's not that late."

"Well, Dan's at the store, and he'll probably be there until late. I did give him your phone number. Sure, I'll come."

Vinny hailed a cab, saying they would be crowded trying to fit into one car. Jen and Megan rode alone in the cab, and the others piled into Frank's car.

"We would have fit," Jen observed. "There's only six of us and that Chevy's plenty big."

"They're just being nice. Or maybe they've had enough of me for a while and are glad to have someone take me off their hands."

Jen was glad to see Megan smile, even though her face was etched with the pain of her mother's death. "Your family seems to be pulling together."

"It's a new family tradition," Megan explained. "I'll tell you all about it later. Tell me, how's Dan? The store? Are you enjoying being a mommy?"

"Whoa, slow down. One thing at a time."

"Well then, let's start with the honeymoon. I never really got a chance to ask you about that."

"Well, you were a little busy when I got back, remember?"

"Well?" Megan insisted, ignoring Jen's remark.

"Well what?" Jen laughed. "Megan, I couldn't be happier. Dan Miller is the most wonderful man in the whole world. He's so thoughtful. He's generous and he's really grown in his relationship with the Lord." Jen's face radiated with pride.

"I'm so happy for you," Megan said. "It's like a fairy tale, you know?"

"Like a storybook ending?"

"Exactly."

"You're wrong, Megan. I'm sure we have some challenges ahead. Just like every other couple. We're barely back from our honeymoon. Life hasn't really settled in yet."

"It seems like a long time ago."

"A lot has happened to you these past weeks, hasn't it?"

"So much." Megan ran her eyes over Jen's clothes. "I'd like to take you up into the attic. Would you mind changing into some of my jeans?"

"Sounds like an adventure," Jen said, gripping her friend's hand. "What are we looking for?"

"I'm not sure."

Once they were in the attic, Megan motioned Jen toward the old mattress. "Make yourself comfortable."

Jen looked around at the mess and surmised that Megan had spent a few hours up here since she had come home. "You live up here?" she asked.

"Not quite," Megan said. "But you might say my life is up here."

"How's that?"

Megan reached for the blue case her father had left her and pulled out the letters, her great-grandmother's rings, and the investment papers. Once they had gone over it all, Jen gave a low whistle and shook her head. "This is really hard to believe, much less understand."

They heard Frank's steps on the stairway. "You girls hungry?" Before they could answer, the smell of pizza reached them. Frank set it on the mattress between them and pulled two sodas from his back pockets.

"Where'd you find this man?" Jennifer asked Megan, flashing Frank a bright smile.

"Down the alley." Megan laughed and Frank responded with a sharp smack across her head with a stack of napkins.

Soon the girls' mouths were stuffed full of pizza, and Frank found a place to relax atop the old trunk. "You tell her everything?" he asked Megan.

"Almost," Megan said.

"You mean there's more?"

Megan glanced at Frank, who nodded his encouragement. She told Jen about the money downstairs in the kitchen cabinets.

"What do you think of all this mess?" Frank said. "I'd like to hear from someone outside the family."

Jen thoughtfully wiped her mouth with a napkin and took a long drink of her soda. "It's kind of complicated. But it does remind me of something else." She paused, not sure how to continue.

"Please," Frank said, "go on." Frank leaned sideways and rested against an elbow. Drawing one knee up, his relaxed position clearly indicated he was staying to hear whatever insight Jen might have to offer.

"It kind of reminds me of God," Jen said. She paused, waiting for Frank's reaction.

"God? How do you figure that?" he asked.

Megan watched Frank's face with interest as Jen continued. "Well, as I understand it, God knew that He needed special plans for us, His children."

"Go on," Frank said.

"So instead of just reaching out and outright rescuing us—"

"You mean by killing the devil?"

"Yeah, or even banishing him to a place where he couldn't reach us," Jen said, "He made a unique plan. He left us letters, just like Megan's father did. Letters of instructions, of course, but also love letters."

"The Bible?" Frank asked.

"Do you have a Bible, Uncle Frank?" Megan asked.

"Yeah, I have Lois's. I've been reading it for years. But I never looked at it this way."

"There's something else," Jen said. "God knew that we not only needed to know what He wanted for us but that He had to have a way to give it to us. So He made provision—that, of course, was Christ."

"Like the seventeen grand downstairs," Frank said.

"That's what I was thinking," Jen smiled.

"You know, girls, I've been thinking about things like this for quite a while. What I can't get through my head is how a person taps into this."

Jen and Megan smiled at each other, and Megan got up and sat beside Frank. "You know, I had a little trouble with that idea myself until I met Jen. I guess it's as simple as this: you don't get it into your head, Uncle Frank, but into your heart." Then turning her attention back toward Jen she said, "It's the same with my papa, isn't it, Jen? I mean, I've been trying to understand not only what he's done, but why. Really, if I could just accept it—I mean really accept it—"

"You don't have to understand it, Megan," Frank said.

"You can spend the money even if you don't know the whys and wherefores."

"It's exactly the same thing, Megan. You see, there is a verse in the New Testament, in Second Corinthians I think; anyway, it says that when we are in Christ, we become new creatures. That the old things in our lives, things that held us down or held us back, all pass away. Then, new things come. It's a wonderful promise of a brand new life. His life in me, and me living a new life in Him."

"It sounds like a marriage, almost," Frank said.

"You're right about that," Jen said.

"But my sisters," Megan said. "I don't understand why Papa didn't include them."

"I guess that's where the analogy breaks down," Jen said. "God offers all of us the same opportunity. We can all tap into His resources equally. The same plan and provision is given to everyone freely."

"Don't worry about your sisters, Meggie." Frank's face revealed his concern for this precious daughter of his best friend. "Somehow I think it will be okay. But for now, why not just keep this between us. I'm not sure why, but we'd better look at the legalities of all this before we share too much information with the family."

"You mean a lawyer?"

"Yeah, somebody who'll know how to untangle all of this." Frank stood and stretched his back. "For now, just know this: your papa wanted a different kind of life for you. He wanted you to be able to make your own decisions. He always said Rosa wouldn't get her way in this. I didn't know how he planned to swing it, but he was very firm about it."

"You look tired, Frank," Megan said.

"I am. I'm going home."

After he left, Megan turned to Jennifer and held her arms open. "I'm free, Jennifer."

"You know, Meg," Jen said slowly, "I can't help but believe that your father isn't really the one who planned this for you."

"I know. I thought about that last night." Megan came to sit close to Jen on the mattress. "Do you think," she said in a loud whisper, "that God could have had His hand in this? I mean, is it possible that He planned this before—"

"Before you were born?"

"Do you think?"

"It's more than possible, Megan. In fact, it's highly probable."

CHAPTER THIRTY-ONE

Following the small funeral and the brief graveside ceremony, Frank herded the family back to the house for lunch. Maria started to put out the food brought in by neighbors and friends, but Frank stopped her. "Let the girls attend to this. Come sit with me on the front porch. The sun is coming in and it's warm out there." He winked at Megan and Sophia, who stared wide-eyed after him.

Dan and Jen promised to stop by, preferring to let the family go to the cemetery alone.

"How'd it go?" Jen asked when they arrived.

"Brief," Megan said. "Uncle Frank advised us to keep it brief and told the priest we needed to get home as soon as we could for Auntie's sake."

When Megan left them to refill the coffee server, Jen glanced toward Dan. "She hasn't asked about him, even once!" she whispered.

"Jennifer, you know what he said."

"I know, but . . ."

"Let it alone, Jen."

Jen shrugged away from her husband.

"Jen!" Although his voice was low, his tone was firm.

"I know what he said."

"Jennifer," Dan warned.

"Okay," she said in a sort of whine.

"That's my girl," Dan said smiling at her.

"I'll do it for you, but not for him," she whispered. Jennifer wouldn't do anything that would risk Dan's disappointment.

Before Jen and Dan left, they invited Megan to come down to the store. "She has an appointment," Frank interrupted.

"I do?" Megan asked.

"I called a lawyer. We're going at four-thirty."

"Do I have to go?" Sophia asked.

"No, just Megan and me. We'll be back later. Say, didn't someone say we needed to have a family meeting?"

"Yeah, but then that was before . . ."

"Well, how about tonight?" Frank suggested.

"As good a time as any," Sophia said.

"Come back for supper," Maria said. "There's enough food here to feed an army."

"This is most interesting." Mr. Chapman, a junior partner at Randolph Packer's law offices looked over the contents of the small navy blue case. "Can we verify his signature?"

"I have letters he wrote to me when we were in the army," Frank said.

"Any other documents?"

"Like what?" Megan asked.

"Marriage certificate, driver's license?"

"I'll see what I can find." Megan made a note on a piece of paper.

"And your mother, did she leave a will?"

"I don't know. We haven't gone through her things yet."

"Here is a list of things I need you to find, if you can," Mr. Chapman said. "This is a difficult time, I know. But as soon as you can, I'd like to have a look at these items."

"Anything else?"

"Are there any other items that I have not seen? How about the safety deposit box mentioned here? Did you empty that?"

"I forgot all about it," Megan said.

"We'll take care of that first thing Monday morning."

"First Bank is open until seven-thirty on Fridays. You still have time now, if you hurry."

"Megan?"

"Might as well," she said.

"This seems to be in order," the attendant behind the counter said. "Follow me."

"How has the fee on this box been paid?" Frank asked.

"A small savings account was set up in trust for that specific purpose. A little unusual, but then I've seen stranger things."

Once inside the cubicle, the woman unlocked the first lock on the box and then told Megan that her key would fit the other and excused herself. "Just push that buzzer when you're finished."

"That must be the passbook savings account I found in the case," Megan said. She opened her purse and found the key she had tucked away in her change purse. Turning it in the lock, she looked at Frank. "I'm almost afraid to look," she said.

"Want me to do it?"

"Would you?"

He lifted the lid quickly and sorted through the contents. "Discharge papers, here's a medal of some sort. The army was always giving medals of one kind or another. Here's something interesting," he said, holding up a small portfolio.

"What is it?"

"Railroad stock. Megan, look here, certificates of ownership in the Santa Fe Railroad. Who knows what these are worth."

"I guess I should take them to Mr. Chapman, right?"

"I remember when we bought these," Frank said.

"You bought them together?"

"No, I bought some and he bought some. I sold some of mine when Vinny was born and then Lois's medical bills took the rest."

"How come we never needed them?"

"Your papa had good life insurance. Double indemnity. That means when he died by accident, the policy paid your mama twice the usual benefit. He also had mortgage insurance. He left her pretty well-off. She didn't know about this stock, anyway."

"You sure?"

"Positive," Frank said. "There's more." Frank pulled out a large envelope filled with small family heirlooms. Joseph had carefully marked each item inside with either Sophia's or Angelina's name. Finally, he produced a large canvas bank envelope stuffed full of hundred dollar bills.

"Not more money!" Megan said.

"A lot more!" Frank whispered excitedly.

"Where'd he get this much money?" Megan asked.

Frank looked at the bills and fanned them, trying to estimate the amount. "You know, I bet he got this when his father passed away."

"Why in heaven's name didn't he put it in a bank account?"

"Who knows?" Frank said. "Maybe the lawyer has an idea or two."

"I'm not taking this home." Megan backed toward the door of the small room. "In fact, I wish we could put the rest of the money here."

"Well, maybe we could." Then Frank had a thought. "Did your mama leave any cash? How are you going to pay the household bills?"

"I haven't a clue," Megan said. "Maybe Auntie knows."

"Did she mention me?" Stephen asked Jen on the phone later that evening.

"I thought you didn't want me discussing you with her," Jen said.

"I thought she might at least mention me."

"Well, I tried to stay clear of the subject."

"She didn't, did she?" Stephen insisted.

"Listen, Stephen, I will talk to her if you just say the word."

"No, don't bring it up."

"You'll be here soon," Jen said, "and you can see her for yourself."

"It could be a few days. I told Dan all about it. I'm sort of stuck here for the time being."

"I'm sorry to hear that," Jen said.

"You're sorry! I'm starting to hate Sacramento!"

"How much longer?" Jen asked her husband after she hung up the phone.

"It could be a week, maybe longer."

"It's really hard not being able to tell Megan he's coming."

"You're doing fine. Remember, Steve has left this in God's hands, not yours."

"But sometimes, I just want to . . ." Jen spoke between clenched teeth.

"Give God a hand?" Dan smiled at his headstrong wife.

"Or just give Him a little shove. Is He sleeping up there?" she said, casting a glance at the ceiling.

"Hardly," Dan laughed. "But there's one thing for certain."

"What's that?"

"He certainly isn't intimidated by your temper."

"So what's this meeting about?" Maria asked suspiciously.

"It's a family meeting, Auntie," Sophia said gently. "We have family business to discuss."

"You want I should leave then?"

"Of course not," Megan said, restraining her aunt. "This is for the whole family."

"I see," she said, looking directly at Frank.

"I'm staying, Maria," he said.

"Auntie!" Angelina spoke up. "Uncle Frank is the same as family, you know that."

"Whatever you say." The hint of a smile on her lips contradicted her curt tone.

"When we planned this meeting, we decided we would tell each other—" Sophia said.

"Without fear of criticism or guilt," Megan interjected.

"Just what it is each of us really wants," Sophia continued. "Whether it has to do with our lives, or where we want to live, or what we want to do with the house—anything."

"The important thing is that we get to speak our minds," Megan said.

"And will we be heard?" Angelina asked.

"Yes, Angie. We want to listen."

"Who wants to begin?" Sophia asked.

After an awkward silence, Frank spoke up. "We might want to begin with Megan showing you what she found in your father's safety deposit box this afternoon."

"How did you find out about that?" Maria asked.

"I found the key in the attic, Auntie," Megan said.

"Going through your papa's things, I suppose."

"It's okay, Maria," Frank reassured. "Go on, Megan. Tell them what you found." He nodded in Megan's direction then toward the large envelope she put behind her on the sideboard cabinet.

Looking around at the faces gathered around the family dining room table, Megan slowly opened the envelope and shook its contents gently on to the table. "Papa left us some of Great-grandmother's jewelry. Here is her watch, Angelina, it's tagged for you. Her locket, for Sophia. A brooch for Angie. Some earrings, Sophie. Here's her little jeweled pill-box, Angie. Here's a hair clasp, Sophie. And a pretty dinner ring, Angie. And Sophie, he left you Great-grandmother's cookbook."

Angelina gathered the small treasures and examined the watch first. "It's beautiful. Are these real diamonds?"

"I think so," Megan said.

"The pin is kind of old-fashioned looking, but isn't it beautiful?" Angelina didn't even notice Sophia's eyes searching Megan's face.

"Megan," the oldest sister asked quietly, "isn't there anything here for you?"

Megan shot Frank a look and got the smile she needed for courage. "Yes, Papa left me Great-grandmother's wedding set."

"Oh, Megan, can we see?" Angie asked excitedly.

"Sure," Megan ran up to her room and retrieved the small box containing the diamond and sapphire rings.

"I was afraid," Sophia said. "There for a minute I thought Papa didn't leave anything for Megan."

"Me too," Angie said.

"You girls know your papa wouldn't do such a thing," Frank said, smiling.

The wedding set was passed around for everyone to get a good look, and when the last comments of admiration died down, Frank cleared his throat.

"Now I know I'm not an official member of the family," he said, looking at Maria, "but there are some practical matters we need to discuss. Maria, do you know if Rosa had any cash on hand, or a checking account, or anything of that sort?"

"Yes, I know."

"Well?" Sophia said.

"Well, what?"

"Auntie, we have to know how much money there is. We had to empty our savings for the funeral and Uncle Frank put up what we didn't have. We have things to take care of."

"She left the money management up to me," Maria said.

"Well, then." Frank smiled in Maria's direction. "She was smart to do that. She wasn't very good at it, as we all know."

"Auntie, are we in trouble, financially?"

Maria stood and walked to the far wall of the dining room. Opening a tall secretary, she produced her well kept records and a small cash box.

"Your father was well insured," she began. "Money was not a problem—at least, not after your mother finally turned it over to me. The way she was going, it wouldn't have lasted this long."

"Well, Auntie?" Megan asked.

Frank shot Megan a warning glance. "Maria, we're very lucky that you could handle Rosa. Not many people here could have done the same."

"She wanted me to turn it over to Megan as soon as she settled down."

"Me?" Megan asked in disbelief. "Why me?"

Maria glanced first at Benjie, then at Vinny.

"She needn't have worried, Auntie," Benjie spoke for the first time. "I have no designs on the family treasury."

"I'm with Ben," Vinny said.

"Well, it doesn't matter now, does it?" Maria said. "She's gone now, and you'll all do whatever you want anyway."

"Maria," Frank said diplomatically, "there's no reason to change the system that I can see. After all, you've done a fine job so far. What do the children know about handling a household?"

"Well, Sophia—"

"No, Auntie. I have my own home to worry about."

"And I don't know what my plans are for sure," Megan added.

"Auntie, you know I'm not prepared for this much responsibility," Angie said. Under the table Vinny reached for her hand and gave it an affectionate squeeze.

"Okay, I'm ready," Angie said. "I want to say what I want."

"Well, let's hear it!" Megan said enthusiastically.

"I want Auntie Maria to handle the household bills and finances. Please Auntie, say you'll do it."

When Maria was convinced the family was in agreement, she consented. "On one condition," she said. "I want someone to teach me how to manage a checking account. I hate having all this cash laying around. The annuity check comes once a month, and Rosa insisted on having it in cash. I think we should make other arrangements."

Frank shook his head in disbelief. "That's a very good idea, Maria. I would be glad to help you with that."

"And there's more," Maria said. "It's these bonds. They just keep coming. Where in the world are they coming from? Who sends them and what am I supposed to do with them?"

Frank took the certificates from Maria's outstretched hand. "These are dividend certificates. There's an investment account somewhere. Do you know anything about any investments?"

"Oh that," Maria said, opening a bottom drawer and retrieving a shoe box. "That must be what these are." She opened the box and revealed even more certificates and a large amount of cash.

"Didn't you people ever hear of banks?" Vinny asked.

"Holy moley," Benjie said in a low voice.

Maria's eyes widened with excitement. "Oh, there's more. In the top of the hall closet, in the little space under the stairs, and—"

"Stop, Auntie." Megan stood and held up her hands. "I want to say what I want." She took a deep breath before she spoke. "I want Uncle Frank to help Auntie Maria go through all this paperwork and come back to us in a week with some sort of a report. Maybe you could talk to the lawyer by then and we'd know where we stand. In the meantime, does anyone object if we reimburse Frank and our savings accounts for Mama's funeral expenses out of the cash we have here?"

The group nodded their consensus and Megan sat down. The family, unaccustomed to such open communication, fell into silence. It was Vinny who finally broke the awkward moment.

"I'm not a regular family member," he said, standing up and glancing furtively toward Angelina. "But I want to say what it is I want." He looked toward his father for support, but Frank avoided looking his way. *You're on your own, son,* Frank thought.

"I want to date Angelina," he said bluntly.

Angie's head shot up, and she stared at him with wide eyes.

"Really?" Megan said, feigning shock.

"Really." Vinny glared at her in silent warning.

"And, young man," Benjie teased, "do you care to share with us your intentions toward our young sister here?"

"I—well, no I don't." Vinny shifted from one foot to the other. "Not before I'm sure of them myself, and certainly not before I tell Angelina."

Megan looked at Frank, but he refused to be drawn into eye contact with any of them. Maria sat with her mouth open, and Sophia laughed.

"Auntie, please don't be shocked," Sophia said.

"I just think you ought to wait."

"For what, Auntie?" Vinny asked. "Angie's not a baby anymore."

"So you finally noticed," Benjie remarked. Sophia poked him in the ribs.

Frank spoke up. "Angie?"

She dropped her eyes toward her hands fidgeting with Rosa's favorite lace tablecloth. "Yes, Angelina," Benjie prodded, "tell us, has this brute been bothering you?"

"No," she said.

"No, he hasn't been bothering you, or no you don't want to go out with him?"

"He hasn't been bothering me," she said, then quietly added, "And yes, I want to go out with him."

"Well, then," Frank said. "I think we should set some house rules."

"I agree," Sophia said.

"Who's going to chaperon?"

"For Pete's sake," Vinny protested, "we practically live next door."

"Who's going to stay with Auntie?" Megan asked.

"I'm hardly needing a caretaker, Megan," Maria scolded.

"And like Vinny says, I'm right nearby," Frank offered.

"So then, it's settled," Vinny said. "Angelina, would you care to catch a late movie with me?"

"I'd love it." She smiled back at him adoringly.

"Wait a minute," Benjie said good-naturedly. "Can't you all see they've been out together before?"

"Settle down," Frank scolded. "You'll not go anywhere tonight. The meeting is still not over. Sophia," he instructed, "we haven't heard from you yet."

"I want my family to be happy," she said. "And I want to repaper my kitchen."

"Well, Benjie?" Frank laughed.

"I don't know," he said. "That costs money!"

"What do you call what you've just been handed?" Maria said, chiming in at last.

"That's my savings, Auntie," Benjie almost whined.

"And what do you think it's for?" the older woman scolded, "Hiding in boxes like Rosa and Joey did? Give her the money, you tightwad."

"That's telling him, Auntie," Megan said. Frank looked at Maria with pleasant surprise. He didn't mind the idea of helping her with the family finances. They both loved all the kids around the table as much as if they were their very own. He always liked that about her—when Rosa wasn't interfering.

CHAPTER THIRTY-TWO

"My best guess," Chapman said to Frank and Megan, "is that Mr. La Bianca didn't want his wife to know about most of this stuff."

"Why didn't he just specify it in a will or something?" Megan asked.

"Who knows?" the lawyer said. "I've seen it all. Some people don't trust lawyers, banks, or politicians. I'll get my fee out of all this, of course, but I assure you, it will be a fair one." Looking over the top of his glasses at his young client, he asked, "Is there anything else I should know about?"

Megan glanced at Frank and laughed out loud. "Oh, yes," she said, "we just don't know how much more."

Frank explained to the attorney the hidden money, the jewelry, and the items Rosa and Maria had tucked in various places throughout the whole house. Mr. Chapman sat back in his chair, removed his glasses and twirled a pen in his hands as he listened patiently.

"I would advise you, Miss, as your lawyer, to gather that little family of yours in one place and form a search party. Turn that house upside down, if necessary. Open the seams on any old mattresses, rip apart any old pillows, and search every box and trunk for false bottoms. No telling what you'll turn up. Call me when you think you've found it all, and I'll make a house call. I think I'd better meet with the entire group next time."

"Can you come Friday night?" Megan smiled sweetly.

"Friday night?" Chapman reached for his calendar. "I think so. You think you'll be done by then?"

"We'll make a point of it," Frank said.

"Come for supper," Megan said. "Auntie makes the best authentic Italian food in the city."

"Do you have a safe place to store all this stuff?" he asked.

"Well, it's been there for years. I think it'll be all right until Friday." Megan stood and slipped into her coat.

"I'll find a way to make it secure," Frank said, shaking hands with Mr. Chapman. "Until Friday, then."

"I think I'd better take a little vacation time," Frank said to Megan on the way home. "I'll see if Vinny can get some time off too."

"Do you think that's necessary?"

"It wouldn't hurt if Benjie was around either," Frank said. "I don't like the idea of you women being there alone. Not even for one minute."

For the rest of the week, the La Bianca house was a flurry of activity. Megan, with Vinny's help, returned to the attic. Angelina was assigned Rosa's closet, and Sophia and Benjie took the basement boxes and the kitchen cabinets. Maria and Frank worked in the dining room going through every last scrap of paper after they searched boxes stored, stuffed, and hidden in the downstairs closets and the pantry. The entire family continued to bring boxes, envelopes, notes, and letters to the table for examination. By the end of the week, the entire house had been searched from top to bottom and back again. On Friday afternoon, Megan finally found time to take a long bubble bath and to try to prepare herself for the full disclosure of her parents' long-running battle and her father's bequest.

Frank tapped lightly on the bathroom door. "Megan, there's a phone call for you. Long distance."

Megan grabbed her heavy chenille robe and ran toward the back bedroom.

"Hi," Stephen said. "Did I interrupt anything?"

"No."

"I can call again later, if this is a bad time."

"It's not a bad time. I'm glad you called. Are you at home?"

"No, I'm in Sacramento. I am at the airport, though, getting ready to take a flight out of here within an hour."

"Finished with your project there?"

"Finally," Stephen said.

"Glad to be going?"

"More than you know."

"I miss you," Megan said.

"I miss you too." Stephen checked his watch. "It's two-thirty here," he said.

"Four-thirty here."

"I know."

"I miss you," Megan said.

"I miss you too," Stephen laughed. "I think we said that already."

"When will you get home?"

"Well, I'm not sure about that," he said. "I was thinking I'd not go straight home."

"Oh?"

"Yeah, well, Redlands is pretty empty since you left."

"Really?"

"Have you seen Jen?"

"Not since the funeral," Megan said. "We've been pretty busy here, with the family stuff, you know."

"And I guess they've been pretty busy too."

"You've talked to them?"

"Yeah, once or twice." Silence. "I really miss you, Megan."

"I think this conversation tends to go in a loop." Megan laughed and Stephen couldn't help but smile. "I wish this was all over," Megan said.

"What was all over?"

"This family and legal stuff," she said.

"Then what?"

"I don't know. I can't even think beyond tonight. We're meeting with the lawyer."

"How's it going?" Stephen asked. "Is everything all right?"

"Everything's a mess," she said. Megan then related as much of the story as she could in a short time.

"Whoa, slow down there," Stephen said. "You think you ought to talk to Jeff about this?"

"I wish I could," Megan said. "But our lawyer seems nice enough. I think we're doing okay."

"Would you like Jeff to call him sometime next week?"

"Do you think he'd mind?"

"He owes me a favor, Megan. A really big one. I'll talk to him tomorrow and find out."

"You'll be home tomorrow then?"

"I'll talk to Jeff, I promise. I'll make a point of it."

"That's not what I asked," she said. "I was thinking of Redlands—and you."

"And us?" Stephen asked.

"Yeah, I guess I was."

"Megan—" Angelina stuck her head in the door. "The lawyer's here and Auntie's ready to serve dinner. Hurry up!"

"I have to go, Stephen."

"I heard."

"I miss you," she said.

"I miss you too."

"Megan!" Angie yelled from the stairway.

"I have to go," Megan said.

"See you soon," he said.

"I wish—" Megan said softly.

"What did you say?"

"Bye, Stephen."

"For now, Megan." Stephen hung up the phone just as the announcement came through the speaker overhead.

"Flight 1247 to Salt Lake City with connecting flights to Dallas/Fort Worth, Bismarck, North Dakota, and Chicago is now boarding. Passengers holding seats on flight 1247, please go directly to the gate for boarding."

Stephen grabbed his small suitcase and headed toward the gate.

"Well, Meggie, I see you've decided to join us after all," Frank teased.

"She was on the phone," Angie said.

"Anyone we know?" Sophia asked innocently.

"No," Megan answered curtly. "Hello, Mr. Chapman. Have you met everyone?"

"Yes, thank you," he said courteously. "This is quite a family you have here, Mr. Petrossi."

"Yes, I think so," Frank said proudly.

"And the food smells wonderful, Mrs. Petrossi," he said to Maria who turned a bright shade of red.

"Oh, she's not Mrs—" Angie started to say. Frank put out his hand and stopped her.

"Maria, call her Maria," Frank said. "We'd like to keep it on a more informal basis, if you don't mind."

Maria was visibly flustered that Frank didn't correct Mr. Chapman. "I'm not Mrs. Petrossi," she said finally. "I was Mrs. La Bianca's sister."

"Oh, I see. I'm sorry."

"Well, now, no harm done." Frank's smile broadened. "Was there, Maria?"

Megan and Sophia looked at each other and burst out laughing.

"Girls," Maria scolded. "Mind your manners!"

"Yes, Auntie," they chorused.

After dinner, Maria and the two oldest girls cleared away the dishes while Angie poured coffee. Finally, the family business took center stage.

Frank explained all that the family had uncovered during the week. "Maria helped me sort it all out, and any sense we made of it at all is to her credit." His comment sent a blush creeping into her cheeks.

"I see," Chapman said, smiling in Maria's direction.

"As you can see," Frank said, "Mrs. La Bianca, Rosa, did leave a will. It was witnessed and properly notarized. Joseph, on the other hand, wasn't as formal. Here are a few letters of instruction; that was all he left. That and the cash, stocks, bonds, and various pieces of jewelry."

"And you have those assets all here and accounted for?"

"Right here," Frank said, pointing to a large trunk they had dragged from the attic.

"You hear about these cases every once in while. Large amounts of cash stashed in a mattress and left in a will to a cat or something."

"We don't have a cat," Angie said.

"Good thing," Chapman responded. "No sense making this any more complicated than it already is." Then the lawyer fell silent as he looked over Maria's careful inventory of all the family assets. Finally he read the will and examined Joseph's letters. "Any way to verify Joseph's signature?"

"Here," Maria said. "On the wedding certificate."

"And there," Frank added, "on his army papers."

"And here," Maria said, "the deed to the house."

"Well, it appears that the La Biancas had some sort of a disagreement on how the family assets would be distributed, doesn't it?" Chapman continued looking at one paper then another. "And you've inspected the contents of the safety deposit box?"

"Yes," Megan said.

"And your satisfied that what he said he put there is really there?"

"Yes."

"Megan, are you aware that unless you marry Vincent in the days remaining before your twenty-fourth birthday you will be cut completely out of your mother's will?"

"Yes."

"What?" Angie gasped.

"It's okay, Angie," Megan said.

"But that's not fair!" Angie cried.

"Angie, I don't want to marry Vinny, for crying out loud."

"But then you won't get anything from Mama?"

"It's okay, Angelina. I swear to you, it's okay."

"I take it she doesn't know about your father's letters?"

"No," Megan said, "she doesn't. No one does except Frank and me."

"I see." He paused then surveyed the small group of people over the frames of his glasses. "Your parents, it seems, were in a battle of wits. Your mother wanted Megan to marry Vinny, we all know that, right?"

"Yes, we do." Megan sighed and smiled at Vinny.

"And your father, it seems, knew what she was up to and didn't want Megan to marry Vinny. Or at least, he wanted her to have the choice." He reached for another paper and then turned to Frank. "Do you have the estimated market value of the house?"

"Right here," Frank pointed to the document.

"I see." Chapman looked over the document then compared two others. "I think he won."

"Pardon me?" Maria said.

"In the battle of the wits, Joseph won."

"What do you mean?"

"I mean, Megan could contest the terms of the will, or she could marry Vincent, which she says she has no interest in doing. Is that correct?"

"That's quite correct," Megan said emphatically.

"You don't have to make it sound so bad, Megan," Vinny complained.

"Now, let me compare this document here with that one—thank you." Mr. Chapman smiled admiringly at Maria as she handed him the paper he indicated. Frank felt the hair on the back of his neck stand up.

"Now, if these figures are correct," Chapman said, "and they'll have to be audited by an objective party, of course—when we put the two wills together, we find that if the property was divided between the two daughters, Sophia and Angelina, as well as the furniture, and the other assets here—their shares would each be almost equal to what Joseph has left entirely to Megan." Chapman sat back and looked at each individual face staring back at him in shock. "He was a pretty smart man, or a lucky one. But in a way, they both get what they want. Sophia and Angelina's portion is in property and valuable stocks, but not readily liquid, I'm afraid. Some cash—that will keep things going here for a while. On the other hand, Megan's portion is entirely liquid. I'm afraid the inequity comes in that Sophia and Angelina are tied down for the moment, but Megan's inheritance releases her from further responsibility or obligation."

"What about the cash in the kitchen?" Vinny asked.

"Oh!" Megan jumped up and Vinny ran after her to get the stepladder. "I forgot about it completely," she said upon their return."

"Seventeen fifty," Vinny said, pointing at the envelope.

"Pardon me?" Chapman said.

"Seventeen thousand and fifty dollars," Megan said. "We found it under Mama's dresser drawers.

"How'd it get there?" he asked.

"Papa put it there. Remember, in his letter?"

"Then I guess it's not as even as I thought," Chapman said. "That tips the scale quite a bit heavier in Megan's favor."

"Can't I divide it with my sisters if I want?"

"You can do anything with it you care to. It's your money." Chapman stood. "I think our business is concluded for now. I'll have an auditor contact you Monday or Tuesday."

Maria walked the distinguished man to the door and helped him into his coat. "That was a mighty fine dinner, Maria. I wouldn't mind being invited again some time."

"Well," Frank said from the dining room doorway, "next time we need a will read, we'll call you."

Maria turned to look at Frank, and Mr. Chapman politely tipped his hat and left.

"I want to finish our family meeting, Maria," he said.

"You mean we're not done?" Benjie complained from the dining room.

"Not just yet," Frank said. "I haven't said what it is that I want." The grown children gave him their full attention. "I want," he said slowly, "Maria's permission to come calling."

"What?" Benjie exclaimed.

"You heard me. I want to come calling on Maria. And I want you kids to give your blessing."

"Auntie?" Megan said.

"Well, I guess that would be nice, wouldn't it?"

"Is that what you want?" Sophia said.

"You know," she said demurely, "I think it is."

"Oh, no." Benjie moaned. "I can't believe I'll have the both of you to watch out for!"

"What do you mean by that?" Frank scolded.

"You *and* Vinny," he said.

"I'll make sure Dad behaves himself," Vinny said with a chuckle.

"That's like the rooster watching over the henhouse, Vin," Sophia said.

"There is only one thing I want," Maria said softly.

"Go on, Auntie," Megan said, "what is it?"

"I want you kids to mind your own business," she said. Frank winked at her, and the blush he caused so easily once again flooded her cheeks.

"Not on your life," Benjie said.

CHAPTER THIRTY-THREE

"How was your flight?" Dan greeted Stephen.

"Long," Stephen said. "I don't remember it being this long before."

"It's the layover. You could get a direct flight from Redlands," he teased his young friend. "You could have waited until tomorrow."

"Not on your life," Stephen said. "I have other plans for tomorrow."

"Megan know you're here?"

"Nope."

"Isn't that a bit risky?" Dan asked.

"I don't think so. Not too." Stephen walked with Dan to a waiting cab. "What time do you need me in the morning?"

"Well, I thought we'd start with breakfast, and I can fill you in on what's happening here and where you fit in. We can do that about seven-thirty or eight. Then I'd like to show you the store and explain the closeout sale and introduce you to the staff. That will be at ten or so."

"Come on, Dan!" Stephen said. "Tomorrow's Saturday. Don't I get a day off?"

"Sure, Sunday." Dan kept a serious expression. "Come on, Steve, we have a job to do here. Megan doesn't even know you're in town. I need you at the store tomorrow."

"Well, you're the boss," Stephen said, not even trying to hide his disappointment.

"That's right," Dan said. He turned his face away from Stephen so he wouldn't give himself away. "Better get some sleep, pal. Tomorrow's going to be a long day."

"What'd he say?" Jen asked when Dan returned to their hotel room.

"He fell for it, hook, line, and sinker," Dan said. "This better work, or you're in big trouble."

"It will," she said. "Trust me."

"With my life, my daughter, my heart. But with my employees? Are you sure?"

Jennifer Miller answered her husband with a kiss.

"I really need you, Megan. Please. No one knows the store like you and me. Just for a week or so. I promise, once we get things rolling here, I'll let you go," Jennifer begged.

"How soon do you need me?" Megan grabbed the clock on her bedside table.

"Can you be here by ten-fifteen?"

"Ten-fifteen?" Megan's voice registered her objection.

"Did you have other plans?"

"No, not really. Do you know what a week it's been? Can't I wait until Monday?"

"I don't think it can wait, Megan. You should see the mess we have down here."

"I wanted to call Stephen this morning."

"You can call him from Halloran's, okay?"

"Okay, Jen. You win." Megan's voice revealed her irritation. "You know, if you weren't such a good friend I'd—"

"But I am, Meg, I'm your very best friend."

"Not this morning you aren't."

"Come to Dan's office. We'll be there waiting," Jen said cheerfully, ignoring Megan's remark.

"Don't rub it in," Megan warned. "I'm not too happy about this."

"You'll change your mind," Jen said. "Once you get here and we get back to old familiar work, you'll see. You'll love it."

"Yeah, right."

"Ten-fifteen," Jen reminded her.

"I heard you."

"Please, don't be late. Dan and I have other meetings right before and right after that."

"Glad you could squeeze me in," Megan said grumpily.

"See you," Jen said. She hung up the phone and rubbed her palms together.

"You're a rascal, Jennifer," Dan said.

"And you love me anyway," she retorted.

"You're right about that," he said grabbing for her just as she scooted out of his reach.

"No, no you don't. You have a breakfast meeting, remember?"

"If I can keep a straight face," Dan said.

"Dan Miller," Jen sternly warned, "don't you dare blow this now."

"I'll try. Come here."

"Oh, no. You accomplish your mission, then you get your reward."

"You're so cruel," Dan said.

"And don't you know it," she said, going into the bathroom and shutting the door behind her. She heard Dan stir, then open the door to their room. Poking her head out, she said, "Remember, Miller, this has to go like clockwork. He has to be in that office by ten. No later!"

"Ten—check!" Dan winked and shut the door.

Over breakfast, he tried to explain to Stephen the ins and outs of closing a retail store. He explained discounts in detail, how every sale marked to below cost had to be written in red ink on the tag and again on the inventory sheets. He talked about keeping employee morale high and how to deal with the inquisitive press and the importance of avoiding leaks to the newspapers about Mrs. O'Halloran's prison term or Joy's whereabouts. When he had gone over everything he had planned to tell Stephen, he checked his watch. He still had an hour to kill, so he started at the beginning and went over it all again.

"Okay, Dan," Stephen complained, "I understand. Maybe I should call Megan before we get started."

"Wait. I thought you wanted to surprise her tomorrow."

"I did, but now that we're in the same town I can't wait. Maybe we could see each other tonight."

"But tonight we have another inventory," Dan fibbed, crossing his fingers.

"What?"

"I'm sorry, Steve. I said it would be a long day." Dan signed the check to his hotel room, and the two men headed for the front entrance. "Your room okay?"

"Yes, I told you, it was fine."

"Edgy, aren't you?"

"Look, Dan. You hired me to do a job and I'll do it. Just don't expect me to be pleasant, all right?"

"Fine," Dan said and looked away.

"I'm sorry, Dan," Stephen said after a few silent moments in the cab. "I just can't wait to see Megan again. That's all. I'm sure you can understand my disappointment."

"It'll be better tomorrow," Dan said.

"I hope so." Stephen sighed. "I don't even know how to get to her house."

"Jen has the address. Just take a cab. I'll even cover it. Put it on your expense report." Dan's smile widened into a broad grin. "That's the least I can do."

"Thanks, Dan, but I can—"

"Here we are." Dan paid the cabby.

"I know, I've been here before."

"That's right," Dan said. "I forgot."

"It's where I met Megan, remember?"

"Hey, that's right," Dan said enthusiastically.

"Where shall we start?" Stephen said as they entered the front door.

"Well, now, let's see," Dan hedged.

"Why not that famous shipping room?"

"Well, we're meeting Jennifer at ten. It's almost that now. Let's head on up."

"Can't she wait a few minutes?"

"Jen?" Dan asked with a high inflection to his voice. "You must be kidding." He grabbed Stephen by the arm and steered him toward the escalator. "You've never seen her in operation before, have you?"

"Back home, she's a whiz, that's for sure."

Stepping off the escalator, Dan heard a commotion below and realized that Megan had arrived.

"What's going on down there?" Stephen craned his neck to see.

"Just some former employee, I guess. They've been dropping by from time to time. It's like old home week, if you know what I mean." Dan gently shoved Stephen toward his office. "We've got far too much work to do to get involved with that sort of thing."

"A regular Simon Legree, aren't you?"

"Well, I try to keep my business and personal lives separate."

"Right, in business with your wife as I recall."

"Speaking of Jen, here she is now," Dan looked at Jen wide eyed, but she looked past him to Stephen.

"Hi there," she said warmly. "Welcome to Chicago."

"Thanks," he said without warmth or cheer in his voice.

"He had hoped to do other things today, sweetheart," Dan said, nodding toward the door.

"Oh, Stephen, come over and sit here," Jen said, motioning to a chair out of the line of sight from the door to Dan's old office.

"Hey, that's quite a view you have there," Stephen said craning his neck trying to get a better look.

"It's just old Lake Michigan," Dan said. "Old polluted Lake Michigan."

"Looks as big as an ocean from here," Stephen said.

"Well, maybe you'd like to take Megan there tomorrow. Here," Jen said, "have a seat."

"I'd like to call her," Stephen said. He started to stand.

"What, and spoil your surprise for tomorrow?" Jen said, gently pushing him back in his seat. "Besides, she has had a pretty rough week. Last night she said she was planning to sleep late."

"Well, I'm here," Megan said, bursting through Dan's office door. "You had better make this worth my while, Dan Miller. This is the last place on earth I wanted to be this morning."

Jen could barely contain herself—or Stephen for that

matter. Megan turned around to face the one person in the whole world that she wanted to see.

For a moment, Stephen and Megan just stood staring openmouthed at each other. Megan drew her hands up to cover her mouth and spun around to face Dan. The tears overwhelmed her and the room grew blurry. She flung herself at Dan, beating his chest with her fists.

Stephen quickly stepped behind her and pulled her away from Dan and into his arms. They tearfully embraced while Dan and Jen stood looking on. Finally, Dan motioned to his wife and they silently left the room.

"Megan," Stephen said.

"Stephen," she whispered through her tears.

Stephen leaned back and gently brushed Meg's wet cheeks with his hand. Then he kissed her.

"We did it!" Jennifer said in a fit of glee.

"Don't you ever involve me in anything like this again!" Dan scolded.

"Oh, come on now," she teased. "It was fun, wasn't it?"

"It was dangerous!" Dan said. "I could have been killed."

"But dangerous missions have the greatest rewards, don't they?"

"Do they?" Dan Miller pulled his wife into his arms.

"Megan, I can't believe they did this," Stephen said.

"I can't either," she cried. "But boy am I glad they did."

"We need to pay them back, somehow," Stephen said. "But I'm so grateful. I've missed you so much."

"Listen, there's a back door out of here that leads through the display department, and if we take the back stairs, we can go out the side exit before they even know we're gone."

"You think we should?" Stephen said.

"You think we shouldn't?"

"Let's go."

"How long shall we leave them in there?" Jen paced in the secretary's area outside the executive office.

"Another couple of minutes—then we need to get to work."

"Right, Dan. Work. You think we'll get any work out of them today?"

"You bet we will," Dan said. "I didn't fly him all the way across the country to vacation on the shores of Lake Michigan."

"Oh, you sound so tough."

"I am, Mrs. Miller, you know that."

"Let's go in," Jen said. Dan loved the mischievous twinkle in Jen's eyes.

Opening the door, she stood aghast. "They're not here," she said.

"No kidding," Dan laughed. "They went out there," he said pointing to the door left ajar upon their escape.

"How could they do this to us?" Jen wailed.

"You don't think we had it coming?" Dan asked.

Together the couple laughed until their sides hurt. "I guess we did, at that."

On the stairs from the second to the first floor, Stephen begged Megan to stop. "Wait just a minute, please," he gasped. "I've got to catch my breath." Stephen sat down on the stairs and pulled Megan down beside him. After a moment, his breathing returned to normal, and he slid his arm around her waist and pulled her closer.

"I missed you, Stephen," she said softly.

"I missed you more."

"How can you be so sure?"

"I am," he said, leaning his face into her soft dark hair.

"Stephen?" she said.

"Yes." he pulled away and looked deep into her dark brown eyes.

"Does it hurt you to be away from me?"

"More than you know."

"Me too," she said softly. "I can't stand it."

"Me either," he said. Stephen moved and squatted in front of her on the stairway. "Megan, I don't want us to be apart, ever again. I love you."

"I love you too," she said.

"Megan, could we get married?"

"I think we should," she whispered.

"Should?"

"I think it's God's will, don't you?"

"I certainly do."

"Then what choice do we have?"

"None," he whispered. "None whatsoever," he said, and he kissed her again.

"How soon?" she asked.

"How soon can you leave here?" Stephen looked serious. "I mean, do you have things to hold you here? Family obligations?"

"No, nothing. I'm free," she said. "Free to make my own way, live my own life—with you."

Stephen pulled her to her feet, and she let her tears fall unchecked on his collar. Closing her eyes, she whispered "Thank You, Father," then added, "and you too, Papa."

CHAPTER THIRTY-FOUR

Sarah had begun planning the moment she saw Megan and Stephen together. She kept her plans to herself, of course, just in case they had other wishes. But when she offered the garden in her back yard, Megan was ecstatic and Stephen, more than pleased.

The California fall day was perfect and the sunlight fading across the back lawn at early evening gave the whole yard a lovely golden glow.

Precisely at six, James knocked on Megan's bedroom door. "It's time, Megan," he said gently. "Are you ready?"

"She certainly is," Jen said. "Look for yourself."

James gave a low whistle and held Megan at arm's length for a fatherly inspection. "Now Megan, you send this one away. I want a word with you."

Jen smiled and gently pulled the door shut behind her, leaving James in the bedroom with Megan while Stephen paced near the arched trellis in the back yard.

"You couldn't have made Sarah and me any happier than if you were our own daughter. Stephen is a fine man and we're proud of you both. I just want you to know, Sarah and me, we've been at this a long time. She's a perfect wife. If ever you need anyone to talk to, I highly recommend you seek her advice."

Megan felt the tear sting her eyes as James continued. "Now, I'm going to call Sarah in here and we're going to have a little prayer with you as we would one of our own."

"Dear Lord," James began. "You brought this precious Megan back to grace our home once more, and for that we're entirely grateful. You've blessed us with many children, though we've never given birth to any ourselves. You had a wonderful plan, and we thank You for it. You knew best, Lord. And You brought the best to us. We now speak a blessing on this, Your daughter, who we love as a daughter of our own. We trust her into Your Sovereign care and ask a blessing on the home she and Stephen prepare to establish. Let them know, Father, that we love them as much as anyone could—"

"James," Sarah interrupted him, "they're waiting out there."

"Guess I'll bring it to an end then, Lord," he said. "In Jesus' name we pray, Amen."

"Come on," Sarah said, "Megan's family is expecting us to come sit by them." Sarah dabbed at her eyes with a handkerchief.

"You'll never make it through the ceremony," James teased her, reaching for her hanky and taking over the job himself. "You have to understand Sarah, Megan. She leaks."

"You're an old softy yourself, Papa James," Megan said. Tears sprang into James's eyes and rolled down his cheeks. "I knew it," Megan said triumphantly as she gently pushed the couple toward the door. "I can't keep him waiting much longer, or we'll end up having the wedding right in here."

Picking up the lovely bouquet of peach-colored roses and trailing ivy, Megan went first to Uncle Frank, then to meet Stephen.

Stephen tried to stand still and be calm, but when he caught sight of Megan, his heart leaped and his eyes blurred.

"And who gives this woman to be married to this man?" the minister asked.

"I do," Frank said proudly.

Megan stepped forward beside Stephen and scarcely heard the opening words the minister spoke to the small group of guests.

"Now Stephen and Megan, if you would, turn and face each other. I believe, Megan, you have a few words to share from your heart with Stephen."

"Stephen," she began, "I love you."

"I love you more," he said. The wedding guests laughed.

"Now Stephen," cautioned the minister. "You'll get your turn. Go on, Megan."

"I love you, and I want to be your wife for the rest of my life. I promise to love you, to cherish you, to honor you, and remain faithful to you and these vows for as long as we both shall live. No matter what comes our way, I am confident we can stand together, and with God's help and guidance, live not only for each other, but for Him."

"Now, Stephen, it's your turn. You may now share with Megan what's in your heart."

"Megan Marie, you are a treasure and a miracle to me. I love you, and I promise I always will. I didn't think I'd ever find anyone that I would so fully and completely love. I thought it wasn't possible for me. But then I met Christ and He led me to you. You deserve someone who will love you, honor you, protect you, and provide for you. With God's help, I will be that person. I give you my word, I will be faithful to you, for you alone hold my heart. I want to be your friend, your partner, and your husband for as long as we both shall live."

Then Stephen slipped on Megan's left hand a beautiful antique wedding set rich with diamonds and sapphires. "Ours, Megan, is a forever kind of love—I promise."

Without waiting for the nod from the minister, Stephen gathered his bride in his arms and tenderly kissed her. The minister said, "Go right ahead, Stephen. Kiss her again."

So he did.